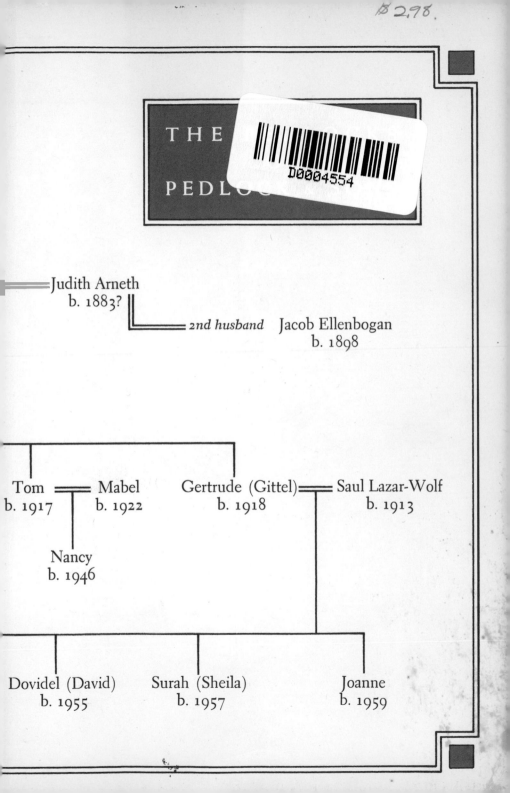

THE

PEDL...

Judith Arneth
b. 1883?

2nd husband   Jacob Ellenbogan
b. 1898

Tom ═══ Mabel   Gertrude (Gittel)═══ Saul Lazar-Wolf
b. 1917   b. 1922   b. 1918   b. 1913

Nancy
b. 1946

Dovidel (David)   Surah (Sheila)   Joanne
b. 1955   b. 1957   b. 1959

PEDLOCK & SONS

PEDLOCK
&
SONS

a novel by
STEPHEN LONGSTREET

DELACORTE PRESS / New York

TO ALL OF MY FAMILY'S FAMILY
who stayed behind and died too soon of
FUROR TEUTONICUS

The Jews have made laws according to
their fashion, and keep them . . .
Gelsus, 178 A.D.

This novel, complete in itself, takes up the
story of some other members of a family
called the Pedlocks, of whom the author has
written before. While it is true to the pattern of Jewish-American life, it remains fiction and none of its people or situations are
to be taken as having any bearing on actual
persons, living or dead. To quote Jacob Ellenbogan, "To us all herring look alike, but
to another herring, ah?"

S.L.

The Messiah will appear only when he is no longer needed; he will arrive the day after his arrival; he will not come on the last of the days, but on the day after the last. . . .

FRANZ KAFKA

BOOK I

GENESIS

CHAPTER 1

◈ When Judith Arneth Pedlock was past eighty and on a visit to the Mandersons on St. James's Square in London, she wrote a postcard to her daughter Gertrude (Mrs. Saul Lazar-Wolf) stating that the weather was rainy—*où sont les neiges d'antan?*—that the stiffness had left her right knee, and that she was bringing back to the old house at Norton-on-Hudson a Mr. Jacob Ellenbogan, whom she intended to marry. The card rocked the entire Pedlock family within reach of Gertrude's Great Neck phone calls.

It was an airmail postcard, but the Manderson housemaid hadn't mailed it for a few days, so Judith, with Jacob, her intended, were on the high seas while the family still thought she was someplace in England, probably with one of her odd friends. Among her family there was even the hope that this was another of her passive caprices, which age hadn't fully removed.

A-Deck. The red-and-green suite of the Cunarder *Queen Elizabeth*, on which kings, unwashed Arabs rich in slaves and oil leases, motion-picture stars and the Mafia crossed the Atlantic. A-1 was, on this westbound crossing, assigned to Judith Arneth Pedlock and her maid, Nora O'Hara. It was a brisk day. The sea had been choppy with whitecaps like whipped cream on the coffee in Vienna, but Judith was a well-seasoned sailor; she never got seasick, only a bit uneasy, the shattered majesty of a King Lear. She stirred in the great bed, felt the ship, felt the sea, felt the earth turn. Memory, reality came back into her mind, limbs, muscles, nerve ends. She

3

awakened, as she usually had of late, feeling irked, feeling heavy. She shouted as she thrashed about in her heavy yellow silk night-gown, angry at her ludicrous behavior. "Nora! Nora!"

Coffee—that was what she needed. Coffee so hot it singed her bridgework, so black that one felt already in *drared*—in the earth. But it pumped blood, bile, life into an old body, gave the illusion of inexhaustible fecundity.

"Nora! Irish, Irish! *Coffee!*"

Nora's crisp Dublin voice was at her very elbow. "Now isn't her-self in a foul mood today. Here's the coffee and it's hot, so mind your mouth."

"Mind your manners, Nora, or I'll have some French bit take your place."

Judith opened her eyes to look up at the peaches-and-cream skin, brass-red hair, shapely features of Nora O'Hara, who, after twenty-two years in Judith's service, was to be dismissed every bad morn-ing and replaced with a Negress or some Gallic tart or other.

Judith took the cup of coffee and blew into it, sipped, swallowed, tears in her eyes. But life came with it. Lord, Lord, bless You for coffee, bless You for life in this crazy world. *Je vis en espoir.* (Her daughter Naomi had picked up this use of French from her.)

Judith let Nora plump up the pillows, help her sit up, run a comb through her dyed red hair, adjust the collar of her nightgown. She held out the cup for a refill.

Nora said, with effusive amiability, "Herself knows the doctor said only three cups a day."

"Don't cross me today, Nora. I'm in a perspiration of agony about how the family will take Jacob."

Nora refilled the cup, pushed up a tray set with silver and china, a plate of *omelette Pavillon*, thin rye toasted just right, stewed pears *St.-Germain*. "We should have come," Nora said, "French Line—the English can't cook an omelet."

Judith looked regal in the bed, like a large Pope by Titian, a backrest against her spine jammed in by Nora. Her face was amaz-ingly free of wrinkles, a good broad face, once beautiful, now merely powerful with purpose, knowledge, prejudices, experience. The eyes were brilliantly blue, the nose straight, handsome, the nos-trils flaring with age. The mouth was sensual but not slack, the chinline strong. But her neck was wrinkled and sagging, with no sign or scars of the face lift gossip said Judith had had every ten years. There was no hint of self-denial or penitence, but one sensed a discipline.

She finished the fresh cup of coffee, the toast and eggs, sighed, and put out a hand for the little black Schimmelpenninck cigar that Nora held ready for her. She puffed it into life as Nora held a small silver lighter to its end. "Weakness, Nora; all my weaknesses win out."

"Man is full of misery at the abjuration of the devil."

They both laughed. Slowly, with relish, the taste of the food pleasant in her mouth, Judith inhaled the pungent smoke, kept it down, then slowly let it escape from her nostrils. She thought: Some sage has said, plant a tree, have a child, eat, drink, make love, die, and a person is fulfilled. I'll save the dying, thank you, till the Messiah comes, thank you. She flicked ash over the bedspread, ignoring the ash tray Nora held out to her.

"Poor Jacob, I've forgotten about him, Nora. The poor man, has he eaten? Has he been at the door? *Je gage que oui.*"

"Herself knows he doesn't get up at the crack of day. He's sleeping, I'm sure. There's an order in the cabin service to feed him."

"He doesn't eat much, unless, Nora, he likes it. He didn't like the French Line. Too much butter cooking."

"Well, he likes to eat in the salon at nine-thirty." Nora looked at her ruby-studded watch, a gift from Judith fifteen years ago. "It's just seven-twenty-two, so relax and I'll slap up your legs. Nothing like a massage."

"A saint, Nora, a man of *yiches,* as the Jews say—good ancestry."

"It's an odd name for sure."

"Mrs. Ellenbogan? Well, it's no title for the *dolce vita.*"

"Herself surprises me, that's all." Nora produced slippers and helped the large woman out of bed. Judith, standing up, was wide and tall, Nora thought, yet herself was all solid, not flab. But there was a lot of her and if she didn't cut down on the feeding and the brandy after dinner and the pick-me-up after lunch, the bit of *pâté* and *fromage St-Marcellin* at eleven when they served only soup and tidbits on deck, *where* would it all end?

Judith started for the bathroom, beginning to pull the nightgown over her head. She never has shame, said Nora to herself, never enough to cover it or them. Here was herself, naked as a jaybird by the bathroom door. Nora turned good Catholic eyes away. Not that the sight of the large, well-formed, solid body was a stranger to her.

She'd bathed it, rubbed it, shaved its legs, served it with enema, forced medical liquids down its throat, cut its toenails, admitted the breasts were still "up there" and that the *tocus*, which was Jew-talk for arse, had a proud curve to it ("the undulation," a now dead poet had called it, "of all breathing things, O Judith . . . ").

"Nora, marriage is God's ordained voice. Damn you, don't sulk. Man does not live by bread alone. That's Bible talk."

"Protestant, black Protestant, talk if you ask me. God bless the Pope and all thieving priests if I swallow any of it."

"You were married once, weren't you, to that rake who drove Nathan's car?"

Nora crossed herself piously. "Was I? Takes me to the Store Christmas party, he does, takes down my drawers in Mr. Tom's empty office, puts his thing to me, knocks me up he does, marries me in the fourth month. Yes, I was married. You know I was, and you know he's dead of drink, and the child, Agnes, is a nun in Rome. You send her presents every Christmas."

"I prefer to call it a Channukah present now. Nora, find yourself a man before the *étagère* dries out."

"Ha . . ."

Judith disappeared into the bathroom, where running water, steam and a cry for the bath salts soon were heard.

Nora paid no attention. She'd find the bath salts and the bath oil where they were, on the tray; and she could scream the water was boiling her like soup; it was the way she liked it: prolonged, retrospective musing in a very hot bath.

Nora laid out the fresh silk underwear, much too frilly for an old party, but then, as herself said, "What the hell." And the sensible shoes with the heels an inch too high, and the blue dress and the scarf and the tight coat bought in Paris, the flat tin of Schimmelpennincks she would smoke up that day, maybe go in debt to a few little cigars from tomorrow's flat tin. Jesus, Mary, Joseph, preserve us all but you'd think she was made of iron except for those migraines that sent her to bed twice a month and the grab of pain in the side when the gas was on her—when Nora had to make tea and put pills in it. There were times now when the breath was out of her and she had to take a rest after a flight of stairs. But she could curse as loud as ever and be as mean as ever and expect you to smile when she called you "Irish Irish, my only friend" and said you were full of little *chochmas*, and forgive a poor old woman whose children broke her heart. Ha, poor old woman indeed, and the children all in their fifties—spoiled as Jew children always are—they went out of their way when she swung her silver handbag at them, the one with the tiger head embroidered on it with the real ruby eyes.

"Nora, Nora! Irish! Where is my big bath sponge!"

Where indeed, Nora thought, with most likely herself sitting on it.

Judith lay back, eyes closed, feeling strong interspatial thoughts coming to her. She brushed them away. They came back. It would be hard to get the family to understand Jacob. She lay relaxed, as if stupefied by some great apprehension. But that would pass as the day grew older and she fed. By the time the ship docked she'd have full control of herself and be able to cow them all. They still depended on her too much. Grown people. She loved them all in spite of the disenchantment they brought her whenever they tried to bend her life to their ways.

They had never fully approved of her. She hadn't been a proper Pedlock, a true Pedlock, for all the years with Mordechai, her husband. Of course those years had been patches of married life rather than a full span. She had left him again and again for Europe; and she had known he'd wait and welcome her back with the placid strength of intellectual bourgeois logic: "We don't want any scandal in the family, and besides, you're more beautiful than ever."

He had come to her that year, to the Hotel Aliberti in Rome, explaining he wasn't spying. He had had to be in Italy for a buying trip. She had shown him incense-saturated churches and Roman ruins and the result was Gertrude, her last child. How clever Mordechai was to understand her so well. With what extraordinary tenacity he had kept her in the family ("more beautiful than ever").

She opened her eyes and looked at the thickening body floating in the pale-blue water. The tragedy of life is not hunger, greed, cruelty, illness or hate; it's getting old. And death gives us nothing; it merely stands there and says, Life is nearly over while I wrinkle you and scar you, blur your view. These are not my breasts and belly or pubic parts—lost to age the grace, the wit I once had. What remains? A few unread lousy memoirs bound in leather with dashes: *J—— P——, the Beautiful Jewess Who* . . . Self-pity is the true Last Judgment. She found the sponge, threw it at the door. "Nora!"

Helped from the bath, dried, powered like a flounder for frying, dressed, Judith stared from the window of A-Deck (no portholes there) and suddenly sighed. "Nora, I'm acting an old fool."

"Don't sweet-mouth me."

"Sit down. Hold my hand. Who am I fooling? You've known me well for a great many years. Under it all I'm weak, given to crazy ideas. I didn't want to marry Mordechai. I was in love with an army officer. From North Carolina. A *goy*."

"A Protestant?" asked Nora, who had heard it all many times.

"Some kind of a deep-dip Baptist. Oh, he was something. Blond, with arms on him. We used to meet under an oak tree and he took my virginity. I was fifteen."

"You said sixteen last time."

"Were you there or was I there?"

"You were."

"I was thinking in the bath . . . all my life a dream, all my doings, what my family said, whatever they said, illusions. His name was Bruce. I wanted to run away to Mexico with him. I was sixteen—all right. But he had his career to think of. *Faire son devoir.* He died years later—in 1917—blown to bits in France. And me? My San Francisco family said the heart doesn't break in a young girl. She marries for the right reason. A Jew for a Jewess. A pair for the Ark, eh? For the first years I thought of Bruce, the nakedness of our pleasures, his expression when we were on the boat going down through the inland waterways, and I said, sure I was a dirty Jew, you bigoted *goy*. Oh, his body! And in bed all the way to Savannah. Nora, I think I'm getting senile. What good is the past?"

"It's your mind running on and the bath too hot."

"So I married Mordechai Pedlock—he came to California on a buying trip—the year Bruce went to the China station. A good man, a fine husband, a kind father. But the truth, Nora, the truth —a dull fellow." She accepted the glass of slivowitz—Jacob's gift —from Nora's hand. "The truth is, my heart, it was always with Bruce. I'm a *Luftmensch* . . . and I've a chance now—only Jacob can bring me a final happiness."

"I wouldn't have thought of him."

"Not my kind, eh?"

Judith began to weep heavily. Nora gave her a second helping of the fiery Polish brandy. This was going to be a bad day, a biological memory of a long-gone menstrual period, Nora had figured out, when herself was a very devil, unhappy, and her life was a burden. But she had seen her through it before. God bless the Pope and the thieving priests, she'd do it again.

"What's the time, Nora?"

"Near eight-thirty."

"Get me the phone. No, he's at prayers now."

"He's a regular cardinal at it now, isn't he?"

"Cardinal? What Jacob Katzenellenbogan knows in one little finger you'll not find in a cardinal's whole body."

Nora drove the cork into the slivowitz bottle with an angry bang. She'd get no more till after lunch.

In Cabin B-22, the little brisk man in his old-fashioned long underwear had washed, recited the prayer for water, donned the *tefillin*, the boxes and straps of black leather that were phylacteries containing holy writing, swung the *tallith*, the prayer shawl with the black stripes, the fringes, over his thin back, recited the sing-song prayers in just the proper tone, swaying to the rhythm. He had kissed the corner of the *tallith*, rewrapped his *tefillin* in their faded red velvet bag with the lion of Zion embroidered on it—his second wife's work. He hummed a little song of devotion: *"Gott fun Avrohom, fun Yitzchok un fun Yaakoiv. Baheet dine heilig folk Yisroel fun alem bayzen"*—God of Abraham, of Isaac and of Jacob. Protect your holy people, Israel, from all evil.

He was a small man with a handsome brown face, just a wisp of graying mustache, a slash of Napoleon III Imperial beard. A likely little goat of a man. He dressed quickly, gracefully. He dug up an amber snuff box, put a pinch up each nostril, gave a great coughing sneeze that warmed his *gavarim*—his entrails—and said for himself *Gesundheit,* and answered himself *guten tonk*—a good thank you.

He wore a shapeless alpaca jacket, lumpy unpressed pants of some gray material (that wore like iron), a black hat with a narrow rim. His shoes were too narrow and hurt his feet a bit. He was not vain but he liked small feet and hands, a good healthy skin. And he felt blessed with all these things. He reached, without looking, for the *mezuzah* that wasn't there on the door of the cabin; the little metal case on all pious Jews' houses that contained the bit of parchment written with the passages from Deut. VI 4-9 and XI 13-21, just twenty-two lines. Every good Jewish doorway should have a *mezuzah* on the right-hand door post, set at a slant. So here they didn't have them and they called themselves a first-class line! In place of it he mumbled a little prayer: *"Shema Yisroel adonoy eloheynu a donoy echod"*—Hear O Israel the Lord our God, the Lord is One. So, no *mezuzah!*

He scampered like an elderly schoolboy down the hall and up the stairs from his cabin, toward the meal of breakfast. His appetite was good, his hunger strong. He'd stop in at the bar and have a *bronfin*—a quick whiskey—that always started one's digestion. He was very much given, as a leading follower of Hasidism, to the uniqueness of awareness.

He did not eat the *trefa*—food—but then he wasn't a fanatic about this kosher thing either. In the dining room, admiring the legs and rumps and *tzitzkes* of the girls and women, he had two hard Kaiser rolls, butterless, belly lox and cream cheese on a bagel, a glass of milk. He peeled and ate an apple, swallowed some grapes and so prepared himself for his beloved, his *kaleh*—bride.

The devil take it, but how it all had happened he didn't know. Shem-hamforesh, as the sages of the Mishnah had written the ineffable name of God (it was his duty as a Cabalist, it was his task, to discover God's true name, for with its supernatural power they hoped to bring the Messiah). He was given to deep thinking, to integrating all experience into permanent form. It had just happened that this fine large woman had captured him, taken him in tow, and he couldn't say it wasn't pleasant. She had the mind of a bright child, but no real sense of God. But marriage? Well, he had to see it as the torah saw it (and when it is given one must take). He had been taken several times in Poland, as a young man had married a herring dealer's daughter, had sired some children when the pogrom killed her. He had gone and married an Italian Jewess of Rome in his middle age, but as God would have it she had run off with some *momser*, a new-type Jew from South America who shaved and carried money on the *Shabbes*, and there had been a ritual *gett*—divorce. After that there was Honnah, who went to a German concentration camp. A man could only count his blessings, and if the Lord said marry, marry, and if he said beget, beget, and if he said *tren*—fornicate—well, not at my age—

even as a cheerful devotee of a Hasidic sect full of pleasure and dancing. Once he hadn't been averse to *trenning*. But—*but*—old bones lack soup. Not that Judith, the Lord bless her name, had hinted at such a thing. He made the prayer for after meals, dipped his fingers in his water glass, dried them on the crisp napkin and bounced to his feet as he saw his beloved coming toward him, her hair dressed, walking with grace for so large a *mensch*. He greeted her with a bit of the Song of Songs:

> "As the lily among thorns,
> So is my love among the daughters . . .
> Behold thou art fair, my love, my love: behold thou art fair:
> Thine eyes are as doves behind thy veil;
> Thy hair is as a flock of goats
> That lie along the side of Mount Gilead."

"Jacob, it's this damn hairdresser on this boat. Did you sleep, did you rest, did you eat?"

"*Shana*—Pretty One—I have." He stood on his toes and kissed her warm dry cheek. He proudly took her arm and they walked slowly onto the deck, followed by Nora ("Look at 'em, Mutt and Jeff") with a coat and a scarf. Jacob admired Judith's figure, took pride in her size, her zeal, the way she looked at him. Oh, she would swallow him up like a plate of black olives—and spit him out, perhaps, like the pits. But a man had to face facts. As Rabbi Isaac Luria, known as Ari Hakodesh, the Holy Lion, had said, "A widow is a rudderless boat. A man does with a maiden as he wills, with a widow as *she* wills." They spoke in Yiddish. Judith's was loud and harsh, remembered from the servants of her childhood.

"Jacob, are you warm enough?"

"I'm warm, I'm warm. The sea never rests. How much longer to this America?"

"We'll get there." She had Nora tuck him in on a deck chair. She gave him a packet of salted nuts, some hard candies. He put them away in a pocket. She sat down next to him and people passed, walking briskly as fools do at sea, back and forth. Judith settled back, lit one of her little black cigars, exhaled and relaxed, holding his hand. So much woman, it was hardly possible, and *all* his. How right was Reb Solomon ben-Isaac Rashi, the great scholar in the days of the cruel Godfrey de Bouillon who had burned the Jews. "Women are treasures that make us enter Hell through their gate of Paradise." He tapped Judith's hand. It was firm, dry, hard.

"Tell me, *Shana,* your children, they follow the orthodox way? I hear America is a land of contending ideologies."

"Jacob, face it. We're not pious Jews. We've been in America over a hundred years. My husband, Mordechai, belonged not to a *schul,* but to a temple."

"Pfeh. Reformed, conservative Jews are not Jews. They are clipped *goyim* pissing at the wrong post. Forgive me the rabbinical language."

"Nathan, my stepson by the first wife, he is for the old forms. But my own children? Marcel is a freethinker; Tom is a whore-master married to a *shiksa,* an Episcopalian."

"*This* I've never heard of. You'll forgive? It's pagan."

"No, it's society Christianity. Naomi, she and Mark Penrose, her husband, are Ethical Culture, I think. They believe only in logic."

"Which is like the donkey dreaming there is no whip."

"Gertrude married a Polack, maybe a *glitz*—Lazar-Wolf, a *bala-gulla*—a laugher but pious. He goes three times a year to *schul,* lights candles to his mother and father's memory, says Kaddish for his father. We're a decadent family to you, I suppose?"

"This Lazar-Wolf I like. As the Misrash says, it's better a clean shirt outside even if the lice bite the armpit. And the grandchildren?"

Judith made a laughing noise and sucked air. "What can I say, Jacob? Marcel's Tony lives only for skis; that's to ride down snow slides on barrel staves."

"*Moisa Rabinou!*"

"Tom has a wonderful daughter, Nancy. His wife drinks. Naomi and Mark, I guess all they do in bed is read long books. Her hips are too narrow to have children. But Gertrude and Saul—Mendes, Sharon, Nahum, Dovidel, Surah, Joanne." The Yiddish rolled off Judith's tongue with pleasure—what a crisp language.

"*Mit nachus,* with pleasure, a fine brood. *Po-po!*" Jacob spit on deck, the proper sign for driving off the evil eye from some one who has just been praised. "Oy, *Shana,* the goddam ship should only stop dancing."

"Nora, the pills for Mr. Ellenbogan. Irish, where are you?" Nora had gone below to have a second breakfast with the A-Deck laundresses from Cork, to nibble on kippered cod and knock back a bit of dark stout. Herself had to rest up for her big lunch. Jaysus, where did she put it all, and stuffing the pore little Jew tad of a feller like he'd been through the famine or done a bit in Montjoy Prison.

The great ship moved on, carrying passengers who refused to fly or those that could afford to keep the past. By now Judith had forgotten her tears, her doubts. Only her loneliness would bring back those things that were her personal horrors; her unnamed yet lurking fears. She lunched heartily. He ate fruit and rolls and honey.

CHAPTER 2

◄§ Gertrude, Mrs. Saul Lazar-Wolf, couldn't at first believe it. Her mother wanting to marry at her age. It was somehow nasty, unhealthy, and yet you could hardly say not Jewish, not that Mama gave a damn about being Jewish.

Something would have to be done—the family rallied, the fact pondered, the thing faced, as they had faced so much from Mama over the years. Even age hadn't dulled her vigor.

It was just an ordinary airmail postcard, picturing the British Museum in rather unnatural color on one side and Judith's *Art-Nouveau* hen-track-styled writing on the other. She disliked ballpoint pens and still used a heavy gold fountain pen that her late husband, Mordechai Pedlock, had bought at the Chicago World's Fair in the twenties. Over the years, Judith's handwriting had fallen away from the proper methods to form the flowing ovals, the perfect letters, the wrist movements, as taught in San Francisco long ago. Her writing had become a series of artistic loops, moving a bit high on the right by the time it reached the end of a line. She never dotted *i*'s or put in the apostrophes. ("What am I? A schoolteacher, a *malamud? Je suis . . .*")

Gertrude Lazar-Wolf, a spreading, Renoir-designed woman nearing fifty, entering her menopause, beat her brow with the shocking postcard and called her older sister, Naomi—Mrs. Mark Penrose—on Sutton Place. It seemed better to talk it over woman to woman, sister to sister, before informing the men that Mama was acting wicked and like a *meshuggener* again. Marrying at eighty! Or was it eighty-two! And to whom? Not a Lehman, a Guggenheim, a Rosenwald, a Strauss, a Manderscheid. No, to someone named Jacob Ellenbogan. Gertrude sniffed, poured herself a fresh cup of strong black coffee as she sat in her Early American dining room overlooking the dimpling sound, the yachts dipping in the strong sun at nearby club moorings. She felt, as her mother used to say, *Je mange de la vache enragée*—I'm having a lean time of it.

As she sipped the scalding black brew and ate a whole shell of Danish with strawberry and pineapple jelly, unaware she was breaking her diet, she could see this Jacob Ellenbogan: an old, bent ancient, yellow as *schul* wax, with a cloud of white beard, a black silk cap on his head, standing before faded velvet hangings, a Chagall prayer shawl around his chicken neck, intoning some bit of Torah in an atmosphere of rotting wood, bad drains, the stale breathing of toothless old men, even a smell of cats and decaying prayer books. She licked her fingers. God spare them all. She wasn't against the older forms; she and Lazar supported a home for rabbinical students in Israel. But *what* kind of person had Mama— once famous in international continental society—found?

Gertrude Lazar-Wolf wiped her sticky fingers, pushed back the bracelet on her plump arm, and picked up the phone from the War of 1812 birch sideboard. She felt one of her hot flashes coming on and fumbled the dialing so that in the end she had to ask the operator to get the number for her. Jacob Ellenbogan, oh God! Most likely the poor man took snuff from an enameled tin box, walked around in heelless slippers, read only Yiddish-language newspapers. He might even insist Mama attend the *mikva*, the ritual bath for wives. Or just suppose he's a cunning old bird, an actor, furniture dealer, black-market *goniff*, and after the Pedlock money, an interest in the great department stores, the real estate or private banking holdings the family had in Lazar-Wolf and Pedlock Brothers. The "full essence of sensation," as her general semantics lessons had it, overcame her.

"Hello, Maude? Is Mrs. Penrose up yet? Her sister calling."

Mr. and Mrs. Mark Penrose, intrinsically alert, polite, decorative, were (to their regret, they always added) childless. They had been married for nearly thirty years—slim, elegant people, wintering in Palm Beach (they never admitted Miami existed), sun-tanned, living in a duplex they owned overlooking the East River, its walls covered with rare Kamakura scrolls, Sung paintings on faded silk, modern furniture holding Tang horses (they properly pronounced it Tong), Han bronzes green with patina. Also their *avant-garde* pride, daring experiments in modern art: a construction of old wood, bits of machinery beaten about, remains of broken violins set in pink and green cement panels. Mark was considering Pop art, a ten-foot replica of a golden dog turd, very *out*.

Naomi wore her short hair in a windblown blue-tinted gray, and her lean, still shapely body was inclined toward simple expensive linens at home. Gertrude envied her sister's slimness. The Penroses were trustees of old Pentland College in upper New York State; they spent the spring in their cottage at Santa Barbara and Mark Penrose never failed to play a round of golf at least once a week or take out his forty-foot ketch if the wind was right. Mark, Gertrude admitted, was a tall handsome man, with his British guardsman's mustache neatly trimmed, his skin glowing pink, his tan even and highly polished; not like Saul Lazar-Wolf, pale, potbellied and bald. Mark Penrose had long since sold his father's business— Moses Fiederbloom: Scrap Metal and Reclaimed Steel—to a Texas combine. (Saul had once remarked, "When someone says, 'Look at the fancy Hebe,' Mark yells, 'Where? *Where?*'")

Mark Penrose was standing on the balcony watching a dirty little tug push a Greek oil tanker along the river. He was thinking of the Pebble Beach golf course at Monterey, when Maude—a beginner-brown Negress, studying art nights at N.Y.U.—said there was a call from Mrs. Lazar-Wolf. Mark took up the white phone.

"Hello, Gertrude? Naomi is still asleep. We were out rather late with the Porters. They are in from Pasadena for a few days, old friends from the coast. *What?*" He listened, pushing his mustache into place with the back of his free hand, his expression not changing. He had long ago decided emotions were bad for a long life, for the digestion and for the nerves. Mark was an intelligent man; he had taken a year to beat down his naturally inherited nervous energy to a slower (more gentile) pace. "You don't mean it, Gertrude. At her age. I mean, why now? Who? No. The only Bogans I know are Irish crumbums up in Boston in politics. Ellen-bogan? Couldn't be! Jacob? Old Testament name. Gertrude, *don't* shout. You can't appoint a committee of doctors to investigate Judith's sanity. Good Lord, woman, she's your own mother, she's a Pedlock. That's why. I'll call Tom at the store."

Mark Penrose hung up after a few more exchanges (how emotional Jewesses were) and stood stroking his mustache. Devil of a thing to come up. The old she-devil, with her short catarrhal bark, her Byzantine-Proustian past, would and could and might go through with it. He hadn't much enjoyed his first interview with her years ago, when he had faced her in the old house at Norton-on-Hudson and told her he was in love with Naomi, and she had glared at him and shouted, "Good God in *Himmel*, what is society coming to when a junk dealer named Fiederbloom has the *chutzpah* to offer himself and his old pots and pans to a Pedlock!" And how the devil did he, *en pure perte*, get into the house in the first place?

It had been a sticky wicket, no doubt about it, but Mark had simply smiled and said that he had an M.A. from Princeton, and that his father's firm, Fiederbloom Scrap Metal and Reclaimed Steel, was on the stock exchange board and had a contract to remove five hundred miles of obsolete trolley-line tracks and ship them to Japan. She had called him a French word (very vile) and a Yiddish word, a *knocker*, and he had had to explain to his future mother-in-law that he didn't understand "the jargon." It was then she had asked him if he was still circumcised. After all these years —even as a Christian Scientist—the memory made Mark Penrose shiver. Now he decided to let Naomi sleep. (She had been fearfully high late in the evening at the Drag Queens night club, and had made matters worse by telling Clarence Porter of the Porter Prize Kennels: "Jews make dogs get fat, you know, and the more Jewish the family, the fewer dogs around.")

Mark picked up the phone and asked information for Pedlock & Sons, Fifth Avenue. He had never called the Store before. As he asked to be connected with Tom Pedlock's office, he eyed an Abstract Expressionist painting of two smears of red on a smallpox background. How dated and old-fashioned it was now. He'd sell it and buy a plaster cast of an ape seated on a real motor bike he'd seen reproduced in *Art in America*. It was all the rage today in way-out art. Still, he missed his Monet "Lily Pond." Naomi was firm. "No Yiddish sentimentality, Mark."

Pedlock & Sons rose twelve stories: glass, green bronze, the newest fashion in Neo-International style. Bright, bold, characterless, so Nathan Pedlock (issue of Mordechai and his first wife) always thought. He preferred the ornate style of the old Store (pure General Grant and O. Henry cast iron) on 34th Street, where marble, stone and iron meant something. Still it had been good publicity to move uptown and build this multimillion-dollar air-conditioned beehive as the showcase for the fifty-two Pedlock & Sons all over the nation. And business here was fairly good.

Nathan Pedlock, chairman of the board, president of Pedlock's Department Stores, was a dumpy, round little man; at fifty-seven he was thin-haired, hawk-nosed, given to heavy English cloth suits and a watch chain across a growing paunch. His new office, all modern corners and glass and hidden lights, was made bearable by his old black teak desk, several oil paintings from the 34th Street Store of New York done in the early twenties by John Sloan, and a carved pearwood fireplace with buffalos, Indian heads and old-fashioned steam trains cut deeply into its surface. His father had bought it when Teddy Roosevelt's effects were put up at auction.

Nathan Pedlock, as he was only too aware, was not Judith's son. He was the product of Mordechai Pedlock's first marriage, a marriage that had produced not only Nathan, but another brother, Charles, now a smug Beverly Hills rabbi who ate *trief*, and Connie, now Constanza, who lived in Rome, a plain *nafka*, a whore with a male harem of beatnik jazz musicians and writers.

The intercom desk box made a simpering sound.

"Yes?"

"Mr. Tom Pedlock is coming up to see you."

"Thank you, Miss Walters."

Tom, his half brother, Judith's problem child, wanted more money most likely for newspaper space or some kockamaymee scheme to go on TV with a news show. That *shiksa* Rita Burton, in advertising and publicity, was behind it. He'd like to throw her out. A married man like Tom, and *against* the Store rules playing around with the help, going out at three in the afternoon for a little *shtupping* at the Waldorf. Grandpa *never* took them above 42d Street.

Tom Pedlock was grinning as he came into his half brother's office. In his forties, Tom looked younger. He was blond. His suit was extreme Ivy League. Nathan frowned. It certainly wasn't a suit from Pedlock's Man's World department. Tom had good teeth and he showed them. He looked around the office, shook his head, took the Dunhill pipe from his mouth and rubbed it against his nose. He wore a Harvard ceramic piggie on his key chain and tried to present a bland mandarin stare to the world.

"Dammit, Nat, this office looks like the old ragbin on 34th Street."

"Tom, I began in a ragbin. I want to end in one."

Tom sat down on the corner of the desk. He pointed the pipe stem at Nathan. "Judith is going to get married, she says."

"*Gott zhul up heaten*—God forbid. At her age! I thought her wild years were over."

Tom, although he was an Episcopalian of the most rigid Anglican congregation in Scarsdale, spoke a juicy Yiddish. "A *hock in kop*—so what's to be done?"

"Nothing, Tom, if Judith has set her mind to it. You know your mother. She always lived with a frenetic license. Poor Papa."

"And she's opening the old house on the river for the wedding."

"So we'll dance. What does Marcel think? He's keyed in on her irresponsibilities."

"He's in Los Angeles. I've got a call in for him. You think she's serious?"

Nathan sat back in his old swivel chair and grinned, looking, Tom thought, like a kosher Buddha. "Serious at the time she decided on it. Who's she marrying?"

"A Jacob Ellenbogan. Not at all from the international crowd she used to run with."

"Hmmm . . . I wonder if he's related to the Katzenellenbogans. Miracle-working rabbis in the Polish villages. All Hasidim. Dancers in ecstasy, drunk on the glory of God."

Tom refired his pipe with a golden lighter. "That's *all* we need. A stepfather who goes along the floors of our Fifth Avenue store trying to get a *minyan* together for evening prayers."

"You could get fine publicity from it," said Nathan ironically.

"Mabel is getting kind of anti-Semitic as it is. Talks like a goddam Bircher."

Nathan made no comment on his half brother's wife, who had a signed photograph of that schmuck Goldwater in the living room. "If this is what Judith wants, Tom, I don't see what we can do, or should do. But there's another problem. Judith holds a lot of shares of Pedlock & Sons stores in her portfolio. Then there's the real estate, the bank, and other things. Your mother is, I hope, not getting flighty."

"You think Ellenbogan is a fortune hunter?"

"I'm thinking if, God forbid, anything should happen to Judith, and if legal protective steps hadn't been taken before a marriage, I mean . . . well . . . " He whistled and knocked out his pipe in a glass ash tray.

"Well me no wells, Tom, *boychick*. Who's spoken to Judith?"

"No one. She sent a card to Gertrude."

Nathan flipped a button on the desk box. "I want to speak to Mrs. Judith Pedlock, in England." He looked up. "Where?"

"With the Manderscheids, the old folks, in Kent, I think. He's Sir Arthur."

"Trace me Sir Arthur Manderscheid."

"I think, Nat, they call themselves Manderson, have since the end of the war."

"Also try Manderson." Nathan hung up, and turned to face Tom, who was blowing his pipe clean. "Judith will, of course, out-live whomever she marries."

"You don't think she'd pick an older man, do you? *Not* Mama."

Nathan made a serious face. "One of those con men, eh? In his early fifties. Slick, hair oiled, carries a cane, kisses the hand over the teacups. I suppose a last romance twinge could penetrate even Judith's good sense. Some greasy Rumanian playboy flattering her. I'm sorry, Tom. I didn't mean Judith was going soft. She's smarter than all of us, believe me."

"I wish she didn't agree so fully with you on her smartness." Tom thought of old photographs of Judith in a luxurious studio on rue Juliette Lambert, of old gossip. "I suppose Lazar-Wolf is the best one to handle this. He's . . ." Tom waved an arm.

"Tougher than we are with her?"

"I didn't mean it that way. But he can use words that Mama sometimes takes with relish. She likes his . . . well, peasant crude-ness."

"I'll switch the English call to him if it comes in. But better get together a family meeting tonight."

Tom looked at his Swiss wristwatch, which intoned a musical

note on the hour. "Not tonight. Miss Burton and I are off to Boston on the five-o'clock plane. Drygoods convention and we're both going to speak. Can't disappoint them."

"You have a grown daughter, Tom. You'll be maybe a grandfather some day. It's a scandal, and with this nothing. A *tocus* and dyed hair."

Tom pursed his lips, looked at the yellow carpeting, kicked at it in an old prep-school football gesture. "Look, Nat, for you the Store and the branches are enough. For me it's a trap. And my marriage to Mabel worse than nothing. I can't divorce her—the girl and all that. Besides, what the hell do you know of the sensual music of mortality?"

"Poetry he gives me. Look, send Burton to the store in Chicago." He put his arm on his half brother's shoulder. "You think I didn't *hock* a buyer from Kansas City in my time? But it's no good. You lose your self-respect, compassion, magnanimity. You feel like sweepings."

Tom turned to the door. "Better call Lazar-Wolf, and I'll phone in from Boston tonight. It's a deranged world, Nat, accept it."

He went out and Nathan sat patting the top of his old desk with the flat of his hand. He told the call box to hold the English call if it came in and to get him Lazar-Wolf and Pedlock Brothers, Wall Street.

He'd be sixty in two years; maybe he should retire then. Take off the blinkers, the studied blindness to the evidence of his senses. Spend the summers in Pittsfield in the Berkshires; travel a bit. But as a widower, and childless, what was travel? What was seeing the leaning towers and smelly canals? And as for churches and cathedrals, he couldn't find anything in them but the horrors of the god whose people had burned, pogromed so many Pedlocks over the last two thousand years. He was not like Tom or Marcel, who could write it off as "history" in their half-Christian lives, moving faster and faster away from Judaism, to those temples with the basketball courts and the modern ceramic classes, talks on birth control and Zen, general semantics, folk singers from the Elizabethan hills of Tennessee. All egregious nonsense for a people who had a Moses.

No, he'd most likely die in harness like old Mordechai, his father, who went out with the figures of the most successful January sale ever in his hands, died happy in the arms of an alarmed buyer of Fruit of the Loom sheets. Or his grandfather, Tobias—one of the few rich Jews of his generation, it almost seemed, who didn't go down on the *Titanic*. Zaydeh, they called him, with the little white beard, who at the end had to be pushed in a wheel chair. He organized the company that expanded the stores west, and east and north and south, and, with his brother, Samuel, he got the bank charter. And great-grandfather Elijah, who had come up from the South as a pack peddler in 1853 and opened a Houston Street dry-goods store, the Bon Ton, then a 14th Street hole in the wall, and later the first of the pushed-together buildings that became Pedlock & Sons. Here they were on Fifth Avenue, and other sons, sons not his, would carry on. Marcel's Tony, Gertrude and Lazar-Wolf's Mendes, Nahum (only *he* preferred to be called Nelson) and Dave.

What did his father sing at Shuvous, the Pentecost (or was it Simchas Torah?), when he was a small boy and Judith was always off to Paris, Rome, Berlin, already a social power to be reckoned with, the feisty fashionable society wife of Mordechai Pedlock off for the stealthy stalking of European watering places . . .

> *V'taheyr leebeynu L'ovd'cho beyemes*
> *La la la la la la la* . . .
> Purify our hearts to serve you in truth . . .

The old ritual text echoed in memory as the call box hissed or buzzed or whatever it did, breaking in on his memory.

"Yes?"

"We haven't been able to get the Manderson call through to England, Mr. Pedlock. But the overseas operator will continue to try."

"Fine. Thank you."

Let Lazar-Wolf handle it. His chest gave an involuntary spasm. Saul as brother-in-law was a little too cynical, too hard, too sure of himself. But one had to face it, he was a solid citizen, a brain, had a way with people. Let him worry over the new wedding in the family. Would it be an old-fashioned wedding? Not for Judith, who once hired the Milan Opera for a gala. A regular Waldorf wedding with cameramen, gowns out of *Vogue*, food French, birthday cake from Sherry's (did one still order a cake from Sherry's?), the young rabbi close-shaven and neat in a Finchley tail coat. You wouldn't be able to tell it from the Protestant weddings.

The truth was you couldn't tell a wedding any more by its guests. The *bubbas*—old grandmothers—in the *sheitels*—wigs—were all dead. The grandfathers with the elastic side shoes were all bones in some Brooklyn burial ground smelling of Con Edison gas mains. Now there were second and third generations, fourth-generation Jews, half Jews, lost-to-the-faith Jews. Blooded by German, Yankee, Italian stock, as tasteless as the insipid white bread they ate, the dreadful Scotch they drank, the television shows they watched.

Yes, he was getting old, all this condescension to the new, but no weddings any more like the old wild emigrant weddings of his youth when the foreman of a shipping department got married on Orchard Street, with green preserved tomatoes and *mondel* soup and *gefilte* fish with the real horse-radish, the stuffed *derma*, and everyone danced, arms around each other, and shouted, sweated and sang, while the children, full of celery tonic, slid across the floors.

> *Alle menschen tanzendik und shpringendik*
> *Und lachendik und singendik.*
> Everybody dancing and jumping
> And laughing and singing.

Judith, most likely, would be married, at her age, privately, in some city official's office, and a simple announcement would be sent out by the Store's publicity genius to the New York *Times* and the *Herald-Tribune*.

In an office paneled in bleached pine and hung with prize-winning advertisements of Pedlock & Sons, a Buffet print and a swordfish stuffed and varnished, Rita Burton pulled her girdle down over her svelte hips and tried to smile at Tom Pedlock, standing close behind her with that handsome smile on his tanned face. Very Cary Grant, Miss Burton decided, swirling her loose strawberry-red hair, every strand in place.

"We should take separate planes, sweetie."

"Goddammit, Rita, I'm not ashamed of you."

"I know, I know, but you're a Pedlock. I'm just a smart *shiksa* ten years out of Smith, and if I get caught up in a hassle here, I'm out on my ass with no job in sight. You Jews stick together so. One nod from old Nat and I'll never get a top department-store publicity job again, coast to coast."

"We have to go together. It would look funny if we didn't. We're listed as speakers at this drygoods clambake."

He kissed her cheek, but she avoided the contact of mouths. She didn't like messy lipstick, and besides the little bitch from Vassar with the tits was just outside the door and trying to get higher in the pecking order. Rita nuzzled Tom with her brow."Where are we staying, sweet, this weekend?"

He sighed. How could he keep her mood just right and still tell her his mother had made a family council important? No weekend. It was all so complicated; enough to send a man back to his wife.

The Vassar biddy knocked and, chest forward, smelling of rosemary, came in quickly. "Sorry to barge in, but you're both due at the policy meeting in the board room in ten minutes."

"Very well, Condon, and stop using that stink water. Pedlock people don't scent that loudly," said Rita.

Condon threw Tom a too casual look with ironic corners in her smile. "I'll remember."

The board room was in the penthouse, where the Store held the yearly Founder's Day prize givings and fashion shows and with persistent intensity promoted all kinds of charity drives with hasty lunches. It was a bit windy, but the great oak table was wiped clean, the chairs were comfortable. The city below the great banks of windows looked fairly unreal—something, Tom thought, out of science fiction. Nathan was at the head of the table. Rita took her place by Mr. Alton Melton, head of advertising, and his goddam charts on a stand. Several other department heads, members of the board of Pedlock & Sons, sat waiting, jeweled cuff links well forward, each on Nat's orders furnished with a pad, a ballpoint pen and a crystal ash tray. ("Never put out an ash tray costing more than a dollar at a meeting; they get stolen.")

Nathan wet a finger, touched a mass of reports in front of him. He wondered who the androgynous youth at the end of the table was; probably the new window designer.

"All right, you all want to get away or are busy. But this horsing around with the Store's policies in the matter of philosophy on sales approach to various groups by income has to be settled. I'm against upgrading our ad copy to a point where even a professor can't read it—getting high-nosed and fancy with the prose, working toward an upper-class customer who will find only one or two of a kind here. We get too exclusive, we're finished. We're a mass-market store even on Fifth Avenue, and the chain, coast-to-coast is folksy, if you like, corny if you want to say so. But it's all Pedlock tradition; savings, fine values for everybody. Melton, you talk."

"Well, N.P., these charts show the index of store buyers' sales from *shlock* to by-appointment-only, broken down by class, salary, city, town and country."

"By who?" someone asked.

"By *whom*! By Broadman and Borindello's public relations survey teams over a period of two years."

"They predicted the last two elections wrong, and didn't they research the Edsel?"

Melton went on. "The trend, as the chart lines A.K. and W. show *here*, is to luxury buying, not rushing for the loss leader any more, not buying the well-made solid product, but the streamlined models, the extra something, the special color, the social-status item. Everything in gas-pressured cans, plastic-wrapped. Form from fish knives to caviar, crystal, from monogrammed silk underwear to gold tie clasps. Fur-lined toilet seats, private bars, iced quail. It's the jet-set group, the duplex world, the hi-fi crowd, the young marrieds in Capri pants and ten-dollar haircuts we should go after. I don't say rush everything over to one side, but think of our ultimate policy. These charts—"

"It isn't easy for our average customer to get away to shop. The *others*, Melton, they shop because they're bored and they expect to return most things they pick out."

Someone at the table brought in the report of the N.A.M. attacking unions, and the snobbery of import labels. The talk fell away to amusing stories of the failure of a sale in a rival store, the trick one shipper had played on a Wanamaker Store in Philadelphia. In the end Nathan rapped for order and sat back in his chair, frowning at the new window designer's silver nail polish.

"Continue with the reports, but I've about decided we'll vote not to increase going after the fancy trade by more than five percent. We have everything they'll find elsewhere, maybe not in such variety. Miss Burton, have some ad copy prepared for test runs and see how it pulls on our antique department, the better perfumes and that Italian line of stretch pants and Canadian fur jackets. So, anything else? Let's all sharpen our heads and think this thing out properly. 'There never was any buyer loyalty once across the Westchester line,' my father used to say."

Melton looked at his unused charts. "Mr. Pedlock, that bronze sign over the Fifth Avenue entrance that we brought up from 34th Street. Suppose we get some fancy artist to do us a striking new design. Is Picasso still alive?"

Tom said as he looked at his watch, "Melton, you're new here. The founder himself had that sign made, pure bronze, and it's a family heirloom. It goes, we *all* go."

Tom Pedlock walked slowly toward his office, his thoughts divided between the trip to Boston and his mother and her idea of marrying. Had he inherited his horny side from her? What did he know of his mother?

A young girl barred his path, looking very pretty but very tail-dragging sad, her face drawn up in a comic grimace; she was wearing figured stockings. Her hair was straight. Kids don't know how to bring out their best points, Tom decided. It was his daughter, Nancy.

"What the hell, sweetie, what are you doing here?"

"Things at home, Dad. The scene got too crowded."

"Oh, it always seems to at times. Then your mother settles down."

Nancy pushed back her hair with the back of a hand and leaned her head against her father's chest. Tom didn't care much for this public display; he had a reputation for liking the chicks and people wouldn't know it was his own daughter. He swung her around behind a collection of smelly marked-down raincoats.

"Sweetie, you belong up in college. What are you trying to prove dragging around—that I'm neglecting your mother? What can I do? I give her doctors, lots to live on. Kid, I won't take all the blame. She was a boozer when I married her, and a lot more a father doesn't tell his daughter." He pressed the girl against him and patted her head and felt the shock by touch and warmth of how mature she had grown in the last year or so.

Nancy said, "Look, Dad, understand, but here I am in the middle. A big house, snotty help, and, well, the bottles rolling under the bed upstairs when things get into a bind. I don't care for the biddies who come to see her, so I run for it. I feel if I'm a Pedlock there must be another life someplace else for me, too."

"What's so wonderful about being mixed up with this rag business? You finish college, go find and love some blond character out of a John O'Hara novel, have Main Line kids, drive your own pony cart, vote Republican, even say some of your best friends are those people. I promised your mother that."

Nancy laughed and punched her father lightly in the ribs. "You're always making out you want me to get away from the family. But it's all such a flop—there isn't anyplace to go that I want to go. I hate Philadelphia, blond men. I think all political parties stink. And what's wrong with being a Pedlock, thick in the family sour cream?"

"Not a damn thing, girl. I was just thinking of what's best. And now Grandma, they say, is getting married. We'll open Norton-on-Hudson and you can wallow up there in family affairs. I warn you, sweetie, it's all so boring and demanding."

"You're kidding about Grandma—I mean the marriage?"

"Wish I was. She was an old rip from way back."

"I haven't seen her since I was a kid. She really made the fur fly, didn't she?"

He kissed the top of her head. "You're a real kook. So serious. It's boring and routine. And as for the family, it's all old folk mostly, and getting older. So let's you, me, have dinner soon. All the works. The Four Seasons, unicorn livers, roast rump of mermaid, huh?"

"Great. Like the time we ate turtle soup in Atlantic City! Tomorrow night I'm free; the bridge club is coming over to the house. Things will be under control there."

"Hell, sweetie, I'll be in Boston for a few days. Call me first of next week. We'll really kick the town over. And get yourself a date."

Nancy scowled. "Yes, sure—a nice blond sex maniac from Penn."

"Aw, baby, it's your old Dad promising. We'll really dig everything."

She turned away. "Don't try to act camp, Dad. You're getting a paunch."

He watched her walk off, so straight, so pretty, *his* daughter.

Damn right he was proud of her. He hadn't wanted children, didn't feel being half gentile, half Jew was such a prize-winning break in society. But now Nancy was grown up, stirring into full life. Well, she was his daughter, and he'd put up with a lot from Mabel because of the growing child. And, let's face it (he started for his office again), Mabel had taken a lot from him, with his tom-catting. Yet Nancy had come up like a rare flower in the muck heap of their marriage. He had patterned out a good life for the kid, in her mother's world, or what was left of it. The best people, the most *goy* college. For years, all those fine, shrill, teeth-banded, Protestant girls they entertained summers on the back lawn. And never kosher cold cuts with their marvelous garlic smell and taste. Always the bland tasteless kind that were like slabs of mush, and the delicatessen stuff that was as if it were made of boiled plastic. Then there was the church she had gone to Sundays—couldn't they keep their own customers in the faith? And he had thought she took a real interest in that camp for halfwitted Negro kids. The only thing Jewish in the house was the Old Testament, and *that* was the King James version. It wasn't that he had tried to keep her from the Jewish side. It was just, dammit, he had so much on his mind all the time. He'd have a real chinfest with Nancy soon and give it to her straight; she was one of those who didn't have to go around with phantom labels on her shoulder. She could move in any direction.

But now there was Mama. He didn't feel they could talk her out of it. No, she'd get her way, and they'd better not interfere.

CHAPTER 3

⚜ The Bank, the family (who had also founded the Store) called it. LAZAR-WOLF & PEDLOCK BROTHERS were the simple gold letters carved into the sooty granite front of the Pedlock Building on Wall Street. It had never been fully modernized except for the IBM machines, computers, air conditioning, alarm systems and files. It was solid grim-Venice-prison in style, nine stories, its facade proudly scarred by the bomb fragments that had struck it when the attempt was made to blow up the House of Morgan across the street in the notorious Wall Street explosion of the twenties. The interior on the ground floor hinted at hope, opportunities, aspirations, befitting an old private bank that floated stock issues and issued bonds for railroads, private and government clients here and overseas. It was a deep gravy brown with a décor of oil paintings too dark to make out. It had the waxy odor that Saul Lazar-Wolf called "the smell of clean money." It seemed to be a combination of deodorants, floor polish, bookkeepers' ink pads, dry cleaning on the garments of the minor clerks (proudly ten percent Negro, but only one percent Jewish; the firm had a policy against Jewish employees, the result of being called "the Yid's bank" during the first Roosevelt's era).

The 1912 furniture was solid, comfortable, ugly. The floors were shiny oak, the staircases and elevator shafts early 1898 and just coming back in fashion. Saul Lazar-Wolf had a breezy corner office on the eighth floor so he could see Wall Street and Broadway. He sat firmly in a deep chair, a solid, short, balding man, eyes small, nose amorphous and large, mouth ironic, sinewed, the hairy back of his hands placed flat on the desk top. He smiled up at James Ashford, vice-president in charge of bond promotion, and his nephew, Dickie Lazarus, legal director. They were in their thirties, with those solemn Harvard faces that were unreadable but always at ease. Dickie's was an act; he had trained his dark handsome features, under a Lennie Bernstein haircut, to appear bland.

"The old families, I keep thinking when things go cockeyed, aren't what they were in the founder's day." He pointed to an oil painting of Samuel Pedlock, brother of Tobias, long dead—the fortunate one who had actually gone down on the *Titanic*—and one of the founders in his youth of Pedlock Brothers Bank. Dickie's smile seemed to indicate better times, more gracious times, and yet hint that if his uncle Saul Lazar-Wolf hadn't come along after the war and married Gertrude Pedlock, and merged the Bank with *them,* it would all have gone down the drain. At least that is how Lazar-Wolf read his nephew's smile.

"The old families, Uncle Saul, all they want is tax-free municipals and no risks."

"I've got another problem. My mother-in-law is thinking of marrying. The family is in an uproar. Dickie, keep the newspaper boys away from it. And what are the Western issues on truck lines doing?"

"Holding up. New high for last quarter."

"Dickie, get me a list of old Mrs. Pedlock's holdings, will you— voting stock, all that."

"Will do." He almost gave his uncle the old navy salute, for Lazar-Wolf was an ex-commander of PT boats in the South Pacific who looked back with pleasure on those wild free days of sudden death, hard liquor, native women and doses of penicillin. What a thanks to God he had come through it alive and whole.

When the first vice-president was gone, Lazar-Wolf sat back in his swivel chair and stared at Samuel Pedlock, preserved like a large sardine in the oil of a bad painting. "Dickie, such sentiment they had in those lazy days, they let the old lady hold on to too much power, too much voting stock. Now Judith is a problem."

"The old gal is tough tittie."

"But marriage, Dickie, at her age." He wondered about the sex habits of the very old, wondered how many more years he had. A lot, he hoped. He had started late. A Polish immigrant shining shoes, becoming a Wall Street runner—running, *running*. Yes sir, and no sir, and thank you for a ten-cent tip. Playing the curb dogs for dollars and sawbucks, running a boiler room with the old Kennedy crews, man, *gevalt*, how you could get away with it then. The war, damn fine war, he had to be a navy hero, even if Lazar-Wolf & Co. was telling him, Why go? ("Somebody had to say you can't burn up a million-odd people because you don't like the shape of their noses.") No. So he had gone on—Commander Lazar-Wolf and the whole goddam dirty Pacific war, faking it, not knowing his ass from a ship's stern at first. Then *bam-bam*. And all the time cabling to Lazar-Wolf & Co. to buy Italian industries, Japanese bonds, Dutch oil, Hong Kong mortgages, Belgian foundry stocks.

Never enough women in his life. Always busy; drunk in Sydney with a few Texans and the Australian whores—God, what size— but the war ended and he came home, rich. Pedlock Brothers Bank was going stale and he met Gertrude at a Friends of Free Palestine meeting to arm the Irgun. One of the great Pedlocks, up there with the Guggenheims and Strausses and the rest of the fancy Hebes. Him holding her hand, him, Saul Lazar-Wolf, war hero. Not only did he get the daughter, but he had to save the old firm by a merger with his own interests.

It had paid off. All those fine children: Mendes, Sharon, Nahum, Dave, Sheila (he had promised not to call her Surah) and Joanne. He and Gertrude had certainly been fertile. Yes, and—

The intercom buzzed on his desk. Dickie took it. "Pedlock Brothers, London." Saul reached for the phone.

A voice like Gracie Fields said, "The Kent Mandersons don't answer. The St. James Mandersons are at Nice. I could put through a trunk call."

"Do that, honey." Saul looked at his desk clock. "It's three-twenty pip emma, honey, here. Be here till five. Miss Monroe will give you my home number for after that. Oh, how's the weather in London?"

"A normal day 'ere, sir. It's raining."

"Thank you, honey." He hung up. "*Nu*, Dickie, think of something bright?"

Dickie admired his reflection in the glass top of his uncle's desk. "Let things happen on this marriage talk. Roll with it. Wait it out."

"She'll do it. Marry some *yold*."

Dickie Lazarus rubbed his nose, the only feature that failed to get his full approval. "I've only met her a couple of times. There's something fantastically wonderful about Judith Pedlock. Any of those rumors true?"

"Which ones?"

"That she used to give the sons gold louis—*louis d'or*—on their birthday, that her bed has real Valenciennes lace spreads, that she was a sort of *grande courtisane* in her younger days?"

"Don't go fancy on me, Dickie. I guess she stepped around a bit. Her husband, my late father-in-law, was a great businessman, but only that."

"I've always admired Jews who stepped out of the tight confines of being Jewish. Got away, you know, from the moral imbecility of being labeled, tagged, boxed."

Lazar-Wolf looked up from a pile of papers he was studying. "Dickie, I don't like such talk. You can be both a Jew and an American. Anybody object to the Irish in green parading on St. Patrick's Day, or the Polacks dressing up in native costume at their picnics?"

"You don't dig deeply enough, Uncle Saul. You like being a solid middle-Jewish family man, owning a double plot in Sinai Grove, that sort of racial cant."

"And you, you young bastard?" He smiled at his favorite nephew. "You are shopping around, if you ask me, for a plastic foreskin? Shame on you, Dickie. Come out to dinner Friday and I'll find you a nice Yiddish Long Island heiress. *Zaftig.*"

"I better go check those Brazilian coffee futures we're involved with for Senhór de Mattos."

When Dickie—what *chutzpah* the young had—was gone, Lazar-Wolf's thoughts got back to Judith Pedlock. He could call the Paris office, the Rome office, but figured it was the middle of the night there; he never could remember if it was later or earlier than in New York. No, he'd let it ride. Every time the Pedlocks got into a jam it was Saul Lazar-Wolf—step in, you Polish *schnorrer*, get the dear old family back on the trolley tracks. Didn't they know there were no more trolleys? He got out a good Havana cigar—the Toronto office saw to it he still could smoke those rich long Havanas —and carefully lit it with a battered old silver navy lighter. Of the few things he took seriously in life, one was cigars.

Lazar-Wolf inhaled the pungent tobacco and sighed. Had he reached the end of his drive? He was a sensual man, loved his wife, his children, good food. The rest of the world he had little use for. He agreed with Freud that most of the human race was trash. As a man of feeling he was sorry for it, pitied it at times, helped it to be better. But there it was, look out the window—trash. Fifty-two years he had faced them, battled them, used them, tried to advise them, heal their wounds, build them hospitals, orphan homes, supplied the Irgun patriots (he had once broken a Philadelphia Jew's jaw for calling them terrorists). And in the end he had found the human race mostly disappointing. Too bad. Life was a fine thing, even if short. The pleasures of life could come to all with a little more effort, a little organizing. But what the hell! Some damn fool Bircher would one day press a button and back to Abraham's bosom for us all. Too bad. They'd have to start Genesis and Adam and Eve and the Garden of Eden all over again. Next time, O Lord, a little more sense, huh? A little less stupidity, and take out the bump of ego, the stain of nationalism, the horseshit about pious cults. All noxious nauseating greeds. He looked at Gertrude's birthday present to him: a clock in a ship's tiller.

To work. He read over the item circled in red in the New York *Times*, left there by his secretary in the place on his desk reserved for pleasant items. Saul Lazar-Wolf, for all his strength, wariness and disdain for cant, had those soft spots that believed in lucky coins, avoided walking under ladders or throwing a hat on a bed. He also believed his great fumed-oak desk had areas on it that were reserved for good news, bad news, and just routine.

PROFIT UP, PEDLOCK PLANS SPLIT, DIVIDEND HIKE

Pedlock & Sons Tuesday proposed a 2-for-1 Common Stock split, voted a dividend increase and reported net earnings for the fiscal year up 20% on a 7% volume increase. The new quarterly rate on the split stock would be 30 cents per share against 55 cents on each share now outstanding. The proposed split will be voted on by stockholders at the annual meeting Nov. 10. The increased dividend would be paid on the new shares about Jan. 2, said Nathan Pedlock, president of Pedlock & Sons.

For the 52 weeks ended Aug. 1, net income increased $2,153,000 to $11,704,000 or $4.98 per share on 2,135,345 shares outstanding from net of $9,551,000 or $4.05 on 2,093,522 shares outstanding in the 52 weeks ended Aug. 3, 1963. Net sales were up to $623,552,000 from $582,906,000 in the preceding fiscal year.

The New York-headquartered department-store chain operates 46 branches in the U.S. and six in Canada. Its stock issues are handled by the family firm of Lazar-Wolf & Pedlock Brothers.

There were, Lazar-Wolf mused, eight other stores in California, but they were experiments called Sunshine Exclusives, very over-priced items with guest doggie pens and bars that served cocktails while the customer shopped in Capri pants and hair curlers.

"Love is a match lit in a dark cave, *Shana,* and often it seems everybody is trying to blow it out."

Judith and Jacob stood at the rail looking at the day dying in the west: level, thin banks of gore-colored clouds, the sky taking on the slate shades of solidity that seemed to hint that space was not after all namely nothing.

Judith, in a long coat, a wide blue scarf, stood holding Jacob's hand. "That sky, it's so damn dramatic, bad art really, yet it's like the end of the world, isn't it?"

"Who says? The world may end with dancing and singing and everybody drunk, marching up golden rays of light. Does it have to end like Dr. Teller says? What can you expect from wormy scientists? Only the few scraps they find lying around. God isn't giving *them* any real secrets. We're a secret of sorts."

"There's a secret me that you know, Jacob. People said to me, I confess, '*C'est incroyable*—what do you see in that little man,' they said. And I smiled and I said, 'I see life. I see mystery.' And that's the truth of it, Jacob, it's the enigma of us that fascinates me. The hope that with it I can become a little like you, face calmly the way things have to be. I've had everything else. Living, pleasures, what some call sins and some call vices and some call— never mind those with *la mémoire de lièvre.* Eating and being, dressing well, and going to strange places. In the end you come out at the other end and *there* you are, empty-handed. That scared me in London. Suddenly everybody seemed so much older, their teeth yellower, their steps more feeble, and I said, Judith my girl, it's all *je vous emmerde,* so take another path, tack a bit—that's a boat-sailing term, Jacob. Look around you, I said, just suppose there is something in faith, in blind faith, knowing one isn't just an animal rushing to its pleasures. I've never met anyone like you. All the power inside, behind the eyes, I saw. I fell in love with you and maybe I wanted to fall in love with believing more than with you. I don't know."

"Why try to know, *Shana?* If I give you comfort, fine. If you find in me a little for laughing, that's good too. If one pinch of snuff is good for one nostril, why not two for each nostril? I don't mean I want you to sneeze out everything you once believed, had or did."

"You know me. I can't anymore repent than I can grow an extra set of legs, but I've never been frightened before. I'm a hard old woman—maybe only agate, not sapphire, but hard, and things bounce off me. But I'd wake up choking, my breath short, trembling, and I'd lie there in such fears *mit gevalt.* I'd ring for Nora, but she'd only give me a brandy, rub my legs. Such fright and no real reason for it beyond the one that I'm mortal and I'll die soon. Don't shake your head; you're not selling me special life insurance. And when I was with you during the day, that night I'd sleep. Even just talking to you on the phone, it was a hell of a kick for me. I never explain these things, I just *know.* I don't even remember when, where, we first met. Tell me, how did we first meet?"

"We met, we met. You invited me to that rich *macher's* house to tea. Tea, they call it? Blue with milk and not a lemon in the house."

"I invited you? Yes. of course. I seem to have been with you for some long time. But you, Jacob. How was it—why?

"For the *noddin*—dowry—it wasn't I took to you. I was never a chappie who has much use to own things. Let's face it, for days I was with my face in the *sidder*—text—and creaking my joints with some scratching old men. Suddenly there's a spark in me again. I was a wild *bucher* once, ah, the blows I got, the kicks I gave. And for me it was God's jest. Why me, I asked, why such a fine *shana* for me, a scholar with dust in his hair? But if it's made some place we should talk, if it is marked down we belong together, who am I to go against what destiny has been sent me?" He put his elbow into her hip for a soft nudge. "And *such* a woman, so much of her. This kind of gift I wouldn't turn down. And if I can help you, isn't that what some are sent here for, to help, others to punish?"

"You're the helping one, I'm sure."

"Who knows his own destiny? We think one thing and we're marked out like garments on a pattern table for other things. Love, we are taught, don't talk about. Take it, wear it, enjoy it."

"*Geteilte Freude ist doppelte Freude.*"

"All kinds of love exist. In youth, ah how we burn, how we twist. Then comes what? Families, mouths to feed, behinds to wipe, faces to slap. Now in the autumn when the harvest is stacked, this is the last of it—it's good too because it's so sad yet satisfying. Nothing burns too much; the eyeballs don't glaze. One can take one's time and look, look at a quiet time. What once was, let it go."

"What a *knipper*—pincher—you must have been."

"What a passion you must have stirred up."

"They'd stare at me and say, '*O la bella putana.*' "

They leaned together; the ship made a slight turn, west-north-west. They felt the boat under them, sensed the boat on the sea, the sea spilling over the planet, and Jacob could have sworn he was looking out into the *comus*, into the hallucinatory universe of the holy rabbis, the sacred words, into the matter of being and the being of feeling. . . . One touches ever so lightly even just one person and the void becomes full, the stranger is no longer the stranger. (One doesn't even need a wise saying to season such a truth.)

Nora found them at the rail, hand in hand, after the first call to the dining room.

Judith sighed. "I'm dying of hunger."

From Marcel Pedlock's journal:

One always needs an excuse to brood, even as a time-binder; we all in a small way make more history than we can consume. When and how should a man try and sum up his impressions, prejudices and patterns? Benvenuto Cellini begins his story boldly, with no modesty: "All men of whatsoever quality they be, who have done anything of excellence, or which may properly resemble excellence, ought, if they are persons of truth and honesty, to describe their life with their own hands; but they ought not to attempt so fine an enterprise till they have passed the age of forty."

As an art dealer I have not much interest in proclaiming whatever I have done "which may properly resemble excellence," but rather to discover in the restirred pool of memory the time and the color of that one individual, myself, who is still in many ways a stranger to me.

People often confuse us with the Joseph Pedlocks, distant relatives. Old Joseph, who originated his family's great copper fortune, was a second cousin to my great-grandfather Elijah, who founded the Store. Most of those other Pedlocks have long since become Perrys, and more or less Christians. There was a Peter Perry, an upperclassman at Princeton, when I entered the school, and my son, Tony, skied with Peter's son, Joey, in some international snow meet in Switzerland a few years ago. They are, I suppose, distant cousins.

I must write of my relationship with my son Tony. At twenty-six, if I remember his birthdate correctly, he is a stranger to me. Polite, soft-spoken, when we are together, but there is no real tie. The fault is mine. I was never a domestic creature, and when early in my one timid plunge into matrimony I was freed of it, I sent the boy first to relatives, then to clean, outdoorsy prep schools, and by the time I was most active as an art dealer (everyone those years wanted to buy expensive modern art suddenly, as tax gimmicks and status symbols), Tony was already an adult and we were strangers. We only shared gossip, mean-ingless pleasantries, rationalizing our dissatisfactions with our relation-ship over Beefeater gibsons in some hasty luncheon place. Then I would hurry back to the galleries to be coldly gregarious with some Bel Air California slob wanting a proprietary share in Matisse or Bonnard or Jackson Pollock. And Tony would go back to what is called, I hear, "his pad" in the Village, to work on what will never be finished, "a definitive book on the art of skiing." It's an amoral relationship we two have, stained with traces, on my part, of an Old Testament conscience, or guilt—Job among the Abstractionists? And is there in him, perhaps, the inner disgust of a false compassion?

Lord, what a time for Mama to seek some recall of her past—wasn't it enough the family had to live through those frantic periods we have tried to forget? She used to say to me when I was a stringy adolescent: "When you sell your heart, Marcel, make them pay for it sixteen ounces to the pound."

Marcel pushed the journal aside. It wouldn't do. Not tonight. As always when his insides were gray, he thought of Tony, a son he had never really raised, a son he had never known, not, he sup-posed, wanted to know until age had come. How does one buy back a birthright? He had always been so involved with the world of aesthetics, abstractions, removed from any contact with people that was not purely cerebral; he could no longer break through the brittle shell to establish the kind of flesh-and-blood relationship he craved with his son. The ground rules of their relationship he had long ago established, and Tony had accepted them. Each succes-sive attempt they made to touch something closer resulted in fail-ure. The conviction in advance of failure was so certain. No, he must keep trying. He would get dressed, go downtown.

Marcel got to the street corner, hailed a taxi and gave an address.

"The Village, huh?" said the driver. "Jumpin' tonight. You want some gay camp, maybe?"

Marcel waved off the suggestion he was a mark; must be the bowler hat and umbrella. When the taxi let him off on the narrow street, smelling of cats and rotting timbers, at Sheridan Square, he looked about him wondering if the Village had ever been all that was claimed for it. He hadn't come downtown often after he had bought the 57th Street galleries of DuVere & Starkweather. (Somehow Nathan and Lazar-Wolf had been against his adding the name Pedlock to an *avant-garde* gallery.)

Marcel mounted the steps of a brownstone house that had been modernized for advertising copywriters, Tin Pan Alley composers, television vice-presidents. He pressed a button under A. PEDLOCK. A latch clicked. The lift, smelling of *cannabis sativa*, took him to the fourth floor. 4D had a red-painted door, and his son Tony (A. for Anthony) stood in the doorway, wearing baggy gray exercise pants, a yellow cable-knit sweater. The light behind him showed his heavy, uncombed head of brown hair. Tony was smiling and yawning at the same time.

"Hello, Dad. Imagine you coming here to the beat expatriates."

Marcel kissed his son on the cheek. "You haven't got company in I believe it's called the pad?"

"Only by squares. Come in, come in. No, no chick, no session. Been working on the book."

"Didn't know skiers could read and write."

"Ha."

It was a two-room apartment, dark yellowish walls with African masks on them, several photographs of groups of skiers, a realistic painting of a snowy mountain slope. A portable TV set, picture on, sound off. Deep leather chairs, the smell of pipe smoke (John Cotten Medium), a white bookcase taking up one wall, its books mostly still in their jackets. Tony towered over his father, and Marcel was not a short man. Tony's brown face was not handsome, but it was solid Pedlock, and Marcel wondered how twenty-six, twenty-seven years ago he had had the energy to marry, beget a son, mourn a dead wife (anemia with complications), all in one year. He had no full image, only a faint memory of his long-gone wife. Ruth, an amusing laughing girl with a too long chin, who collected old Lautrec posters, sold ceramic things from Mexico, once had a shop someplace near here, did drawings for a Hebrew-language magazine of arts and letters that Marcel had helped to support (in fact, that was how he had met her).

Marcel looked around the room as he sat down. No picture of Ruth (nee Silverstein) or of himself. Always pictures of bull-like males and malelike women in ski togs, climbing, rushing down slopes. He remembered old times in the Village: sandals and eurhythmics, the first Freud, first Joyce texts, Gurdyieff diets.

"We had a family meeting tonight at Nathan's."

"The clan, Dad, must be something huge by now. Care for a beer? No hard stuff in the joint."

"No, you go ahead. Tony, let me send you down some Redon prints or a few Hokusai drawings."

"They'd get stolen." Tony went into the kitchen and came back with a can of beer, strip-top torn off. He sat down, long legs out, sucking the beer from the can. He belched and laughed. They were still reconnoitering—both wary.

"Must have been something solid, Dad, to bring you down here."

"Your grandmother is getting married."

Tony popped his eyes, beer can halfway to his mouth. "*That* must have caused a balls-up hassle! Well, good for her. She never understood me, you know, Dad. I wanted to go into the Store when I was a kid. Or down to the Bank. She wanted me to compose or paint. But I like the old gal. She's all right."

"She didn't want me to become an art dealer. Said we ate dead artists' bones. But I conned her. You're too damn independent, Tony. You don't use your Pedlock charm. Get out of the Village, find a publisher—is there really a manuscript?"

"Eff my charm, Dad. And being a Pedlock. It was always a pain in the rump. At Princeton the boys at Cottage always wanted me to get them dates with the salesgirls in the Store's jewelry and silk drawers. I said my Uncle Tom had the nookie concession there. . . . So Grandma is getting married again?" Tony finished the can of beer and aimed it at an overflowing wastebasket and got it in. "Two points. Well, it's your problem. And it's her wedding. I'll come to it, of course."

"Why don't you move in with me, Tony? The big apartment on 57th over the galleries is large. I'm not in town too much; you can ball the jack there. I'm going to Paris soon to buy some Arp bronzes."

"No, Dad." Tony frowned, lit a cigarette and slumped deeper in his chair. "The family would try and capture me. I'm not against the Store, business, banking. They're real fascinating. But I want to be free a few more years, know what I mean? Go places."

"The national ski bum?"

"You talking like a Jewish father, *you*."

Marcel laughed. (Play *his* game—be the stuffy Hebe.) "I am at that. Maybe it's just I think this whole Village set-up is phony, a self-immersed society of misfits. And to me you're real."

"Of course it's as fake as a new folk ballad. The pansies, the studs, the johns, the chicks, the junkies, the smokers of pot, the dykes and the bad art and Zen writing. But it's also, for all the jet-age beats, the copywriters and the TV whores, the fancy-sounding crap, a place where you do what you want."

"I remember Paris when Gertrude Stein—she's your grand-mother's second cousin—and Hemingway and Joyce and that *putz* Ezra Pound were trying to live like that. But they had a kind of quality, a deep but cheerful insouciance."

"That's just nostalgia, Dad. Hemingway tagged it. 'We all had a girl and her name is Nostalgia.' "

"Maybe so, Tony. But the Jews, the wonderful Jews in Paris then. Pascin, the whoremaster; Chagall, the good cubist one, not the later hack who overworked his old themes; Soutine, who stank of the dead chickens he painted; Kisling and his redheaded women; Lipchitz carving stone; and people who really remembered Modigliani charging into the White Russian anti-Semitic cafes shouting: 'I'm a Jew, you Slav bastards, I'm descended from Spinoza.' "

"And what would happen?"

"He'd get beaten to a pulp and tossed out. . . . Well, Tony, it's been good seeing you. You need any money?"

"Next you'll be offering, 'Have a piece of fruit' and 'How about a Jewish girl with money.' "

"What a strange picture you have of me."

"I've enough money, Dad. I sold a story about skiing on Mount Whitney to *Sportlife*. I'll manage. And I've got the book half done. Well roughed in."

"I know Bennett Cerf if you need help. Is a lexicon of skiing what people need?"

"Can't I get you a drink, really?"

"I'll have sherry."

Tony laughed. "Sherry? You must think I'm an interior decorator. Look, let's go find a drink. Let me take you out on the town. It's changed since you knew it."

Yes, why not. I'm getting through to the boy. There is still hope.

Marcel smiled as he got out of the too deep chair with the busted springs stabbing at his kidneys. "Why not."

They both switched to scotch at the Cafe Au Go Go on Bleecker Street; and at the Bon Soir on West 8th Tony invited two chicks to have a drink—brassy girls in pageboy boots, fluffy sweaters, Alice in Wonderland hair long and lank down their backs. They said they'd like to smoke pot and hear the Second City at the Square East on West 4th. But Tony said he'd rather hear Miles Davis at the Village Vanguard. Somehow, to Marcel's amazement, one of the girls was suddenly a Negro in drag and they lost it (him or her) and went on and on. Marcel had to admit two hours later, when he shook Tony's hand in the taxi, "It certainly was a different evening. Have dinner with you soon."

Tony leaned into the cab and kissed his father's cheek. "Don't forget to invite me to Grandma's wedding."

Marcel, his head clearing as the cab went uptown, the open window bringing in night smells, decided he'd not be able to sleep much. Drinking always brought on his insomnia. He'd work on his journal. Maybe someday Tony would read it. Tony was a fine son. Had he made any progress tonight with the boy?

When the family heads had to meet—in complete commitment —for crises personal and emotional, it was tightly secret. But sometimes minor members were called in—"How could you help it," Nathan would say, "with such a family"—and such social position, so many facets of business, charities, obligations to clients, blood ties. Things had to come to a head, and then the whole family would assemble and talk things out. Such as the time the Pedlock Foundation was sponsoring a study of ring-wing hate organizations. Mark Penrose and Naomi had been against it: "After all, it's time we lost our Jewish attitudes to social things and supported cultural things like, say, a national art project, or perhaps consider restoring that water mill in Vermont." It was Nathan who spoke up that time. "Morris, I think you better get up a project for Jews who don't like Jewish organizations, for yourself and your friends."

Now there was a gathering in Nathan's big, twelve-room apartment. Nathan had been a widower for twenty years—an only son had been lost in an air strike over Berlin in 1944—oh, the black year. The family assembled in the old-fashioned apartment with its very high ceilings, over-rich wood and too solid furniture—all very good pieces that had been brought over by Nathan's father and grandfather on buying trips to Europe. On the walls hung Impressionist paintings his half brother, Marcel, had sold him a long time ago, and Marcel no longer showed any interest in them. Hard to think you could live long enough to see people turning up their noses at Renoir, Monet, Pissarro (the Pedlock Pissarros of the various hours of the day on Paris boulevards were legendary—and never loaned for exhibit). But all this, Nathan knew, was out of step while a *narr*—a fool—like Mark Penrose filled his house with art objects made of crumpled auto fenders and old burlap sewed together and called a picture. Yes, yes, to catch content without essence is failure. So Nathan never went *avant-garde*. God forbid. His problem was that he fought a demon of doubt within himself. Had he sacrificed his life for the family? The Store?

Nathan walked through the large gold living room, the old-rose library, the big dining room of the wrong Chinese period—Ching not Sung—noticing the Spode laid out for late coffee, the silver tray of little sandwiches with the chopped *pâté*, marinated herring slices in sour cream, rye bread cut very thin. "Heartburn Alley," Tom called Nathan's snacks. Nathan served his guests what he liked; they could at least try it. He had no time or taste for such nonsense as smoked oysters, caviar *frais*, paper-thin imported ham and other *trief*—unkosher—tidbits. Nathan didn't himself keep a strictly kosher house, but pork and shellfish he found stuck in his throat.

In the gold living room under the famous "Twilight Hour on the Boulevard Neuve-Luxembourg," Pissarro's greatest painting, many thought, stood Marcel Pedlock, looking up at the painting, amber-rimmed glasses on his thin hooked nose, very slim in his Ivy League tailoring, seeming frail and feeble, the remains of his blond hair twisted like whipped cream over a dull tanned skin and delicate angular jaw. Ha, Nathan thought, Marcel must be nearly his own age, fifty-five to his fifty-seven, a half brother, Judith's first-born. Odd he had turned out so frail for a breast-fed baby.

"Marcel, it's holding up, the picture?"

"Very well. Painted thickly and firmly. It should be revarnished. I'll send a man from the gallery for it."

"I like it, getting old like this. After all, who isn't getting old? You're a bit peaked yourself. You look 'friendless and alone in the common day,' as the holy writ says."

"It's a hectic life on the West Coast. Before anyone with new money buys a painting these days you not only have to assure them it's very up to the moment, but no one around has one as big."

"Who builds for permanence any more, Marcel—not even painters."

"What do you think of Mother, Nat?"

"Like always a *bren*—a fire, but a little old for it, you know, for all her strange compelling individualism."

"At her age, really." Marcel paused to let one of the servants, the male member of the two old Swedes who took care of the place, hand him a very dry martini.

"Jus the vay you like it, Mr. Marcel."

"Thank you, Olaf."

Nathan waved off the tray. "Frankly, Marcel, she's older than we think. I had to get some papers out of the old house vault at Norton-on-Hudson. She's eighty-three, not the seventy-eight she claims."

"There has never been a birth certificate. The San Francisco fire took care of that."

Saul Lazar-Wolf and Gertrude came in shedding coats, shouting greetings. Gertrude was a bit too big for her black silk dress, but smart in a plump, careless way. Lazar-Wolf was smoking his usual cigar, a bit of shaving cream by his right ear; he had a heavy blue-black beard and had to shave twice a day. The protrusive nose had a Medici dignity; his eyes suggested a predominance of irony.

"Marcel, Marcel," Lazar-Wolf shouted. "I thought you were becoming a Californian. The rumor is you are closing the gallery and going to be a yogi. For oranges it's all right out there. For human beings, I doubt it."

Marcel smiled and shook hands with his sister and her husband. "I may retire there someday. Right now the art business is the greatest social climbers' tool among West Coast Jewry. Gertrude, you look glowing."

"Glowing? Fat as a goose. Nat, you should have this place done over. Reeks of the twenties, and Papa's furniture reminds me of us playing games on Saturdays when we weren't allowed to go out in the park. Naomi always skinned her knees."

"It will outlast me. That's all I want. I don't change anything."

Lazar-Wolf carefully deposited ashes from his cigar in a mutton jade ash tray. "I've heard from Judith."

Nathan leaned forward, hands clasped behind him, and motioned no with his head at the Swede offering him a tray of little sandwiches. "It's nine o'clock, I've eaten the big meal of the day. You spoke to her, Saul?"

"No, but I spoke to Artie Manderson in Nice. I better save it for the rest. Only Judith could do this to us."

Mark and Naomi Penrose came in, suggesting, Marcel thought, a dated Noel Coward scene: faultless evening clothes, Mark in tails, Naomi in a silver silk Paris gown, the good diamonds at her throat ("The first team," Tom called them). They had been to a party for the Indian ambassador at the United Nations. "*Au beau milieu*," said Naomi, as she let her silver mink fall back into the waiting arms of the female Swede. She adjusted her well-set hair with a too thin arm.

"Utterly fantastic the news here. Mama and some fortune hunter?"

Lazar-Wolf grinned; his twinkling crinkly eyes, his mocking sardonic grin, annoyed the Mark Penroses. "He's no fortune hunter, Naomi, he's a very famous Talmudic student, a sort of Hasidic seer, monkeys a little with the cabala. These things seem to go together. So there you are, Judith has deserted her fashionable set of *goyim*."

Mark Penrose shook his head as he rejected a black olive. "She can't be serious, marrying some senile old poop."

Gertrude looked away from the trays of food. Her tight girdle was warning enough. "Mama isn't picking anyone with a foot in the grave. He's younger, Saul says, than she is—*much* younger."

Nathan motioned them to sit down on the overstuffed sofas with the Roman lace on the armrests. "Worse and worse. She's still formidable—but this religious thing is new." Saul Lazar-Wolf shrugged. "He's no boy, you understand. In his sixties. But twenty years between them at least, I'd guess."

Naomi tasted a bit of *pâté* with the tip of her pink tongue. "Don't make Mama older than she is. I'm wrinkling into a hag myself." Mark kissed his fingertips to his wife. She smiled.

Lazar-Wolf said, "If you don't want to face the facts, go on dreaming. Judith is in her eighties and she's stubborn. This Katzenellenbogan . . ."

"What!" Marcel stood, mouth open.

"That's right. Full name is Jacob Israel Baal-Shem Katzenellenbogan. But he calls himself simply Ellenbogan, Jacob Ellenbogan in England. Born in Poland, I gather."

"Where, *where*," asked Gertrude of the painting, "did he meet Mama?"

Lazar-Wolf was enjoying himself; he put his hands out in the air palms up. "That we'll soon know. Judith plans to sail home with the bridegroom. She says she wants the wedding with the entire family present."

"Where's Tom?" Naomi asked.

Nathan pursed his lips. "Had to go to Boston. Addressing that drygoods convention."

"Ha," said Gertrude. "He's with that *nafka*, that Rita Burton. You'll see, there will be a scandal yet. Mabel hardly ever sober. What a wife, what a husband! Comes of marrying outside one's class, one's faith. Not that I'm bigoted, but what's to happen to Nancy? She's still a child."

"She's twenty at least. So her mother drinks."

Nathan closed the doors as the Swedes left after depositing the coffee service on the low table before the gold couch. "No side issues, please. There are two paths open to us. We accept Ellenbogan, or we oppose him. Judith is not related to me, but I'm a Pedlock. It's a serious family problem. Anybody wants to talk—go ahead."

Mark Penrose inspected his gold cuff links made of two Roman emperor's heads. "What do you mean *talk*, Nathan?"

"You decide. How we act. What we do."

Lazar-Wolf smiled his special smile again, the one he used when the family got a bit too stuffy. "He means, Mark, we could get Judith examined by a group of competent medical men for an opinion of her senility or sanity."

"Head shrinkers?" asked Gertrude, pouring coffee.

"I suppose so," said Lazar-Wolf, studying their faces. "And there could be issued, privately, with the utmost discretion, a document certifying her as mentally unable to function or protect her interests."

"Saul Lazar-Wolf!" shouted Naomi. "*This* is truly revolting!"

Marcel rubbed his long fingers together. "In the end we'll maybe all have to face this thing in this light, so let's not protest so loudly just now. Just *what* is Mama's state of mind?"

Nathan passed around the filled cups taken from Gertrude's hand. He stared at the red sliver of ribbon of the Legion of Honor in Marcel's lapel.

"I mean," said Mark Penrose, "it's a sort of senile infatuation. I mean there can't—well, you know, *all* that sort of thing one heard about Judith when she was younger."

Nathan carefully handed Mark Penrose an overfilled cup of coffee to keep him busy. "You mean like going to bed together, the 'sex act' as they call it these days?"

"Nathan," said Gertrude, "*you* stay out of this. Sex act! When is she going to settle down!"

"Impossible," said Naomi.

Lazar-Wolf got rid of his cigar. "I am informed by solid medical men that a person's sex life can last well into old age. The senior citizens, as we've come to call them, can be just as feisty and erotic as young people, *if*, as Dr. Newberger put it to me this afternoon when I called him, they're a little patient."

"*Risqué*," said Naomi and stared over the top of Mark Penrose's head with a cool look. She considered it a rather undainty duty to sleep with Mark once every two weeks. A hasty, easy, casual brushing together in the king-sized bed of their well-cared-for bodies—usually to music; he preferred Chopin, she Ravel—after two very strong gibsons and an evening of bridge.

Lazar-Wolf took his coffee with cream and sugar, Gertrude took hers black. She watched her husband over the rim of her bone-china cup. That Saul, he didn't hold with nonsense, and she had learned from him and general semantics that most people always walked around a problem and stared at it rather than face it. There was some cruel finality here—some potential drama to play out.

Lazar-Wolf made a loud sipping noise and set down his cup. "There are only two ways of facing any crisis, they taught us in the Navy—retreat, or plan an attack. So who's for accepting the facts as they are and we'll all dance at the wedding. The ceremony will be private and quickly over. So?"

No one showed any signs of voting.

"All right, who's for going to our lawyers? After all, we pay Addison, Foote and Kalish a hundred thousand dollars a year retainer. They can get us the best legal and medical action." He looked from face to face and no one moved.

Nathan said softly, "I don't have the right to vote. I'm concerned mostly with the Store and the stores. But as a Pedlock I've thought—it's only a suggestion—Gertrude, try the strudel slices— Judith is an old lady. So what's the loss if she has a few years—till a hundred and twenty—with this rabbi. Is he, Saul, a rabbi?"

"Rabbi—shmabbi." Lazar-Wolf clapped his hands together. "The loss is she owns a huge block of stock in the stores, in Pedlock real estate, a neat bundle of Lazar-Wolf & Pedlock Brothers. And the Foundation; somehow she is in full control of that. How the money is spent and where. Judith could cast a solid golden calf a hundred feet high and present it to the city of Jaffa or force a merger of the stores with Macy's or Goldwater's, God forbid . . ."

"That's what to lose," said Lazar-Wolf, taking a new puff of a new cigar before he put it down in the mutton jade ash tray. "What Tom would say if he were here, I don't know. Somebody make a solid suggestion. After all, you're all her children, sons-in-law. All but Nat; he's the stepson. And he's for letting her have her way. Come on, Mark, stop goosing your cuff links. Naomi? Gertrude?"

They all failed to find an appropriate answer.

Lazar-Wolf gave it up and slapped his heavy thighs with the palms of his hands. "It's what I expected from you; you don't run a tight ship. But we've got to issue a statement to the newspapers soon."

"I'll talk to Miss Burton when she gets back from Boston. She's wise in these things: publicity, press reports."

"The *kurva*—the harlot," said Gertrude. "I'd have her out on her twitching tail if I were running the Store."

Nathan said, "Let's not antagonize Tom. These things sometimes work out for the best. Saul, suppose we wait till we have a talk with Judith. Marcel, how's Tony? When is he coming into the Store?"

"He's living in the Village, writing a book on skiing." Marcel looked at a wafer-thin watch he took from his waistcoat. "I've thought it best to open the house for Judith at Norton-on-Hudson. If the thing has to be done, it's best done there."

Lazar-Wolf looked, without expression, at the art dealer. "Yes, behind the stone walls, the fancy iron gates, behind the English boxwood and yews. We could even call it a cook-out, or a barbecue in cowboy hats."

"No jokes, Saul," said Gertrude. "After all, it isn't your mother."

Lazar-Wolf was suddenly fed up, worn out. The hell with them. Let the Pedlocks stew in their family problems. What were they to him? It was his son Dave's birthday next week—ten years old already—and he wanted to talk to Nathan about the right English racing bicycle for him from the Store.

He walked into the library with its uncut red leather-bound books, the charming Degas drawings of ballet dancers, the collection of Roman and Greek coins (old Tobias Pedlock had collected them when such things could still be found reasonably). The fireplace was laid but not lit. Nathan had followed him in, while the Swedes, at some hidden signal, were back in the gold living room with fresh hot coffee. The Penroses were leaving; there was a late party at the Actors Studio they had to make. They were supporting an off-Broadway production of Chekhov—*not*, they said, *The Cherry Orchard*.

"It's better, Saul, believe me, not to make firm commitments tonight. It's all too grotesque to them still."

"You can't run a brokerage house or a bank without commitments. And no horseshit about people aren't banks or stocks. I know that. But why do they always let Judith scare them so? They're full-grown, potty-trained—adults."

"Because, Saul, she scares us all. A brandy? They call it Napoleon, but Napoleon it never saw. Still, it has mellow characteristics."

They stood looking at the amber fluid in the huge crystal glasses. In the next room, Marcel was talking of the rotten state of art collecting in Los Angeles, where the whole thing was still mere prestige, social status and tax write-offs.

Lazar-Wolf swished the brandy through his cheeks. "So we'll wait. I'll get Gertrude home—the kids have colds."

BOOK II

JUDGES

CHAPTER 4

◄§ From Marcel Pedlock's journal:

I can't sleep. The meeting about Mama's coming marriage at Nathan's upset me. And the Village tour with Tony the night before keyed me too high.

For years I've collected notes on the Pedlock forefathers. Perhaps this is a good time to put them in order.

They were men of long robes and great beards who trembled for their lives in half the courts of Christendom. And practiced science and healing arts between pogroms and burnings and tortures and rapes. Even with the comfort of their God it was a horrible life, often cut short like a butcher's product. It produced us: me, Mama, the family.

The Pedlocks, in the tribal progress after being expelled from Spain, had been driven deeper into the ghettos and rancid corners of Europe. Driven from Spain, from England. From France. Murdered by Jesuit fanaticism on the lips of holy hangmen. Burned, broken and flogged with mad mockery in the name of the Great Jew of the Cross. They came to the schools and museums of mankind. To teach again the old and sacred tongues of Hebrew and Greek. To speak of the Talmud and the Testaments in their original texts. And as doctors to hold up the crusted urinal bottle and mumble medical terms into their newly cropped and stylish twisted beards. To take up their mathematics and knowledge of Semite-Arabic figures and signs, and try to foster schools where they were still ignored as human beings and permitted only to function as lesson givers. The ache in the bones of Abraham's flock was bittersweet at times. But that's too romantic-sounding. The smell, the terror is missing.

They settled in rag-filled groups in shabby parts of the Eastern European cities. Their wonderful women spawned and spawned, their wombs a powerful secret weapon (yet I have only one child, Naomi none, Tom one—only Gertrude is fertile).

Some drifted east out of Europe. The Holy Crusades hunted them down like prey. Hundreds of thousands died by Crusaders' swords, fire, rape—they set the early Nazi pattern. They were victims of an ironic, bloody historical shift. As if even history could not spare them more than a kick in the ribs. It was a time when the Czars had defeated the Turks, partitioned Poland and dissolved the free Cossack settlements. The Russ held his knout ready from the Ukraine to the Black Sea for any Pedlocks. With the gobbling up of Poland and Lithuania the Czar found himself rich in Jews, and certainly rich in Pedlocks. Mangy, tired, beaten people, living in the mud of the crossroads. Standing in village streets full of wind and rain, praying in tattered prayer shawls. All now good new subjects of the Czar. *Gospodi pomilui!* Some fled to Austria, to Hungary—these were the Joseph Pedlock branch of the family.

The Czar helped their misery along. For he was a good little Christian and aided his fellow man in his own way. By the ukase of 1804 he forbade the Pedlocks to exist in certain trades. He lured some deeper into Russland by offering them the wilderness of Kherson and Ekaterinoslav—those sparse unsettled Ukrainian provinces. Here some dug up the wilderness and became farmers, herdsmen and taxpayers. Here they lived and grew old and died, and gave the land to their sons. It was all a game of diseased insane Czars. Most of the Pedlock land was taken away from them by Alexander II, the Samoderzhetz. A new ukase forbade Jews to rent, lease or buy land. Our brief day as Russian farmers was over. The mightiest of the autocrats had spoken.

So again packs were roped on thin backs. Again the terror and mud and fleeing. Now the savage Cossacks and the police tore at them. The Czar, called *Rodnoi Otets*—Our Dear Father—had a pogrom whenever he felt the nation needed one to take its mind off other problems. Many Jews drifted back to the west, and Middle Europe shuffled them back and forth like a tennis ball.

They died of disease, filth, rape, pogroms (hot or cold), lung trouble, lack of food, in fear and in courage. They died in jails, in cellars. They said their prayers for the butchered dead, and heard the mobs howling for their own thin tired blood.

But their women never stopped breeding. Sex was the Jews' pocket gold mine. In the cities of Mittel-Europa they were allowed to rest a little while, and the women had many children. As if the wombs puckered so long in fear were making up for generations spilled in so many unmarked places. Sometime the most beautiful of children appeared. In them were the dropped seeds of the lusts of barons, Cossacks, lecherous prelates, of sudden pogrom, of hasty and hot rape. Women's bodies under sweet layers of fat felt the ultimate sword of the Crusaders, a weapon more feared than the iron shafts of the battlefield. Ready always to implant a seed in the accidents of human endeavor. All things, the Talmud said, are part of the reproduction of this world. The Pedlocks cherished and brought into this world many children.

The Pedlocks, when they needed the stuff to live and eat and breed by, they went into dangerous trade. They gave a prosperous glow to the hard serf toil of the peasants. They moved the foodstuffs, the grains, the horseflesh. They dealt in woolens and the finest silks and the hottest spices for the cold and damp stone pig kennels of the castle lords. Into the icy and dreadful terror, the muck and mire, they brought a little comfort. A feeling for the tormented scar tissues that man had become in those long Christian wars over the shape of crosses and the proper ways to cross oneself. Outsiders took the glory and wore the silks. And in the end carried off most of the clipped and golden coins. I can picture them, these bearded robed Pedlocks, already storekeepers, yet more.

What small thing was left, the Pedlocks and their people used for a little fish and braided *chollah*, the clean white bread, and a brass candlestick or two for a Friday night, so a rusty group of elders could keep the holy word in circulation on the Sabbath. They wanted only a chance to breathe—a place to lay their heads together with the mellow bodies of the daughters of Zion, who were so wonderful to grind in God's good work of replenishing the earth. The women often worked in the market, heavy with child so that the fathers and sons and brothers could spend more time in front of the Ark, swaying in their zigsewn shawls under the sacred scrolls of the marching torahs. Was it worth it to produce us?

Some were rebels. Like great-grandfather Elijah, father of Tobias, who fathered my father, Mordechai, who married Judith Arneth. Elijah heard new talk and thought new thoughts. He felt new ideas pumping the thin lean bodies of his fellow students. New libraries, new books. A whole new world of volumes and manuscripts. Saved from the fire and living among the horse manure of shifting barbarians and the bonfires of armies, Elijah dreamed of new worlds. All this was good to minds trained on the sacred scrolls. And so in 1840, Elijah came to Boston, went south as a pack peddler, and in 1853 opened the Store as *Pedlock & Sons*, although his own sons weren't yet born. Was it worth it?

Elijah grew up, my grandfather Tobias told me, in the Austrian Empire, which his father called the Tibet of Europe. A mixture of Magyars, Czechs, Poles, Croatians, Germans, Italians, Slovaks, Slovenes and Ruthenians. All were kept as ignorant and illiterate as possible—a plan laid down by Prince Metternich as the best way to keep the common people loyal and religious. The Jews refused to fit into such an evil and simple conception of ruling power. But the black and yellow Imperial colors and the bugle calls (beautifully composed by the great Franz Josef Haydn) excited young Elijah. They sent him scampering after the white-uniformed troopers on the royal horses as they rode toward Schönbrunn.

Nothing could keep Elijah from the royal trooping of the colors. It was no secret that the emperor had inherited a strong strain of imbecility on his father's side, and paranoia and other neat, pathological tendencies from his mother. Yet the royal show was very impressive to a small Pedlock. Interbreeding among the three related dynasties of Europe on the stern order of the Church had tainted and warped the royal stock, the *schul* gossip said. Everyone was everyone else's uncle or aunt. "Besides which there were even," my grandfather Tobias used to chuckle, when he looked up from his books, "several uncles who thought they were aunts."

Young officers with their cruel jests: window breaking, drinking, degeneration. Elijah listened too much to the pranks of the Counts Coudenhove, Sylva-Tarucca and Clamm. He discovered that the interbreeding of the Catholic dynasties and a tendency toward cretinism in the House of Habsburg-Lotharingen caused the horse to be worshiped rather than the man.

Austria was the last nation of Europe where horsemanship was the major test for character. Early in life Elijah planned to become a great rider. Horsemanship as practiced by the hypersensitive neurasthenic, genetically degenerate, or the brutal barracks-room bullies inspired the boy to spend many days at the horse barracks. Riding the wild colts shipped in from the Hungarian plains with the stable boys, he became by the time he was ten a boy who could cling to the back of the wildest colts. His family never knew how close he often was to death. The laughing officers urged the boy to dangerous tricks with the madly thrashing colts.

Later he went out to the hunting boxes in private parks with other children of the streets, performing small services. He wore a faded red coat and picked up bird life murdered in mid-air by the royal court and its huntsmen. Once the emperor shot a little too soon. Elijah felt the heavy hunting slug hiss by his ear, just missing him.

One of the fat gamekeepers gave Elijah fifty gulden and said it came direct from the royal purse. It was a sort of honor in those days, he later found out, for a Habsburg to shoot a beater, horsewhip a groom, insult a woman, or give anyone a venereal disease. A few gulden made the event more memorable.

Elijah took the fifty gulden home, buried them in the cellar and never went near them again. They were for America.

After that, he stayed home more often and studied. His first encounter with death had not been pleasant. "Is this the end of Elijah?" he had asked himself as he turned in horror when the slug whizzed past him and he looked into the mutton-chop whiskers of the Apostolic King. He gave up the wild riding of colts and the hunting parks, but he still planned to join some regiment of riders as soon as he was of military age. He didn't tell his mother or father about this. He collected pictures of Hungarian grenadiers, Ruthenian fuseliers, Hungarian hussars, Moravian dragoons and Tyrolian riflemen. It was a delightful hobby he shared with his king. All the time he grew taller and leaner.

Deborah, his mother, cherished Elijah like a Christ Child. She taught him his first letters, and when he knew Hebrew and had been confirmed at thirteen, wondered what to do with him. Elijah solved the question two years later when he broke the jaw of a Hebrew teacher, a little yellow-and-green-faced starving Pole with a whipping arm. He had tried to lash Elijah on his bare white buttocks one cold morning; it was the teacher's only pleasure.

Elijah ran away with an "American Wild West Show." When they found him two years later, he had a golden earring drilled through one earlobe and was riding two horses bareback in a fleabitten circus in Berlin. He almost died of a filthy fever. Deborah brought him back in a wagon filled with straw. They treated him with bleeding and cupping until he almost died again.

At eighteen he was with a failing linen merchant. (In America he'd have real shops, bigger, better ones.)

Back in Vienna with a scar across his once handsome nose (a market-day brawl) he joined the Kaiserchritzen Regiment. He rode a black stallion and wore a red coat with heavy gold braid. He studied military history books with ideas of becoming a general in the American armies and growing great red mutton-chop whiskers. On a Christmas night the soldiers celebrated the birthday of the Great Jew by a drunken orgy that was to end in the killing of a Jew—any Jew. Elijah was the only Jew present. They put their hopes on him. The use of a heavy chair saved him from becoming the sacrificial object of the evening. A man related to the Prince of the Bedchamber almost died.

Elijah was young enough to sob when his mother burned his red coat in the kitchen stove and hid him in damp and stinking cellars for a week while the police hunted him as a deserter. He joined some Russian Jews making their pitiful way to Hamburg and freedom with laments and groans. He had never seen such Jews: a beaten and broken people, who kept their eyes low and went in fear. They had welts and empty eyesockets to show the reason for their behavior. Feather-bed bundles (clouds of duck's down) were their main possessions.

He saw the floating hell of the Hamburg-American Line into which the Jews were pitched, with their stinking and brawling infants, their small bundles of decaying herring and wormy bread. He would go on. His life had been, for all its turmoil, a place of grace and courage, a world of color and understanding and knowledge; of simple desires and some sin. These herded fellow Jews made him feel something he had never felt before, and he didn't like it.

He decided to resign from the Jews, my grandfather told me. Resign for good. It took several years before he understood that one did not resign from a people the way one did from a club or a horse-racing society.

Elijah went to England with a cargo of Hungarian woolen cloth. He spent two years in a great store: Sterling & Condon, Ltd., by appointment to H.M. Here he learned the store business.

England was green and cold and damp. For Elijah it lacked bite and humor, but he became a man who knew all about running a great store. He went to Liverpool to board an ancient iron steamer that carried great sails just in case its power failed. Elijah spent two weeks in the reeking hold. He was twenty-three. His beard was stylish and small, his great dark eyes big and wide as they gulped the surging commerce of

Boston. He invested part of his little horde in a pack of pins, buttons, lengths of cloth, notions, mirrors, apple corers, graters, and went South. The Store would come.

The South, though still barbaric, was a land of cotton kings, tobacco kings, black slaves. Elijah walked thousands of miles, pack on his back, through the ante-bellum South. It had, for him, a vicious, gay charm and countinghouse life. He never found the sensual, romantic actions of later generations' historical novels. Yet there were certain Faubourg St-Germain manners and morals he enjoyed. He bought a horse, a cart. He moved on. He came to New Orleans with two wagons of goods.

An epidemic of yellow fever had just passed, and the natives, pale and bilious, drank a great deal of cheap distilled spirits and talked often to Elijah about making money. Lots of money. Elijah opened the Bon Ton Store on Royal Street. On the side, he haggled over cotton bales from the Bayou Lafourche parish or reeking hides or barrels of rotgut whiskey (floated in flatboats by hairy folks from the upper reaches). This appealed to him. It meant a bigger store. He never rested, nor invited his scientific soul to find something to sorrow over.

He invested in a small river railroad that crept and leaped across the soggy delta bottoms. It delivered small carloads of bales and boxes and barrels to the docks. He was cheated by his partners—gentlemen. He killed two in duels and went to Charleston.

Not yet the Store. Was it worth all the hard years to produce us?

Judith and Jacob were playing cards in her cabin. She was in bed in her pale-rose night robe. He was seated cross-legged on the foot of the bed, cards in hand. Nearby was a tray of over-ripe hothouse fruit, a decanter of brandy, a littered ash tray for Judith's little black cigars.

"You cheated, *Shana*. So badly, too."

She laid down cards. "Gin! I always cheat if I can. Games are foolish but they pass time."

"I must confess, from boredom I cheat a little too. But not with you."

"A fine one to yell cheater, *mon cher*."

She seized his hand and put it between her large breasts. Age had not wrinkled, time had not marked them, only expanded them, drooped them a bit, but they were alive and warm and smooth.

"I can't say it isn't delightful, *Shana*, but at our age stirring the ashes isn't going to help."

"How do we know? Sparks last a long time."

"Your deal. Shuffle them for real."

She dealt the cards across the bed cover, inhaled, mashed out her little cigar, took a sip of brandy, then leaned back smiling, the glass at her lips.

"Always I get a feeling there is some magic in you."

"Why would you think that? Play."

"Such a small package—very attractive but *no* Greek marble. You look as if a small breeze would blow you away. And I'm mad about you. That's magic. What card did you put down?"

"Look and you'll see. *Not* that one."

"Oh, hell."

She threw down her cards as he said, "Gin."

She moistened a handkerchief in some scent and rubbed her brows. "Yes, magic. The Cathari in the Middle Ages burned Jews like you for having meetings called *synagoga Satanea*."

"Grandmother stories. The damn Cathari were demonic swine. They taught there were two deities, one good, one evil; they reverenced one and said they detested the other. But it was the Devil they worshiped in secret. Satan, they wrote, came to them as a goat, and he taught them magic for obedience and sacrifices, mostly of their bodies. I ask you, who needs excuses like this for a little buggery, a *little* . . . well, so you don't want to play cards."

"I was hoping for some magic." She looked at him. Am I just going along for the ride? Or playing for power? Obviously not completely. Why did I select you, Jacob, as the road back? What is my attitude toward your ritualistic way of life? What sort of Talmudist are you? Is the joy of Talmudic reasoning and argument an end in itself for me, or do I regard it as a kind of mechanical means to help guide me back to Abraham's bosom? What does your dream of a Hasidic foundation in Israel really mean to me? What, for that matter, does it mean to you? This is not a Svengali-Trilby relationship. But the real basis? Jacob's influence and control, his compelling force? How can I resolve them to myself? "I'm thinking foolish thoughts, Jacob. Sing me something. Hand me a little cigar."

> "*Du maydela du shanas, du maydela du fines,*
> *Ich vel deer eppes fraygen a retenish fines.*
>
> Pretty little girl, good little girl,
> I'm going to ask you a hard riddle.
>
> *Vos far a vaseer is ohn a zamd?*
> *Vos far a maylech is ohn a land?*

What kind of water is without sand?
What kind of king is without land?"

Judith had fallen into a doze, leaning back on two pillows. She said in a mumbling manner, eyes closed: "Land? Tomorrow we'll see land. The golden land, Jacob, it was called in the old days. . . ."

CHAPTER 5

ARRIVING THURSDAY ON QUEEN INFORM FAMILY
TIME AND PLACE TO WELCOME JACOB

JUDITH

§ Doomsday. D-Day, Judgment Day, Zero Hour, Blast-off Time.
Nathan ran all these images through his mind as he fingered the
radiogram from the liner already approaching the American shores
in the mist beyond the Kill Van Kull. He went over to the Store. It
was after midnight, but Nathan, when he had a problem that kept
him awake and restless, when something came up that lodged in
his mind like a bit of irritating matter, always found the best thing
to do was to go down to the Store, no matter what the hour.

The windows were still lit; the lights would automatically go out
at one o'clock. Inside there were work lamps here and there; the
cleaning crews were busy, or as busy as their unions permitted
them to be. Labor, Nathan had told the board, was a conflict between getting things done and the game of coffee breaks and free-
loading.

Nathan let himself into the Store by ringing the side-street night
bell that brought old Magnin, the watchman, to the door.

"Haven't seen you, Mr. Pedlock, for some time. Coupla weeks."

"Felt restless, Tim, just restless."

"Anything I can do?"

Nathan waved off the offer. He knew every corner, every twisting
shadow of the Store. And he wanted to be alone. He inhaled slowly

the atmosphere of cloth-draped counters, the menacing stance of full life-sized dress figures looking like ghastly waxwork horrors in the strange night light. He walked past a crew of West Indian charwomen, not on hands and knees with buckets, but pushing purring machine scrubbers, dryers, waxers. Indifferent Indian and Congo faces with cigarettes dangling from wet lower lips; but he knew better than to point out the nonsmoking rules; he had had two meetings with union grievance committees already that month. One just had to get used to the modern philosophy that no one wanted to do his job any more, and that the union heads were making a fat thing of fringe benefits, medical care, pensions, vacations and committees on toilet paper and hot coffee.

Nathan inspected the long rows of covered cases, the silent watching humps of the cash registers. Gods of some Egyptian tomb. He felt under the counter of the machine in the leather department. Just as he suspected: chewing gum again stuck there in thick wads. He went up the now unmoving ramp and stood between a display of silver tea services imported from England and a menacing jungle set in which a girl's wax figure in shorts and tight sweater held up a best-selling novel ("Makes *Peyton Place* read like *Rebecca of Sunny Brook Farm*"). Hardly what Nathan called a clever display, but then he belonged to the old school—crowd the counters and give them bargains. A freight elevator hummed to a stop and he got in beside an unshaven man in coveralls who was chewing tobacco.

Nathan did not address him, and the man, half asleep, didn't care to talk. A folded copy of the *Daily News* was stuck in a back pocket. On the upper floors Nathan, moving as if on wheels, flitted about, a portly ghost. Few lights were on, but between the racks of coats, the shine of reproductions of period furniture, among a forest of lamps and shades, beyond the hall of mirrors in which he saw himself—a stocky furtive figure moving in a hundred fragments of his own image—here he began to feel calm and collected. The smells of clean linen, floor wax, spilled spices and stale grease from the test kitchen, all were like a lullaby to him. He found that one of the fire doors was jammed, and that someone on the third floor —in Stretch Pants and Sports Outfits—had left a half-eaten corned-beef sandwich and the wrapper of a chocolate bar in a large plaster vase, and ants were there! Six stories up, solid steel and concrete—

yet *ants!* He made a mental note about the lack of taste in the outboard motor section, the disorder in the back of the rug department (he suspected a hasty lunch-break fornication). He sat down in a chair in Unfinished Furniture (SURFACED, READY TO PAINT, SAVE 40%). Nathan huddled in his topcoat, head turtled down; he sensed an awe, felt the whole building, its many floors, a living thing. The cleaning machines hissed from below, the elevator groaned its electric heart out. Somewhere solid heels tapped on the floor as a watchman passed, carrying his check-in clock. The Store had been designed to be full of automatic alarm systems, protective gadgets. But Nathan had insisted on watchmen as an added protection.

He felt himself calming. He went to his office and lay down on the long wide couch of fine black leather from the old Store. He unbuttoned his vest, kicked off his shoes. He'd have the family at the dock in time even if no final plan had been worked out about the marriage. He heard the stock trucks deep down under the city come in with loads that would be placed in their proper departments before the Store opened at nine-thirty. He heard the cleaning people going higher. Out in the dark street, the city sanitation crews, riding hoses, were plashing the avenue clean.

Nathan slept and came awake in panic, then calmed. Heat was rattling in the steam pipes. The sound of traffic and life began to breathe itself into the Store. The building had lain almost dormant all night. Now bells rang, speedy passenger elevators moved with polite hisses as the employees (in the old day they were "the help") hurried to their departments. The sounds of plumbing added to his living image of the Store with its uncomfortable miles of wiring, drains, pipes, the blood vessels, digestive tracts, nerve clusters that would—he looked at his father's heavy butter-gold watch—would in twenty-two minutes activate itself as an insucking, outbreathing thing—the Store.

Nathan got up and went to his private bathroom and inspected his need of a shave, exposed his teeth (too many inlays), felt the remains of his hair. He saw himself not as the brain or the dictator of the Store, but mercly the tiny spring that reacted to the time-bind and threw the switch. Below him the special open-the-doors bells were ringing, and they let in the customers. Now the building was fully alive, an animated creature on many levels.

One of the bars of the *Queen,* the Mahogany Pub, was aglow with overpolished wood and pictures reminding the passengers that there had once been an Empire and that India had been one of its jewels. It was the night before landing, and people who would never see each other again were exchanging addresses, dry kisses and sentimental pats on the back. Jacob sat in a corner sipping sherry, waiting for Judith. It would be a sort of last celebration, she had said, before he became one of the family.

A thin rake of a man, red-faced, some of his too long teeth outlined in gold, stood over the little table, a stubby fist outstretched.

"You'll pardon me, I just couldn't stay away, Reb Ellenbogan. I said to myself for three days now—there's a real Jew."

Jacob looked up at the *schlimazel* beaming at him, his eyes taking in the Harris tweeds, the crumpled shirt, the rayon necktie. "You guess right, a Jew I am, and if I'm visible to you, I'm real."

The man sat down, mopping his brow with a silk handkerchief scented with sandalwood. "Bogel is my name, Bernard Bogel, editor, publisher of a Jewish newspaper, the *Zion Express,* at Biami West in Texas. Believe me, *rebbe,* there, I said, is a Jew, and proud of it."

"I'm not a *rebbe.* I don't think so any more. And what's to be proud of being a Jew? A human being, yes."

"You've been to Israel? I've just come from there—three glorious weeks, saw everything, did everything. Milk and honey. And I wrote a poem about how I felt: 'Oh My Dead Father, Rejoice, Israel *Is.*' "

"You write poems too?"

"The kosher Keats they call me as a joke at the B'nai Brith. I'll send you a copy of my book of poems: *The Star of David Rose,* by Bernard Bogel."

"Bagel?"

"Bogel. A vigorous Texas Jewish newspaper, always in the fight for the true Jewish life. We're firm against intercreed marriage, temples that serve unlicensed kosher food, the sale of beef not inspected by the Union of Ritual Drovers and Sacrificers."

"I know those *momsers.* Racketeers, chappie, believe me—all those unions, guilds, little fancy groups of penis clippers, cattle killers, chicken pluckers, *mikva* sealers, and the graveyard burial-parlor pirates stealing the dead peoples' gold fillings . . . *all* of them against the wall," said Jacob, feeling the three glasses of sherry, still poker-faced. "Shoot them down to the last *nafka*."

Jacob watched the publisher's shock. He wanted to burst out laughing. He had met so many of these lice that fed off American Jews: pompous, self-appointed guardians—ghetto-conditioned to try to find a romantic past in a mean and cruel poverty. Oh God, he couldn't hold back his laughter at the dismay on the face of this idiot. He had to let go. And a great wind went up in Jacob's throat, the laughter came loud and sustained.

The man just sat, growing red in the face. Then he stood as in a trance, as if he could not move. "Look, *look*, I'm a respectable man, looked up to, you can't laugh at me . . . you . . ."

Jacob controlled himself. "Mr. Editor, Mr. Publisher, Mr. Poet, you're a plain and simple *putz*. Now go away. *The Star of David Rose!* Ha!"

The man fled. Jacob wiped his laughing eyes with the back of his hands. He felt fine, and stopped a bar waiter in neat white. "Chappie, ask the man at the bar if he has some Polish slivowitz. This *pishochs* is like nothing."

"Yes sir, of course."

Judith appeared in her best traveling jewels, her hairdo fresh from the ship's beauty parlor, the Emma Hamilton Salon. She pressed his shoulder pleasantly with strong fingers.

"You didn't dress, Jacob."

He looked down at his lap. "I thought I did. You mean the monkey suit like a *shommas* wears? Tell you the truth, *Shana*, I look like a waiter in a Warsaw restaurant in it. All I can say with it on is: 'You want the hot borscht with the cold potato, *or* the cold borscht with the hot potato?' No, I'm dressed enough."

Judith sat down and lifted a signal finger to the bar waiter. "Champagne . . . You still see women in a Queen Mary toque on this boat. . . . One of the good Rothschild champagnes, waiter—and be sure it's properly iced. Jacob, you'll please join me."

"I asked for some slivowitz."

"All right, dear. I'll drink for both of us. Jacob, are you as nervous as I am?"

"I'm not nervous. And you, *Shana*, if you are, they'll have to dig for it. It doesn't show."

"I've done so many strange things in my life. What if you were to turn out to be the most foolish? Love in an old woman is sometimes as insane as a dog dancing on its hind legs. Sometimes *ce monde est plein de fous.*"

"Frankness for frankness. If it's a mistake, look at the world. A mistake from the beginning. But how many fine things have appeared on it. How much joy there has been, how many children have sung, how many maidens have gone to bed with the *Song of Songs* whispered in their ears, their wombs the secret weapon replenishing the earth. Making man and woman was a mistake from the start. Who couldn't have done it better? First take the plumbing—on the economy plan, serves two purposes. Then wasn't the egg system better? Why this *swenngering* for nine months, and the woman looking at the man as if he planted pine cones in her, and—"

"Jacob, you've been drinking down here, how long?"

The bar waiter was back, a thin glass of nearly pure-white liquid and a pint bottle of champagne on a tray.

"The bar 'opes, sir, this is the right thing. Madame, shall I pour?"

Jacob held up the slivowitz and Judith her glass of racing bubbles in the amber wine. They touched rims.

"Jacob, I've forgotten all the clever toasts, but here's to a sense of being and a companionship. May you be my truest teacher."

"*Shana, Shana,* you talk as if you regret your past. Listen, when Moses was old, he asked God to forgive him his sins. And God—in those days he was a real voice, not just a recording—He said, 'Your sins, Moses, shall not be forgiven you, so that all the people shall know that the Lord does not even discriminate in favor of someone with whom He spoke face to face.'"

"The Lord has bad manners and often a rotten temper."

"Who's perfect?"

Judith smiled; he *was* drunk, he really was. And her heart went out to him and she smiled over the rim of her glass. One of the ship's boys in a tight red jacket was at Jacob's elbow. "Mr. Ellenbogan? There's this package for you, sir, I was asked to deliver."

Jacob took the little flat package and tore off its covering of blue paper. It was a small book, *The Star of David Rose*, Poems of Bernard Bogel. He opened it, wrinkled his nose and read out loud, slowly: "To Jacob Ellenbogan, a great sage of my people, who growled like a lion at me because I offended him. In admiration, from one brother in Zion to another. Bernard Bogel."

Judith set down her glass and took the book from Jacob's hand. "No, don't read tonight." Overhead a siren sounded, feet pattered politely across the deck. "Jacob, it's the Last Night party. Can you dance?"

"Was there ever a true follower of the Hasidim who couldn't?"

CHAPTER 6

◆§ Norton-on-Hudson, twenty-two minutes by train to Grand Central Station, more fashionable once than any of the other towns-on-Hudson, faced the river from a high series of ridges, staring across at the Jersey Palisades with a kind of rich indifference. Norton-on-Hudson was not what it had been in the post-Civil War years when, as Marcel said, robber barons, admirals, generals, inherited money, political graft and boodle had built a series of monstrous big houses which had charm and nostalgia when painted white, copper roofs patinaed a goose-turd green. They fitted the landscapes of oaks and maples, elms, and grassy sloping lawns. The pioneer Dutch patroons had long since left; only their names remained: Ver Planck, De Wandelaers, Van Rensselaer, Van Cortlandt. The native stock, former city dwellers who had interbred, smoked pipes, wore imported tweeds, played Goren bridge and golf, and were now defending the Jockspur and Tiller Yacht Club against Catholics, Jews, Democrats and actors, while standing siege under a leaking roof by their boathouse.

Negroes were moving into the decaying backstreet Victorian houses: slum dwellers on rich dole doing over the decaying servant quarters near the tracks of the New York Central. Norton-on-Hudson had come on some prosperous days, but they were, Nathan Pedlock said, the days of the speculators, real-estate sharks, smiling hucksters and hustlers who were bulldozing the Washington Irving hills beyond the town, covering brooks, shattering old oaks, creating their versions of Levittowns and Disney ranch-house

66

estates on thirty-foot lots. The parking meters on Main Street, Nathan noticed on his rare visits, serviced Hondas and Ramblers. The Jags, Bentleys and Lincolns were fleeing north. In the supermarkets, tasteless, plastic-wrapped, overpriced items were replacing the smoked eels. The last sturgeon had been caught in 1916 by Mordechai Pedlock. The shad run produced barely six diseased fish a year. Condoms and offal from the yachts often stained the rocky fringe of river frontage below Pedlock House's columned porticos and herb-bordered promenades.

Pedlock House jutted a bit farther into the river than its neighbors, stood a little higher. It covered four acres. It had been built in 1865 by Elijah, the founder of the Store, of solid granite with the big porches of the South, which Elijah had seen during his pack-peddler days. Over all a slate roof, copper-topped towers out of Sir Walter Scott, a deep cellar dug into the ridge's rock, and gardens and coach houses, stables for matched grays, strong-hocked mares long since gone, several hundred trees already overaged. Elijah's son Tobias had added, in 1881, such items as a better heating system of forced air, so, as Nathan remembered as a boy, one stood over a grating on cold nights and the warm breeze ran up pants legs to warm the ass and cause groans of pleasure. The large marble fireplaces were of Italian stone and ate logs. The ceilings were twenty-two feet high in the main chambers. There was, of course, a ballroom, a billiard room, a glassed-in sun porch for growing exotic plants. Mordechai, the grandson of Elijah (Time flies? "No," said Judith, "We fly—time stays"), when he took as his second wife Judith Arneth, wired the entire place for Mr. Edison's Mazda magic. The coach houses and stables were already being called garages. Nathan remembered the marvelous cars the years brought: the air-cooled Franklins, regal Pierce Arrows, Stearns-Knights, Hayneses, Paiges. The drives were repaved. The ballroom became an art gallery.

For Judith, Nathan himself added radios, washing machines, a series of telephone extensions in house and grounds. Judith sent the herd of iron deer on the lawns into exile.

Most of the time the old house was closed. Two caretakers were kept on the grounds. Storm windows were in place. An old couple in one of the towers saw to the shrouds on the furniture and to the temperature of the art gallery where the paintings of the Second Empire, the Hudson River School, the Pre-Raphaelites, grew darker and cracked and showed mold spores. Marcel had long since given up trying to get Judith to show any interest in Impressionism, Postimpressionism, Cubism, Dada, Surrealism; and as for Pop or Op art and such things—"Marcel, me hammer holes in *my* walls for such *drek!* A *meshuggener* I'm not. Really, this fashionable new art detests good taste as if it were a bad smell."

Now the window boards were taken down, the porches swept, the drive regraveled. Gertrude Lazar-Wolf, a one-woman house committee, got to Pedlock House at seven of the windy day the *Queen* was to dock. The storm shutters were latched back, the gardeners were raking leaves. Several grocer and caterer pick-up trucks were in the back unloading crates, wicker baskets, tins and extra chairs.

Gertrude parked the Lazar-Wolf Silver Cloud Rolls by the chinaberry tree she remembered from her childhood. Judith disliked the new Rolls—"When people themselves drive their own Rolls-Royces, it's the end of the world if you ask me. A Rolls was never meant to be driven except by some hired *balagulla* with slim hips. Ha, next you'll be doing your own laundry, carrying an electric hot plate in your luggage." The truth was the handyman, Saul's ex-navy bosun, took Lazar-Wolf to Wall Street and the Bank; the rest of the time he polished silver or helped the housekeeper check the wine in the Great Neck cellar. One didn't, in the atomic age, drive with a chauffeur to go shopping any more.

Gertrude adjusted her girdle, looked to the stocking seams on her solid but shapely legs, and walked up to the big porch of Pedlock House with its white brick columns in need of paint. She felt a stab in her womb and secret parts, for mostly when she had come here to visit her mother she was pregnant. Always carrying a load under her heart, and Saul always eager for more children. Well, that was past, even if the hot flashes still bothered her. She could do without the panting and red-faced emotions on the Everest mattress, thank you. One did one's duty, a man's a man, and children, God bless them, are children, but enough is enough. She had the Hadassah, the U.J.A., Zen and general semantic classes, doing over the country club's décor (there was talk of admitting a few select gentiles); that was enough for one woman, even a Pedlock.

The big doors were open, the ghost sheets of linen were off the furniture, maids were dusting and men were waxing. Her brother Marcel was pointing to where the cut flowers in Tiffany vases were to go, and in the Chinese red-velvet drawing room with its view of the Hudson through its bank of windows, the long table was already laid with damask and places of heavy silver were being set. She decided the only true heritage we leave is a spectator's eyeview; she must bring that up at the next general semantics meeting.

"It's good, Marcel," said Gertrude, rubbing her elbows after dropping her mink on a chair. "It's the only thing I remember from childhood that hasn't proved a disappointment."

A young girl with that sly grace of just-lost adolescence had come in and stood in the hallway, hands in the pockets of her green knit jacket. It was Nancy, Tom's daughter.

"Nancy darling! What are you doing here?"

The girl shrugged her shoulders and smiled. Marcel smiled back and said, "Couldn't resist the old family lair?"

"That's true, Uncle Marcel," said the girl, pivoting around to look at the walls. "I haven't been here since I was very small. . . . They say when you come back to some place you once loved everything is smaller and meaner. Well, *not* here."

"It hasn't let you down?" Marcel asked. "What luck."

"No. It's bigger, wilder, much more charming, in a heavy solid way. Sometimes I dream about it, and Grandma, and I wonder if it's really here. I've been kind of drifting around, restless, you know, like a creep nobody has room for. And I thought I'll just drive up here for a look-see from the road. I didn't mean to come in but I couldn't stay out. May I smoke?"

"Of course," said Gertrude. She was about to ask how Nancy's mother was but decided against it. "Of course. We must see more of you, dear."

"Now you're being nice." She lit a cigarette, and hands back in her pockets she looked up the staircase. "Man, that Sargent, he could paint. This de Kooning stuff doesn't come near him for brushwork."

Marcel went to her side. "That's the kind of talk I like. Yes, I'm banking on a revival of Sargent. He could out-Pop and out-Op them all, and action painting too. You've grown so, Nancy."

"That's nature's trick." She sniffed the air, fine nose way up. "I like it, the smell. The half-musty odor of old parties, old voices, almost. I'd like to come here a lot. Would anyone mind?"

Gertrude was near tears: *oy oy*, this *Kind*, this poor lonely *Kind*. But general semantics had taught Gertrude not to gush, not to be emotional about things, not right away. Try not to react at once, her swami had taught her.

"Nancy, of course no one would mind. Why don't we have lunch? And, if you want to know about the place, I can tell you things no one knows. Maybe only Marcel. He was very close to Mama."

"The mystery of a house, Gert, is best left mystery."

Nancy sat down on a red-carpeted step. "She's really getting married?"

"She appears to be," said Marcel. "No one knows for sure if she was jesting, serious, or just, well, feeling her years."

"Oh, she couldn't be senile, Uncle Marcel. She'll just sail on and on like a great ship and disappear beyond the horizon." Nancy lowered her head at this speech she hadn't really intended to make out loud. "Well, enough of my gush. You're busy. If it's all right, I'd like to go down to the river. There used to be shad in it."

Nancy went out through one of the French doors in the back of the hall. Gertrude heaved a great sigh. "There's a girl who's looking for something. And *what*, I'll tell you—"

"I'm sure you will, Gert."

"A family. They've kept her at arm's length from us. Held her up, as it were, overhead, out of reach. Now she's looking for warmth. Tom, he's no father, he's a—"

"We know what Tom is."

"And that *one* he married—well, if Nancy wants to be with us now, I'll make it my business to see she's—"

"I'm sure you'll make it your business."

Nancy stood by the river wall, by the old lead garden statues of a girl taking a thorn out of her foot and a little boy's wee-wee in danger of being snapped off by a goose. The river sounded softly as a barge went upstream loaded with old bricks. The New York City of her childhood was being torn down: Sherry's, the Plaza, Saturday afternoon at the old Met. It was being pushed upriver to fill swamps for more conforming little towns and big conforming towns, all alike, all seeing the same television, reading the same news weekly, eating the same hormone-injected roast from the supermarket, dieting on the same no-cal cola, and all very much involved with culture: Buffet prints, old Irving Stone, Saul Bellow best sellers placed just so on the hi-fi, everybody just hot for the newest weird group from England: the Four Masturbators, or the Queen's Own. A bit of wife-swapping and a cozy boff once a week after a take-home Chinese meal, a little sneering at Jews and Catholics, but a cute house guest at times: race (Negro), references (writing a thesis for his Ph.D: "Homosexual Themes in the Western Films of John Ford").

Lord, how flip she was, yet she didn't want any more of that highbrow culture, that kind of life. Better middlebrow Mabel: seeing her through a big monthly bat and two weekly hangovers— Sunday to Tuesday, Wednesday to Friday.

She picked up a stone, flat, smooth, warm to the touch. She felt lewd and shy and sensual all at once, and her breath was tight and her body reacted there and there. She threw the stone toward the river and cried out:

> "A woman is a branchy tree
> And man a singing wind;
> And from her branches carelessly
> He takes what he can find."

In the house Gertrude wiped her hands together. "So?"

Marcel said, "There is a lot to be done."

"No matter what we do Mama will find fault."

"That's her way of showing her affection. Just keep her warm."

"Can we?"

"The furnaces have short-circuited, there isn't enough fuel oil, but it will all be working by noon when Judith gets here."

"You can't get an honest day's work any more out of anyone. They just break things, Nathan says, and sit around, double-time, portal to portal."

Marcel smiled and rubbed dusty fingertips. "The age of the common man, and he's in the saddle. Perhaps the Pedlocks would have been better off and smarter to stay in the ghetto and join the International Ladies Garment Workers Union and get fringe benefits and pensions too."

"You talk like a Communist, Marcel. I don't know whether you're joking or not." She looked into the hall at the grand staircase. "We used to slide down the banister and Papa said we'd get a *tocus* full of splinters. Papa, *olva scholom*—entertained Zionists and Teddy Roosevelt and William S. Hart. How many trees did Papa plant in Palestine?"

"Three million, but in the wrong places. The Arabs cut them down for firewood. And here the gallery is a mess. The Boucher nude is badly cracked and the Pre-Raphaelites, the Burne-Jones, Holman Hunt, Millais, all need restoring. As for the Blakelocks, well, they're all really no great loss, but Mama and Papa liked them."

"Me too, Marcel. You knew what you were looking at. Solid painting. Solid. Is my taste in art poor?"

"Yes," said Marcel, turning away. He knew Gertrude and Lazar-Wolf collected dismal late Chagalls and anything with rabbis or wineglasses. Yet their tastes were no worse than the Texans who wanted Remingtons and "hosses, lots of hosses."

There was a crash. A shower of silverware came cascading down the side stairs near the pantry. Two middle-aged maids were holding an empty and shattered rosewood box lined with yellow silk. Local help. They merely giggled.

"Ma'am, the handles were that worn. Just busted out."

"All right, all right," said Gertrude. "Just pick them up and get them polished. Marta, Marta!"

A middle-aged woman with brown hair cut short, great fat arms, thick torso enveloped in an apron, wide androgynous face sweating, came out of the swinging kitchen doors, armed with a long ladle.

"*Yoi istenem!* I try cook, I try work. Always somebody crying out—all *bulunds* shout shout."

"Marta, Mr. Ellenbogan is sort of kosher. I mean no mixing butter with meat, no cream in the coffee after dinner. You understand, Marta?"

Marta Nemenyi, the cook, Hungarian, touchy-tempered, suffering from heartburn, bunions and the heat of the kitchen, lifted apron, dress and petticoat to her face to wipe it, revealing torn black stockings, huge garters, pink thighs like—Marcel thought—scalded pig carcasses.

"*Yoi istenem! Buss meg a sonya! Zhidos Zhidos!*" The cook disappeared beyond the swinging doors to shout shrilly at Willie for some mishap in the kitchen. Willie, ageless, of no known nation, small, cunning and handy, had been with Pedlocks for thirty years, since boyhood.

Gertrude turned to an older woman with a crooked mouth who

was testing the top of a sideboard for dust. "Mrs. Fields, all the beds changed? All the linen fresh?"

The housekeeper's mouth curled a little further as she spoke with a slight Southern drawl, "Yes'm, Miss Pedlock." Mrs. Fields, the housekeeper, had never fully accepted Lazar-Wolf as a member of the family—"You can't tell me he isn't some kind of a *glitz* or *litvak*; one of them pore-white-trash Jews."

Gertrude took out her cigarette case, a gift from the Bank when Joanne was born. She and Marcel lit up and, smoking, sat on blue-velvet-covered chairs inhaling their long-ago childhood with a sense of the sadness of time passing and the gladness at being still alive.

"She'll disagree with everything we're doing here today."

"It makes her happy. How's Tony?"

"Fine. Did the Village rounds with him the other night."

"*You?*"

"You think I'm something belongs in museums?"

"Ha, who knows anybody. But why don't you get married again?"

"Judith is enough. I never really cared for it."

"Marriage or sex?"

"Both. I let Tom handle that end, no pun intended."

"It's crazy the way Tom was always chasing *and* catching too. Remember the redheaded Polish maid?"

"She seduced us both when Tom was fourteen. But now, looking back, I think Tom started it all."

"So what about Tony marrying? Listen, there's a girl on Long Island near us—the Sylvester Guggenheims, charming, contact lenses, Smith graduate, raises dogs, so you see not *too* Jewish. I'll have just a little dinner and you and Tony—"

"Don't. Tony is living his own life."

"Level with me—twenty-six, not even engaged. He's maybe just a little bit a fairy?"

"Good God, no! I mean how the hell should I know? Really, Gert."

"The in-groups, they're all homos these days. Theater, books, the press. Nice Jewish boys—lots of them. When I see them I want to go up to them and say, how can you do this to your own mother, your own father. Jews don't become alcoholics, fighters in the streets, so why *this*, why?"

"I'm sure you'll come up with an answer."

"Is that supposed to be a witty remark? Some classic ploy? Hand me the ash tray."

"Sorry, Gert. I suddenly feel I never left the house. And we were so happy here. There were no unresolved dilemmas. It was all a purely sensory enjoyment, and Mama one summer driving us around the grounds in the wicker-chaise and the smelly pony."

"I'm not promoting for Tony, but there are a lot of fine girls of the best Jewish families around."

"Really, Gert, the Pedlocks never went in too much for this Jewish society nonsense."

The Hungarian cook was back, some butter on the end of her nose. "*Istenem! Istenem!* Come look at ducks they send. No ass on them. This is duck? This *is* . . ."

In a cloud of Hungarian obscenity Gertrude rushed the cook back into the kitchen for them both to face the butcher, who was delivering improperly made birds.

Marcel sat alone, feeling the atmosphere of the old house enter his body like some invisible fog, and he remembered his father in one of those bad days when Mama had suddenly left again for Europe. Papa saying: "So, Marcel, what is life? Three days of poor food in a second-rate hotel." Poor Papa. Why did no one say "poor Judith" of their marriage?

In the morning mist on a choppy sea—a Camembert-green day —the *Queen Elizabeth* approached the shores of America, slowing somewhat to make contact in the low-lying fog with the pilot boat off the Kill Van Kull, a riptide sucking in toward the Narrows. Salt spray had formed a crust on the ship's rails and funnels. The decks were damp. Below there was activity as passengers swore eternal friendship with people they would never see again. Ship-met lovers stared at each other in saturated silence—half hope, half regret.

Jacob Ellenbogan inspected himself in the small mirror of his cabin. All right, he'd wear the new blue suit, he'd stand for the white too soft shirt, the simple string of black tie. But the shoes he'd keep, the old ones—not get into the orange *mameligge*-colored ones from Bond Street. The socks would remain white and garterless, the underwear long, and he'd put on the black homburg. But the pince-nez on the long black silk cord, no! Good enough the cracked lens in the silver frames for his eyes; glasses bought for a few francs from a barrow in the Paris flea market. Jacob smiled at his image. *Azoi vee a zelner far der teer?* What is a man? A reflection in a pool and God stirs the pool and *where* is man? Ah, as Hittel put it, was even the pool an illusion? The cabala was the clue he needed and had studied so long. He sang through his nose: "As the hart panteth after the water-brooks, so panteth my soul after Thee, O God." Yes, the true cabalist must blot out the world, all its traps and its sensual content, replace them with reason and intuition. The flesh with spirit, the visible with the hidden, the known with the unknown. So far, so far he hadn't been able to do it. The material world seduced one. Here he was, nearly a bridegroom again, and the cabala (in Hebrew "the received"), the Hidden Wisdom had not prevented this thing. Ah, but perhaps he could study in peace now, inside the embrace of Judith, work his way through the Zoroastrian, Pythagorean, Neo-Platonic emanations. He had brought his bride only his books, the Sefer Yetzura— Book of Creation—and the Zohar, the Splendor. Without them life was a lost tit in this America. As he was busy reroping his book box, the Irisher came in buttoned up in a gray coat with a red fox collar like on the hats of the Polish rabbis.

"Mr. Bogan now, you'll stop that. The stewards will handle the baggage."

"A *shvariz migilla of dere.*" His Cockney-learned English was shrill. "I think I didn't bring the Simon-bar-Yohai text."

"Your heathen things don't interest me. But herself wants you properly dressed. The shoes, those *shoes.*"

"*Lig in drared,*" said Jacob Ellenbogan, "*mit dein kup tzvishin.* The shoes I keep as they are. Have I feet or stones?"

"Come along then. Don't be hanging back, man."

He followed Irish up the stairs, a nice bit of flank on her. He almost gave it a *top*—a feel, a *joup*—pinch—then sighed. "All flesh is grass, but before it was grass it was a sinner."

Judith was on A-Deck facing a sharp wind in a sable coat. She wore a yellow scarf tied over her head and a tall black fur hat. She strode back and forth as if she were docking the ship herself—seaman's heels, she called them. She rocked with the motion of the boat when she stopped to make a turn back. Her face was a little overcolored, and any idea Jacob might have had about getting her to cut her hair for the ritual wig—the *sheitel*—or bathe in a *mikva* he gave up. With a bit of red paint and lipstick and God knows what else women trick themselves up with, he'd have to take her the way she was. Even Rabbi Israel Baal-Shem-Tov, founder of Hasidism (blessed be his memory), was once driven from his own house by his wife's broom, and he explained to his followers that being himself among the *tzaddikim*, the broom had been bewitched in the strong hands of Honnah his wife. But the black eye he couldn't explain.

"Jacob, soon you'll see land. A return home—how we're tied and bound to our memories."

"It frightens me, *Shana*, as if when I touch the alien land I'm dispossessed of some magic, exiled in a Babylon."

Nathan Pedlock awoke at dawn, shaved, showered, had a light breakfast of a boiled egg, toast and coffee. He was not a lonely man. He had many friends at card clubs, in the organizations he belonged to to preserve old landmarks, to train young men for fields and machines, transport those on the land to the city, and those in the city to the land. (It was certainly a topsy-turvy world.) But he had few real friends. His true life was the Store; the two other children Mordechai, his father, had had by his first wife, Nathan's mother, were far away.

Nathan swallowed two digestive pills and went down to the blustery street, where old newspapers were flying, for a taxi. Nearby, the bang of pneumatic jackhammers, the shrill cry of iron cranes. They were tearing the fine old city apart.

"Hudson River, Cunard Line. The *Elizabeth*." He wondered why any change of daily pattern made him suffer so. He belched lightly as the cab hit crosstown sections of torn-up street paving. He tasted egg, toast, coffee and whatever was in his pills.

Tom Pedlock felt dry, so dry; he was crawling across the Great American Desert—the wind, a *bossa nova*, beat in his ears—crawling on his hands and knees, and the sands smelled of sandalwood perfume, stale cigarette smoke, the unwashed body of a woman. He opened his eyes. It was painful, and the half-dark of pulled shades and drapes made it seem some lost place, not desert any more, but a strange room. The bed vibrated; his skull ached with extraordinary tenacity, and the pain over his eyes pressed down. He was in Rita Burton's bedroom on East 80th Street, and she was next to him, pressing close, pore to pore, breathing with her mouth open, a slight difficulty inhaling through her nose. Her bronze hair lay wild over the pillow. There was a musky smell in the air from the night, the half-empty glasses, the ash tray of their last cigarettes. Tom had to wrinkle his nose at the memory hovering in the air of their drunken love-making. Not that it had seemed anything revolting then, but, face it now, he just felt too low and hungover.

His throat was dry, and he stood up naked and saw himself in the mirror—at forty-eight still in shape despite the start of a paunch. He felt a sense of malaise, lassitude—yes, like a crumbled Jew, let's face it, he thought. And something banged in his head as he sipped rancid water from the container on the night table. Rita Burton stirred and said an obscene word in a fastidious Vassar accent, then laughed.

Tom Pedlock snapped his fingers. "Mama!" Today, his thought processes signaled—sometime this morning—the *Elizabeth* docking—Cunard Line—with who—some old Hebe—marrying. He snapped his fingers again. Rita opened her eyes; she had been too emotionally involved to remove her false eyelashes. One had become unstuck; she pulled it off sadly.

"Lovee, I hope I don't look as bad as you."

"It was a big night." He patted her behind as she turned away to yawn and stretch. She had a magnificent body. The throat a little puckered, the under-the-eye discoloration showing the effects of their three-day bat. "Listen, honey, I just remembered. My mother is coming in today."

"Who? What? Look, lovee, go put on the coffee. You know where everything is." She cupped her breasts with her hands, then scratched her ribs, remembered something and smiled, eyes sticky, half closed. "It's been a something, a *something.*"

"I'll see you later at the Store. Where the hell are my pants?"

"The coffee, Tommie. We undressed in the living room, remember? Say, did I bite you? Where?"

Tom felt a sore earlobe. "Living room?"

"Very vaguely it seems so."

"I must go—family hassle."

"Give us a kiss, Tommie."

"It's nearly ten. The *Queen* may dock, have docked already."

"They never dock on time. *Um um* . . . What makes me like this with you? You're married, Jewish, a lousy lay. All right—*ouch*

—I take that back!" Rita laughed. "*Mmmm*. Come over on this side. *Ah*."

"Rita . . ."

"We're both nuts. This can't go anyplace. I'll get fired. Your high-assed wife will strip you clean if you step out of line. Crazy crazy. Tommie, Tommie. Get me a Kleenex."

"Don't cry."

He avoided her gravesite breath—his must smell like a kennel too. He buried his face in the nape of her neck as she turned and twisted.

"Touch me there."

"There?"

"Oh *there!*"

Naked body to naked body, wet, steeped in the scent of her, his mouth found her breasts, found one, shifted to painful bites on the other, and all the time her grinding under his touching, but he delaying the final pelvic plunge; they had learned it was better to wait until every pleasure nerve screamed and every muscle was hard, solid with desire to function in the final parody of the reproductive act.

Now he turned her over and bit at the base of her neck (*her* spot of ecstasy), and she muttered those fond obscenities that love play brought out in jaded people. She was rolling over and her legs flew up as if seeking firm ground.

"Oh Tommie, *don't* hold back, *don't*."

There was the raised fury of despair that always came over him before he entered a woman, and he knelt between her spread quivering legs and he saw the shaggy moist arch, that spring which had excited him since his groping schoolboy days and had been the only comfort in his life. She reached for him and held his sex in her hand, and he looked down at her, the object of his love: her. Mouth open, breathing hard. And they were as if together planning some cruel ritual rather than the act of passion.

Their love at such moments was never tender, only the cruel drive of their mindless bodies, engorged organs, the play of their trembling hands on each other. By fingers, by teeth, by tongue they built up their pressures, and when he launched himself between her legs, their cries were like the agony of condemned prisoners who felt at last the release, the peace of the ax on their necks.

But the play had just begun as he entered her; mouths glued

together, they rolled and thrashed, legs interlocked, the scent of room and bed and bodies a musk stronger than anything else, the whistle of their breathing choked with half-words.

He thought of all the times they had been like this; he wondered what Mama would think if she could see him now, see what he was doing, they were doing, with what brutal impatience, with what a feeling of despair, of sensual charge, a kind of desperate ferocious hope. . . . *Now!* They lay still, eyes closed. A little light came around the drawn shades and drapes.

Tom Pedlock began to count to a hundred silently. He got up at one hundred and one, rose and went into the living room. He began to dress quickly, standing on Rita's ocelot coat as he got into his pants.

CHAPTER 7

～§ Mark Penrose, filled with a Petronian sense of logic, stood on the terrace of their Sutton Place apartment. They had bought it with some G.M. stock of Naomi's years before, and while it cost twenty thousand a year just for maintenance and carrying charges, he was proud of the place, a duplex full of art. He cut a flower for the buttonhole of his Italian woolen jacket, a white carnation that had survived the chill mornings. He inhaled, exhaled, carefully adjusted his very expensive salt-and-pepper toupee, in which he lived and slept, changing each week to a fresh one and sending the last out to be cleaned and rewaved. Glued to his head, just the proper shade, it gave him with his high color, his good tan, the appearance of a man in his middle forties. He was fifty-three.

Mark went back to the living room, admired Hokusai's print of the "Great Wave," and went into Naomi's bedroom after a delicate tap on her door. They had not shared a room for twenty years, and his rare moments of passion (no, not passion—biological recall, he preferred to call it) usually took place in the afternoon, when the help was off, on a sofa in the library, cheerful, jolly, most friendly, under the eyes of the Han bronze pots, if those things were eyes.

Naomi, in gray robe, gun-metal stockings, carved lapis-lazuli earrings, was just lifting a neat litle gray hat onto her hair. How slim and young she looked. They'd do. If they could keep the calories away, they'd make a fine couple for a great many years yet.

"I've ordered the car from the garage, Naomi."

"There's bound to be heavy traffic. Wouldn't a taxi be better?"

"Judith deserves a little traffic fighting. *Chic.*"

"The hat?"

"The entire ensemble. Heels a bit high?"

"I can handle them. Sleep well?" She offered her made-up face and he pecked at it from an inch away. He knew better than to touch the carefully brushed-on face. He was reminded of Saul La-zar-Wolf's vulgar remark the other night— "You know what a nymphomaniac is? A Jewish woman who will sleep with her husband the same day she's been to the beauty parlor."

Rather good, but low, like Saul himself.

Naomi snapped on a green-stone-set bracelet. "Let's break away early if we can. I can't stand the old house. It plunges me into depths of reveries Dr. Shindell says are bad for my analysis."

"We'll not get away before the dinner. Even your worldly mother has the old racial habit of offering the fruit bowl and pressing you to eat. In her case it's a tureen of *foie gras.*"

He didn't like the way Naomi smiled at the mild jest only with her teeth. That sonofabitch Dr. Shindell and his Freudian trash was perhaps going too far.

Lazar-Wolf's Silver Cloud Rolls-Royce darted across the Queensboro Bridge, sparkling in the strong cold sun as the shadows bent before it. The car bravely entered the 59th Street traffic. Their exnavy man, Rodgers, drove. He wore only a chauffeur's cap, refusing to put on the full uniform. At Rodger's side sat Mendes, down from M.I.T., with a sore throat, at seventeen too tall, too thin, his nose that of a mature man. In the back between Gertrude and Saul were Dave and Sheila, and on the two folding seats were Sharon, feeling at fifteen this was—oh Gawd—pretty square; and Joanne, at five, feeling that it was pretty swell. Saul held a cigar in his mouth unlit, still in its cellophane wrapper. Gertrude didn't like the smell of a lit cigar in the Rolls; it made her carsick—God forbid—like the morning sickness of her many pregnancies.

Joanne said, "Grandma coming?"

"Yes, dear, don't get your nice new shoes dirty."

Sharon, a pretty girl with good skin and too long teeth, said, "She's wiping them on her dress; oh Gawd, kids!"

Mendes turned to face them from the isolation ward of the front seat. "You think I can get to see the engine room?"

"Don't breathe on the children."

"I want to inspect the generators."

Gertrude adjusted Dave's necktie. "You're there, Mendes, to welcome Grandma, not to be a tourist."

Saul Lazar-Wolf picked up the car phone and proceeded to get the Bank and his nephew, Dickie Lazarus. He chewed on the encased cigar and discussed the opening market prices, city bonds on the West Coast, and warned Dickie to keep his eye on any new statements from the Lancia firm in Milan, which seemed either to be merging with Fiat or about to sink. "And check on what Ganzler Fairs Stores are doing."

He hung up the phone and Dave said he had to go. Now. Lazar-Wolf smiled. "A phone yes, a radio yes, but a *pish teppel* in this Rolls-Royce, no."

Tony Pedlock, in a heavy round-necked cable-stitch sweater, blue slacks, the windbreaker of balloon cloth open, ran across the street toward the pier, narrowly missing being run down by a lumbering Diesel sixteen-wheel truck carrying crates of live chickens. In the smells of bird droppings and the dirty river, the sound of the driver cursing, Tony got to the shelter of the pier entrance. It all added to his early-morning difficulties. He hated to get up early and hated to get to bed until late. Most of the night he had been at a jazz session taped at Newport, at the pad of a Madison Avenue copywriter who had all the new Coltrane recordings and the latest Diz, something good on the piano by Monk, a few old Bird things that hadn't been commercially issued. (One just didn't, he mused, use full names in way-out-jazz circles. It was Myles, or the Duke or Jerr.) Not that Tony felt he was a jazz nut or cared too much for the cool, but it was a good excuse not to go to his place in the Village and go to bed. The girl from Bennington he had been living with was getting married to a boy whose father owned the Beth Sholom Cemetery in Chicago and was rich enough to be in trouble with the income-tax department.

Tony had been madly in love for the first few weeks, but now he felt almost sure he was relieved. Tess Goldfarb had given him back his Princeton ring, the book on mountain climbing and a little advice. "Look, no matter what a decent Jewish girl says in bed, she's always *thinking* of marriage. Goodbye."

The *Queen* was just rounding the end of the pier, being shoved by two groaning tugs, moved around like a huge invalid by the three hooting little guardians. Tony liked the excitement of docking, the tall gray wall of the ship, rusty water running dull red from some vent, the smell of sea, paint, the roar of steam in some petcock, smoke being torn by a wind in which geeking gulls wheeled crying their desolate call. He laughed, remembering someone saying last night, "The human condition is hopeless but not serious."

The jet set, the U people Tony knew, traveled only by the fastest, most modern planes and thought of all ship people as prehistoric and drips. Tony had a shamed feeling he preferred ships himself: the leisure, the grace, dignity, rather than smelling the stewardesses, fear and Kotex at forty thousand feet. He looked around for his father. Marcel wasn't in sight. Progress, progress; they were creating snowless ski runs, and soon instant skiing would be everywhere. He waved. Uncle Nathan stood behind a bank of glass windows watching the docking process. He turned and pressed Tony's shoulder with a yellow-gloved hand.

"Tony! A surprise. Not climbing an Alp?"

"Not today, Uncle Nathan. I almost sent flowers. But I figured Grandma might think I was wishing she were dead."

"Ah, here's Tom. *Oy*, look at him. That *kurva* has been with him. Take a lesson, is it worth it? Hello, Tom."

"Hello, Uncle Tom."

"Lo, Tony boy. Nat."

Tom was very spruce in a too narrow-brimmed hat with a pheasant feather in it, a well-cut London topcoat, pale pigskin gloves; the trousers were a bit wrinkled. His face was professionally freshly shaved and powdered, his eyes deep in dark wrinkles and full of pain. "Made it. Tony, I thought—"

"Thought I was climbing an Alp. How do we get aboard?"

Nathan looked with pity and a kind of revulsion at Tom. "I've arranged for everything. Tom, you have breakfast."

"Coffee."

The Lazar-Wolfs began to yoohoo from the pier entrance.

Tom waved back. "Mabel couldn't make it. Nancy is coming down from school."

Soon, of Judith's children, only Marcel was missing on the Cunard pier.

Marcel still slept in the apartment on the fourth floor of the DuVere & Starkweather Galleries on East 57th Street, south side. A very imposing gray-green stone front with its bronze plaque: *DuV.& S. Est. 1870.* Two small windows done in black satin, two little gold signs, nothing else: DUV. & S. ART: TRADITIONAL. MODERN. No need to say more. You knew DuVere & Starkweather, were recommended, perhaps had a family heirloom painting to sell, or your late aunt's Cezanne. It was not offensively brusque like the new places.

DuVere was dead, had died, Marcel would explain, in a socially important Palm Beach auto accident in 1935. Starkweather was on the island of Majorca, a loose-limbed, big-mustached sufferer from asthma, no longer active in the firm ("a friend of Noel and Cecil and Christopher"). Marcel Pedlock was president, director, owner and chairman of the board of DuVere & Starkweather. He was thinking of inserting his name either between or at the end of the firm's title. It was a problem he often thought of when too tired to write in his journal or while waiting for his two sleeping pills to take hold.

It was the sleeping pills that had caused him to miss the arrival of his mother on the *Queen*. Doctor Newberger had changed brands on him. Marcel had worked late on his journal; the new pills seemed to drive him deeper into unconsciousness. He slept now while the *Queen* whistled from the Hudson and was moored to the pier. Marcel, wraithlike, drugged, in yellow Sulka silk pajamas, surrounded by the dark blue of the bedroom walls, in the wide brass bed he had removed from Pedlock House years ago. The apartment was large; Stanford White had designed the building at the turn of the century. It had proportion, height and ease, the vestigial remnants of forgotten graces. The bedroom contained no art objects, no paintings, just two walls of Marcel's favorite books —Pepys to Stendhal. He was going through a recurring period of dislike of art and art talk and art buyers. It came on him, these extremes of response, regularly with his attacks of shingles; all those games of playing with lumps of mud or pouring metal or making colored messes on canvas or marks on paper then seemed the ultimate foolishness. He would agree with Freud, who had once told Marcel that all forms of creative art were merely little games moral men play with themselves while waiting for the final annihilation: the proof of their nothingness.

Marcel stirred and moaned as if trying to avoid some last extremity. The drug still held his mind locked in sleep, and his body and his tissues and his electrochemical makeup (Marcel was a non-Aristotelian and believed man was not just a mind *and* body). When he slept all of him slept; when he was angry all of him was angry; when he was in love all of him was in love. But he had not been in love for many years. His vitality was low, his sensuality almost zero.

Buddha appeared: "We must unburden ourselves of matter." Marcel was aware he was waking slowly, slowly, coming from a great dark, coming into a warm blue, rising like a cloud of chrome yellow from some deep. First the shapes of the two Chinese lamp bases (Sung), the pale-blue shades. The photograph of his son, Tony, in his Olympic team sweater, smiling into a wintry sun, skis over his shoulder. The old Chippendale set of drawers with the ritual brass candlesticks some Pedlocks had carried into exile and used every Friday night when they lit ritual candles. Marcel's eyes traveled, still half glazed, to the wide muffled windows; beyond them the traffic of the day was like the roar in the seashell held to an ear—a shell his father had once bought him in Atlantic City. River sounds, the hiss of the elevator taking some customer to the second or third floor where the drawings and the Rodin and Henry Moore bronzes were displayed. River sounds? Lord, Mama, *Mama!* His eye leaped (no; *not* leaped; Marcel hated literary terms for things or movements); they went directly to the gold traveling clock in its yellow leather stand. Eleven-twenty-two. Mama was in, passing through customs, landed. He not there. He sat bolt upright and rubbed his thin bony chest, feeling each hard rib. Mama would raise holy hell. H-E-L-L.

Coal dust, gas ordors, sea rot, old wood smells came from the city and pier to meet the ship nudging its mooring lines. Porters, sailors, bath maids, one of the ship's officers stood around Judith Pedlock and Jacob Ellenbogan on A-Deck. She had refused to stay below to wait for the family. Now they flung themselves at her: Gertrude, Naomi, Lazar-Wolf, kissed her cheek. Tom held his breath and brushed his lips to her fur collar. Mark Penrose asked about the crossing. Tony grinned. Nathan winked.

"Enough, enough," Judith shouted. "Go see to the bags, the trunks, Tom. Wait. This is Jacob Katzenellenbogan. But Ellenbogan *de bon augure* for short."

The little bright-eyed man with the wispy mustache, minuscle Imperial on chin, face under the new homburg, in the still-uncreased blue suit, smiled at them, shifted his furled ancient umbrella and shook hands here and there as Judith made introductions.

"What a *banda*, what a tribe," he said. "So Lazar-Wolf, so Tom, so you're a son-in-law chappie?"

"Moses Fuderbloom," said Judith grinning maliciously at Mark. She pulled Tony's ear. "This is Tony."

Tony was delighted with Jacob. "There are a lot of us."

"And who's the pretty one?"

Tony turned. Nancy was pushing her way toward her father. Yes, she sure was a pretty cousin. "That's Tom's daughter, Nancy."

Tom smiled and pressed his daughter's arm. "Well, knock me over."

"You look as if I could," Nancy said. "Come on, let's talk to them."

"Mama, you know Nancy?"

"Another *shiksa*?"

Nancy laughed. "I'm your granddaughter." She leaned over and kissed Judith. "How flattering, you thinking I was one of Dad's dates."

"I should have known such good taste he hasn't got. Jacob, a granddaughter. Tom's."

Jacob put her offered hand between his two. "I knew, beginning with Judith, the family beauty had to seep down."

"You're saying all the right things, isn't he, Dad?"

Tom was watching his daughter. Somehow he had never imagined her in a family setting, the Pedlock side. Yet here she was at the pier. He put his arm around her. "Sweetie, I should have thought of telling you to come down."

"You're just a rotten father and I love you anyway."

"I want to know what you're doing away from school, appearing here, there, around town."

"How about talking about it at that lunch?"

"All right. Not today, but soon."

"Oh sure." She let her voice slide away as people crowded toward the engaged couple. Lots of Jewish-looking kids, pampered a bit, overfed. Their mother must still tuck them in nights, kiss them pleasant dreams, even leave a night light burning. Lucky little bastards.

Judith said, "Fuderbloom, step aside."

"Grandma, Grandma! You bring presents?" shouted Sheila and Joanne almost together. Nora kept them from pressing herself too closely.

Two men with cameras came forward. "Just a few shots, Mrs. Pedlock."

Tom wiped his damp brow in the chill air. "From the Store, Mama. For the papers."

Judith waved her well-gloved hands. "The other side, gentlemen, the good side. This side makes me look like Laurel, or Hardy, which is the fat one?"

"Well, Nahum, go kiss the *bubba*."

"He looks thin to me," Judith said. "Gittel, he looks starved." (Gittel for Gertrude was Mordechai's idea of a name.)

Gertrude protested that Nahum was eating like a colt.

Saul Lazar-Wolf managed to offer Jacob Ellenbogan a cigar. Nathan tried to light it. "I hear you come from Zhitomir, Reb Ellenbogan."

"Where else, Lazar-Wolf, and you?" His Cockney English seemed out of place with his appearance of a Hasidic saint.

"From Bialystok; my grandfather was the Rabbi Seoram, who edited the *Mahzor* of Rabbi Ammon of Mayence."

Jacob smiled. "Ah, a breath of something fine in all this nonsense." He pointed to the city, to the passengers.

A young man with a pad pushed his way forward. "Mr. Bogan, I'm from the *Jewish Welt*. What do you think of modern Judaism in America today?"

"I think I don't. I think I don't know nothing, chappie. I haven't seen it yet."

"And the American Jews' place in the modern world?"

Jacob turned to Lazar-Wolf. "*Wus hockt er mir a chinik?*— What is he hitting me on the teakettle for?"

Lazar-Wolf pushed the young man aside. "The Store will have a formal press conference. Not here, young fella."

"Mr. Bogan, will you and your wife, when you're married, keep a kosher house? Our readers want to know."

The answer, if it ever came, was lost as Judith, among grand-children, children, in-laws and Nora O'Hara (carrying jewel boxes), suddenly shouted: "Marcel! Where's Marcel? You don't want to tell me, do you? Any of you?"

Gertrude grabbed her mother's gesturing right hand. "Tell you what, Mama?"

"He's dead, that's what. Marcel, he's gone. He was always not strong. I didn't breast-feed him long enough like the rest."

"No, no," said Tony. "Grandma, I phoned the galleries. They said he was still sleeping."

"Those pills he takes, a sign of moral insufficiency. Jacob, take my arm."

Naomi said, "*Au plaisir de vous revoir.*"

Judith answered, "Bad grammar, Naomi."

There were other groups leaving the *Queen*, but Tony doubted if any were as loud, as large, as colorful as the Pedlocks. He loved the old gal and wondered why Judith's vitality sometimes embarrassed the rest of the family. Tony hoped she would act the *yenta* a bit more to set Mark Penrose back on his heels. He noticed Nancy had slipped away. He had wanted to talk to her.

The customs section had been alerted. Pedlock & Sons were important importers, and while they never bribed, customs officers could get a bargain, twenty percent off, at any of the Pedlock stores when they showed their service cards.

The large Irish customs officer shook hands with Judith, "Welcome back, welcome back," and looked over the filled-in form Nora handed him. "And that's it, McMertry. Herself always has all the bills and check stubs if you want to put eye on them."

"Now, O'Hara, I never question any list of hers, darlin'."

"Don't blarney me, McMertry."

The two always played a bit of low Irish vaudeville like this. It was their act, and Nora went along with it even if she knew McMertry was north of Ireland and a Black Protestant bastard whose brothers had shot many an I.R.A. in their time.

McMertry was about to make his usual mystic chalk marks on luggage and bags when he saw the battered wooden trunk wound in rope, its brass hinges sprung, Hebrew lettering on its side.

"Yours, Mrs. Pedlock?"

"Mr. Ellenbogan's. He's with me, here on a student's permit."

"A student? *You*, sir?"

Jacob shrugged his narrow shoulders. "Who isn't a student of life, Mr. McMertry?"

The customs officer looked at the little old Jew with doubt.

Lazar-Wolf handed the customs officer a cigar. "It's a mere formality. He's marrying Mrs. Pedlock. That will give him certain rights beyond that of a mere student."

"Saul," said Judith crisply, "I don't want a public discussion."

"To be sure, to be sure," said the customs officer. "Mr. Ellenbogan, what's in that trunk?"

"Books, scrolls, manuscripts, prayer shawls, torah covers, very old ones."

"You've filled out a form?"

Judith said, "Yes, yes. It's all antiques. Duty-free. Damn it, Nathan, what's holding us up?"

He said, "Just a minute more."

The customs officer avoided Judith's stare. "Mr. Ellenbogan, is there anything of an obscene or pornographic nature in these volumes as defined by the Ordinance of Section 106 of the revised Manual of Imports?"

"Just books, chappie," said Jacob.

Lazar-Wolf stepped forward again, cigar case open. "Chief, this is a very great rabbi, I mean like a cardinal. He wouldn't be carrying anything of an erotic nature, I assure you."

Jacob was pursing his lips, fingering his little beard. Behind him the family stood, some pressing forward, little Dave picking his nose. Jacob said, "Erotic? Oh yes, lots of it. The Song of Songs that is in Solomon. Ha, and the Cities of the Plain in the Old Testament as you call it. To us it's, in a way, oh, yes . . ."

The customs officer frowned, made chalk marks on the battered trunk. "That's all right, Mr. Ellenbogan, the courts declared the obscene stuff in them texts you named are okay." He touched his cap. "And a happy married life, Mrs. Pedlock."

"Thank you, McMertry. Come, Jacob."

Lazar-Wolf said softly, "Gertrude, Joanne has just wet in her pants."

Tony took Judith's free arm. "Fabulous sacred obscenity."

"There is something sick in this country," she said, smiling.

Judith, arm-in-arm with Jacob and Tony, marched toward the exit, and Joanne followed, steaming in the chill dank air of the pier. Near the entrance a taxi was just ejecting Marcel Pedlock, hair carelessly combed, tie poorly knotted. Judith let out a small cry of satisfaction."So you're not dead after all?"

"No, Mama, no." They hugged and kissed with loud smacking kisses. "You look damn poorly, Marcel, and your color—Oh, this is Jacob Ellenbogan. My son, Marcel."

They shook hands. Nathan said, "We have enough cars?"

"Gittel, take the child indoors. She'll catch cold in her bladder. Nathan, is the house ready?"

"Yes." He motioned to the black Lincoln waiting with its motor running, smoke purring from its exhaust. The car pulled up. "You'll go direct to Norton-on-Hudson, Judith. You too, Reb Ellenbogan. I'll ride with the driver."

Judith, her bulk halfway into the car, said, "Marcel, you ride with me. Which is your boy?"

"Tony there."

"Yes, yes, of course. Tony. He can press in between Nathan and the driver. Inside, Tony."

"I'm in."

Nathan said, "I'm dropping off at the Store. See you, Judith, at the dinner tonight."

Judith seated herself, wriggled, grunted, "Good to be home. Nora, hand me the jewel cases. You follow with the luggage. All right, see the rest of you tonight. Naomi, you're showing too much bone. Mark must like a *zaftig* bite now and then. All bone, no. Jacob, what's holding you back?"

"I was talking to Lazar-Wolf, ah, a real Jew."

"And what are we *de bonne volonté*, Cossacks?" Judith waved, Tony thought, like the Queen of England, as the door of the car was closed and she settled back, crowding her companions. "They don't make cars like they used to. Old Tobias, he had a Pierce Arrow you could have a *minyan* in it and have room to hang Nasser. Jacob, you properly settled?"

"I'm all right, *Shana*."

"A bit of a frail thing, Jacob, but a head on him, a plethora of wisdom. The Pope would like to own it. Nora, my shoes are murdering me."

Tony said, "She's in the next car."

The Lincoln moved off and went quickly uptown. The family, left like shipwrecked sailors, moved toward their own cars. Lazar-

Wolf nodded. "The little guy, he's all right. If Judith doesn't crush him into her own pattern."

Tom put his hands deep into his coat pockets. "I don't understand it. She always traveled with the best people. He's got her bewitched, if you ask me. Why would she want to get married again?"

Naomi said, "It was a good idea opening the old house up *there*."

The Penroses departed; the Lazar-Wolfs departed, Gertrude wrapping damp Joanne into a car robe. Tom was left trembling. He went into a snack shop and asked for a cup of very hot black coffee and two aspirins. After swallowing the pills he sipped the scalding coffee. Around him dock workers, little strange-talking importers and exporters, civil servants, made a hasty starchy breakfast, or was it lunch? He looked at his watch. He wondered if Rita would raise a stink about his not taking her to dinner tonight. Papa used to have a saying in the Store: "Never sleep with the help. You'll end up having a shrew at home and a shrew in the office." Rita hadn't reached the shrew stage yet. But they always did; say in four months, after exhilaration or exhaustion. And if this came to Mama's ears, man! She hadn't been pleased about the little Italian art student who designed the Fifth Avenue windows, and had had to be aborted. Even though he swore to Judith he was sure it was the damn football player in the sports department who had impregnated the girl at the Dartmouth Winter Carnival.

He finished the coffee and went to the phone booth to call his wife. Mabel *had* to be at Mama's dinner tonight. Had to. Damn it, it was the only wifely duty he expected from her. As he dialed he wondered where Nancy had gone to. He must really look to having lunch with the girl. Having a daughter that pretty was a problem when they reached the filling-out age; an old rip like himself knew that better than anybody.

"Hello, Mabel? Oh, where did she go? I mean, did she look . . . she wasn't feeling too well, and . . ."

BOOK III

ISAIAH

CHAPTER 8

&§ The huge brick-walled kitchen at Pedlock House at Norton-on-Hudson had been in use all day. As the dinner hour neared, Marta Nemenyi was moving and cursing, a ball of sweat and suet wrapped in white, a cruel pronged fork in one hand, a heavy pewter ladle in the other. *"Yoi istenem!"* she shouted, calling on God to witness the fools and cripples that she had to work with. A bank of gas ovens was active, boiling, broiling, stewing and steaming copper pots. On an open charcoal hearth heated cherry-red basted joints were swinging on spits.

"The salad, the salad," she said to Willie, a stocky man with grease-spattered shoes, his body tight in a too short white jacket, his torso almost lost in several large salad bowls in which vegetable life just removed from cooling compartments was being mixed. Willie had been in Judith's service for many years. He had no official title but loved food.

"The garlic fine, Willie, the wine vinegar fine, but *tha bulond* no saffron! Herself she kill anybody use saffron. Willie, Willie, you *nem yoh*—you no-good. Not that soup tureen, the big blue Delft one *mit* the river painting on it. Where the pepper mills?" She darted to the stoves to sniff at the clear soup *mit Markklossen,* peer at the *Salzgaroffel,* and move a pan of *Königsberger* meatballs off the flames. And Judith expected a *gigot d'agneau en croute.*

"Willie, the *Königsberger Klops,* quick to the table. They are having cocktails. *Yo yo lanou,* girl, what are you doing to the *pallotini di salmone?"* She rescued a braised shin of beef, pushing aside

95

the help especially hired for the dinner. "Where is the Bordeaux, Willie? The Moselle?"

Nathan Pedlock, in well-cut evening clothes and a waistcoat that accented his paunch, came into the kitchen. "Ah, Marta, like old times, the smells."

"The quality of things, not like old times, Herr Pedlock."

"Marta, do me a favor." He leaned toward her as if they two had to decide the fate of an international conference. "Herr Ellenbogan, he's from Poland. He's asked for a little *grechnevaia kasha*—buckwheat."

Marta tried to reach her blond hair tied up in a white kerchief to tear it out. "Yo, now he asks. Willie, Willie, the *kasha*, where it is?"

Willie wiped hands dripping with olive oil, garlic sauce and vinegar on his white jacket. "I'll get it."

Marta watched the soup being ladled into the blue Delft. "Herself how did she like the hors d'oeuvres? The avacado puffs, Herr Pedlock? The herring salad?"

"Just fine. We're sitting down. Marcel is late, he had to pick up Tony. We'll start without him." Nathan left, nibbling.

There was a loud tingle in the call box over the big icebox just to the right of the meat safe. The card that slid into view in the slot read DIN. RM.

"The soup, the soup!" shouted the cook.

The soup tureen went out the swinging door through the pantry, where the cakes waited with the fruit jellies and the pickled green tomatoes, stuffed eggplant, calves' brains, and the planked carp *Polsku* on its platter waiting for the almond sauce.

Marta questioned the two waitresses, got ready the *caneton aux oranges* for those who ate only kosher, examining each bronzing duck through the open oven door like a pious Jesuit a heretic on the fire.

The swinging door opened and Lazar-Wolf came in carrying a basket of dusty wine bottles. "Marta, I bring these late, but better than never. Mrs. Pedlock's taste in wine is what I'd call the best. The burgundy is a good year, the sauterne is extra special, and be careful of the cognac, it costs like gold. Keep Willie from it."

"I'll use some for the *crêpes Suzette*."

"It's a shame to waste it on food. But you know best, Marta. You run a tight clean ship here, Marta."

"How was the soup?"

Lazar-Wolf kissed his finger tips and dipped a hand in chestnut purée and rolled his eyes. "I'll have to go back on my diet—toast and skimmed milk after tonight." Marta began to mix the sauce for the carp. "Ah, Herr Wolf, a man should have a bit of belly, no?" She quoted an obscene Magyar proverb about the size of the genitalia matching the size of the gut that swung them. They both laughed as she tasted the sauce and cocked an eye on the bottle of Grand Marnier and added two dollops of it to the sauce. "Can hurt nobody, *nem?*"

Nora O'Hara in a neat dark evening gown came in, flushed and rosy from the heat of the candles and the excitement of the event. "Where the hell is the bloody *kasha?*"

"I only got three hands," said the cook. "Coming, coming."

"The auld man isn't happy, and when he isn't happy herself isn't either."

"You want I stop now? I take off apron? I'm *nem yoh?* All right, Irish, I quit right now. You finish dinner. *Ha!*"

Lazar-Wolf patted the cook on the rump and Nora on the cheek. "Let's all have a quick one and go back to work?" He poured three glasses of champagne and they smiled at each other and sipped. The signal box buzzed twice. "All ready," asked the cook, "for the carp?"

Nora smiled, refilled her glass and winked at Lazar-Wolf. She had taken on a few already. "Herself is driving the buzzer tonight. She's hungry. Nibbled her way across the sea. . . . *Lachaium.*"

"To life."

The meal progressed; the *kasha* was sent out steaming and butterless as was proper with a guest of honor who did not eat *trefa*—mixed meat and milk dishes.

Willie came back with the duck and veal platters. "The Wolf kid, she tossed her dinner."

"That Joanne, if she don't eat her food, she pee on rugs. Get mop and scraper in closet. Clean it neat now, Willie. Don't act like you shoveling horse manure."

The silvered steam engine that was the coffee machine was sending off vapors from an escape cock. The cook ran a test brew, rolled the scalding stuff around her yellow dentures and tossed the machine a pinch of salt.

"No cream tonight, no butter, cheeses. *Nem!* Holy Jew fella here tonight. *Yoi istenem,* how I going to cook when they married? Ha? How you make a meat sauce no butter, how *oeufs en cocotte* no bacon drippings?"

The desserts went out to the dining room. The huge Russian silver coffeepot was filled, the demitasse cups of Royal Doulton, forgotten in the table setting of Wedgwood, were rushed out to replace full-sized cups. The *crêpes Suzette* in their blue burning-brandy flames were among Marta's masterworks. The pots were off the flames, the stacked soiled plates and dishes were in the washing-up room. Underfoot, lettuce leaves, carrot tops, slippery kitchen debris was being stirred by a broom in Willie's hand as he chewed on a duck leg held in his strong teeth. He stopped from time to time to insert more of it into his mouth. Most of the help were on the back porch smoking cigarettes, smelling like sweated horses in their soaked, melted aprons and shirts, slyly depositing full wine and brandy bottles in the shrubbery to tote away with them. Greasy paper bags contained whole duck carcasses, filets of veal, a few cigars, more tins of English cigarettes. Marta shrugged it off, the toting was their sacred privilege. She had two bottles of champagne and a fifth of rare brandy herself, set aside in Willie's pantry. All she counted carefully was the silverware, the number of small cups, so easy to slip into one's drawers or pants, and the little salt cellars of Imperial Sustrain crystal.

One of the waitresses was kept busy at the coffee machine. Hot water and Earl Grey tea were sent in for Marcel and Mark Penrose.

In the washing-up room the clatter of dishes and steaming water mingled with the laughter of the dishwashers, who were getting rapidly drunk on the mixings they made in an ice bucket of all drinks left in the glasses or cocktail shakers. Marta would have to go in soon and sober them up with a little shouting. But they were not yet at the stage of breaking things. She counted the fruit knives, the fish forks, and locked them up in the silver room, for which only she and Willie had the keys. It was time to slip off her shoes, flex her toes.

She and Willie sat under the dying breath of the coffee machine, Willie smoking one of Lazar-Wolf's best cigars, Marta a hand-rolled Turkish cigarette she made herself; she couldn't stand store-bought. Willie filled two water glasses half full of brandy and they toasted each other silently and sipped. Gertrude in her gold lamé gown came through the doorway a little stiff from sitting in a too tight girdle. "Ah, Marta, Mama—she's tired from a long day—she wants you to know the meal was just perfect, better than perfect. And Mr. Lazar-Wolf would like some more *crêpes Suzette*."

"So would Willie and me, Mrs. Wolf. But no more batter."

"Can't you mix some more, dear? I mean Saul always looks forward to extra *crêpes*."

"Ha, Mrs. Wolf, you think any great artist he just mix colors, slap on paint any old time? To make good *crêpes*, no, must take time, to think, to make true mix, to feel like. *Tudum*—understand?"

"Of course, Marta, of course," said Gertrude, backing out and away.

"That's the *Zhidos* for you, work your ass off you let 'em."

"I'm a *Zhido*," said Willie, grinning.

The goodbyes in the dining room, candles expiring, were beginning as the coffee grew cold. The Lazar-Wolfs had already left with their brood—little Joanne smelling of digestive acids, wrapped in a blanket, Gertrude fearing the child had fever and the hint of a rash. Judith, who dreaded all diseases as the by-products of too close human contact, had waved them off, leaning away from Gertrude's kisses. Nathan put down his coffee cup (the third), admiring Judith; she had vanity and character but no coquetry.

"Judith, it's good to see you back, good to meet Mr. Ellenbogan. And it's late; you're tired and I have to be at the Store early. So—"

"Put away your watch," said Judith, her color high, her girdle unhooked. "Good of you to come." Nathan kissed her cheek and shook hands with Jacob Ellenbogan, who seemed content, eyes half hooded. It had been a revealing gathering, this dinner, this family dominated by Judith. He released Nathan's hand.

"You must show me your *schuls*. Not the fancy ones, but where Jews haven't crystallized into deceptive shapes yet."

"I know," said Nathan, and he nodded to Tom and Marcel and Tony and left. The wind from the river was cold, and leaves were rattling across the lawn, beating like moths against the windows. He was still puzzled by the apparent inconsistencies between Judith and Jacob.

In the library Tom reached for the brandy and poured a stiff shot into his coffee cup. "I'm sorry Mabel couldn't come. She has these damn migraines. They come on suddenly, with blurred vision—"

"She's allergic to me," said Judith, picking up a handful of walnuts from a silver sailing-ship model in front of her, her hands gleaming with diamonds in turn-of-the-century settings. "To all old Jews."

Tom sipped his strong drink. It had been hell over the phone with Mabel before dinner, talking to Scarsdale and trying to get Mabel even to come to the phone. She had at last, and had said in a whiskey-slurred voice that she'd be goddamned if she'd be trotted out to a family dinner and be treated like a goddamned poor trash *goy* relative and as for Tom, he could—well, he knew what he could go do for himself, and he didn't have to come home either. She had hung up with a bang, and he had thought—phone in hand— of loves lost through bad judgment, unfulfilled promises, weakness of character *and* through kindness.

"Mama, it's not like that."

"You're not getting on with Mabel, eh?"

"She's been upset since her operation."

Jacob asked politely, trying to hide a yawn—it was past his bedtime—"An operation?"

Judith said, "A hysterectomy. Very *déclassé*. You ask me, it's too much cocktails and sitting over bridge tables. Give a dull woman a half dozen children and problems and she doesn't have to be hollowed out by surgeons like an unfilled pastry. All right, all right, you can go, Tom. I see horses are pulling on you. You, too, Naomi."

"Oh, Mama, it's just you must be tired."

Mark Penrose brushed invisible crumbs from his lap. "Judith, you're looking fine. May we wish you and Jacob the best."

Naomi kissed her mother's cheek. Judith took a deep breath. "You smell wonderfully dimensionless. Send me a bottle of it?"

"Just an amusing Chanel."

Marcel and his son, Tony, made no move to go after the others had left. They remained seated while Judith cracked walnuts and fed herself and Tony the nutmeats. Jacob asked for more coffee.

"Doesn't it bother you?" Marcel asked.

"I sleep like a demon after a trance. Coffee never keeps me awake. Sometimes I feel the rotation of the earth a bit—but not too often."

Marcel leaned forward on his elbows. "You're a fortunate man, Jacob."

"Of course he is," said Judith, cracking a nut by pressing it against another nut. "He's a remarkable scholar, a wizard, if you must know. What he doesn't know isn't worth knowing." She smiled at the little man.

He smiled back, shrugged. "That much I'm not sure of, *Shana*. But if you think I'm a wizard, so I'm a wizard."

Tony held a light to the little black cigar Judith had taken from a jeweled case. She puffed it alive and pinched Tony's cheek. "That's right, take care of your grandmother. Life can be over—" she snapped her fingers—"like that, and it's worth living. Well lived it animates morality without preaching to it."

"You'll outlive us all, Grandma. Can I try one of your little cigars?"

"Go on. Your growth you no longer can stunt. He's a fine boy, eh, Jacob? Splendid stock, genes, coloring."

"A very tall one and wide as a Polack. So tell me, chappie, you ski all over Europe?"

"Yes, I'm going over soon on an exhibition tour."

"You'll go behind the Soviet curtain? To Rumania, Poland, places like that?" Marcel was aware of the deep-set earnest eyes of the little scholar—out of some painting of Faust.

"Yes, we have State Department permits."

"So Judith told me. Tony, I have a daughter somewhere in there. Maybe you'll do me a favor."

"Whatever I can, Mr. Ellenbogan."

Judith sighed and wriggled in her confining gown. She had eaten well, drunk well, and her bulk was uncomfortable. "We'll talk about it some other time. Marcel, what do think of the wedding plans?"

"The truth is, Mama, I don't know what they are, We all congratulated you, but nobody wanted to talk much about it. *What* are the plans?"

"Jacob wants to find a proper rabbi. None of those young wet-noses with basketball courts and folk dances, art lessons. A *tzaddik*, a member of the modern Hasidim, to perform the wedding. Am I right, Jacob? And a small wedding. Nothing of a blushing virgin. And I'm not too young, either, *jeter de la poudre aux yeux.*"

Marcel said, "You'll have to have blood tests, all that."

Jacob said solemnly, "A little blood we can spare."

"Just the family," said Judith. "A few close friends. Perhaps fashionable absurdities we can avoid. A little music. The children of some of Mordechai's old friends. The old German-Jewish society, Strausses, Lehmans, that sort. I can't overlook the older Store people who have served so long, can I? They'll come from miles around to see me re-enter the wars again. No offense, Jacob."

Marcel shook his head. "Of course the old families, but you've outlived most of them." Tony tried to keep from smiling.

Judith gazed into the tobacco smoke. "And some of the fancy rabbis, the ham actors, they'd be hurt if I didn't introduce them to Jacob. I want him to see what a few generations does to a class."

The little man rolled his head around and reached for his coffee cup. "It doesn't sound such a small wedding. In Poland a wedding was an excuse to feed poor relatives—but *here?*"

Judith showed her ringed hands, palms up. "I suggest a hundred, hundred and fifty at the most. That many. I'll have the cake made at Sherry's. No lard, of course. All *milchedikeh*, don't worry, Jacob. And the children we must have at the governess' table. After all, they're my grandchildren. You think Joanne has something? I swear I saw a rash. I forgot the Greencrest Club. Tobias himself founded the damn club, and Mordechai was on the building-fund committee for the new clubhouse."

"It's now the old clubhouse," said Marcel, enjoying his mother. Of all her children he was the closest to her and needed her the most. "They built a modern building last year. They've let in a few gentiles."

"Only the officers. That fusty old lady, Rifka, who was attendant in the baths there if she's still alive. She kept me limber and active. I suppose she's gone."

"Man is a moment, a breath in one nostril of God," said Jacob. He sounded sleepy.

Judith nodded. "Yes, Jacob, I've thought of that too. Marcel, I'm going to endow a school of Hasidic study in Israel. Most everything I have, I leave to them. You're all provided for, I'm sure. It's my wedding gift to Jacob. You may not know it, but I was sunk in despair till I met him, heard him talk."

There was a snore. The little man had fallen asleep. Marcel was looking at Tony with a frown. Judith cried out, "Nora, Nora! Irish!"

"He's only sound asleep," said Tony. Marcel said, "It looks like a sort of trance."

"He doesn't travel well," said Judith. "He's frail, mere bones and tissue. Irish!"

Nora appeared, arms folded in front of her. "It's time herself was asleep."

"When I need to find out when I need sleep I'll wear a sign. Help the rabbi upstairs. He's got the Yellow Room in the tower."

"I'll help," said Tony.

Between them—he and Nora—they lifted the slightly protesting man to his feet. "A *cholem*, a dream. I'm all right, I say."

When Tony and Nora had started Jacob upstairs, Judith turned to her son Marcel. "Don't sit there staring. You think I'm mad to get married, setting up a foundation for a place to study for the Hasidim?"

"I don't care what you do, Mama, as long as it pleases you. But you know what this could do to the Store, to the Bank, the real estate? You're the major stockholder in so many Pedlock projects."

"Don't worry over that. That's for Nathan, Saul Lazar-Wolf and their lawyers to work out. It's not as if I'm selling out to Gimbels, God forbid, or going into an Omdurman harem. It's just I want to live a little longer—not sit in a rocker."

"I tell you, Mama, it's all turmoil."

"A *tummel* never hurt anyone. Come kiss me and tomorrow take Jacob to some of the real *schuls*, the proper sights. He's a clever little man—don't think he cares if I'm rich or poor. *Je ne sais trop.*" She let out a roar of laughter. "He said when I asked him to marry me: 'Can a hungry man refuse roast goose?'" She patted Marcel's hand. "It's lonely being old, it's dreadful and it's dark. The strength will go, the limbs will tremble, but not from passion, and what's waiting? A return to grass. But that's talk for poets. A poet once said he'd die for me—he didn't. For death is waiting. To become nothing, *nothing*. If I fear anything I fear old age, the joints locking, the breath stale. Ah, pour me a brandy. If Jacob were the devil I'd still see him as my light, my hope for a few more years that make sense, without too much agony. . . . Go, go . . . I'm drunk."

Tony came downstairs and he and his father kissed the old cheek and went out into the crisp night, Marcel feeling Judith was trying to slough off the past like an old skin.

Tony drove. Marcel did not trust himself too much as a driver at night. He turned to his son. "She's dropped a bombshell."

"He's not a bad old man, Dad. I rather like him. He's Jewish; so many of the Jews I meet, they don't seem very Jewish any more." He grinned. "Like you, me. We're colorless, invisible Jews, some kind of pliant plastic we can paint any color."

"I don't mean the old man. He's strange, unreal, shadowy yet substantial. This foundation for a crazy university in Israel—Judith would have to sell some of her holdings to build it. These things are bad. A rumor of something like it on the market and the family holdings could drop in value. Well, it's Nat's and Lazar-Wolf's problem, as she said."

"He's so frail, the old man, just bone and tendons when I laid him on the bed. He called me *Chayyim Alkabez*, the champion, who would bring his daughter to him."

"Maybe he's arranging a marriage for you, Tony."

"She's fourteen, he said. Grandma looked solid as a rock and mellow on brandy. Is she really in her eighties?"

"Nobody knows. Her birth records were destroyed in the San Fransisco earthquake. She doesn't tell. Have dinner with me to-morrow?"

"Like to, Dad, but I'm going out of town—up to Maine to a sports meeting. Call you when I get back. I'll make the wedding."

"Do that." Marcel closed his eyes and saw a much younger Judith bending over him, telling him his bellyache would go away. She was going to the opera, smelling of furs and perfume and the white liquid women used then on their bare arms and back. And beyond her the polite bearded face of his father, and he had cried out, for this was the man who took his mother away from him so often. So often, so often . . . By the time they reached Manhattan, Marcel felt lost in the dimensionless despair of a childhood stolen from him.

Alone in the high-ceilinged dining room where she had gone for more brandy, the candles beginning to gut and smell, Judith sat in a kind of exaltation over a melancholy thought, and she drove it off. How does one achieve Goethe's dignity of significance? How? Here she was still alive, alert, deep in her seventies—even to herself she had to lie a bit—and what was really ahead? As Jacob said, "The end of everything is forgiveness."

She stood up, balancing all her limbs in delicate precision. Nora must have fallen asleep in her chair waiting for her. Judith looked around the room and crossed to the hall, and she heard music in her mind at the steps leading down to the ballroom; she knew it was only ghost music. But as another Marcel had said to her—a French one—"There can be music without sound." She entered the great ballroom. It was 1917, the nation at war, and she had danced in the arms of the officers, and she remembered acts that were or were not ever committed. It seemed favorable to the war effort. She had been faithful—*nearly* so. What was the use of thinking of old adulteries? In the end she had won a kind of victory over her body. Nietzsche came back, as quoted by that captain of the white Pacific liner when she went to Japan and India in 1924: *Was mich nicht umbringt macht mich stärker*—what does not kill me makes me stronger. The ballroom tilted and she was in his arms again at the party the night before they sighted Yokohama. She danced and laughed and looked about her and saw in the bank of ballroom mirrors only a very large, very old woman in tight silk with jewels on raddled weathered skin. She blew the poor old bat a kiss and lifted the train of her gown over one arm and slowly, slowly, she accepted the homage of the ballroom, the ships salon, the memory of something far off, a perfect waltz. She had always been a fine, well-muscled dancer ("long American legs growing out of your shoulder blades, *ma cherie*"), and she circled the room again, light seeping in from the hall, the ballroom in gay orange shadows. She whirled faster faster as if the past would remain, bowing and nodding, if she didn't stop; the ballroom so big and mirrors showing a half dozen reflections in their fragmented, left-handed world. Judith waltzed on. Alone, silently, in the old house.

From Marcel Pedlock's journal:

In what a mystic (St. John of the Cross) has called "the dark night of the soul," unable to sleep, I comfort myself by recording family history from notes made years ago.

Elijah did a lot of moving on before the Civil War. It was a new land, America, and he had fallen in love with its spread, its crudeness, its vitality. Unlike Charles Dickens, as Elijah's letters in low German still say, he was not shocked at rural democracy and tobacco juice. The light peddler's wagon and "the Ethiopian Abner" moved along yellow-dust roads and by riverbanks in high flood. He was in love with the touch and color of things. He knew many backroads, shattered rock paths, odd discolorations of the landscape. Elijah traded and bartered everywhere.

When he needed money for stock he repaired the new-fangled farm tools or the hammers of silver-mounted shotguns. He understood the mechanism of clocks and once, in Virginia, repaired a huge one that told the hour and day, the month and year, to a family so sunk in drink and incest they were too tired to care.

He made markings on maps and years. Later Nathan was to own some of these maps with inkings of roads and paths along the wild Natchez Tract, the twisting Wilderness Road. They sang their names in my head when I was a boy: Yazoo, Jackson, Tupelo, Nashville, Tul-lahoma, Cobin, Roanoke, Durham, Hamlet, Greenwood. And Raccoon Key, where there had been a false rumor of Spanish silver coins, and Charleston, where the surf ran high and the gray horizon seemed to sag.

The wagon needed repairs, the horse some rest, and Elijah a new outfit. Elijah went into the junk business, waiting till he could afford to open his Store. Near Isle of Palms he had found a rusting pile of ship's gear and old iron from steamboat disasters around Charleston Harbor. These he carried off as salvage or bought on credit and pure nerve. He got a forge and some Negro blacksmiths as help. It was soon easier to get a gate or an almost new lock from Pedlock's yard than to have one shipped over from London or down from New York.

Mornings he sorted and hammered on old iron or copper, wrote letters to Hamburg jobbers, Manchester cotton mills. Afternoons he walked the shores and the rice fields snapping a fine borrowed gun at ducks and geese and river fowl, and counted the roads a storekeeper could wheel on in trade. Evenings he sat in some inn watching the flares of market life, hearing the shouting and singing of the market folk. In the inns he met the gentry with whom he did iron-mongering business. They liked him. He was in a business that was not rice or indigo or long-staple cotton, so they forgave him.

One day he rented a neat white house in the bend of Church Street. He called it his home. Charleston, with the spires of St. Paul's and St. Michael's fingering the sky, pleased him. It was a patchwork city built on rice, its major crop; the great houses and families were almost all based on a wealth brought by rice. To Elijah's eyes the city had gay spots and sad spots—such as Catch What You Can Alley, which was like the slums of some European city, populated by dark natives. Elijah liked to ride on the horsecars that traveled the Blue Line along Broad Street and Rutledge Avenue, and often, late at night, he would stand on the platform, smoking a strong stogie, the salt breeze from the harbor cool on his face. He was to remember Charleston more vividly than any other way station to Pedlock & Sons.

It was a city of simple and lazy pace. Drinking water was fetched in great jars by Negro girls from the city well at Meeting and Wentworth streets. An old black man stood all day at the yard well pumping bath water into the hotel's great roof tank over the bathroom. Lamplighters came at dusk to light the smoky oil lamps, each street standard proudly topped by a brass eagle. Buzzards were really the town's birds. They were the cleaners of streets and alleys. Even on the stylish Battery, where weekends the quality and the gentry paraded, they swooped and dived. The shadow of the buzzards' wings often circled Elijah's imported beaver hat.

He established the Bon Ton Store: E. Pedlock, Prop., and the ship builders and railroad families opened accounts. He saw his dray pulling crates and boxes over the Belgian blocks and cobblestones of the city. The beautiful iron balconies that overhung the paved blue limestone of Union Street (name changed to Old State Street after the fuss with Abe Lincoln) were backed by Pedlock curtains of printed madras. Elijah often attended stately funerals at St. Finbar's Cathedral for the burial of victims of dueling or overeating or the dull knives of local surgeons. But the Bon Ton, he saw, would grow no bigger. Its trade was stabilized.

So Elijah became a barterer of plantation products. Even in the wild Tennessee hills his light traveling wagon went hunting for loomed cloth, old clocks, hill tobacco. He moved among the hookwormed, pellagra-tormented people of the hills, shared their chitterlings and hominy, their fleas and pine-needle pillows. He saw signs of coal and iron in the hills, but how to dig it or smelt it or process it he didn't know. But someday, someday, someone would. He would come back from the hill counties with a wagonload of cloth and untaxed whiskey, his boots worn out, his horse unshod, and Abner shaking with "the miseries."

He went the rounds of the plantations with his bolts of calico, trying to interest the rice growers in refurnishing their homes. But they were interested mostly in rice and indigo and long-staple cotton; the old firms in England got their quality trade. They lived a fine life under their live oaks. The mist from the cypress swamps was like perfume to them. They hunted mangy fox and treed possums and ate suckling pigs. They drank corn-mash tipple until the red glands on the backs of their necks swelled. Bizarre, provocative men, they held to many evangelical sects. They respected their women and produced yellow girls in the slave cabins. They sat on their piazzas, dressed in spotless white, offering him cheroots, taking the tinkling frosted drinks from the hands of silent servants. They cursed the "damn niggah that crushed the mint leaf instead of gently bruisin' it." They were a brave and handsome and foolish race, Elijah found. Brave beyond their needs, and they ate fire and cursed the North. Their minds and manner of life made a sport of conflict, as under the walls of Troy.

In the end he gave up trying to develop a quality trade. He settled down to wait with the Bon Ton. He danced at the great balls, drank with them in great drunks, stood one morning ("how could this happen?") under live oaks covered with whiskers sighting along an etched pistol barrel because some handsome young fool had discovered that Elijah resented being called a "louse-bellied Jew," and had remarked to him, "Damned unmannerly for yo' folk, like that thar Judas, to have betrayed the Lord with a kiss. No suh, no real gentleman could be that rude." (It's there in one of those long letters now yellow as ritual wax.)

Nothing came of his play at *code duello*. The handsome young man was too drunk to hold his pistol. Elijah handed his back unfired and offered to stand the party a breakfast at Shepherd's Tavern. They ate oysters and shrimp and hotcakes and drank mulled ale (*"Trief, trief—* unkosher"). The handsome young man cried on Elijah's shoulder.

Elijah imported goods and waited. A rich and not too ordered business in shipping went on all along the coast. Past reefs and sandbars, ships slipped into the fruit-green harbors, crossing the shifting river heads, trying to avoid old wrecks and uncharted currents. Elijah regretted that so much of this shipping did not come to him, but the Bon Ton could not sell mule collars or Queen Anne tables. The people who filled the ships' holds were contented and happy on their own land, overseeing their fields. The building and manning of ships they left to Yankees and Limeys. Cargos and invoices were work for sailors and clerks.

Too often these ships wrecked themselves in wind and tide. Then Elijah would be on the scene. If the wreck was not worth salvage, he would buy its iron and brass fittings, oak beams, chains and skylights, and even the old cannon balls, veterans of Waterloo and Spain. Old cannon balls were used as ship's ballast. Elijah bought them and piled them neatly in his Bon Ton yard. Later they were to see Manassas and thunder for Jackson in the Shenandoah Valley.

It was the captain of an English bark, gone on the rocky shoals and beaten to splinters by a Hatteras wind at Stone Inlet, who said to Elijah, "You Americans, Mr. Pedlock, live it pretty fine here."

Elijah, who was writing a bill of sale for the wreck's stores, looked up at the captain, his fist around a glass of hot toddy.

"You said, *we* Americans?"

The captain sighed. "You American chaps do yourself proper, all right."

Elijah put down the pen. Inside himself—he wrote in a letter—he felt something very big go off. "I had never really felt anyone else would notice I had already become an American. . . ."

CHAPTER 9

⋙ Nathan Pedlock and Lazar-Wolf sat in Lazar-Wolf's office after a too large lunch at the Brokers' Club. Lazar-Wolf held up a newspaper clipping. "This is what the Ganzler Fairs Stores are doing. Peanuts it isn't."

"You think Pedlock & Sons can still merge with them—swallow them?"

"A big lump. Listen." Lazar-Wolf read aloud:

" 'Annual Meetings two-for-one stock split approved by Ganzler Fairs. New York—The tax cut is beginning to stimulate retail trade, Dov Ganzler, president of Ganzler Fairs, told the annual meeting here Wednesday. Shareholders at the meeting approved a previously proposed two-for-one stock split and increased authorized shares to twenty million at two-fifty par. Record date for the split is June sixteenth. He said the tax cut had no influence on the February to April volume of the fifty-eight-store chain, but sales in the month of May were eight percent higher than last May even though there was one less selling day in the period.' "

"They did that well?"

"Yes. ' "On a comparable basis," Ganzler said, "this represents an increase of almost twelve percent." The stores earned thirty point six million, or four twenty-three a share, on sales of seven hundred and twenty-three point seven million in the year ended January thirty-first. Profits were up twenty-four percent on a two percent sales increase.' "

"We've been buying up their stock."

"Not enough. Listen: 'Ganzler Fairs, which has opened seven stores since last August, will open "another large branch" next fall and "expects to continue thereafter with the opening of four or five new branches a year," he said.' "

Nathan Pedlock helped himself to a cigar from the rosewood box on the desk, carefully cut the tip with a gold cutting tool and slowly lit the end until it glowed just right.

"We must buy more Ganzler stock. Slowly, carefully, so Dov Ganzler doesn't know it's us. He may be from Lumsa-Gubernia, but he's smart and he's mean."

"We have the proper dummies. We can do it."

"What's this talk of Judith starting a Hasidic foundation in Israel?"

"So let her, Nathan. I've had the lawyers and Dickie Lazarus draw up a document where she'll be able to use only the income from her holdings and her stock will be voted for her by Lazar-Wolf and Pedlock Brothers. Satisfactory?"

"I wouldn't want to see the stock in the hands of those Israeli beggars. They *schnorr* with one hand and insult us with the other."

"It doesn't leave America. Worry more about the wedding. They've found some bearded Hasidic saint over in Brooklyn. It was set for Wednesday afternoon. But Gertrude said that was *too* hasty."

Nathan looked up from his cigar. Lunch was settling well. The Store sales were excellent across the country. "Saul, understand, the family isn't trying to stop the wedding."

"If they could, believe me, Nat, they would. But what chance have they?" He slapped Nathan's knee. "What chance with a man-eater like Judith? What a creature of fire and cream she must have been in her prime. They say she had an affair with Stanford White, the one Harry Thaw shot on a roof garden."

Nathan flushed, his face and neck turning red. "Look, Saul, we're not her sons. But it's lies. All gossip, all lies. She was a good Jewish wife to my father, a wonderful person. Flighty in her youth, they say, but she made a good home, was a fine hostess. Don't you believe this talk. Absurd, ridiculous yellow journalism in the Sunday papers."

Saul lifted his eyes to the paneled ceiling. If Nathan, that *yold*, wanted it that way, all right he wanted it that way. He, Saul Lazar-Wolf, certainly didn't think less of Judith for all the old newspaper gossip. He turned to a report of a flurry in copper stocks where Pedlock Brothers was involved with the Guggenheims.

Back in his office at the Store, Nathan tried to keep his mind off the talk about Judith's past. He had plenty to do at the Store. Customers who saw the bright, clean, well-run departments were unaware that Nathan felt the continuing conflict that went on to keep this army of employees doing anything at all. The warehouse men were always thinking up new schemes with false papers to carry off truckloads of valuables; some of the sales help added a bonus with a pair of nylons rolled up in their drawers or a necktie placed in a hip pocket. It was a daily war between management and hired hands. There had been a conflict between the Teamsters local, who delivered the rugs, and the Sales Workers Guild as to who had to roll them into the trucks for shipment. There were two grievance committees waiting to see Nathan, and he couldn't stall them much longer or they'd throw down order blanks or sales books and picket.

Then there was the weather for the big sales to mull over. Last year a blizzard had blown a two-hundred-thousand-dollar loss into a week's sale of food stuffs and seasonal gear: advertising and publicity wasted, extra help and warehouse space costing like pure gold. And two newspaper strikes had made a morgue of the top floors. With no newspaper advertising (television time was money wasted), those two strikes against the New York newspapers had cost the Store half a million dollars.

The rising cost of packing and exchanging home deliveries was a grim problem. Tom had the idea of starting a discount section of low-priced goods, no exchanges, no services, cash and carry. But that, Nathan feared, could ruin them in their fixed-price sections and make them look like a loft *shlock* house, with crumby cartons all over, no counters, the section looking like a distressed area. He'd vote the idea down and advertise: "Nobody Touches Bottom Prices Like Pedlock & Sons—Always Discount, Always Service." Let Macy's make something of that.

The comparison shoppers were lying down on the job. From various stores they were exchanging each other's notes and spending their time in Schraffts or at the Museum of Modern Art.

Vos taig der leben—what's life worth, he thought, as he sat back to await a grievance committee of the Stock Clerks and Packers Local.

He let them wait a few minutes in the outer office. Not too long or they'd use dirty language, and that called for a union trial, which the Store hardly ever won; the local's justice was like a white jury in Mississippi. Justice wasn't dead, just cockeyed.

After the grievance committee filed out, the callbox announced that Matt Wilson, head of policing, wanted to see Nathan. *Urgent.*

Matt was big and lazy, but bright on most subjects, and his staff —football players, retired cops and ex-marines—kept shoplifting two percent below the city's average. They hadn't demanded more fringe benefits for three months. It must be the mild blackmail of the Employee Ball and program advertising.

"What is it, Matt?"

"Well, Mr. Pedlock, look at these. We found them in the Czech glassware counter and tucked into the Polish hams."

Nathan looked at small cards with printing in red on them: "Pedlock & Sons is happy to serve you Communist-country products." Others read: "Pedlock & Sons calls your attention to the support it gives our Red enemies"; "Pedlock & Sons sells America short and uses your money to aid Red terrorist nations and world Communist takeover here."

"Who?" asked Nathan.

"Don't know. Could be Birchers, Nazis from Yorktown, Christian Defenders of One True Americanism, even the Daughters of the War of Independence. Or . . ."

"Or?"

Matt rubbed thumb and forefinger of his right hand together. "We may get an offer of an anti-Red service for so much, and all that, and no more cards on the counters."

"Find out who's behind this, and if it's one of those big sick groups, we'll have Addison, Foote and Kalish get injunctions and start a libel suit. If it's a shakedown, the answer is *always* no."

"You're so right."

Nathan laughed. "Matt, who you fooling? You've been an Americanization Forum man for two years. Half your men are."

Matt joined the laughter. "We don't bring our politics, Mr. Pedlock, to the Store. How'd you get this information?"

Nathan smiled and shook his head.

CHAPTER 10

&§ "It takes a great deal of religion to make a little bit of God,"
said Jacob Ellenbogan.

The Shem-Meforah Cemetery was a forest of tasteless stone
monuments, granite tablets, marble columns, bronze chains, the
English and Hebrew inscriptions going back in the older parts of
the place to 1857. Thousands of Jews, six to eight generations, were
here, an army of Hebrew immigrants and refugees, scholars in
flight, pants pressers who made it big, journalists, Yiddish novelists,
housewives, premature hopes of children, Kaddish sayers who died
young in four wars; all were laid out row on row between ragged
maple and pine trees. "So *close* together," said Jacob Ellenbogan as
he walked with Judith up a graveled path, almost touching shoulder to shoulder. "And such heavy stones, as if the relatives were
afraid the dead could get up and walk home to haunt them. *Shana*,
only the kindness of strangers is to be believed."

Judith was happy. It was her wedding day. Behind them walked
Nora, carrying a car robe, and the *shammes*—sexton—of the old
place, an old bent Jew with a wet nose, a greedy eye, a battered
top hat on his disordered white hair.

"Ah, Mrs. Pedlock, so happy so happy to see you," he said in
litvak Yiddish. "We're ready for you, don't think we're not. An
honor." He offered an amber snuff box to Jacob, who joined him.
They put the powder up their noses and sneezed together. They
wished each other *gesundheit* and *sholom aleichem*. Jacob added,
"The Reb Moses ben Maimon, that some call Maimonides, says

the soul leaves the body for a moment through the nose when we sneeze, and if one is not careful it can re-enter the nostrils of a stranger."

The *shammes* muttered a prayer against that evil. "Ah, here we are. Pleasant, isn't it? A pleasure just to look at it. And to occupy it, a *ganedden*—paradise."

They had come past the boulevards of stones, of close-packed plots of entire families in an eternal togetherness, and were viewing a slight rise under fine elms where several spacious areas had been fenced off by impressive stone walls, bronze chains and some gateposts, each section of which bore the name of some well-known family: Strauss, Warburg, Lehman, Wise, Cahn; department stores, copper, junk, garments, furs, banking, art collecting, the early films, the stage, fashionable temples. The Pedlock plot was a full half acre, mostly still green turf and rosebushes, but there were the graves of the families of Elijah, Tobias, Mordechai, their various wives, children, an old aunt or two, a gambler suicide, some small stones to babies who died early; all made up a cozy corner, as the *shammes* with the knobby features expressed it.

Judith led Jacob up to a low horizontal stone on which PEDLOCK was cut deeply in Roman lettering. The names of Mordechai and his first wife, Rose Rochell, were marked on the left-hand side of the stone. Judith pointed to the blank section on the right. "And here, Jacob, there is room for your name and mine. Napoleon's generals had it no better." She took his hand, pressed it.

Nora O'Hara came forward and slipped the car robe over the old woman's wide shoulders. "A fine way for a wedding day."

Jacob looked around him, walked about, hands clasped behind his back. "The best people, but you know they should have started burying from the right, not from the left. It should go—even underground—like Hebrew text, right to left, not left to right. . . . So, so time gives definition to everything."

The *shammes* wiped his nose with a sleeve of his black broadcloth coat. "A *tzaddik*, only a *tzaddik* would have known that."

Judith said, "I thought, Jacob, this would be my first wedding present to you. Am I a fool?"

"No, *Shana*," said Jacob, nodding and smiling at the old *shammes*. "Even Him up there can't give us eternity."

"Now," said Judith, shaking off the rug, "We've got people com-

ing and the wedding is strictly set for two o'clock. Irish, button
your coat, it's cold here."

"And herself not using the car blanket."

"I'm never cold when I'm walking."

"A fine honeymoon. Herself sneezing with a cold, her feet in a
tub of hot water."

The old *shammes* accepted the dollar that Nora as banker
handed him. Judith and Jacob walked down the path to the exit
gates. The old man said to Nora O'Hara, "So that's a *kolah*, a
bride? By me she's no *kolah*."

"Shut up, you dirty old man," said Nora with calm dignity.
"Herself always knows what she's doing."

Jacob was happy as he briskly kept up with his bride, snapping
his fingers, inspecting the inscriptions in English, Hebrew and Yiddish to Sarahs, Shirleys, Rifkas, Mendels, Moseses, Morrises,
Harrys, who had been recorded as loving wives, faithful husbands,
beautiful children; there were also various rabbis who had been
pious, holy, learned, missed and mourned.

He didn't mind the bad taste, the ostentation, the expensive
carvings and letterings. It reinforced his own philosophy of the fu-
tility of all human endeavor. Only to enjoy and enjoy, to lament
and lament was right, even for those who did not know the cabala.
("We don't think, we only think we think.")

"You're pleased, Jacob?"

"Impressed. To be planted here with people who wouldn't in
life offer me a glass of tea. And such stone luxury, such stylized
grief."

Nora gave a sob. "I can't think of herself here without me."

Jacob winked at Judith. "We could bury you across her feet like
the Irishers used to bury the king's dog."

"Ha," said Nora, who had a down payment on a plot in conse-
crated Holy Cross of Mercy Acres in Brooklyn.

The *shammes*, who had stopped walking after them, did not
bother to wipe the drop from the end of his nose. He made a
snorting noise in his toothless mouth. "Some bride."

The wedding at Norton-on-Hudson did not get off at two-thirty
as planned, but it went smoothly at three-ten. Old Reb Baal-Shem-

Tov, imported from a *schul* in Bensonhurst, a proper Hasidic *roff* picked by Jacob himself, married the couple under a canopy of flowers erected in the ballroom. The "little private wedding" had expanded to two hundred and eight people, not counting a few children. The caterers had been brought in, chairs hired; and in the dining room, library and sun porch, tables were solid and ready. There had been no scurrilous jests.

Judith was married in a pale-yellow gown, kicking at the short train with a skill that showed she was not nervous. Marcel had outfitted Jacob—who looked like a haunted visionary—in wing collar, striped trousers and morning coat, and had even lent him a black pearl stickpin. But Jacob balked at the gray topper and wore his homburg, somewhat creased but proper. Once he corrected the rabbi's Hebrew (*"B'shuv adonoy"*), and when Judith had trouble clearing her throat for response to the ritual, he patted her back to help her get her breath. Jacob neatly crushed the napkin-wrapped glass with a sharp stab of a heel, wondering to himself at this nonsense of breaking: Did it signify the destruction of the Temple by the Romans, or the penetrating of the maidenhead—hardly of vital interest to himself or Judith? With this ancient ritual, the ceremony was over.

Judith kissed him. He smiled as the sons came up in round-cornered frock coats, the stepson Nathan in a four-button frock coat. Everyone was shouting, "Good luck, good luck, *mazeltov, mazeltov,* good luck, good luck."

The musicians in the glassed-in garden room beyond the palms in brass pots simpered and tootled some pale version of a wedding march. Jacob's memory spun back in time as he stood there, a glass of brandy in his hand. Had he really once lived in a Polish village, and at his first wedding was he a snot of student of the Talmud, aged fifteen, his bride a year younger? The fiddler, old Yankel Kalish, who repaired clocks for a living—"Call them clocks? call it a living?"—Old Yankel, over half a century ago in time, playing a Yiddish wedding song: "The Youngest Daughter Married Off." *That* was music. The warm spring night in the feather bed, and for his living there was his wife selling salt herring from a barrel in the market, while his ear curls grew and he sat all day in the *schul* mumbling over the Midrash . . . long, long ago, or was it all only a dream . . . long, long past . . . and had it never happened? Belka dead; the children dead in the pogroms; concentration camps and Germans, those foul people, nation, race . . . better it never was . . .

Jacob took a swift swallow of the brandy to burn out the idea he had a past. He was not a human, he was a *Luftmensch*—created of air.

Lazar-Wolf slapped Jacob's back. "Ah, to hear the old Hebrew read properly. The new rabbis they read like Cary Grant."

"The old man is wonderful," said Jacob. "In his little *schul* he's one of the few real rabbis left. In America most rabbis live enclosed in social parentheses."

Jacob moved down past people well dressed, healthy, prosperous-looking—gentiles, Jews, he hoped a few infidels, free thinkers—the stale road of the possible dogma was dull—past Tom Pedlock, looking pale, a very pretty blond girl by his side.

"Jacob, my daughter Nancy."

"So, Nancy. We met, no, at the boat?"

"Hello there. You really put on a show today!"

"Thank you, thank you, Nancy." She was so young, so beautiful, that butter-gold hair, tall with a dainty body, lip salve, eye shadow; still it didn't take away from her. A maiden for the feather bed. He took her hand, placed it between his two. "So, Tom's daughter?"

"I loved it. I've never been to anything like it before."

Tom said, "I'm sorry Mabel, my wife, couldn't come. She threw her back out playing golf."

"Mom, Mr. Ellenbogan, she just doesn't understand any of this. You know how these things are."

Jacob kissed her cheek. "I understand you're alive." He passed on to where the Penroses were entertaining some of their gentile friends.

Nancy hugged her father's arm. "Say, he may be old, but did you see his eyes? Charles Boyer mixed with Dracula."

Tom patted his daughter's hand. "I'm pleased you like it all, Nancy. Your mother's friends think Jews still belong in long beards like Fagin and Shylock."

"You forget. I've got a few mixed-up genes."

The smooth young man with the dark hawk's face, curly black hair so crisp it hardly seemed possible to comb it, came over to them.

"Hello there, remember me? I'm Dick Lazarus, Uncle Saul's nephew. We were introduced before the wedding."

"Of course. You know my dad?"

"I work for his bank. Mr. Pedlock, it's all right if I ask Nancy for a dance?"

"Ask her."

Several young couples were already dancing, others were drifting to the food tables. The buffets were being loaded with steaming dishes. Judith had insisted on informality—"*Kalbsbraten, lamproie, Bordelaise,* or chicken fat, let's please everyone."

Nancy and Dick Lazarus moved onto the waxed ballroom floor. He danced well, and Nancy danced close and with interest.

"Your grandmother is some gal."

"She hasn't a hair out of place. Say, most bankers dance like a rinky dink. But you really get with it, Dick."

"It's a good band. Not Coltrane or Dizzy or Kenton, but good for dancing."

"That Coltrane! When I hear the girls at school—I'm at Smith, dammit—talk of Dixieland, I absolutely want to scream. You for progressive?"

Dick smiled. "As they say, the most, Nancy."

They danced on, talking of recordings, sessions, sides, stereo and woofers with the seriousness of philosophers bolstering up an absolute.

Donald Kalish—a distant cousin of Nathan's mother's family—of the firm of Addison, Foote and Kalish, the family lawyers, was trying to get Judith away from some elderly women who were shouting like schoolgirls after a bit too much wine and cognac—"A *cluck iz tsu mir,* Judith, if you're not the most beautiful one here."

Marcel took his mother's arm, kissed her cheek. "Now, Mrs. Ellenbogan, please, a moment of your time."

Donald Kalish, fortyish, bald, a bit walleyed, took her free hand. "Aunt Judith, we *must* see you a moment."

"Really—I have guests. It can wait. Willie, the Mums champagne—tell the old ladies it's Mogen David!"

"Just a minute, Mama, please."

"All right, but where?"

Judith nodded at Nora in a neat silk dress, Nora wiping her eyes with a lace handkerchief held in a gray-gloved hand. "Oh it's a beautiful day, so serious and churchy."

"Yes, yes. Nora, please come in and unhook my brassiere, it's killing me *de gaieté de coeur*." She turned to Kalish. "You don't mind?"

"Not at all. This way, Aunt Judith."

The little room off the library that had once held Tobias' collection of coins—eyed by Brandeis, but since given to Harvard—was off the hallway. The Queen Anne table held some bottles of brandy. Nathan Pedlock and Peter Addison, senior partner of Addison, Foote and Kalish, were sipping cognac and nibbling on honeycake.

"Mrs. Pedlock, I mean Mrs. Ellenbogan, what a splendid day." Peter Addison kissed her hand. Addison had a serious old fox face, as became the senior partner of an important firm, white hair, a neat gray triangle of mustache, a red cocktail drinker's skin, blue eyes of icy deepness. He had been, she guessed, a rider to hounds in his youth. She suspected he had never regretted bringing a Jew into the old firm his grandfather had founded the year John Brown was hanged.

"My dear Judith, I never expected a wedding."

"Ha, Peter, you're a mean widower. A chippy will get you yet unless I can fix you up with some of my girl friends. Their first appearances can deceive you."

"I haven't your vitality, my dear." He fingered a family seal on his watch chain: *Decori decus addit avito*.

"Patience, patience. Someone not too long in the tooth. I'll introduce you. Nora—just open the top hooks."

"Here?"

"Here. They've all seen a tit before. So?"

Lazar-Wolf slipped into the room with Donald Kalish in turn and pushed the latch closed. Behind the walnut paneling, the Cole Porter dance music and the chatter of guests came through as if from a distance—like across a lake, Judith thought as Nora put a hand down her back, in the Berkshire summers of long ago, a banjo sound, deep blue shadows dimpling under a moon as vulgar and direct as early love.

"Now, Judith," said Kalish, wiping a bald brow covered only with a thin fuzz. "We left some papers with you a few days ago. I hope you've gone over them with care."

"The truth is, Donnie, no. Papers, let Saul or Nathan take care of it for me."

Nathan shrugged his shoulders. "Judith, you must realize the stores, the bank, the real estate, you own a good share of it."

"Not today, Nathan. Please don't start on holding companies, mutual trusts, all that *chazzereye*. Where's my bridegroom?"

Lazar-Wolf rolled his head from side to side and saw her grinning at him through the smoke of his cigar. "Darling, it's a big family and we don't any of us have the secret of eternal life."

"Yes, we're all getting on. Nathan, Tom, the girls."

"The papers Peter and Donnie have drawn up protect the family holdings, so that no matter what we do with our interests, the stocks, bonds, shares, the whole *magila* is shipshape, is kept in the vault of the Bank. Never transferred out of the country."

"Ha." Judith folded her arms as Nora worked on a stubborn clasp behind her broad back, loosening straps and zippers. "Ha, *oh*, Nora, *that* feels good. What's this legal mumbo jumbo you're trying to bamboozle me with? You all have the expressions of carnivores—why?"

Peter Addison swung gold-rimmed glasses over his classic nose and took some papers from a calfskin bag (*not* pigskin—Addison prided himself on a proper touch with clients).

"We are not a firm that bamboozles, Judith. The Pedlocks are more than a family, more than an institution, stores, banks. They are a kind of . . ." He searched for the word, a discernible pulse beat on his temple. "A sort of . . ."

Kalish helped: "*Projection* into the future?"

"Splendid, Donald. Yes, a sort of projection into the future. When we're all gone, the family will still be. Pedlocks. Not the mere money, the assets. No."

"Then what, Peter? All right, Nora, I can breathe now. Go see they haven't smashed the wedding cake. And I'm doing the cutting." She turned to face the men looking at her as Nora unlocked the door and went out. The music was louder for a moment, the babble of voices stronger—like, Judith thought, the continual sighing of sea tide. "I don't want to get angry, not on my wedding day. So someone better talk fast or *bonsoir*. The cake can't wait."

"I didn't know. I mean . . . how stupid can you get."

"What?"

"Jews are such fun. I once thought they were just nice and dull about money-making."

"No, we're like anyone else."

"Listen, Dick, you must think I'm some kind of kook."

"We're all kooks. How'd you like to have dinner with me? Get some tickets for a show. Or you want to make the scene at Birdland?"

"You think we'll break up here early enough?"

"We can just slip out, Nancy."

"Look at Dad. He looks as if somebody had put ground glass in his martini."

"He's carrying a big load at the Store."

"He's cheating on Mom with some bitch at the place, that's what, and he's getting rocky. Isn't he handsome?"

"You look a lot like him. I mean on a girl it's even better."

"You should have seen Mom before she began belting the sauce. She was a champ tennis player—Santa Barbara—what legs."

"Like yours?"

"That's what I like to hear, Dick."

"Somebody should have warned you against us Jewboys."

"Don't stand with your faces hanging open like recalcitrant children. A fool I'm not, even in dotage. Sign *here*, sign *there*, sign on my aching arse. I'm signing nothing. It's too late to teach me new tricks. I was running everything, Store, Bank, when Mordechai had that first heart attack and you men were nothing. I had to wipe your noses. I don't think you are any smarter than I am nor have more fidelity to the family. All right, all right. So I'm old. So I'm a feisty old *yenta* with a big tongue. But it's too late to change me. You must trust me, that's all. I don't go for the fallacy of sentimentality. I don't sign. I don't promise. And now I want to dance at my own wedding. Put away your papers. Stop speaking through your sinuses. Saul, you're a married man; see if you can reach this zipper—I'm still choking."

"The truth is I've never really noticed regional Yiddish cultures," Tony was saying.

"Ah, chappie, everybody is alike, but everybody is different. It's a kockamaymee world, and you're too young to know life can be vicious to itself. You have problems?"

"I should be thinking of what I'm really going to do. I can't ski all my life."

"You want to become like the guests?"

"Why not?"

"Do they look happy? Your Uncle Tom, a face like he was weaned on a sour pickle."

"I'm very ordinary and I know it. Maybe I was born to fit into the Store."

"Don't *hok mere a chinik* with what youth thinks is life. Live, don't reason with it."

"There must be a reason to things, or do I sound like a college freshman?"

"No, no, Tony . . . Have I been drinking too much. Come nearer. The answer to the riddle of the universe is promised by the text of Sefer Yetzira. Really, chappie, the full answer will be revealed to us, he says, on a Tuesday at two in the afternoon. It doesn't say on *which* Tuesday. You're laughing? That I like. Look, you're going to Europe soon?"

"In two weeks. Traveling with an ice-sports exhibition, skiing, sort of a cultural exchange project."

"Behind the Iron Curtain, as they say?"

"Yes, our passports are good most any place in Europe. Not Russia."

"Poland?"

"Yes. As a matter of fact the Poles are fine skiers."

"Ah, Tony, *boychick*, I told you about my daughter, Leah, must be fourteen now. Someone must go in to bring her out. Judith says she can get the proper release papers, entry permit here—all that."

"Anyone can get her out then?"

"No, some mishmash, a relative has to sign there for her. The *momsers* don't make it easy."

"I doubt if I could find the time."

"We were just talking of time, no? It's not in a box, it's not cut to fit like an overcoat. Ha, you ever read Gogol's *The Overcoat?* You ever figure our clothes, in a way, have an immortality that's denied to us? The Czar is dead, but his coat is in a glass case."

"Somebody bungled this. Donald, I fear you were the butter-fingers."

"Why me, sir? Judith walked out on all of us. I mean, you all were here."

"All right, don't bubble like a *teppel* soup, Donnie. She knows what she holds and she isn't having anything done to it. Nathan, you she likes and trusts. Why not try and talk to her later. After, pardon the expression, the honeymoon. A family is—"

"Like a tight ship, I know. They're going to Palm Beach for a week."

"So you fly to Miami and drive up."

"Thank you, Saul, but I'm also permitted in Palm Beach."

"Gentlemen, why don't we go and enjoy the cutting of the wedding cake. Your personal family matters . . . I'm sure you know how to—"

"To find a common denominator, sir?"

"Kalish, I believe I can find my own texts. Saul, you're the man to sway her."

"Pete, don't get a wild hair up your prat. Judith isn't easy to turn from her purpose."

"What are you looking for, Tony?"

"Well, Uncle Tom, I thought I'd dance with Nancy."

"You're a little late."

"I got involved with something for the family. Jacob was giving me a pitch about an errand he wants done in Poland."

"I think Nancy left with Dickie, Saul's nephew. Never liked that little sharp cookie."

"Oh, Dick's all right. He's trying hard to become a type."

"Why don't we all have lunch sometime, you, me, Nancy?" Tom laughed. "Me and my lunch bit. Right at the last moment I'd have to say I can't make it. Remember the summer Nancy was about four and you had a twenty-two rifle some fool gardener put into your hands? No one knew it was loaded. You shot Nancy in the foot and thought you had killed her?"

"I don't remember much about it."

"You ran away, were gone two days. The state police found you on a sand barge out on the river, in the hold. And you yelled out, 'Don't send me to the 'lectric chair, don't send me to 'lectric chair.'"

Tony frowned. "I don't really remember it. I do remember hiding in wet sand, though. It was dark and so cold, and I remember vaguely some enormous crime, but I suppose I've blotted out the details. How old was I? Six or seven? Was Nancy badly hurt?"

"No, just a bit of a powder burn. You weren't a good shot."

"No wonder I'm sorry I didn't manage a few dances with her before she left."

"They're going to cut the cake—no butter, of course, and kosher. The cook is a dreadful liar, always was."

"It's a shame, *Shana,* to cut into such a fine cake. So pretty."

"Jacob? Where are you? Let him up here. Here, put your hand on the knife. A wish—not to be better than we are, but just to be ourselves."

"*Shtarker fraylech du dee malkeh, Ich der maylech.*"

"Jacob, sweets, you're drunk."

"Pish-pah drunk. An old wedding song. Come on, *rebbe.*"

"*Hecher, besser dee rohd, dee rohd, mach gresser . . .*"

"*Rebbe,* you're drunk too."

"*Ach du lieber . . .*"

"Who wants the first slice? Plates, Willie, plates!"

"*Wie Gott hut mich matzleach gevane.*"

"Somebody catch the *rebbe!* He's drunk as a Polack!"

The last guest left the house at two in the morning.

The newly married couple had gone to bed, each to his individual bed, at midnight, with guests still stirring. Jacob kissed his wife on the cheek in her bedroom and she kissed him in return and said, "Good night, Jacob."

He smiled and said, "Good night, *Shana,*" and went to his own room down the hall. Judith, her hair combed down by a yawning Nora, was helped into a batiste chemise with a furred peignoir over it, was at last supine in the big family bed, tired, dazed, happy, and, she hoped, ready for sleep.

Nora went out after a husky, "Sleep well. It was a grand affair. Herself never looked better."

"Herself, herself! Herself looked a hell of a lot better once."

Judith lay on the wreck of her combed-down coiffeur, satisfied that she had done what she had wanted to do. She had found a hope of salvation: not a complete salvation, she thought, but then, while she had always been superstitious, she had never been ardent about religion. That would come slowly, through Jacob, her love. She relaxed, limb by limb, remembering that we begin with hope and survive by learning how to live without it. At her age, hope was long gone. Just peace and a bit of wisdom would do, and the love of Jacob. And an accepting. She had never been able to accept things as they seemed to others. She wanted life in more glowing colors, in sharper detail, in leisured intimate contact. That had been long ago when she had the face of a Nefertiti. You could almost hear her beauty, and as the poet has said, "All the heavens were a bell, and being an ear."

She turned her head to one side, burrowing into the pillow, and began the slow soft descent into sleep. It would take a good half hour to reach, but it would come. She smelled to herself of emollients and astringents and of the scent that was Judith. She was her own good company now at night, unless terror came in some cauterizing bad dream and she should wake, calling "Nora, Nora!"

To desire and to despair. That was living. For her, happiness had not been merely prudence, or complete passivity. Jacob, my love. She thought of the little man, so alive, so sparkling, so full of those things that would make her old age bearable. He had told her: "For most there is a ravine that separates us from a universal life. One must forget the opiate of the past to cross it." How right he was. She dwelt too much in her own past. Sometimes it seemed that she was happiest there in her past. Missing the today, the *now*. Jacob. Jacob. She thought for a moment of getting up and going to him. To hear him say again, "Even a ten-thousand-mile journey begins with *one* step. *Shana*, your steps go backward. It is maturity to find the past inadequate."

She would go to him soon. Listen to him, believe in the still-vague immanence of God. She delayed rising, or finding her slippers, perhaps touching up her face in the mirror of the vermeil toilet case. She delayed, and dozed. But sleep would not come tonight. Too much food, drink, dancing, talking. The slightly epicene face of the lawyer, the overexuberant mood of music and young people . . .

She would think of some old song and hum it till she slept: an old sleep trick, a deviation from thoughts. *Adieu mon amour, adieu douces fillettes, adieu Grand Pont, halles, élus bains* . . . the birth of Marcel . . . Steinhager gin and *aatsuppe* in Dresden that strange summer . . . shift the pictures again . . . afternoon tea on deck H.M.S. *Audacious* off Spithead . . . the thinning pompadour of Mordechai on the honeymoon . . . such boisterous weather outside and the day of the bad blood-pressure reading

. . . she knew her grown children seemed strangers . . . what had happened to her babies to wrinkle and gray them, age them, make of them ninnies or poltroons or foolish serious wives and poor husbands . . . it hadn't been easy to hold them together, to keep the family as a family . . . *adieu Paris, adieu petits amis* . . . Jacob hold me tight or I'll fall away away . . . And she slept, snoring loudly.

BOOK IV

JEREMIAH

CHAPTER 11

⋅⊰ Archie Gillman, roving reporter in Europe for the *Yiddish Velt* of New York City, was a shabby young man with a face spoiled by old acne scars and muscles built up by a hitch in the U.S. Marines. He called himself a Brechtian man "of two dimensions clawing at the veil of appearances." He was a drinking man, and his reports at space rates to the *Yiddish Velt* didn't bring in much income. He had other sources of income. He could find a fake Picasso, Japanese cameras at cut rate, a fur coat that was nearly mink.

At the Bayerischer Hof at Immenstadt in the Tyrolean Alps he found just what he was looking for: the name of Tony Pedlock, who had just finished a ski tour on the Mädelegabel near Oberstdorf. Archie hitched his shabby trench coat tighter and went into the elkhorn-hung dining room. He found Tony at breakfast.

"You may not remember me, Pedlock, but I covered the ski season in Oslo."

"Did you?"

"Archie Gillman, New York *Jewish Velt*. But I don't suppose you read the Yiddish press?"

Tony grinned. "I don't even read the New York *Times*, but my grandmother's husband does."

"Your stepgrandfather, if there is such a term?"

Tony went on his guard, looked toward the kitchen to see what was keeping back his breakfast. "I suppose so."

"Look, my editor knows what you're going into Poland for. We want to help you."

"I don't need any help. I have the proper papers to—"

"To bring out a great rabbi's daughter. Don't you see it's a story to delight every Jewish heart. Even *Look* or *Life* would eat it up."

"You're beginning to bore me, Gillman. I'm hungry and I want to eat alone."

"Pedlock, going into Poland, it's not like going for a walk in the park."

The waitress brought Tony's food: four eggs and some of the dark northern ham, crisp white rolls. Archie—he had been on a bat—looked at the food with a shiver of distaste and ordered some toast and jam. He took a newspaper from his coat pocket. It was the *Regensburger Anzeiger*.

"Pedlock, I love the rotten German press. They hide the news between cornplaster ads and coy invitations to go to Swedish massage parlors. Not like the direct push of the American press, eh?"

Tony ate with relish, breaking the egg yolks, sopping up the ham fat and egg with the white roll. Archie refolded his paper.

"Pedlock, you need help on what you're planning."

"I don't know what you're talking about."

"I talk Polish. I've been all through that country."

Tony stopped chewing and reached for his coffee cup and took a slow deep swallow. "Stay out of my affairs, you hard-nosed bastard."

"I know the ropes, the right officials."

"I'm meeting a buyer from the Rome office of Pedlock & Sons. So I don't need you.

"That's not friendly, *landzman*."

Tony motioned the waitress to remove his plate. He felt his pulse beat in his forehead. He tried to remain expressionless. It was bad enough to have accepted this thing from Jacob Ellenbogan— but *this* pest . . .

"It's a great Jewish story, Pedlock, and I want it. American Jews are very sentimental. They cry at art movies, and this is a story to choke them up. The rescue of a little lost Jewish girl from behind the Iron Curtain by a former Olympic champion, a member of the Pedlock family."

Tony turned to the waitress. "A slice of *Apfelstrudel*. "Gillman, you go get your own story."

"I'm going in with *you*."

"Maybe I'm not going. Why should I?"

"Of course you're going. Look, I'll arrange everything. *Everything*. Planes, cars, hotels, whatever schmearing is needed with minor or main officials. All I want is the story and pictures, exclusive for the *Yiddish Velt*."

Tony watched the waitress set down the cut of strudel. He pushed a fork into it but didn't eat any of it. "It isn't that good a story."

"I'll eat that cake, Pedlock, if you don't mind. You're ruining it."

"Go ahead."

His mouth full of strudel, Archie waved the fork at Tony. "The exclusive story. Nothing to break in print till the girl is safely out of Poland. It's all part of friendlier relationships between nations. Don't struggle—give in."

"The Polish security police are, I hear, very good."

"That's why all of this has to be aboveboard."

"And you really speak Polish?"

"Sure, Pedlock."

Tony looked up at Archie Gillman, in need of a shave, his shirt collar grimy, a button missing. "Gillman, what's really in it for you?"

"Call me Archie. A story. The hearts of American Jews love this kind of feature. I'm the Marine Corps *goniff* to dig it up. Blessed are little children, for they shall make the best journalism. Jesu, Maria *und* Joseph. Not to forget Moses and Abraham."

"The person from the Rome office gets in on the afternoon plane. They buy products from Poland. You can go to hell. I don't want any part of you."

"*Schrecklich*," said Archie in his dismal German accent. "I'll get seats for us on the Munich-Cracow plane leaving at seven tonight. My passport, Tony, should be ready at noon. I'll pick up your Rome contact. No bother, as I'll be arranging passage."

Tony watched a man wearing a hat with a chamois brush carefully wipe the forks at his table.

Archie stood up. "Must go cable the office everything's solid at this end."

Tony wanted to shout something in protest, in anger at this ex-Marine, but didn't. He picked up the newspaper. Archie had circled a news story in red. Slowly Tony read, translating from the heavy German prose.

JEWISH DOCTOR DIAGNOSES OWN CASE

DOCTOR SPURNS HELP, DIES OF GUN WOUND

A doctor who reportedly shot himself in the chest with a revolver Wednesday turned an ambulance away from his door with the comment: "I can diagnose my own case." An hour later Roth Semmel, M.D., 65, of Bodenseestrasse was dead and police were resummoned to the house. Semmel was once an inmate of the Buchenwald concentration camp. Detective Hans Tren at the Police Station said he got a call from the doctor's wife at 11 A.M. She reported her husband had shot himself. A radio patrol car, detectives and an ambulance sped to the hillside home. Tren said that when they arrived Dr. Semmel refused to accept medical attention and told the officers: "I'm a doctor and can diagnose my own case. My lungs are filling up and an ambulance won't do me any good." The patrol car remained as the detectives and ambulance left. Tren returned when the report came in the doctor had died.

He tossed the paper aside. Maybe he *could* use help. Europe was not a happy garden for Jews, and Germany still brought the odor of a beast pit to Tony's nostrils. Suddenly he felt too alone—too much alone; even Archie Gillman looked good. And big tough Archie was no beauty.

Munich airport crouched under a pall of cold biting rain; the slush of an earlier snow had been washed away by the ground crews. Tony stood alone in the waiting room, Archie having gone to phone some mysterious news source. Tony's head was sunk in the collar of his heavy leather coat, hands deep in its pockets. In a kind of dismal despair he watched the red and yellow lights blink off and on on the runway. Everything was shiny and reflected back in distorted pattern by the mirror of the black rain. Some actors— judging by their made-up faces—were rushing to catch a small two- motor plane waiting for them, shouting to each other and to the people who had come to see them off: "*Hals und Beinbruch!*"

A hoarse voice came from the public-address system, but Tony didn't bother to make out the pebble-rattling message. His German was feeble. Their plane had been delayed for half an hour. He could still not believe he was embarked on this foolish and danger- ous thing for Jacob Ellenbogan. The ski group back at the hotel had remarked that Tony was going after a dame, or maybe acting as a secret agent—ha ha! The parting from them had been hard, but the friendship was all worn out of it once he had said he wasn't going on a new ski tour.

Tony lit a cigarette. Beyond a pile of magazines and newspapers across the waiting room he saw Archie Gillman, muffler in disorder inside his shabby coat collar, a battered black hat set back on his head. Archie was holding the arm of a tall dark girl wearing a red oiled-silk coat and a high sable hat. Archie was never predictable, apparently. This tramp newspaperman didn't seem the type for this kind of woman.

"Tony boy, this is Asta, Asta Chauessian. She's from your Rome buying office. Ran into her at the passport desk. Asta, Tony Pedlock."

Tony became aware of the hard falling rain outside the drafty waiting room, Archie smiling, the tall girl looking at him, poker-faced, her shoulders crosshatched with straps from which hung fashionable bags. She certainly wasn't Jewish. He wondered what the policy of the *Yiddish Velt* was on that score.

She held out a strong, long-fingered hand, like a baseball player's Tony thought, and she said in a heavy, accented English: "Sounds crazy to me. This trip, the things I do for Pedlock & Sons."

"The New York office insisted I contact you. You've been in Poland buying for the stores."

Her voice was very deep and low, her face too long. Not much makeup, pale skin, hair heavy and blue-black, cut short and pushed over her high forehead. She looked able, wary, bright, and if the mouth was any indication, sensual; the kind of woman Tony mistrusted, avoided. A hip babe. He wondered if she was Hindu, Rumanian, Gypsy, or from the heel of Italy; from her name, most likely Armenian. He had seen beautiful stone heads in museums that had her features—half Greek, part Turkish.

"They'll never take off in this weather, Archie."

"Sure they will, Tony. I have a bottle of slivowitz along for company. We'll be snug."

Asta hunted up a handkerchief from a bag on her red oiled-silk shoulder. "I hope I'm not getting a cold. In Poland you're down with lumbar pneumonia before you know it."

Archie said, "Polska winters *are* cold."

A porter in a heavy black raincoat and rain hat came up to them and touched his hat with raw red fingers. He said their baggage was aboard, their plane was loading, to have their passports ready. Asta took Tony's arm. "Let me hold on. If I trip with all my gear, it could cost a few bucks, and those *momsers* try and jew you down on all assignments. Oh, sorry."

"*C'est selon. . . .*" Tony answered.

Asta was certainly a tall girl, Tony decided, slim but swelling in the beam like most Armenian women, shapely legs pacing along with his in the boiling rain with a flash of gun-metal nylons and flapping overshoes. He hoped she had a fur-lined jacket under that red raincoat. Poland this time of the year, he had heard again and again, could really crack trees apart by just freezing the sap in them. As a boy, Jacob had told him, he had often found hawks and other birds of prey with their feet frozen to the boughs they had settled on the night before.

The jet was warming its engines on the off side—thundering blasts coming from its jet pods, throwing the rain into spattering fury. Inside the plane there were only nine passengers, among them an old lady whose face was tied up in a yellow scarf as if she had a toothache, and a Rumanian smelling of scent and shoe polish. The jet engines blasted on, and Tony motioned Asta to a seat by the window. She shook her head. "I need sleep. You take the window. It vibrates."

Archie settled down behind them and poured slivowitz into paper cups. Tony had forgotten how potent the fiery plum brandy could be, but Asta swallowed hers at a gulp and showed no reaction. She settled her bags around her feet and without taking off her red raincoat or tall fur hat, she closed her eyes and seemed at once to fall asleep. Her mouth had opened a bit and her breathing was audible, her head tilted way back. Tony removed her fur hat and saw that her ears had been pierced for earrings but were bare. She stirred slightly in her sleep and without waking muttered in what sounded Italian, "*È meglio donare la lana che . . .*"

The plane began to move for takeoff. The rain became stronger and darker. The jet began to gather speed, yet never seemed to lift. When at last they were airborne the field lights below faded too quickly into darkness. Everyone settled into sleep.

Tony came awake, feeling sticky inside his clothes. The jet was just putting down its flaps to approach Cracow. Somehow it seemed the world already smelled like Jacob Ellenbogan's stories of Poland. There was little to see, just a snowy landscape, some factory chimneys, the roads with a few cars and sleds. Ahead was a tower, a wind sock, what had once been Pilsudski airfield. Jacob had bewitched him, put a spell on him; how else explain his being here?

He turned to Asta. She was awake, staring down at the landscape through the tiny window. She had discarded the red oiled-silk coat, was wearing a leopard-hide jacket. Her hair was in tumbled disorder, her breath was strong. She looked at him—how amazingly long her inky eyelashes were, how large the slightly bloodshot eyes.

"I need a hot bath. I feel tacky."

"You look fine."

"Jesus, don't start flattery. Just tell the main office in Rome I try. I need the job."

Tony turned his head. Archie was still asleep in the seat behind them, his face twisted into some agonized grimace as if he was suffering through a baffling dream.

Asta said, "He's drunk. The bastard killed that bottle of slivowitz."

"I'll shake him awake."

"*Das frait mich.*"

Tony wished the Rome office had sent a more agreeable person. But Archie seemed pleased with her.

CHAPTER 12

ᴇᵺ The landing was bumpy as the plane dropped from the silver Cracow sky. They taxied a long way over the bleak ground before they came to a low iron-roofed building. A few soldiers stood before it with rifles on their shoulders. A little fat man told them in Polish to have their passports ready. Passing customs was not difficult, but it was bone-biting cold in the place. Their visas were stamped, they were advised of the rules on smuggling and currency exchange and warned against listening to the wrong people, the *stanszlach*—the gentry.

On the way to the Huzarska Hotel in the big, rattling fifteen-year-old Buick, Archie sobered up and said he needed a hair of the dog. Asta adjusted her fur hat. "You revolt me."

"I'm too sick to defend myself." Archie looked really dreadful, a pale green in color, hands trembling, licking his dry cracked lips, his body loose in his rumpled, stained clothes.

Asta said, "Here's the place you want, Tony. I better go with you." She tapped on the glass separating them from the driver.

"I'll go alone. Don't worry. Meet you at the hotel."

"Sly," said Archie. "Real sly. You'll get lost."

"No."

Asta, examining a run in her stocking, said, "Remember, don't get me in trouble with New York. They better have plenty of hot water at the hotel. I always catch cold in these Mittel Europa dives."

The driver pointed to a building, and Tony got out of the taxi as it pulled to the curb. He watched it rattle off in a cloud of blue smoke. Happy to get rid of his companions, he looked around him. Everybody was hurrying along in the cold wind, well bundled up, showing a red cheek or ear tip or end of a nose. The shop signs in Polish made no sense; letters, it would appear, announcing a drugstore, a herb shop, a leather store, a place that sold tea and certain things he had never known: *babka, kwaśne mleko* (sour milk). He stood staring at a big *tort general Iwaszkiewicza*. He hadn't seen one of those layer cakes for a long time, not since Judith's last birthday. His mouth watered, but his feet were freezing, and he looked down past the shape of the church of the Ecumenical Patriarch.

311 Stephan Bathory Street. Past Kosciusko Square. The People's Artists building of gray stone was in need of paint but in good repair. Inside, the overheated hallway was hung with coats and scarfs, crowded with overshoes scattered underfoot. A lean blonde with silver-rimmed glasses, who spoke a poor English mixed with a Kasube dialect of Polish, said for Tony to ask for Pan Ozinski on the second floor, the proper man to see.

The marble staircase had once been a fine one and was still impressive, though the red carpet was worn. People carrying battered brief cases were hurrying past him, smoking long cigarettes, half paper tube, looking preoccupied and busy. The Ozinski offices were crowded into a corner of the second floor, and as Tony entered he was assailed by the heavy smell of wet wool and leather. Several people were drinking the *herbata*—a native tea—from a battered silver service, and from the smell in the air and if his guide book of Polish phrases was right, there had also been some *krupnikof* punch consumed.

Pan Ozinski was a little round man with the greater part of his hair gone and his upper teeth outlined in gold. He was very pleased to see Tony, shook his hand and pulled him into an inner office. His English was slurred but very good. He pushed some newspapers and magazines off a black leather chair and asked Tony to sit down.

"To see such a ski star—ah. Ah, *życie*—life is real again. I saw you win the jump near Oslo. Yes, I did. Shall I send out for some *zakonshi* to an hors d'oeuvres shop? No? Sit, sit. The weather is *chlodnawy,* cooler, eh." Tony sat smiling. "You'll do a ski exhibit for us? Ah, the People's Artists would be proud to show you off."

"No, I'm sorry, I can't. I'm due back in the United States. I'm on a strange mission. For a relative—he married my grandmother."

Ozinski just rolled his head a bit. As if he didn't want to say yes or no. Tony took out his papers and explained in detail about the daughter, Leah. Ozinski listened with care, nodding in the right places, as he touched his fat legs, his little paunch, rubbed his round pink chops, smoked a cigar in a white holder and showed less of his gold-edged teeth as Tony went on.

When Tony was done, the little man jumped up. "Ah, Pan Pedlock, always trouble, families, children. The damn *szlachta*—gentry —have left us in a mess. All the *ludzie bezdomny*—the homeless drifting among us." He was like an actor playing a part. He almost wiped back a tear.

"You'll help me find Leah Ellenbogan?"

"But of course. The Lupescu Ice Show and Circus, you say? With them she ice skates? Of course. Make yourself at home, Pan Pedlock. I'll go check our records. I'll send in a drink of kvass, *our* Coca-Cola, eh?"

He was gone a long time. Tony felt too warm in the little overheated office with its dusty pictures of Casimir the Great, Ladislaus, and new ones of Lenin and a few faces Tony did not know. He was almost asleep—he had slept badly on the plane—before Ozinski was back, smiling, rattling papers on his desk.

"I don't know where Jacob Ellenbogan got the information the circus was performing just now in Polish villages. I mean this season. It was here seven months ago. Our records are well kept, regular Lankski style. But the show went into Rumania then, and it's not due to play in Poland again till . . ." He rattled the papers again, peering nearsightedly at them. "Ah yes, March first. Wait, there is a note it may get back before then and we'll pick up some bookings for them—that's stage talk; it means playing dates."

"No one here knows where it is?"

"I'll get in touch with those bastards, our comrades in the Rumanian People's Artists. Full of *Zydzis,* and you'll not hear from them till *Wielkanoc*—Easter."

"What about that Siberian tour?"

Ozinski showed his hands palms up. "We are only loosely connected artistically with the USSR People's Artists groups."

"You'll try and get some information for me, Mr. Ozinski? I'll be at the Huzarska Hotel."

Ozinski seemed to want to keep Tony in his office. He suggested lunch, posing for some pictures. He began to sweat and pat himself with nervous gestures. He seemed relieved when there was a brisk knock on the door and a thin young man with red hair came in. The redhead opened his black fur coat, stomped his boots and said in poor English, "Pan Ozinski, you overheat offices, waste people's fuel."

Ozinski smiled and rolled his eyes. "Our guest, Anthony Pedlock. And this is Comrade Kura. Shall I send out for some *nalewka* or vodka?"

"*Nalewka*," said Pan Kura. "And go see it's the good brand."

Ozinski smiled and went out. Tony looked up at the tall redhead with his knobby country-boy features, bright-blue eyes, mouth that turned up at the corners in a lawyer's or judge's way.

"You're the police, Pan Kura?"

"Captain Kura, the Security Police. Pan Ozinski had to report you here, but I knew you were in Poland from the airport list. Do you know an uncle of mine, Harry Goldman—in Cleveland?"

"Sorry, I've never been to Cleveland."

"My mother's brother. So. Your record is good. You have never acted against the people's interest, never plotted against us, have not lied about us in other parts of the world."

"That's correct, Captain Kura. I am here, believe me, only to get Jacob Ellenbogan's daughter and reunite her with her father."

"We Jews—eh—great family people."

A girl came in with a tray holding a bottle and glasses. Captain Kura slipped out of his fur coat and sat down behind the desk as the girl left.

"Did you ever think you were being used, innocently on your part, in some *other* scheme?"

"Good lord, no!"

Captain Kura sighed and rearranged a little glass ball, an ivory penholder, a tiny statue of an eagle on the desk. "I am even assuming that you did not know that Archibald Gillman is a suspected black-market money smuggler. I fear it's bad for the Jews—you understand?"

Tony's reaction, his open-mouthed state of shock, was almost comic. He could only sputter and wave his arms. Captain Kura handed him a glass of colorless liquid. It burned all the way down.

When he found his voice, Tony said, "Damn it! How could that be? Archie Gillman?"

"A perfect agent. As a tramp newspaperman he can go almost anyplace, file his silly little gossip stories. His appearance and way of life certainly don't make him suspect."

Tony had to agree. He looked up angrily. "Why should you tell me this about Archie?"

Captain Kura smiled and knocked his drink back swiftly. He looked like a good-natured farm boy who had grown up into a simple adult. Only the eyes seemed out of place: direct, overshiny, steady, like the irises of a hawk Tony had raised as a boy.

"Pedlock, that is a very good question. If we have this agent here and if, as you claim, you know nothing about his true standing, why should I tell you?"

Tony accepted a cigarette and coughed as the harsh Balkan tobacco was lit for him by Captain Kura's brass lighter. "Yes, why tell me? I don't like him—I don't give a damn what happens to him."

"It would be easy to toss you three in prison and keep you there. On any of half a dozen charges. But what good would it do us? We wouldn't know *why* he is really here. What your plan is."

"Me? You know. I'm here to get Jacob Ellenbogan's daughter."

"Suppose I believe you. Jew to Jew."

"Why shouldn't you?"

"Say I do believe you, you're still part of a party that includes an American black-market money smuggler." He looked at a bit of paper he took from his pocket. "And Asta Harootunian Toovanda Chauessian. Assistant manager, Pedlock & Sons buying office in Rome, via della Croce forty-two. Right?"

"Oh come now, is she a money smuggler too?"

"Born in Thessalonike, what you Americans call Salonika. Of French mother, and Armenian father—by the way, shot by the Greeks as food speculator. Educated in the Convent of the Sacred Heart in Lutz, Austria, *and*, ah, Mills College in California." Captain Kura looked up, filled the glasses and smiled. "We are rather proud of our files. I just picked this up on the way over. She worked for R. H. Macy's in New York, went to Paris for Wanamaker's buying office, then went to Rome to work for Pedlock & Sons. Is this her picture? Yes. Personal details. Married to Edmund Ali Sethos,

former Egyptian consul in Naples. Divorced. Then to Max
Schahner, former Nazi S.S. officer, salesman for Volkswagen motor
cars in America. Lives in an apartment on the via Condotti."

Tony looked at his smoldering cigarette—what vile tobacco.
"She seems to be what she claims. A buyer for our stores."

"Yes, it may all be very normal. But report to me or to whomever I assign to you the daily doings of Gillman and Chauessian."

"What do you mean, report?"

Captain Kura sighed and stopped smiling. "I have to work with
what I have. You're not, I agree, at all the agent type."

"You're so right."

"My dear Pedlock, it's all very simple. I *must* keep your friends
under surveillance. Find out why they're really in Poland. You
must help us." He made a sad gesture. "*Please*, don't make me
outline threats of what *can* happen to you."

"I want to find Leah Ellenbogan and get the hell out of all this."

"You have my word you will find Miss Ellenbogan. Drink up.
Now go back to your friends—act as if none of what I said has
happened. Find out what they are up to. I will be in touch with
you to find out what you discover for us. We trade you information
for Leah, a *Yiddische Kind*."

"I'm a fool," said Tony bitterly into the glass. "I didn't want any
part of this thing. Not even, frankly, getting Leah."

"We will find out where the ice show and circus is. You make
your *wyzwolenie*—deliverance—and you can go back to being on
skis. Ah, we had fine weather for skiing in Listopas, November.
Now the snow is a little too rough."

Tony was listening to the palatal sibilant sound of Captain
Kura's accent. He wanted to cable to Judith, to his father, but
knew he mustn't panic.

"Suppose I refuse to spy on them?" Tony stood up, a bit woozy;
that *nalewka* was like missile fuel.

"Terrible stubborn *boychick*, are you? You like to see a warrant
for your arrest, orders for you to be held in Zemsta Prison under a
number only, no name, and permitted to see no one but Security
Police?"

"Frankly, no," said Tony. "May I go now to think it all out?"

Captain Kura spread his arms wide and smiled again. "My dear
Pedlock, but of course." He pressed a button on the desk. "This
damn pig Ozinski, messy desk he keeps. These artist fellows are all

soft as the old ruling class we got rid of. You are taking all this very well."

"I'd like to see how you'd take it, Captain Kura."

"Interesting idea."

Ozinski came in, trying to look happy but standing stiffly facing the police officer. "Yes, Captain Kura, at your service, Captain Kura."

"Get a car to take Pedlock to his hotel. Help him any way you can. He carries news of the pride and honor of a free Polska wherever he performs, all over the world."

"Captain Kura," Tony said, "you're a charmer."

He shook hands all around, and when he was in the street getting into a gray Russian copy of a no longer made Packard, he discovered he was trembling, as he often did in a nightmare the night before a big meet, dreaming of great canyons opening up in the snow before him just as he leaped off into space. There was a Turkish song on the car radio.

CHAPTER 13

੩ The high-ceilinged lobby of the Huzarska Hotel smelled of the decaying deer heads mounted on the walls, of *kasha*, carp *Polonais* and damp overshoes. Tony was taken up to a fine suite on the second floor. Archie Gillman was in the living room, sprawled in a deep, silk-upholstered chair under a chandelier covered with cheesecloth. Two double-sashed windows looked down on a snowy square where women wearing headcloths and knee-length boots were clearing paths with snow shovels among the bronze statues to new heroes.

Archie said, "Tony boy, this is living, isn't it? The old Imperial Romanov suite. All gold and moth-eaten *drek*. Your room is the third door to the left. Asta is in a lousy mood. Felt you didn't trust her, going alone."

Tony stared earnestly at the newspaperman, not really believing this large shabby individual was engaged in black market activities. The interview with Captain Kura was a fantasy—a joke being played on him by bad actors.

"Asta? She's worried, I suppose, that I'll tell the New York office something not flattering about her?"

"She's got personal troubles, too. Some guy she's in love with but isn't any more. You follow the whole *magila*? She tried to phone him in Paris and couldn't get a line through."

"She's married, isn't she?"

"Twice, I gather. But this is some French creep she never wants to see again—so she told me. Go figure out a dame. How was your visit?"

"The Lupescu circus with which Leah is skating is most likely in Rumania. The People's Artists office will try to help us."

"Were they snotty about it? Oh, an airmail letter was here waiting for you."

Tony took the letter and saw his father's art gallery address on it. He studied Archie's heavy-lidded eyes, scarred face. "No. I'm a hero to them. I skied in the Olympics against a Polish hotshot."

"Sure you're a hero. I'm going to get some sleep."

"Don't you want to see the city, Archie? What are your plans?"

"Easy," said Archie, standing up, blowing cigarette ashes off his jacket. "You sound like the old Deuxième Bureau Interrogation working over a suspect."

Tony turned away. He certainly hadn't acted natural asking questions in a hurry. How was he going to find out anything to con Captain Kura along?

"See you, Archie," he said and went to his room.

It was small, blue-papered, oak-floored, very ornate; a badly gilt Louis period in robin's-egg blue. The bed was comfortable for all its obscene sag, and he washed up at a marble sink, deciding to shave later, and lay down on the bed, the letter in his hand. His mind was like a bad montage in an arty movie: Archie; Asta of the roving international buyers offices; Captain Kura's so simple Jewish farm-boy face, the red hair in disorder over his brow; a wind whistling through the birch and alder trees in the parks; the *chłopi*—peasants, as the guide book said—people singing *Przedwieczny*; he recalled a prison in Austria where he had once visited a skier named Billie Leech, who had gotten drunk and smashed up a cafe owner. There had been a smell of decay and offal in the cell. Better read his father's letter.

The sight of the fine letterhead printing, *DuVere & Starkweather Galleries*, helped bring back reality, or if not reality then a world with which he was familiar. There were no corrections in his father's neat small penmanship anywhere in the letter.

DEAR TONY:

I sometimes think you are on a fool's errand, but when I consider Judith's comment and pressure if you had turned down this task put on you, I think you're better off doing this thing than facing her resentment. She seems full of irrepressible naïveté, but in fact is hard as steel.

Here there is little peace in the family. It's all rather complex, but I gather from legal talk that Judith holds a vast portion of the Store and Bank shares in her own home and is involved in some dream of a school in Israel for the mystic cult in which Jacob is a sort of high priest. I don't know too much about it except that I find him a fascinating character—there is something fey about him at times, which is nonsense, and also something graceful, swift, small. He's like a bright supernatural creature that seems to mock us mortals, run among us and observe us, offer wise sayings from tattered texts. He told me, "Chappie, the failure of experience to remake you may be your true tragedy."

This Jacob Ellenbogan is a strange old man. He fascinates me. Sometimes I wonder is he alive, or is he a *dybbuk*—a possessed spirit. But a cigar-smoking, herring-eating *dybbuk* in modern New York is nonsense.

I do like being with him now that the marriage has shaken down a bit. They headed for Palm Beach, but Judith wanted to show Jacob the West Indies. They started out, but on the ship Judith was taken with food poisoning, claiming it was a bad lobster, and she insisted the ship put back to shore and she be flown at once to Johns Hopkins. Radiograms came pouring in on Nathan and Lazar-Wolf to stop the ship and make it return to port. But the captain would only take her to Bermuda, where she made a marvelous recovery and hired a horse and cart to drive Jacob over the island. They came back, breathing hard, to Norton-on-Hudson, which is to be their permanent home. Jacob comes into New York twice a week to lunch with me; he's doing some mysterious research at the public library and at the Hebrew Institute with the quixotic expectancy of finding the true key to the cabala.

Meanwhile, Judith will not guarantee that her holdings after her death will stay in this country, and the lawyers are delving into those dank wells of intrigue that lawyers always seem to be able to dredge up to subdue a client. I keep looking at the prints of Daumier's lawyers that hang in my office; the breed of these shark-headed monsters hasn't changed much. But Nathan tells me tax laws, estate problems, business relationships are so complex now that only a herd of lawyers can keep any firm or fortune afloat these days against the greed of the taxing power—a sad commentary on our times.

Do you find Poland cold? Unfriendly? Some Pedlocks for generations suffered there; pious murders, Christian pogroms, beatings, deaths, first by the nobles, then by the peasants, then by various governments. Those that survived died under the scientific skill and knowledge of the Germans, who go insane—the entire nation—every thirty years. Check history. Very sad story. Jacob knows so much of it. And the horror is this: There is no horror in the world really about what was done. The Germans who ran the Krupp-tooled camps, the police, and the torture cellars are now in control of Germany again,

East and West, and we hug them as allies. What caused me to digress? Jacob's retelling of this history.

Back to the family. It's not so frightening, but you know domestic alarms and laments. Little Joanne Lazar-Wolf was rushed one night to the hospital and had her appendix removed. Tom's wife is making dreadful trouble. They are separated and he's living with some woman from the Store's publicity department. Lord, how I sound like Samuel Pepys relating the court gossip, but it's no gossip. Tom and Mabel are separated, but if it comes to a New York divorce it can be nasty with Tom's adultery so well known. And just when there is talk of a raid on Pedlock & Sons by the Ganzler Fairs group. Nathan says a scandal now would really affect our stock and give Ganzler a chance. But this is beyond me. I sell reglazed old masters and second-rate moderns, hoping to find better work here and there. (By the way, there are some Brueghel drawings loose in Poland; if you hear of them appearing for sale, let me know.)

So while Mabel drinks and is a public drunk at times, if she sues Tom on the only grounds in New York State, adultery, the sacred Pedlock name would be dragged in what is referred to as the mud—although the city is well paved except for Con Edison digging here and there. Tom is a fine man but has a moral insensibility.

Tom's daughter, Nancy (you met her at the wedding), is going around with Lazar-Wolf's nephew, Dick Lazarus, or rather Lawrence —he changed his name again. He was originally a Lazar-Wolf, but changed to Lazarus when he entered the bank, claiming he didn't want to carry the firm's name. Now he's Lawrence. Next he will probably do over his nose, or be fitted for a plastic foreskin. (That's a bad joke, but it's written down, so let it stay.) Actually Dick is a fine, driving young man, solidly educated by his uncle, an asset to the Bank. He's a climber. Like Saul, I suppose; being born in poverty and into a minority is a combination that does affect one's habits and one's dealings with the world. He and Nancy are not engaged. Mabel says she'll be damned before she'd allow "another Hebe into the family." Nancy is pretty firm and amusing and I think very beautiful—one of Goya's young duchesses. I like taking her and Dick to dinner before some successful but poor play on Broadway. I'm lonely, Tony, and I suppose I lost you long ago.

Maybe this isn't the age of fathers and sons, or if it is, only à la Turgenev. I don't know. When you were a child, even when you were growing up, I felt you interfered with my way of life. I write this in bed, on a board on my knees (actually a portfolio of Klee prints). I've had two big bourbons, so if I say anything out of place, ignore it. As I write to you, the loneliness of approaching old age has made me look around, and I've sort of adopted Nancy and Dick, at least till you get back. I'd like to know you, know what you want, what you are, why I failed you.

Nothing dates one so much as being abreast of only one's own time. Somehow it suddenly seems to me that all we went through as Jews for a few thousands of years—all the agony, the torture, the fearful horrors —wasn't worth it. What has it produced? American Jewry? The Pedlocks? The smug, sleek, upper-middle-class rabbis? The bland cant of Reform services as tasteless as white bread? In my journal—yes, yes, I've kept one for some years, and just now, in it, am I able to break out of the skin of my daily existence and find something to put down that is often what I haven't dared to say before. In my journal, then, which I will destroy someday, for unlike Walpole, Pepys, the rest, I don't write with one eye on publication or a presentation to some university, I scribble nights (a little loaded on bourbon) of a hunt within myself, and of the family. I'm getting involved in a kind of evanescence and emptiness, like Henry James, who was taken seriously when I was at Yale. But I'd better close this letter and get it off to you in the morning, before I give in to the idea that if one waits long enough nothing holds together; everything falls apart.

I go once a week to Pedlock House with as many of the family as put in an appearance, and most do (or get fantastic phone calls from Judith the next day). There is a warmth in the old house again, and she, your grandmother, has dug up from the attics many of the old discards, which are fashionable again: bentwood rockers, Biedermeier tables, old sofa covers that are like Pop art, only mellowed. Judith is battling with the cook, Marta, and it's a real war. Marta keeps sneaking butter into the fried cutlets that Jacob enjoys and refuses to understand that the dishes with the blue-pattern rim are for dairy dishes and the red ones for meat. So we go on clinging to the veil of appearances.

So much for news here. Send me a few hundred words. And if you need anything, I've contacts with most of the great art dealers in Europe, who have connections everyplace, and there is my half sister, Constanza—born Connie—from Mordechai's first marriage, who is in Italy someplace, Rome or Venice. We are not totally alienated.

Your father,
MARCEL

Tony folded the letter and carefully put it away. Marcel wasn't such a fancy old crock after all. As for being a father, well, maybe it was too late now, maybe not.

Tony dozed. He dreamed of stale prison clothes, bad breath, damp walls with a kind of black moss growing on them, and his skier friend's trouble came back. The cellars of the Security Police of Captain Kura would be no better, probably worse. How could all this happen to a man who didn't even cross streets against the lights?

Tony moaned and opened his collar and lay spread-eagled on the bed. He decided none of this was true to his time-bind; none of this could be happening.

He dozed off again. The room was icy cold. The heat vent in the wall seemed to be blowing Arctic weather into the room. He slept in a fitful tossing of limbs, coming awake again and again, finding a thin blanket to pull over himself, falling away into troubled sleep to mutter and to toss. He was skiing down a very steep and dangerous slope of flint snow, and behind him were a dozen skiers—Polish Jews, in police uniforms. He looked over his shoulder and they were all Captain Kuras, and all were shouting, *"Ucho igielne! Ucho-igielne!"* Tony panted for air, bent lower, skied faster; then ahead of him the entire slope began to shake like jelly and dissolve into a kind of smoky-white version of Pedlock House. He slipped and was falling for a long time into the void.

He could only cry out as he smothered in the clinging liquid, "Grandma, Judith." But no life remained, only a smothering of all sensation. The dream seemed to be shaking itself apart, and he heard Jacob Ellenbogan laughing.

Tony opened his eyes to find Asta, in a finger-length bed jacket, standing over him, one hand on his shoulder, shaking him.

"What? What?" he called out, feeling a dryness of mouth and tongue.

"You were shouting so, I thought you were having a fit."

"No—no fit."

He sat up cross-legged on the bed and wiped his face with the back of his hands. Lord, what fine long naked legs Asta had; they seemed to grow out of her shoulder blades. She didn't appear to mind the cold. He looked away as if he had been peeping through a suddenly opened door.

"I must have been having a bad dream."

"Have you any aspirin? I've a doozy of a headache, and I can't get them to understand what I want on the phone. Would you believe it, my room has a rosewood Sèvres bidet but no aspirin."

She had been weeping, his casual study of her showed. Her dark eyes seemed darker, her nose was tinged with red. She was marvelously alive under the short bed jacket, and was apparently unaware just now of how short the jacket was. Tony pointed to a brown canvas carryall on a chair.

"The lower right pocket. It snaps open. You'll find a bottle of aspirin."

"Thanks. I never made a buyer's trip just like this before."

She took two pills in a cloudy glass of water from the tarnished pitcher on the night table. She sat down on the edge of the bed and rubbed her brows slowly with her long baseball player's fingers. The robe gaped open. She had the high hard breasts of young Mediterranean women in some of his father's paintings—Renoirs. Later, he had heard, they would sag and spread if she was true to type. But then her mother was French. French women were supposed to be chic and pert often into old age. She closed the robe and went on rubbing her brow.

Tony asked, "You know Archie long?"

"Not too long. The Rome office hands him a story once in a while. He's a notorious free-loader." She rubbed her brow more slowly.

"What does he do besides write for his paper?"

"Drink mostly, I guess."

"I wonder why he's really here in Poland." Lord, Tony thought, I'm going about this all thumbs. What giveaway questions.

"The story. These newspaper nuts, the story is everything to them."

Was she too putting him on? "He's shady in some way."

Asta shrugged her shoulders. "Who isn't, in some way? Oh, my head!"

"My grandmother has a way of rubbing out a headache. She says it's all from the nerves and muscles going tight in the back of the head and the neck, where the blood goes up into the brain. She uses a hand pressure, a downward stroking. She's a big strong old lady. It works."

"Sounds reasonable."

Asta turned her back to Tony. The robe slid off her shoulders and her naked flesh was facing him, giving off a kind of fragrant warmth, smelling of Asta and bath powder.

"I'll try anything to get rid of this ache. Stroke."

Tony put his thumbs up to the base of her skull, felt her crisp curly hair, the top of the spine, the strong muscles of her neck. He stroked downward and pressed, felt the stiffness leave her slowly, the tension soften, relax, as he continued the stroking and rubbing. Asta moaned, then sighed. When he had been working on her for several minutes, she seemed to purr like a cat, as if a small motor inside her were on.

"That's it. Just *there*."

"Feel better?"

"It's going away."

"Hurt?"

"Don't stop. *Umm*."

In five minutes she rolled her head from side to side. Tony held his hands flat against her shoulders, feeling vitality pulse in the warm body. They leaned against each other in a kind of trance, neither speaking. Asta stirred at last, head down, eyes closed.

"The robe."

He set the robe back in place against her neck and shoulders. She tied it up in front and faced around.

"Thanks. Your grandma had a real system."

"You feel better?"

"Deep ache is gone, just out of range of pain. I feel it there, throbbing, but no stabbing pain."

"Happy I could help."

She looked at him closely; he wondered if she was nearsighted, with those very big eyes.

"Tony, I'm in great trouble."

Tony stiffened. Back to lousy melodrama. All his thoughts and doubts turned to worry.

Asta said, *"L'amour."*

"Oh."

"L'amour. I'm no girl. I've been married. But let's not talk of that. What I have to talk about to someone is deep, you understand, very personal."

"Cigarette?"

"No. As the French say, *avoir du guignon,* to be unlucky, that's the way it is with me in love. At sixteen I was in trouble by my father's lawyer. It was taken care of. At nineteen married to a fool who liked choirboys. One learns about life. And now there is Jules. Works in Pedlock & Sons Paris office. He's five years younger than I am. He's married, a rigid Catholic, in politics. You know the French—hate the priests, send the women to Mass. Two darling children. Jules is tall for a Parisian, a blond, thin as a swordsman, a guardsman's mustache, carries a Bond Street umbrella, wears a homburg. Marvelously detailed in *l'amour.* An aunt had him when he was fourteen, you understand."

"I know the type," Tony said weakly, folding his arms. He was a bit of a puritan. He wondered how his Uncle Tom would have reacted to this.

"We met first at Pamplona in Spain. I was buying leather handbags. He was there for dry fruit packed in woven baskets. It's rather tasteless. I didn't want any affair. Jules didn't either. It was the real thing. He went to a bullfight. We could not resist each other. He turned me on. You know the phrase?"

Tony said he did, it was used in the Village.

"We saw it was impossible. My job in Rome, his family, his wife, the children, the Church. So I took this goddam assignment with you to get away. But it's very hard once you're turned on. I tried to call Jules this morning."

"The phone service is poor."

"Yes, thank God, the phone service is in dismal repair." Asta took Tony's hand, pressed it hard. Her mouth was wet and open. (Boy, would the ski club believe this?) "You must help me. I must have help."

"Look," said Tony, getting off the bed and adjusting the wall vent that now was sending a tepid wind into the room. "Aren't you cold, Asta?"

"I didn't notice. You're a nice guy. What were you asking me about Archie?"

"I just wondered if he did anything more than just act like a newspaperman." That tore it again. If they, Asta and Archie, were working together, he was sure he had given the game away.

"You hear stories, Tony. Nothing solid."

"I don't like him."

Asta shrugged her shoulders as her stomach rumbled. "You don't have a bottle of Entero Vioform? This local water can give you the intestinal trots."

Tony said he might get some. He'd look. When Asta had gone back to her room, he noticed for the first time that there was a connecting door between their two rooms.

He sat down in a deep armchair and tried to sort out his thoughts. The first thing he had to admit to himself was that this thing was actually *happening* to him. He had always practiced the habit of disbelieving most of the stories he heard about people. Besides, what had happened? He had rubbed a headache out of an employee of the Rome office of Pedlock & Sons. . . .

He slept solidly.

CHAPTER 14

⋖§ In the cold Polish day Tony Pedlock dreamed nonsense of agents, espionage, plots, counterplots existing in paperback books that one bought in airports or hotel lobbies and read quickly, smiling at the childish nonsense created by armchair authors, stories spun out of thin air. The dreams tried to catch onto some book plots, but all that came through were women with Lugers carried in their douche bags and fantastically unreal love-making by agents called 007 or Mr. X.

The phone rang. It was Captain Kura's voice in Tony's still-unfocused ear.

"I've been taking a nap, Captain Kura."

"Why not? Comfortable rooms, I hope."

"Oh yes, the former, pardon me, Imperial Romanov Suite."

"Anything you need, please feel free to call me."

"I wouldn't want to bother a busy man."

The voice changed, became serious and slower. "Now, tonight, Pedlock, you have a good dinner with your friends at Przedswit Cellar. I recommend *pierógi z serem lub jagodami*. Take the huckleberry filling. Afterward a night spot? The Mazzona—the Man and Wife, a holdover from other days, amusing."

"I'll see how they feel about going out, Captain Kura."

"And have you kept your eyes open?"

Tony leaned closer to the phone. "Nothing out of the way."

"And the Chauessian?"

Tony grinned. He felt like a prep-school boy snitching to the headmaster about the games played after lights out. "Just broken off with someone called Jules, a Paris buyer in our offices there."

"What's his full name?"

"Don't know."

"Have either of them a numbered account at the Banque Crédit Suisse, Zurich?"

"I don't know. What about Leah Ellenbogan?"

"You hear soon from Ozinski."

"I'd like to put a call through to my father in New York."

"We don't impose any restrictions."

"Miss Chauessian couldn't get through to Paris."

"You're not Chauessian, Pedlock."

He decided to test the captain for a reaction. "You'll be listening in?"

He heard Captain Kura laughing. "Don't even try, *boychick*, to make a career in security intelligence. You've just no knack for it. Be in touch."

The phone connection clicked off in Tony's ear. He sat a long time looking at the soiled red carpet. Good, the captain thought he was a dope—in Judith's words, a *schlemiehl*. He called the long-distance operator and asked to be connected with New York—Mr. Marcel Pedlock.

It took half an hour to make the connection. There had been questions of a visa number, hotel-room listing, a lot of crackling on the phone. Then a faroff voice that could have been Captain Kura's. And a click like a tape recorder being switched on. A thin female voice said they would call Pan Pedlock when they got a clear connection.

Tony paced the room, smoking a frayed cigar Archie had given him on the plane. In twenty minutes the phone rang. The thin-voiced female said the connection had been made.

"Hello? Hello, Dad?"

A sleepy voice answered, "Who the devil is this?"

"It's Tony, calling from Cracow."

"Tony. Good to hear from you."

"How's the family?"

"Fine—I mean, confusion. And you? How's Leah?"

"I'm good so far. The show is some place in Rumania. But expected back. The People's Artists office has been very helpful. Look, Dad, maybe I'm jumpy, but I might be, well, arrested."

There was a loud intake of breath on the other end, a groan as Marcel must have shifted his position. "What the devil for?"

"It's just my imagination, most likely."

"Tony, Judith sent you on a simple errand and you—have you been drinking the Warsaw vodka? It's plain poison, I hear."

"No. I just ran into some local rumors. Good to hear your voice, Dad."

"Look. I'll call Senator Goldstein in Washington."

"No, no. Take care of yourself, Dad. I'll call you as soon as there is something new on Leah. I was just lonely, I guess. Goodbye, Dad."

"Goodbye, Tony. Be careful."

After his father hung up Tony kept the receiver to his ear and heard the click of a recorder being turned off, if it was a recorder. Lord, he had acted like a panicked ten-year-old. He decided not to play around with Captain Kura if he could avoid it. He was suddenly bone-weary, drag-tailed tired. He slept without dreaming till it was dark.

He came awake to a knock on his door. Archie Gillman, shaven, in a fairly neat brown suit, came in. Under his eyes the skin was loose and wrinkled, and he had cut himself on the chin. A tiny fragment of tissue paper was stuck over some dried blood and shaving soap.

"Asta is stirring. I figure, *yingle*, we might make a night of it. Dinner, the way-out dives, *if* they have any."

"Ever been to Cracow before, Archie?"

"The sooner we get Leah Ellenbogan and get out of here, the better. They really have tough winters here."

"Yes."

"This is just a mild thaw. Wait till it gets to be a really Polish winter. Auto oil freezes like water."

"Does it?"

Archie went to the connecting door and knocked. "Hey, Asta, shake your beautiful tail. I'm hungry."

Her voice came back. "No native goop in sour cream. What about some *côtes de boeuf*?"

"I doubt it." Archie kicked the door. "You dressed?"

"I'm afraid to use the plumbing. It looks like one big germ culture."

Archie grinned as he tapped on the door with large nail-bitten fingers. "Millions of Poles around to prove you can outwit the germs and outlive them." He turned back to Tony. "Some *zaftig* broad, eh? Don't let me drink too much tonight." He held up a shaking hand. "A beaut, eh?"

Tony went to put on his dark-blue suit and blue necktie.

The dinner had been very good: a roast called *pieczeń Huzarska*, a fine wilted *salata* and a pale-green wine that was faintly Rhenish in taste, but a product of Poland. Tony paid the bill and Archie settled for two small brandies. They went on to the night club in the hired car. Asta was feeling moody. She didn't say much but smiled sadly—Mona Lisa in modern lipstick—at Tony from time to time, looking very elegant in a well-fitted snuff-colored-and-tan dress with a long dark-brown fur coat over it—"Wholesale from the Rome buying office." The cold, crystal blue, had really come down over the city, and everyone in the street was preceded by his own visible breath. Outside the night club, behind great drifts of snow, Asta pointed to old posters flapping loose on a brick wall. One of them was fluttering looser than the rest in the chilled wind.

"Lupescu Circus is all I can make out."

Archie peered at the poster in the underwater glow of blue and yellow lights over the club entrance. He translated from the Polish letters on a black-and-red picture of a line of girls on skates kicking high in a can-can on ice: " 'The great international Lupescu Ice Show and Circus. Greatest of all events on a frozen stage. Ballet, sports, drama, art. The People's Artists presents the greatest collection of stars on the ice anyplace in the world. Company of two hundred, Starring Masha, the Cat Queen.' "

Archie shivered and lowered his head deeper into his coat collar. "That must be Ellenbogan's sister-in-law, Masha. 'Children's ballet on ice with Leah, world's youngest People's Artist, in her sensational ice waltz and . . .' "

Asta tried to crouch down to get more of her fur coat around her nylon-covered legs. "Let's go in. I've begun sneezing already. *Where* can I buy long underwear?"

The steps down into the club were wooden, covered with a blue rubber mat. Inside, brick arches had once been whitewashed and cracked walls were covered with Abstract Expressionist and Pop art paintings copied from tired New York styles. Pink lampshades with long fringes covered unfrosted light bulbs. A small band, in

forest-green uniforms, was under the impression it was playing Dixieland jazz. The low-ceilinged room was fairly well filled, mostly by
very young people standing in couples on the small dance floor,
hardly moving to the music, just staring into one another's eyes.
Several elderly people sat. There was a jowled Greek with a girl of
twelve, a portly Jew with two redheaded Rumanian tarts, a couple
of middle-aged women, built like wrestlers, with long jade cigarette
holders and the roving eyes of huntresses. In a corner, Tony saw
Ozinski from the People's Artists. He smiled at Tony but made no
further sign of greeting.

"Funky," said Asta as they were seated fairly close to the band.
"Very funky. And I bet fleas in the chairs."

A plump girl on the bandstand began to sing: "*Mój Swiat.*"

"*Champagne en tout cas?*" asked the waiter in very poor French.
Archie nodded. "Of course, Mac."

They sat drinking the flat tired wine. The young people danced
slowly. Tony watched Ozinski, who was drinking cognac and smiling more and more as his eyes began to lose focus. Great blasts of
cold air rushed in every time a door opened.

The jowled Greek came over and asked Asta to dance. She shook
her head and turned to Tony. "I promised it to you, didn't I?"

"Did you?"

Tony got up and took her arm and they went out on the small,
packed dance floor, standing among the young people wearing
Levis, beatnik outfits, moving a bit to the music and keeping their
legs in shuffling position.

"A dive," Tony said, choking on Asta's perfume. He stood over
six feet himself, and Asta with her high heels came up against him,
her head nestling against his chin.

"They're all dives, Pedlock. Every one. Why can't people just sit
around and say something honest to each other? This crazy trip
depresses me. I want to be in Paris." She moved her head to Tony's
shoulder and began to weep. "I know if I could just talk to Jules
once more I could break it off short. You think that's crazy?"

"Asta, I might get your phone call through to Paris. I have some
connections." He rubbed his chin on the side of her head.

"You mean it?"

"I'll try," Tony said.

"You don't know what it is—what this love thing does to you."

After five minutes of standing in each other's arms to music they went back to the table. Asta said the cold had been so biting she had to go to pee. The waiter pointed: *"En queue."*

Archie Gillman was not at the table. Neither was Ozinski in his corner. Tony decided he didn't give a damn. He was thinking of this love thing. In the hired car going back to the hotel he kissed Asta and she pushed him away with a weary gesture.

"There will be none of that, sweetie. Christ, Pedlock, haven't you got any respect for the way I feel?"

"I'm sorry. Call me Tony. I know how it is. There was this Chicago girl."

"Poor guy. Hard, huh?"

"Well, you know . . ." What was he saying? He had actually been happy it had ended!

She patted his hand. "I know. But just don't try to move in; this happens to people like us. Shared misery."

"Yes."

"It's no good, Pedlock."

Tony was conscious in the deep cave of sleep that he was very thirsty, and he came awake, for the moment unaware of where he was. At Pedlock House? His apartment in the Village? Then he knew he was in the Huzarska Hotel in a Polish city—Cracow—and a white night was filling the world outside his window. He also knew he had had too much to drink at the night club; that was causing his thirst and the mean throbbing in his head. And he had tried to make a pass at Asta—not at all his type. He put on his overcoat and went to the window. It was a clear night. Outside everything was silent and still in the snow that covered the city. It must have fallen earlier on the older soiled snow. The statue of Ladislaus II wore a white cape.

Tony turned to the night table and poured himself a glass of water. It certainly tasted as bad as Asta had said, and he drank it slowly in little sips, thinking of her, puzzled by her, aroused and not liking her for all his desire. He had always prided himself on the kind of women he admired, and Asta was not—*hey!* Who was in the suite he shared with Archie Gillman?

He could hear someone walking about the suite, moving drawers, opening and closing closet doors. Tony sensed a stranger, and he stood still, the glass in his hand halfway to his mouth. The sounds continued, but he could not tell from just where in the suite they came. The truth, he suspected, was that he was still slightly drunk.

He put down the glass and opened the door to Asta's room; after all, she had the only valuable things in the suite, jewels most likely. A feeble bed lamp was on and Asta lay asleep on her face, her body turned, outlining hips and thighs. Her clothes and fur coat, stockings, shoes, were all scattered, as if she had gotten into bed as boozed as he was. No, she had had a few extra drinks. She lay sleeping, mouth slightly open, her pale naked shoulders above the rumpled blanket that covered only part of her legs. Tony went to the bed and tenderly kissed her cheek, touched her breasts, smelled her breath, and pulled the blanket into some sort of order. He stood smiling like an idiot, watching her sleep, deeply, fully, as if she were engaged in some serious task—which, he thought, sleep probably was for her. The sound of the intruder came again. He had forgotten for a moment. Sex really bollixed one up.

Archie Gillman had not returned with them to the hotel. Tony went out into the living room, and this time the sounds were clearly from Archie's room. Someone was moving a suitcase by the sound of it. There was the click of locks being forced. Tony picked up a small bronze statue of a greyhound from the table and crossed to Archie's bedroom. The door was ajar and he looked in. The moonlight and reflection of the snow made everything in the room stand out as if carved from bone ivory. A small man in a checked cap, with the speed and dexterity of a ferret, was moving his fingers through the contents of Archie's bag. Of Archie himself there was no sign. The little man had his back to him, so all Tony saw was a long sheepskin coat with the wool worn inward, a checked cap with its fur-lined ear muffs, baggy pants pushed into worn boots.

Tony lifted the bronze dog as if to enter the room and strike down the intruder, then decided against it. The drinks were still active in him and he almost giggled. He really had an edge on. None of this was real, of course. Just a dream.

CHAPTER 15

&s This moment was, Tony felt, all against Pedlock logic or reason. The intruder must be one of Captain Kura's stooges. Tony decided he was tired of Kura, Archie, the whole trip. He'd capture this fellow. It seemed a grand idea in Tony's still alcohol-touched mind.

Tony nodded in agreement with himself. Smart, very smart. He went back to his room and began to dress. There was plenty of time. The intruder still had to go through a canvas carryall that Archie had along. Tony, a little clumsy, put on ski trousers, two shirts, a leather jacket; he wound a knit scarf around his neck, pushed his way into the fleece-lined walking boots. A woolen snow cap completed his outfit. He grinned at his reflection in the hazy mirror, waved his bronze weapon and went back into the living room. Well, this was action.

He was just in time to see the intruder slip out of the suite door into the dimly lit hall. Damn. Tony peered about him and then slowly opened the door a half inch. The checkered cap of the intruder was just disappearing down the hall. Tony followed, past numbered doors, and came to a tin-covered door which had a pane of cracked, unwashed reinforced glass set in it. He opened it and was hit by an amazing breath-burning cold. The wind was gone. The night was white and calm, but the cold bit at once into the bone. Checkered Cap was just turning into a cleared path past the gray cement-block garage. Tony went down the cast-iron stairs, slippery with frozen slush and new snow. He dashed by the garage, panting, and saw the intruder moving at a dogtrot down an ash-covered path between birch trees that led to a small park. Suddenly Tony felt nearly sober, foolish to be in this crazy race. The Freudians would say he was running away from Asta—all women—some crap like that.

How still and cold it was, the stage set of a dream. Somewhere a church clock rang out a muffled hour; a steam train far off coughed and began to chug. Otherwise all was still, the pale streets blank, the snow-smeared park empty. It was easy to keep Checkered Cap in sight. He had no idea he was being followed; he never looked back. Tony wondered why he followed the shadow ahead. Go back? No.

Once past the park, the street twisted and turned. It was lined with shuttered old houses, the sidewalks banked with snow so high that only the checkered cap was in sight between snow piles. A freezing mangy cat tugged at an old herring spine in the ice. A tin sign creaked overhead, and Tony saw a German text: Apotheke Drogerie—H. Weiner. Beyond was a movie house, silent and unlit, starring Pan Gable and Pan S. Tracy in *St. Franciski*. Checkered Cap had settled down to a good dogtrot, and Tony was pleased he was himself in ski-run condition. As they moved along a tall brick wall, they came to a cold copper cross set in an arch. Beyond it, a series of ugly dark nineteenth-century buildings, and Tony made out some faded gilt letters on a black panel set in a recess of the wall: "*Order Cenobites*"—and words that could translate as "Poverty, Chastity, Obedience." *Dei memor, gratus amicis.*

The alcohol was leaving Tony's system. This was no cockeyed dream. The long chase, the fast pace, was clearing his mind. It was a damn fool stunt to have come out in the white night. The intruder moved among the monastery paths between outbuildings and sheds. Tony followed, fingering the bronze greyhound in a fist pushed into his pocket. He increased his pace, narrowing the distance between himself and Checkered Cap, and as he came around an open-faced shed in which some bicycles were stored he found himself facing the man, who was waiting for him. Tony flushed and felt ashamed at being caught so easily. Checkered Cap's eyes were expressionless but he was breathing hard; it had been a fast pace from the hotel to the monastery. He spoke in the precise English of a schoolteacher.

"So hunted and hunter change places?" said Checkered Cap.

"What now?"

"Come in, Pan Pedlock, it's very cold out here." He pointed to a yellow brick building with a ghastly tower of early twentiety-century design. Under the crest of crossed keys of the Holy See was lettered: *Deo adjuvante non timendum.*

The man took out a brass key, opened a narrow door, and motioned Tony to enter ahead of him. The gray hallway smelled of careless boys, oil stoves, stale food; a monkish sourness that Tony remembered as characteristic of any large place inhabited only by men and boys. It was dimly lit, with small yellowish light bulbs set in a raftered ceiling. Checkered Cap stopped at a brown oak door and tapped lightly. Someone said, *"Kto tam"*—who's there, as the guide book put it—from the other side, and Checkered Cap opened the door and motioned Tony in. As he did, he removed his cap, revealing a shaven head, a greenish skin and almost no eyebrows. An old man with a thin gray beard sat at a desk under a wall of old religious paintings of saints enjoying their deaths—all gone to ruin. He wore a black skullcap and a heavy monk's robe. The room contained, besides the desk, a chair, a narrow iron bed, a wooden crucifix, and a small table radio set on a shelf attached to the plaster wall.

The monk, who was reading from a tattered volume in Gothic type, looked up. He was a stern old man with a hard thin mouth; the lively eyes were flecked with gold. Checkered Cap said softly, in German, "Father Herodias, Mr. Pedlock followed me."

The old man waved off Checkered Cap, who went out, closing the door behind him. Tony, for no good reason he could think of, asked in his college German: "You have no heat in here, Father?"

"Not in my cell." The old man's German was very good. "Sit on the bed, my son. Brother Minski moves very quickly, doesn't he?" He added the formal Polish greeting: *"Bardzo mi przyjemnie"*— honored to meet you.

"What was he doing in my hotel suite, Father Herodias?"

The old man frowned, closed his book, and rubbed his red horny hands together. " 'And the rough ways shall be made smooth. And all the flesh shall see the salvation of God.' That's from the Gospel according to Luke. I prefer the Gospel according to John myself. 'Then gathered the chief priests and the Pharisees at council.' My advice, my son, is to forget what happened tonight. Do not become involved. It is not to your interest."

The cell was so cold that Tony, sitting on the hard cot, wondered if the old man wore another heavy wool robe under the solid-looking garment he sat in. His pipestem legs were naked, pushed into felt boots.

"I am involved, Father. I'm puzzled, too. What was the man doing searching the baggage of an American named Archie Gillman?"

"I will tell you if you want to know. I do not think you will betray us, for it would be trouble for you too.

"You have heard what the church does here against the People's Nation. Some of it is lies, some is true. Many of us get into trouble. Then we need help from the outside. We have been trying to arrange to get some of our assets out of Poland before the police find them."

Tony almost shouted, he spoke so quickly. "Currency, gold smuggling!"

The candle wavered in a gush of freezing air.

"Your friend Gillman was to come here last night. He didn't. We began to suspect perhaps he wasn't actually Gillman. We hoped to find in his baggage some clue as to who he really was. Who is he, my son?"

"He's Archie Gillman, he claims, Father."

Father Herodias began to finger a rosary of heavy dark beads. "I am a practical man, too practical for my soul's good. I am in charge not just of spiritual things, but of buildings, of churches, of schools. Before I was God's, I was a very material man. I ran great organizations, industries. I was unhappy. Now I am a Benedictine with a motto: *Domine—Deo—Optimo—Maximo*. In confused times I try to stay unconfused. It is not so easy as buying a million *pud* of herring."

"Why is it so important, this currency and gold smuggling?"

"Don't ask too much. What has happened to Gillman? We promised to release some Jewish ritual treasures." Father Herodias took up a tin snuff box and took a pinch. "Treasures left here during the war—torahs, Talmuds—in return for his help."

Father Herodias sneezed. "My only weakness, Copenhagen snuff. I cannot give it up. 'Who is worthy to open the book and loose the seals thereof.' I was just reading that in Revelation. We are all worthy to try—if we remember the original sin we are touched with. If you can't help us, don't hinder us. If Gillman fails us, we are all in danger, believe me."

"I have no idea where he can have gone to. He speaks Polish."

A bell was ringing deep in the moldering walls of the grouped buildings. The old man said, "It's the call to the first mass. *Prze-praszam*—excuse me. The brothers are a lazy lot if you don't stir them up at all hours and make them face God. It's not easy to keep them to their task. We don't get the best—the state does. But I am talking like an executive again." He lowered his head, the features strong, worn, the face raddled and roughened by weather, the neck thin as an old turtle's; this was a very old, harsh man.

He began to pray in a low rasping Latin. He appeared to have lost interest in Tony. From somewhere the flawed voices of the monks could be heard. It was wretched singing. Tony got up off the cot and went out into the hall. Yawning, scratching figures, still smelling of sleep, were passing, some holding candles. They ignored him.

Tony moved down the hall and took a wrong turning. He saw a deep vault behind gilt wooden screens picturing St. Stephen being stoned. The smell of candles and morning breath was stronger. A lean monk with wet lips and a great growth of black beard was reading. Tony tried to catch the meaning of the old Latin.

> "He was led as a lamb to the slaughter,
> And like a lamb numb before his shearer . . ."

Tony fled toward a distant door that admitted daylight as two old monks, their heavy work boots stained gray-green with old cattle dung, came in, obviously from the barns.

> "And who shall discover his generation?
> For his life is taken from the earth . . ."

It was still a white world outside, but a wind was rising and Tony walked quickly away, so chilled he felt that he would never be warm again. It had been a foolish night. The effects of alcohol had all worn off, and he felt the lump of bronze in his pocket and grinned. A crazy night. Crazy crazy. He wondered if Archie was still missing, if this melodrama of currency smuggling and old Hebrew ritual gear left with the monks was real.

Tony was tired by the time he got back to the hotel. The night clerk in the lobby didn't seem to be surprised at his coming in so near the dawn. In the suite Tony looked into Archie's room. He was not there. A faint and healthy musical snore came from Asta's room. It would be fine to hold a woman in his arms. He undressed, put the bronze dog on his night table and got under the blankets of his bed. He shivered for some time, and the image of Father Herodias grew hazier in his mind. When at last he slept, his sleep seemed scented with cheap church candles and the smell of breakfastless men. . . . Poverty . . . Chastity . . . Obedience . . . A million miles away were Judith, Dad, the Store, the Village, the unfinished book on skiing. . . . He put himself to sleep repeating: Pedlock & Sons, founded 1853, Pedlock & Sons, founded 1853 . . .

With morning, the sound of sleds passing in the street started before the early cars with chains on their wheels. The Diesel buses began to snort in the square by the park. Tony slept on, undisturbed by the rising day and morning noises.

Coffee. Real, well-brewed coffee. Brown, very hot, steaming. Deep in his inner core, wrapped in sleep, he smelled the coffee. He came awake, remembered the night's strange dream. Running in the snow after a man in a checked cap, meeting an old monk, hearing talk of hidden ritual torahs and Talmuds. Only was it a dream? Or wasn't it? Like the damned Chinaman who dreamed he was a butterfly *or* a butterfly dreaming he was a Chinaman? He sat up in bed, pushed his disordered hair into order, put on a robe and followed the smell of coffee into the living room of the suite.

Asta, her fur coat over her nightgown, was seated at a linen-covered table on wheels watching a glass coffee maker perk and steam over an alcohol flame. She looked beautifully disheveled, unwashed, desirable as a legacy.

"These lamps never heat fast enough. How's your head this morning, Pedlock?"

"Not too bad, considering I've had a hell of a night. If I told you you'd have me in a laughing farm."

"Sit down. I carry my own coffeebeans and glass brewer. You'll like the way I make it. Room service this morning wasn't too bad. Lift a lid and try some food. What were you saying?"

"You're damned cheerful this morning, Asta."

"I feel taut and good. I didn't develop the cold I thought I was processing."

Tony sat down, accepted the first cup of dark rich coffee, took a deep pull on it and burned his mouth. "Archie Gillman is missing, Asta."

"He may be tomcatting around town."

"We're doing everything but finding Leah Ellenbogan."

"Relax." She smiled at him. Later, as she aged, he thought sadly, she'd get fat, grow a dark mustache, waddle ungracefully on flat feet, but now she was desirable and near. He helepd himself to the *nalésniki z jablkami*—baked pancakes with apple filling. He thought of Asta's first husband, her second husband, her lover Jules, the fruit buyer for Pedlock & Sons in Paris. That helped to calm Tony's passion. They sat sipping coffee and chewing food like any long-friendly couple. Asta picked up a folded newspaper beside her plate. "Can you read this, Pedlock? It came with room service."

"It's Polish. Of course I can't read it."

"I can talk it a bit. Reading is harder."

"Try, Asta."

"The people of the world are marching to freedom and true socialist democracy under you know *who*, it says. The American President, it is said, made a warmongering speech to the D.A.R. What's D.A.R.?"

"You went to school in America."

"I forget."

"They're old ladies who don't admit their ancestors were the scum of the New World, yet brave enough to fight to better themselves."

"Soviet scientists have exchanged heads on a donkey and a zebra. A Russian married couple with their two children are planning to go into orbit."

"That's better."

Asta began to translate a new column: "Polish men indifferent to wedding age. Young Poles don't seem to care whether they can wed at eighteen or twenty-one, and Radio Warsaw is disturbed by their apparent apathy. A new marriage law, still in draft form, proposed raising the minimum age at which a man can go to the altar—and in Poland most of them do go to the altar as well as to the Registry Office—from eighteen to twenty-one. For girls the limit will stay at eighteen. Radio Warsaw commented: 'Once upon a time our grandparents fought for the privilege that "Nothing which concerns us can be decided without our participation." Today, young men, the citizens of People's Poland, take note of a draft proposing a limitation of their civic rights as far as marriage is concerned with absolute lack of interest. Does socialist democracy lower the sexual urge?' "

Tony looked up to find Asta weeping softly, her head down on her arms, her breasts quivering with her agonizing sobs.

"It's not that sad."

"I was thinking of Jules."

Tony got up and went behind her chair and put his arms around her. "I can arrange a Paris phone call to him at the buying office."

She tilted her head back and looked at him with wet eyes, tears on her cheeks. "No, you mustn't. I must get over it, Pedlock. Help me, help me."

"I'll try, if you'll call me Tony."

"*Il n'y a pas à dire.*"

Tony thought, How would my Uncle Tom, a notorious wolf, handle this? The image of Uncle Tom faded from Tony's mind as he decided to proceed on his own with Asta.

Tony lowered his head and kissed her on the mouth. She struggled and tried to turn her head away. He held her very firmly, and after a while she stopped struggling and Tony rolled his mouth over hers. A far-off sea seemed to run in a hiss of surf in his ears.

Archie Gillman's voice was like an indoor clap of thunder. Tony nearly wet his pants. "Is there any more of that coffee?" He was standing in the doorway of his bedroom wearing only long gray underwear, a crosshatch of court plaster stuck on his bruised forehead.

Tony stood up, feeling all thumbs. "Where were you?"

"I had to try and see some people. Ran into a lamppost."

Asta calmly filled a cup and held it out in Archie's direction. "You're lucky there's some left."

Archie eyed them, took the cup and sipped the coffee, the cup clattering on the saucer in his fingers. The morning light showed red blood vessels under the skin on his face, and some were broken. "I made progress on our problem last night."

Tony wiped his lips on a napkin and looked at it. Asta hadn't been wearing any lipstick. "What kind of progress? Leah Ellenbogan progress?"

Archie smiled into the coffee cup. "Don't get clever, *boychick.*

That's my department. Did you enjoy your visit to the monastery school and Father Herodias?"

Tony said, "Get dressed, Asta."

She went out, carrying her cup to her room.

Archie was eating half a cold pancake. His eyes were closed as if he were in deep thought. A thin edge of blood appeared from under the court-plaster patch on his bumpy forehead and formed a red bead.

Tony said, "You must be crazy, smuggling gold and currency in or out of Poland. The police know."

Archie touched his head. "I didn't get this at a Bar Mitzvah."

"You've involved me. That's a lousy thing to do. And Asta."

"She doesn't know anything, so don't alarm her. Look, for doing this for the church, what the hell, they'll turn over to an Israel *schul* a treasure of very old torahs, their fittings, rare versions of the Talmud. What's the matter, Tony, aren't you a Jew?"

"I'm not a smuggler."

"Oh shit, don't act so like a Pedlock. You're in this. So come off the high horse. Act human."

"Aren't Pedlocks human?"

Archie sighed and belched. "I can't tell you much. So you'll remain in the clear. Me, I'm a tough ex-Marine. I'll take care of myself, I hope. I didn't do two hitches being brutalized for old glory in boot camp for nothing. Anyone who survives their sadist camps can survive anything. I'm still hungry. Order some food."

"Phone down yourself."

Archie grinned. "I can't. The police, *boychick,* are in the lobby listening in."

Tony felt his hand tremble. Oh how we lack the courage of our platitudes. He went into the bathroom and threw up. He felt near an imminent collapse of his nerve. Yes, the Pedlocks had gone very soft.

BOOK V

JOB

CHAPTER 16

◄§ Judith Arneth Pedlock Ellenbogan was exercised over Tony's disappearance. She roared through Pedlock House at Norton-on-Hudson, through the offices of Nathan and Tom Pedlock at the Fifth Avenue Store, waved her gold-headed cane (a bit of stiffness in her right knee was back) in the halls of the United Nations, wired strong night letters to United States Senator Sol Goldstein:

IMPERATIVE MY GRANDSON ANTHONY PEDLOCK NOW HELD PRISONER BEHIND IRON CURTAIN IN POLAND BE FREED BRING ISSUE BEFORE STATE DEPT OR USE FORCE DO YOU WANT TO KEEP THE NYC JEWISH VOTE TO BE REELECTED AS DEFENDER OF AMERICAN CITIZENS OR NOT QUESTION MARK
                    JUDITH PEDLOCK ELLENBOGAN.

The truth, as Nathan Pedlock knew from many calls and personal appeals, was that no one in Washington knew if Tony Pedlock was alive, dead, or under arrest. Marcel, in a meeting with the Polish consul, a Jozef Brodzinski, got very little real information. The sleek Pole with the oily black hair, sitting under an old ikon of the Virgin of Lvov and a photograph of Lenin, refilled his cigarette holder and smiled. "There is really nothing, Mr. Pedlock, on which to base the assumption that your son is in Poland, or if he is there that he is in danger. So?"

"I can't accept the evasion of responsibility on the part of your government."

"We assume, on your word, that the man who entered Poland with the papers was your son and that his mission was legitimate."

"You know that for fact."

"We don't know if a person presenting such papers was actually your son. We are checking. We don't know if he is still in Poland."

"But where would he go, or why? It's nonsense. Senselessly demoniac."

The Pole shrugged in Slavic doubt with every muscle of his back, every tendon in his arms, and lit his cigarette. "These are the things we must find out. Why, where, who. Patience, Mr. Pedlock, patience."

Marcel scowled, thought, rose, went out. He could not, like Judith, continue to bluster and apply pressure. He was dizzy, nauseated over this arrogant treatment of Tony's disappearance.

Marcel drove crosstown to the galleries and entered the dark, slightly scented front showroom (Constable, Degas, a doubtful Cézanne), went past a hall full of minor old masters, passed through the yellow wing, where the Postimpressionists eyed with wonder the American hard-edge Expressionists, already dated, old-fashioned. Marcel was stuck with them, and he knew they'd sell in time for a good price to the culture vultures among the new Texas and California millionaires and the second-generation Chicago hard boys, former ghetto types buying their way in. He didn't give a damn about the inventory anyway. Tony. Tony.

Marcel went up to his office and said he'd speak to no one on the phone but members of the family and the Polish Embassy in Washington. He took a small drink of brandy, although he had no liking for the stuff.

Tom Pedlock was announced on the intercom. Tom was well dressed, a bit pale and drawn, but as always the most sporting and best tailored of the Pedlocks. Marcel, who took pride in his own clothes, thought Tom overdid it a bit. Too showy a fold of handkerchief, the French cuffs too long, the cuff links of old Greek coins.

"Any news, Marcel?"

"Nothing. After that phone call from him a week ago, it's like, well, it's unbelievable. I mean these things don't happen in real life to people like us. It's a bad Hitchcock movie. Life can't be like that."

"Was it Tony you spoke to and was the call from Poland?"

"Yes, it was Tony and the phone company's overseas office says it was directly from Poland. Look, Tom, some of the Pedlocks came from Poland, didn't they?"

"They certainly passed through there, and some stayed for a couple hundred years. What has that to do with *this?*"

"I wonder, did they do something against the present government that Tony's name could be connected to?"

"I doubt it. Most of the Polish Pedlocks died in concentration camps, gassed by the dear Germans. Look, Marcel, Washington is doing all it can. Judith is threatening to see the President."

"She would. That damn Jacob—his diabolical errands. Kind of you to drop in, Tom."

Tom took out a tan pipe and filled it carefully from an oilskin pouch. "Marcel, I'm in a hell of a spot myself. You may not know it."

"I know, I know. *Die teuflische Venus.* You're living with the big redheaded *shiksa.*"

"Well, I've need of some love in my life. Mabel is drinking harder than usual. Don't think she became an alcoholic over this. It goes way back." Tom lit his pipe, but he didn't seem to be enjoying the taste of it. "The fact is, unless I make her a big divorce settlement, Mabel will sue me for adultery in New York State. Not just that." He slowly waved out a match with which he had relit the pipe. "But she'll dig up back history. Name names. That sort of thing. Respectable married women, important families, like—"

"No names, Tom."

"Of course not." He looked hard at a Toulouse-Lautrec drawing on the wall. "I need money, Marcel. Lots of money. And all I have is my stock in the Store. I sold my bank holdings to Lazar-Wolf long ago."

"I didn't know. That fox Saul. He's really greedy."

"Not important now. His nephew Dick is running around with my daughter. Mabel wants that stopped too. She, she—"

Marcel said softly, "She doesn't want any more Jews in the family?"

Tom turned away from the drawing. "Will you buy my Pedlock & Sons stock?"

Marcel inhaled quickly and whistled. "Nobody sells their share of the Store. It isn't done."

Tom almost snarled. Look at him, thought Marcel—the gentile clubman, church member, Scarsdale citizen, with his country-club scatological vices; all the veneer of thirty years now cracks.

"I haven't the cash, Tom. I've bought a whole series of Monet canvases, water lilies, magnificent things, but they're big and move slowly. The collapse of Pop art caught me loaded. Why not Nat, or Naomi, or Gertrude?"

"Why not the Pope? Nat, I don't want any favors from. He'll only warn me it's all my fault. I don't want the truth—I want cash. Lazar-Wolf would grab at it, but he's afraid of Judith. And Penrose, that *putz*, is only investing in stocks that will help him get into the better golf and hunting clubs. I'm desperate, Marcel. In a bind with Mabel. Rita isn't going to control her temper much longer." Tom released a string of obscenities and then knocked out his pipe bowl in a crystal ash tray on the desk. "You, Marcel, don't have my problem, do you—the smell of a woman's skirts, dirty little hotel rooms, wet armpits, meetings in crumby eating places where nobody will know either of you. It's pure hell. What's the matter with me?"

Marcel stood up and patted his brother's shoulder. "You're a sex maniac, a type very acceptable socially these days, or more likely you're proving something by trying to sleep with every *goya* who twitches her hips at you. Maybe you need the Freudian couch instead of the king-sized bed. I'm not being flip—you do need help."

Tom unscrewed his pipestem (symbols, symbols) and blew through it to clean it. "Well, Herr Doktor, thanks. I'm sorry about Tony. But it's going to be all right."

"Tom, I'll try to help you—with money. I'll see old Sam Spitzbalm, the art collector, the man with all those uranium mines in Canada, I'll see if he'll make me a loan on some of the pictures in our vaults. How much do you need right away?"

"About three hundred thousand. My holdings in Pedlock & Sons are worth a devil of a lot more. I'd pledge them for a loan, but that would really ring the panic button if it got out."

"All right, Tom. I'll call you in a few days."

"In a couple of days."

They shook hands and Tom went down the elevator to the street. He stood at the curb, half filled with self-pity. (My failing is that anyone can recognize his vices and himself in me.) He could go back to the Store, but Rita Burton at her job there wasn't in too good a mood these days. She was busy on the Store's quarterly house flier—a mailer—that went out to all the charge-account names. And she had missed her last two periods, and even if they were sure it was just a case of nerves . . . He'd better come to some agreement with Mabel. He crossed to the Plaza and went to the off-lobby bar and had a scotch, then found a phone booth and talked earnestly, smoothly, to Mabel. She didn't make much sense, but told him what she thought of him, Pedlock & Sons, and no daughter of hers was going to marry into a nest of—what followed wasn't very nice, kind, or polite. Tom hung up and had another scotch. He'd have to talk to Nancy and tell her to break it off with Dick Lazarus, or whatever the hell his name was these days. Tom didn't care much for Dick—too earnest, always in a hurry, quickly educated to basic cunning, always with an eye on the main chance, always trying to come up through the best Jewish society of four or five established generations of good traditions. Tom laughed out loud. Christ! He was no better than Mabel. What difference did it make: One generation from a cold-water flat with a grandmother who spoke only Yiddish, or five generations with family silver and letters from Lincoln, portraits by Sargent and grandmothers who had Rolls-Royces. In the end we all become, as Jacob said, tasteless conformists.

The barman said, "Is your drink all right, sir?"

"Fine. I was just laughing at something funny."

"Yes sir, Mr. Pedlock."

Yes sir, Mr. Pedlock. That's what I've become—headwaiters and barmen know me by sight.

Judith rested on the terrace of Pedlock House, watching the river mutter and flow beneath her, smelling the Jersey shore, the river muck, the special odor of trains from the N. Y. Central line that ran below the estate and along the bank. Trains always had special smells, and now people were outgrowing trains. Too bad. The nights all *andante con moto* on the International Express, with caviar on ice and the best wine in white linen napkins. The Kaiser in silver breastplate, boarding at Baden; the finery of the waiting crowd in the Rome railroad station when only the best people went to Rome—unless they were pilgrims going to kiss the toe of the Pope. The fast shrill little trains that carried one down from Scotland, the grouse shooting and the long weekends; Edwardian houses and one lover in a nightshirt, hunting the bathroom but ending up . . . well, never mind . . . those shrill little trains, the Royal Scot and others, carried us all into World War I and old age and the burial of so many friends and men in gray toppers with waxed mustaches, cultured accents, the slurred vowels of sports lovers. Trains—later they took some of them to Dachau, Belsen, Buchenwald.

She remembered she had said to Proust—she had named her oldest son after the neurotic little monster in his cork-lined bedroom doctoring himself with strange medicines—she had said to the thin figure in the bed smelling of stale sheets and quack drugs, his little fox face under its already graying hair, skin shiny with ill health: "Marcel, it's more than people getting old; it's a world making more history than it can consume. But I feel we're too civilized to spoil things."

"My dear Judith—" how accented his English was—"we all invent a religion that permits us to endure." He reached out a clawlike damp hand, patted her wrist, and added he had to make a note of their talk—he could work it into *Le Côté de Guermantes*. (He said so, but he never did.)

The past was past, even for trains—life was here and only too late were we aware of its metaphysical nuances.

Jacob Ellenbogan came out on the terrace wearing a flannel nightrobe over his old-fashioned European underwear, which he wouldn't change for jockey shorts or whatever they were called. His ritual fringes of frayed cotton, which the true Jew wears under his shirt were exposed, and he was scratching himself under his belly with a sighing, audible pleasure—not that he needed to scratch; he was a clean old man; but as he explained, it helped him think.

"Have a cup of coffee."

"*Shana*, I need more than coffee. I've lost a daughter, and you've mislaid a grandson."

"You think I've just sat here? I've done things. You pray and I'll raise the roofs. And no philosophy."

"We all have a chink in us in which we see the worm. Yours, *Shana*, is a fear of philosophers." Jacob smiled and accepted the cup of coffee and watched as Judith spooned in three heaps of sugar. He was very fond of sweet things. "You think prayer helps?"

"Jacob, it doesn't do any harm, does it?"

"That's the most sensible thing ever said about it." He patted her knee. "How's the pain?"

She smiled at his interest. "I'm paying no attention to it. It doesn't order me about, so I'll let it stay. You'll eat something?"

"I'm eating too much—it's choking me. I'm a small package. What does a man need here below? The tail of a herring, a few black olives—you can't get the real *maslinas*, the wrinkled olives— and a crust of cornbread."

"Marta can fry a herring in onions, turn out a good *mameligge*. Just ask her, Jacob."

"No, no, this and a bit of toast is enough. I don't need much. And too much food, it gets in the way of my brain. . . . Ah, to see my Leah again. Ten years I haven't seen her. My sons, their children, wives, all gone, gone into German furnaces at Struthof, Oranienberg and worse." He shook his head. "It's good the Reb Baal-Shem-Tov is not alive any more; the worst he could predict was someone would drown or be drafted into the Czar's army. Not the Germans. Those sentimental stinkers. Now atoms!"

"Don't fret, Jacob, I'm sure things will work out. Tony will be with us. But they'd better hurry. I've been arranging so we can go to Israel to establish your Hasidic school."

"How, *Shana*, how? The Hasidim here feel so *aleyn aleyn*— alone. This is a place of timid Jeremiahs."

"Why bother your head? It's legal and business nonsense. You go work on your manuscript: *The Age of Tashlik*."

"Ah, tashlik. It began, you know, this ritual of tashlik, of casting out, when the medieval Christians were burning Jews like candles. So on the first afternoon of the first day of Rosh Hashana the pious Jews would go to the banks of a stream, a river down to the sea, but only a place where there was running water and fish live. The Jews shake out the contents of their pockets into the water, whatever there is from lint to coins, old sins, bad luck, troubles, *kilas*—bad times."

"Jacob, you've explained it all before."

"They recite the verse from the Prophet Micah: 'And thou wilt cast all your sins into the depths of the sea.' *Shana*, you must come to a tashlik."

"I promise."

He sat, cup in hand, his eyes looking faraway. He seemed in a trance, deep in the seething irrationality of his prodigious thoughts.

Judith touched his arm. "Jacob, Jacob. Your *nashuma*, your soul, it's leaving your body. I can see you have inexplicable gifts."

Jacob shook himself and smiled. "We shook out our demons, our bad fortunes, our foolish vanities, and the *goyim* said we were throwing poison into the wells. Ah." He shivered. "I better go get dressed. I'm having lunch with Marcel. He's puzzled by life at times; wise and educated as he is, he's like a child wanting to know why things happen. He doesn't understand that the wisdom of the serpent includes its poison."

"He was always my favorite child. I tried to hide it from the rest. He belongs to a time of my life when . . . Go get dressed, Jacob. It's no time to listen to me *en déshabillé*."

The skipping little man was gone. How lovable he was, how comforting and wise. Judith sat watching the river. And how banal people were to compare life to a river. Life was more like falling down a long long flight of stairs, which were sometimes padded. But sometimes there was a nail to catch at one; there were times when falling downstairs (she yawned) was amusing, exciting, entertaining. But always one fell down *down*, and along the way one drank champagne and made love. Or thought of the better things with serenity and detachment—and of the worst habits. She saw (she was dozing) jewels and palaces, and was laughing with other laughing faces, crying with other crying faces. Yes, it was not lonely then, even if there were stretches when one was alone. In time one would come to the bottom of the stairs (she was dreaming) and there was darkness, perhaps worse. By the time one reached the bottom of the stairs one had been worn away, rubbed down, crumbled into the dust from which we are made. And that was a satisfactory dream, for dust does not think, does not feel, and best of all has no memory, like the descendants of the Levi reading from Leviticus—we were once strangers in Egypt.

Nancy Pedlock waited at a good table at 21, happy at her own reflection in a mirror, pleased to be in such a slob and snob trap with all the big-shot television wrecks in their fancy Ivy League tailoring, looking tanned but ripened with ulcers. She was pleased by the visiting alcoholic movie stars from the coast, and the rich white trash that had swindle sheets and could use them here among continental whores, and the hillbilly types from Congress. A girl could get to see a lot here. She was sorry for Mommy and Daddy as she sipped her vodka Bloody Mary. She smiled as Dick Lazarus (or Lawrence) came in. She hoped his hair didn't fall out, that he wouldn't take his Arab nose to a plastic surgeon. She had doubts about Dick, and she didn't want them enlarged.

"Love you, gal, love you. You look damn cute."

"Sit down, Dick. I like to watch the gold-plated bohemians here. I'm sorry for them. They've all been injured by the bitch goddess, but they'll die before they'll let themselves be moved down one rung in their lousy pecking order."

"Bitch goddess? Where you learn all this doubletalk?"

"At college—Contemporary American History III. And it's William James' expression: the Bitch Goddess Success. You should read more, Dick, you're damn ignorant."

"I once read part of *Marjorie Morningstar*. Now there's a great theme. How to protect the orthodox Yeshiva—blessed maidenhead."

He smiled at Nancy as he sat down, took her hand in his, snapped fingers of his free hand at a waiter, nodded to several people, who gave him back the short hardly moving wave of a hand, done with the elbow held very close to the hip. He banged a pack of cigarettes on the table and lifted one from the package with his teeth.

"I like your hair, Dick, the way it comes down over your forehead like Lennie Bernstein's."

"I'd rather you'd think of Cary Grant." He lit his cigarette, took her hand again, ordered lamb chops and salad with very little dressing. He was, he said, watching his diet and not drinking much.

Nancy ordered a broiled Maine lobster. "This makes me hungry."

"That's my girl." He looked ardent, eager, happy, wary.

"I'm sure of life. Not of you, Dick. I've got uncertitudes about you."

"Uncertitudes? Man, those college words. Why?"

"You really changed your name to Lawrence?"

"Yes. We immigrant pack-Jews never had last names till the tax collectors came around in Shylock's day and said get a last name for our tax lists. So it isn't as if we went on the Crusades—unless as spies, ha ha—and made our forced names famous. Lawrence is as good as any for the end run from Jehovah to Unitarianism."

"Dick, promise me one thing?"

"You name it, doll."

"Don't ever go to a surgeon with your nose. It has character."

He grew serious, stopped playing with a book of matches to look at her, smiled, showing very white strong teeth. "You'd marry me, sheeny hook and all?"

"I'm not committing myself *that* far."

"You want to call me Moishe, go ahead."

They ate slowly, with relish; Dick weakened and also had a Bloody Mary.

"I know about your mother and how she hates the idea of us. Hates the Pedlocks at the Store. They don't jump for joy either at the idea of me in the family. My uncle is enough of our breed, they feel. Well, I don't much care what they feel."

"Daddy hasn't really said he didn't like you, Dick. . . . Say, is that Tallulah?"

"Tallulah *who?* I'm kidding. Yes. Listen to me, doll. I'm not going to stay much longer at Lazar-Wolf and Pedlock Brothers. For me there is only so far to go there, know what I mean? Then Lazar-Wolf's kids will come into the Bank, and Tony Pedlock most likely—if they ever find him."

"Isn't it dreadful, not a sign of him or a word?"

"So I'll just be the poor relative. Oh, a vice-president taking on minor trusts, estates, watching the dog stocks on the curb. No, I've been prospecting. Came up with a few things for Dick Lawrence."

"Your eyes, what color are they? Gray-green or dark olive and brown? I trust eyes."

"Pick your own color and I'll match it. You're not listening to me." He took her hand. "We'll make it together—our escape from Pedlockland. I swore to myself when I ws a lousy kid on Orchard Street stealing orange crates to heat our dirty cold-water flat, going to school in my mother's old shoes with the heels broken off."

"Spare me, Dick, the square corn of your early hardships. You and Abe Lincoln, walking ten miles in the snow, barefoot, to return to a one-room schoolhouse. Don't you see it's just crumby ghetto romanticism, fit only for Hollywood hacks?"

"All right, Miss Rich Bitch, with the grandfather who didn't chicken out at Gettysburg and the three-thousand-dollar teeth-straightening job, the Smith-Vassar wax finish—nongloss style. But now I want to talk about the golden-haired princess I knew I'd find someday."

"Oh brother!" She put her face in her hands. "You sure you didn't have *Marjorie Morningstar* bound in red leather?"

"You think I need polish? All right, doll, you have a job."

Dick snapped his fingers at the surly waiter and ordered coffee, one black, patted his stomach to see if it was still flat and hard from handball. It would remain flat and hard, he had promised, for the next twenty years on Christian tennis courts. A man had to have a plan and a wonderful girl to share it with.

"You have to understand me, Nancy. On the surface bright, cunning, which is the same thing, in love; and I think your William James was a kind of nut. But inside I'm not all what I act and talk. I'm not after material things alone; they're only what you have to use to make yourself. Don't frown, makes wrinkles. What's for this afternoon?"

"How about the Museum of Modern Art? Or are you going to be the *only* rich Jew without an art collection?"

"Try again."

"Your apartment." She gritted her teeth together, looked over the rim of her coffee cup, her gold-flecked eyes firmly holding his attention.

"Not a chance, doll. You throw too many sparks. Remember? *This* boy wants all the bridal rice, organ music, "Oh Promise Me," and a bride in white, *real* white."

"You're assuming a lot. I'm human, damn human."

He motioned to the waiter for the check. "And if you don't mind, we'll be married in your fine Episcopal church at high noon."

She knew then that it was all over.

CHAPTER 17

ᴥᴥ§ Nathan Pedlock in his speculative calm was a genius. He knew, he said, he could not play a fiddle like say Heifetz, paint like Chagall, tell jokes like Milton Berle. But when it came to running the Store, he had that skill, ability, an uncontaminated mind, knowledge, sixth sense and sixteen hours a day that made the Store the best, most valuable in assets, of the city's department stores. And the most publicized. Though, he had to admit, even as a keystone in the chain, not as profitable as it could be. It was over-staffed, over-fixtured, and committed to too many public services.

Nathan was on the job (not position or office, just job) at nine-ten every weekday morning. He nodded to Miss Bambi Nelson, his secretary. (How he regretted cockeyed, skinny Miss Murmellstein from the old Store—but Tom was keeping the Jewish help down to a quota to remove the old libel of being called the Yid Store. Besides, Miss M. married her foot doctor.) He had already break-fasted on two pills, half a buttered egg matzo, fat belly lox, and a cup of coffee that would set up heartburn in half an hour and require another two pills. On his desk the morning mail was laid out, having been sifted from those that went to Tom (depart-ment routine), various vice-presidents, heads of departments, pub-licity—a black year on Miss Rita Burton, *ah cholleria ef err pupik* —and to Complaints and Returns.

Nathan had glanced through the New York *Times* at breakfast, at the opening market prices (he was only in blue chips, those stocks that were his special interest). Ganzler Fairs stock was down half a point. Pedlock & Sons should buy more of it. He'd call Lazar-Wolf if Lazar-Wolf didn't call him. He'd call Marcel to see if there was any new word on Tony, and Judith to see if she was in the proper mood to sign the legal papers the lawyers wanted. And she should make a new will. But she wasn't his mother. Nathan checked the proof sheets for the ads for the weekend papers with his silver pencil. They were stuck with a lot of *shmattes*—rags—in modern college clothes. They were hiring ten tall skinny Negro girls to dress up the jewelry department. Tom hoped to set off the cultured pearls and the gold-washed "Jet Age Jewels" bracelets they were featuring with big tits. He hoped Tom wouldn't try to change his luck in that department. He penciled out some lapidary French in the book-department advertising. Sounded dirty. ("A copious, coarse masterwork." Prescott—*N. Y. Times.*)

Nathan went over a list of items that were to be priced lower and gotten rid of. He disapproved a window sketch showing nude male and female figures in a summer landscape, featuring only sports hats and men's capes. Last month he had pulled a window done in drag. He sighed, polished his glasses, and dialed Tom's extension. Tom hadn't come in yet. He called Marcel's galleries and then the apartment. Marcel sounded sleepy and Nathan hoped he hadn't been drinking. What was the world coming to? Jews as drunkards? A small *bronfin* after prayers on Friday, all right. A little schnapps with honey and almond cake after services on high holidays. But this highball, cocktail guzzling—there was a lamentable venality loose in the world.

"Anything, Marcel?"

"A news agency—Beaverbrooks, in London—says one of their men in Warsaw, Poland, saw Tony four days ago in a night club. With a woman."

"That's children—at his age what's on his mind? His father, his relatives? No. A *shtickel shtuppin.*"

"I've been unable to confirm it with any other news service. But it's a sign. You coming to dinner at Mama's tomorrow night?"

"Friday night I always, if I can, go to Judith's. Listen, Marcel, I think we better raise the money Tom needs, as you suggested. It wouldn't surprise me if he got desperate, even sold his stock to Dov Ganzler."

"You're jesting, Nat."

"Jesting? I never use the word. So good luck with Tony, and tomorrow at Judith's."

Nathan hung up, felt the belly lox, the coffee, turn to acid in his stomach, took the pill, and went down three floors one by one, inspecting each department. Not that he said anything; he merely nodded greeting to older department heads, smiled at the help, felt a few fabrics, motioned the rug section to be in neater condition, made a note—an elevator in the east bank had old chewing gum still on its floor. He went into the men's room in the Squire's Country section, where the unemployed chorus boys and the Yale dropout salespeople stood around examining their fingernails by college colors and shirts piled on transparent plastic counters. Nathan always needed to use a bathroom about this time of the morning. His kidneys and bladder were not what they once were. The prostate's uncertainties had caused Dr. Zimmerman to go *tut tut*. As Nathan inspected and used a gold-colored urinal, he thought of a new lighting system in Antiques. It would cost like gold. He worried over a stock raid by three other big department-store chains besides Ganzlers. He dribbled a bit as he stood there, revolted at his body's slowing functions. He zipped up and went out past the *feigilas* and Joe Colleges and took the elevator to Tom's floor, trying to keep an uncontaminated mind about the employees: They were becoming, against his will, the enemy.

Tom was sitting at his modern desk, fingertips to his lips, whistling silently, his handsome face expressionless, the bags under the eyes more pronounced, some lost precision of rhythm apparent.

"Tony?"

"No news."

"Nat, how are *you* this morning?"

"Well as can be expected. I'm an A.K., face it. And I'm talking to Lazar-Wolf today about a loan for you to get you over your difficulties."

"I think I'll take over the Hawaii store. Maybe I'll live there after . . . after all this is settled. I'm in a damn apathetic frame of mind."

"Believe me, Tom, Hawaii, it's nothing. Coney Island with palm trees. Everybody a grafter, cheating the tourists, the climate muggy and full of bugs. And where are you? A million miles from faces you know. And who can stand that music?"

"And no good kosher delicatessen, I suppose?" Tom laughed.

"Don't joke. We're in a series of crises. Judith's marriage and her refusal to sign the lawyers' protection agreements for the family. Tony missing; but there's hope there."

"I want Tony to date Nancy when he comes back. I've got to sink this Dickie Lazarus thing."

"First cousins, *fehh*."

"Anything to take her mind off that stinker, Dick Lazarus. That's one of the conditions Mabel insists on for a settlement. All I want is to get Nancy interested in other men. I don't want her to get married just yet. I fear she has some of the family's latent intensities."

"Speak for youself, Tom. Our major problem just now is Judith. With mergers and raids in the department-store field, even we are in danger of some pressure play, and you know how many millions of dollars your mother's holdings are worth? Preferred stocks, special bonds in the Store and Bank, the buildings?"

"I don't add so well these days. Nathan, you've always been the real head of the family holdings. I mean after Judith. I know Mama has held us together as a family. Who'd have expected it after *her* strange life? But you've got the head for it. I'm going to shock you."

"Shock away." His bladder needed attention again.

"You think Mama is not feeling her age? I mean, after all, it's been a long active rich life, full of events. I'm sure you've heard rumors of some of her reverberating exploits when she was younger."

"*Bubba meinsahs*—old granny stories."

Tom examined his well-cared-for hands. "You think today—now —she's fully aware of events, of happenings, of consequences?"

Nathan said softly, "You're trying to make out your mother is senile? That's what you're trying to make me believe. Shame, Tom."

"I'm saying nothing. But suppose, because we are so close to her and she's so strong-willed, suppose we don't see that she's incompetent to carry on all her burdens, obligations. Don't look as if I didn't fast on Yom Kippur."

Nathan shook his head with bleak disapproval. "You've been talking to those dirty shysters, Addison, Foote and Kalish. Don't ever dare mention it to me again, Tom. Don't. Where's your heart, your feeling?"

"Here." Tom touched his left pap. "And thank you and Lazar-Wolf for bailing me out with a loan."

"You'll be at Judith's tomorrow night?"

"I'll certainly try and make it."

That was not good enough, but Nathan gave up. "Mind if I use your bathroom a minute, Tom? I think I've picked up a bit of a cold in the bladder."

"You should go down to Palm Beach for a few weeks, soak in the sun."

"Next you'll be asking me to knock a little ball around on a golf course."

"You're too compulsively a methodical man, Nat."

Tom watched his half brother go through the door to the silver-and-black bathroom with its full-length mirrors, the electric horse, the glass-walled shower in the center of the room. Poor old Nat and his dubious Yiddish puritanism. Nothing mattered to him but the goddamn Store. No wife, no kids. Just a crumby big old apartment on West End with other Seventh Avenue types and those two creeps for help, and going to *schul* on the high holidays and sitting on the board of some greedy high-pressure Jewish college. But a sterling character, a guy you call on and get help from, a good Joe; he never let anybody down. Maybe just himself. Duty's child.

After Nathan left, Tom dialed Rita's department.

"Yes? *Mr.* Pedlock?"

It was a phone line that went through the main switchboard. He'd have to get some private lines put in. "I'd like to talk to you, Rita, about the spring layouts. I'm not satisfied with the dummies of our direct-mail booklets. Too much chic and not enough selling points. Tighten up layout and copy. For publicity we need something flashy. Yet class—like a festival or a Paris originals show."

"How about a public burial at high noon in Central Park of some prominent society queen? She can be laid out in one of our Paris originals after having her hair done and her face made up in our own Milady's Miracle Beauty Department."

He gritted his teeth; those bitches on the switchboard must be busting a gut. "Let's not be *too* amusing this early, Miss Burton. We'll lunch at the Colony and go over your department's apathy."

"Yes, *Mr.* Pedlock."

"Oh, any change in routing of *that* item?"

"Ha!" And she hung up. Tom played with the battery of pens in his silver desk set. How can you know, without making a medical fuss, if a woman is actually pregnant or just play-acting? No way; that's how.

"All right," said Nancy, answering the playroom phone. "I forgive you. I forgive you."

"That's all I ask. What you're forgiving me for, I don't understand."

"It's not an engagement. We're not engaged. Understand?"

"I understand, dammit. All I'm asking you is to see me, have dinner with me. And—"

"And I'll get to love your charm, your approach to things?"

"Now you're putting me on, honey."

"Look, Dick, Mother isn't well. Things are all bollixed up here in Scarsdale. It's World War Three, so I've been a little jumpy."

"Sure. I've been talking to your old man, and—"

"He's *not* old. He looks better than you do and he's a good twenty years older."

"Boy, is that one right between the eyes. I mean, honey, I've been talking to him and he's in a state. He has big problems."

"Don't I know it."

"How about dinner tonight? Pavillon?"

"That should keep you from ordering steak again."

"I happen to like steak. But I'll taper off. Look, don't make up your mind about me, Nancy. I'm working on some amazing projects. And—oh, what the hell, you don't like this kind of talk. Meet you at Maxim's Spot for drinks, say seven-thirty?"

"Say eight o'clock. Yes, Mother, I'm through talking on the phone. Just somebody. No, nobody you know. Gotta ring off. See you."

"See you. Wear the tight black silk."

"Don't wear that old school tie."

"CCNY has an old school tie?"

Oh damn, Mom has fallen out of bed again. Will I, too, ever fall drunk and cursing out of bed because I hate my husband? Do you call this any way to run a world?

From Marcel Pedlock's journal:

Now that there seems a tiny sign Tony is alive (the State Department wired this afternoon that Tony had reported to an American consul he's all right), I still can't control my jitters. (What an out-of-fashion word, jitters, like my memory of heebie jeebies, nifty, solid senders, snazzy. All out of my prime and as dated as oh you kid and twenty-three skiddoo.)

I find great comfort in this journal—more, a safety island. Not keeping it with any sense of purpose, but just when the insomnia, as tonight, is thick on me, it's pleasant to sit and write with the unneeded luxury of a coal fire in the Adam fireplace before me, the scratch of a pen on paper (not a ballpoint) as I put down, I suppose, my traumatic vision of the universal rock pool.

I've become fascinated in a strange way by Jacob Ellenbogan. Or Katzenellenbogan, which I gather is the fuller, more proper name for him. Someplace from the Russian villages, from the Polish plains, he has wandered, married, begot, become a true mystic, a seer, acted out the philosopher of some odd exuberance, and I still think of him as a *dybbuk*, or demon, some supernatural being certainly, not a human at all, but a projection of some damned Jewish *Mensch*—a cursed soul or rejected angel. I don't always think so, because he's fully believable in the daylight, a lonely little old man, lively as a grig with his little wisp of mustache, finger length of beard. Alive, unanesthetized eyes, shaking his finger, a too high voice. Bringing a theme to a point, tossing in a quote from some rabbi that most likely never existed. He's made Judith happy. He's brought her back to an interest in things that had slipped away from her, I suppose. But who can fathom her? Mama sits like a great kosher Buddha attended by Nora of the pendulous washerwoman's breasts. Mama who could make Gertrude Stein seem like a blushing schoolgirl. She's been our strength, our will, kept us together, herding us with her gold-headed sunshade all these years. Without her Nathan might have retired to chairman of the board, Tom gone abroad with one of his women, the Penroses fled to Nice or Carmel or Majorca. Lazar-Wolf would have swallowed up everything in his strong, healthy, vulgar grip, aided by his nephew Dickie. They circle us like real wolves in a Russian fairy tale at times. Or so it seems. Playing at being tame doggies, but under it I feel Saul and Dickie are only waiting to leap at our jugulars. This is more of my imagination. Lazar-Wolf has power, has the Bank with us. But it needs him. Gertrude has a fine brood of kids. They'll all in time go into the Store; sons and sons-in-law. . . . So for the first time since I was a young man, this year I've begun to doubt, to doubt the importance of the family, the things they own. . . . Judith was the solid thing in our lives. But how much longer can she control us with her frown? How much longer will Lazar-Wolf, Tom, Naomi, fear her?

CHAPTER 18

⌐⌐§ To dilute any gossip of conflict within the Pedlock family, and to show the company's and corporation's strength in its rivalry with Ganzler Fairs Stores and their president, Dov Ganzler, Nathan had Pedlock & Sons show its best face to the public. The *Times* reported:

PEDLOCK PREDICTS VOLUME OF $781 MILLION

New York—Nathan Pedlock, president of Pedlock & Sons Department Stores, predicted Thursday his company will have record sales of $781 million during its current fiscal year.

Pedlock said the total would be 8% above last year's $724 million.

In an address to the New York Society of Security Analysts, Pedlock said the increase is the greatest percentage since the firm took over the Ankrum-Faulkner department store firm in Baltimore. Pedlock said the company is investing $25 to $35 million a year in new stores, shopping centers and other facilities. Five branches under construction will open this year. The Pedlock chain's only major rival is the Ganzler Fairs Stores.

The presence of Jacob Ellenbogan at Pedlock House did create changes, wrinkle old family habits. Friday nights, the *Shabbes* ceremonies were brought back in stronger detail. The *milchedikeh* and *fleishadicha* dietary rituals were nearly always observed by the cook. Even the old custom of inviting pious and needy guests to a Friday night was recalled. Jacob had gone down to the Lion of Judah Sanhedrin Home for the Hebrew Elderly, ("No nonsense, *Shana*, of calling them senior citizens—they are just *alte kockers* there.")

He invited two oldsters with mighty beards to come to a *Shabbes* service. "Listen, come—the only reality, our youth is over. And you'll get fine *chollah.*"

Jacob went everywhere around the city and the countryside, as if trying to discover a new youth—visiting the strange little splinter groups of Jewry in Bensonhurst, in Brooklyn, where the men lived in wide black hats, long ear curls and elastic-sided shoes, existing as strangers among the Negroes of the neighborhood. He found the farm youth training for the Israel *Negev* on New Jersey tomato fields. Best he liked the little *schuls* set up in crumby slums, in old stores next to gypsy fortunetellers and Chinese eating places. Here old men came for an hour or so to escape from living with sons-in-law, from their little soda stands, from setting the pages of the dying Yiddish press. Others were sent out from the house to *shep luft*—get aired. They were on the way, or waiting for admission, to an old-age home. Jacob sat in the store-front *schuls* with them, spit, took snuff, played at cards, listened to fearful stories of pogroms, lost fortunes and opportunities, of sons who were doctors, lawyers, movie producers, television muckamucks. ("Regular *goyim*— matzos they eat with oysters.") Daughters there were, too, who never ate so as to keep their figures; grandchildren who ran like Indians wild in the streets, had no respect for age or a beard, didn't know a word of the *mama lushin*—the mother tongue. ("For *this* forty years bent over a sewing machine?")

Jacob was respected like a seer, a prophet bearing wisdom and gifts: a bag of bagels, a waxed paper of belly lox, a peck of apples, a bottle or so of brandy, a greasy paper of *maslinas*—the black wrinkled olives.

In the dusty store of his favorite Bensonhurst *schul*, with the torah's ark covered, the curtains drawn, the dust rising like God's word on motes of sunlight, rats frisking in the foundation, the old men sat and talked, quoted holy writ, obscure wisdom. Jacob offered his full snuff box, and with sneezing from hairy nostrils and tears from old eyes, they went into mystery, dogma, ritual, the failure of youth to understand, of age not respected, the true text of Onkelos bar-Kelonikos, the Proselyte.

Jacob would come back from his tours of the cabalistic and Hasidic centers to find Judith taking her late-afternoon nap. He would go to his room, just across from hers, for his own *drimil*—snooze.

At night, if he woke for a drink of water and *pishen darf men nit*, he could hear her snoring and his heart would light up, for she snored with a healthy steady beat and it gave him deep comfort. To be near *Shana*, to know one mortal loved him. To feel here was a moment of safety in his destiny, an oasis in the journey of his long task. He had no false hopes that this mating of dried sticks would last for any length of time. This world, as some *rebbe* had said in his comment on the Targum Onkelos, is a wheel—who is on top now is on the bottom as the wheel turns.

In the late afternoon, Jacob would tiptoe past Judith's room and hear her splendid snoring. He would go down to the sunroom and sit facing the Hudson, the great stone cliffs like the walls of Solomon's Temple across the river. Perhaps God had handed down the stones marked with the Commandments from such cliffs. The sunlight dappled the waters of the river into coins of gold, or scales on a great fish, and the little waves of the river moved toward Pedlock House. Everything is constantly undergoing change, even concepts, sensations.

Judith did not sleep deeply in the late afternoon. She moved fitfully on the sofa, for she did not undress or get into the big bed; that was not what one did in the daytime. God forbid. To be in bed with daylight would give the impression one was ill. ("Sleep, Jacob, should be a seeking, rearrangement of attitudes.") When she dozed she dreamed mostly now of food, of rare dishes of other times when the food and the company had been more exciting. Lobsters and Lambrusco wines. Such worthless dreams. She noticed that as she had grown older, food, the process of eating, had begun to fill a great deal of her random thoughts. As her taste grew weaker and her sense of smell somewhat atrophied, memory served almost as much as actual feeding to comfort her.

She stirred lightly in her sleep, her face faintly sweaty in the overheated bedroom, shades drawn, lavender smells coming from the chest of drawers where two generations of linens were stored.

Someone near her ear was quoting La Rochefoucauld: "It is not enough to have achieved personal happiness. . . . One's best friends must also be ruined." Someone in pin-stripe trousers, carrying a Briggs umbrella. They were entering Rosa Lewis' Cavendish Hotel on Jermyn Street. It was before the Great War. Her hair was done up in Anne of Austria spitcurls; she was wearing her chatelaine diamond watch. They had a private room and were served woodcock *flambé à la riche,* goose liver *ballotine,* and there was a magnum of champagne with Whitestable oysters.

Judith stirred in her sleep. A sense of nearly sin intruded. The scene shifted. Lord Joseph Duveen handed her into an early motor car; César Ritz showed her the truffled *foie gras,* poached turbot, Salisbury duckling. ("A Musigny '07, milord?") The archduchesses were smoking cigars at Sacher's in Vienna. ("Love, my dear, is only social hygiene.")

She stirred again and woke in fear, panic, a taste of despair. She lay staring at the ceiling and knew she would never get rid of the past; she had found something else, perhaps better, a return to the ways of her family and the mystic world of Jacob. Jacob! She missed him and sat up and rang for Nora. She could still taste part of her dreams; the high teas at Brown's Hotel on Dover Street, she and King Edward in the slowly rising lift, he pinching her, well, her arse. Fog moving slowly along Albemarle Street, the Ladies' section of St. George's Bar as she waited for the man with pin-stripe trousers and the Briggs umbrella . . . My tragedy was never tragedy—just compromise.

Nora came in chewing something, wiping one corner of her mouth slyly with a finger.

"Herself had a good sleep of it?"

"Who needs sleep? Shut off the damn heat. They always over-heat in America."

Nora held out a blue robe with some lace on the sleeves and collar. Judith got into it, her bulk and size threatening its seams. She stood turned away from the pier glass. After a sleep, a meeting with the past in her dreams, she didn't want to see this old hulk. "Reminds me of those old battleships, Nora, that they push out to sea to sink with honors."

"Will herself wear the tight girdle tonight?"

"Irish, you hinting I'm still gaining weight?"

Nora said nothing. She took back the emptied glass and got out the hairbrush to comb some reflected light into herself's hairdo.

The two old men from the Lion of Judah Sanhedrin Home for the Hebrew Elderly were a little confused. They had been sud-denly aroused from their twilight fog at the home, dressed, brushed, given their best sets of teeth, told to behave themselves, and carried off by a great snorting chariot to a land they hadn't seen before. They were exposed in a great house from which gentile noises and smells came—furniture wax, flowers. They stood in a hall where servants like pogromists pulled off their scuffed rubbers, took their charity coats, and pointed into a room where a great table was set.

They were, muttered Chaim, "In *Ganedden.*"

"Paradise," agreed Hersh.

"What hangs on a wall, is green and whistles?" asked Chaim as they stood as if waiting for a blow. "A riddle passes the time."

"What?"

"A herring."

"Herring doesn't hang on a wall."

"Who stops you hanging it there?"

"A *green* herring?"

"So paint it."

"But it whistles?"

"*Nu,* so it doesn't whistle."

Jacob Ellenbogan came toward them. "Good *Shabbes,* Reb Chaim, Reb Hersh."

"Good *Shabbes,* Reb Katzenellenbogan."

Jacob led them to the table; the ritual candles burning; the woven *chollah,* the braided bread, varnished in egg white and seeded; the red horseradish sauce—as all Friday-night meals should be.

Chaim asked, as they donned their little silk caps, "They're gentiles?"

"No, no, believe me, Jews," Jacob insisted.

"The hats are where? The women aren't even wearing shawls."

"It's America, Reb Chaim."

"America?" Chaim's mind was a little confused. Memory was dim. But the food was fine-looking. The old men said the proper prayer, put their beards in order with old twisted fingers, hands flecked with liver spots. They drank the little glass of *bronfin* ("Lachaium!"), smiled at a mountain of a woman gleaming in jewels, over-life-size teeth. They nodded to shaved men, young girls. Their mouths watered as the *gefilte* fish was served, entombed in aspic and rings of carrots. "Ah, this is a Jewish house after all," said Hersh.

"Even if it's a trap, eat."

They ate the *mondel* soup, the chopped liver, the *Kartoffelpu-ree, Koftsalat, Dampfnudeln Krappels,* and only after the *tzimmes* of prunes and carrots did they wipe their sweating faces with a corner of the tablecloth and insist, "Too much is enough, enough."

Chaim said, "I haven't room even for a *grepz*—a belch."

Nathan was pleased with the old men, Marcel admired their beards, Nathan and Saul tried their Yiddish on them. When the old men could look up from their food, Nathan talked to them in a singsong language, a Yiddish he hadn't used in years. Nancy, sitting with Dick Lawrence (formerly Lazarus) was fascinated. Except as a child, she had been to Pedlock House only once before, and she pinched Dick's arm. "Jews are so fascinating. These two old characters there, they're making the scene, know what I mean? They're not shy."

"They're just a couple of holy free-loaders Ellenbogan found."

"No, they're grand. I like them."

"Just all new to you, honey. Remains of something that has no more value, or much meaning. Even in Israel these old coots would be something for a crumby museum."

"I'm beginning to dislike you again."

"Better," said Chaim as Dick scowled, "a Jew without a beard than a beard without a Jew."

Hersh said, "It's not a shirt, but it's sewed. Not a tree but it has leaves, not a person yet it talks sense."

"So what is it?"

"A book."

Tom Pedlock looked across at his daughter and decided he'd let her do what she wanted. If she wanted this slick shyster, let her have him. Mabel could be made to accept it if there was enough cash—after Mabel took a drying-out treatment at Dr. Welp's sanitarium. He turned to his mother. "I'm sorry Mabel couldn't come."

"She never does."

"It's not as if we were on the best of terms."

"Tom, you're holding back."

"I think we're breaking up."

She took her son's hand. "Don't make a fool of yourself trying to have every woman in the world. You think I don't know you? I know you *en tout cas* like I know my toes."

"You do."

"Where are Mark and Naomi?"

"They went to Palm Beach," Nathan said. "Mark's sinuses couldn't take the cold weather."

"A coward, a brace of cowards. Nathan, they don't want any part of the family quarreling."

"Judith, we said no talk of the legal papers till *after* dinner."

"Now, later, you're barking up an empty tree."

"Reb Hersh, Reb Chaim," said Jacob, "a little brandy? We wanted to make you a *chullent*, but didn't have the right oven."

"What does a deaf man hear from a dumb man?"

"What?"

"A lie."

Marcel leaned over to Chaim. "You're from Poland?"

"Eh, eh? No, your honor, I'm from Pippachuck, a little town in Rumania. Chaim, he's from the Polacks, a black cholera take them all."

"It's a cruel place?"

"The peasants pull your beard out for fun on market day, hair by hair, and you have to laugh and dance while they kick you."

"When were you there last?"

"Ah, who can remember it now. 1915? 1918?"

"No, no," said his friend. "It was at least, eh, 1928. . . . If you're dreaming of a sinking ship, and your child, your wife, your best suit, a wonder-working *rebbe* are there too, you can only save one. Which one, eh, would you save?"

"It's a problem," said Marcel. "I don't know. What should I do?"

"Wake up."

The two men cackled and pounded each other on the back and began to cough and hawk. The candles dropped wax tears, the black coffee was served. The old men said a prayer of thanks for the meal and smiled at Judith.

"That's what I call *tzitzkas*, Chaim."

Marcel watched the old men, his questions about Poland put to one side; they could tell him nothing about his son. Tony was in some danger, but the news was better; the American Embassy had had one of its men talk with Tony. Marcel looked from the old men to Jacob. These were the ancestors of his race, the old wise tribal leaders. He knew he had had too much wine, but he was feeling mellow and would sleep tonight for the first time in days without having to write in his journal.

Lazar-Wolf was matching riddles with the old men. Gertrude wiped the chin of one of her children. Joanne was at home; there was a suspicion the child was coming down with some sort of a rash—"German measles, perhaps." Jacob said he didn't want the word "German" used in *Shana's* house in front of these wonderful old men.

Lazar-Wolf left the old men to Jacob's bantering and wise saws and slowly sipped his coffee. His two oldest children quarreled softly over the nuts and dried fruits. He looked over at Judith, and he knew Nathan was foolish to think the lawyers could break Judith down on that matter of her holdings in the Store and the Bank, real estate, who knew what else. No, she was a firm old biddy, and in her day—ah, *her* day, what a day it must have been; beauty, money, a busy distracted husband, hot breath; yes, *what* a day. She wasn't one to change her iron determination. There would have to be something else. He looked at Tom on his third big brandy. Skirt-crazy, but a gentleman. What had he hinted to Nathan, and Nathan had told Lazar-Wolf in horror? Declare her senile? In a few years Judith would be ninety. The big body, the *décolleté* bust and shoulders, could last to a hundred and twenty and he'd not wish her less. But the mind, that cool lambent mind; perhaps a few trained Freudians, Jungians, Adlerians should have a look at it—just a report. But how, *how?*" She'd tear the house, the hill, down before she'd let the head shrinkers come near her with their notebooks, their dirty tricks. Saul smiled at his mother-in-law and held his cup for more coffee.

Nathan swallowed two pills in a glass of soda water, feeling better than he had in some days. The quarterly totals on the stores were even better than expected. He remembered a talk with Jacob, who had said it wasn't a matter of money, it was an understanding of spirit. "If they give, you take; if they take from you, yell. It's good of Judith to think of giving for a Hasidic center, but first I must find the old men, the old young men, the *tzaddickim*, the *minyans* I need to found such a school. That takes years."

Nathan sat back, hand across his stomach. He'd have to do

something about the paunch, but the *tzimmes*—he couldn't resist two heaping platters of it. And the goose, well, it didn't come around often this well cooked. He smiled at Judith. Without her it could never be the same here in the old house. But then, who would think she was mortal? Not Judith, certainly. Opulence, order, a justifiable complacency came from her. It spread to them all.

Chaim was gasping a bit for breath as he began to sing.

> *"Hava nagila v' nismcha,*
> *Hava n'ran'na v'nism'cha!*
> *Uru achim b'lev samayach!"*

Jacob translated, taking up the tune:

> *"Let us be of joy and jubilate,*
> *Let's sing, rejoice!*
> *Awake, brothers, joy in the heart!"*

The two old men staggered to their feet and Jacob seized their hands as they shuffled together in a dance. Nathan joined them in the ring. They sang and made bolder dancing gestures.

> *"Artsa alinu artsa alinu*
> *K'var charashnu v'gam zaranu*
> *Aval od lo katsarnu!"*

> "We have gone to the land,
> We have plowed and sowed,
> We have not yet reaped!"

Nancy got up. "Come on, Dick, this is something."

"Sit down, honey."

"I'm joining in."

Nancy pushed herself between the two old men, grasped their horn-hard hands and kicked off her shoes. "Stomp it!"

Lazar-Wolf clapped hands and sucked his cigar into brighter life. His children broke away from the table and joined the dancers. The old men pranced, panted. Judith banged a silver knife on a wine glass; she didn't want the old men to drop dead in her house in all their transient joy. Jacob had promised the Lion of Judah Sanhedrin Home for the Hebrew Elderly a safe pick-up and an early delivery, "Good as new."

Nancy, on nylon-clad toes, danced wildly, laughing, mouth open.

All those years in Scarsdale she had never had any idea what it was like to be a Jew. She got a hand free and waved at her grandmother.

"What can sit in an elephant's eye and blow down trees?"

BOOK VI

ECCLESIASTES

CHAPTER 19

◄§ Now that for some mysterious reason their Polish house arrest in the hotel was over, they decided to do some sight-seeing. Asta, dressed in her leopard-skin jacket with high fur hat, heavy ski pants and boots, carried her camera. Archie Cillman's teeth chattered in the biting cold outdoors. "She's a kook for picture taking. You'll see."

The hired car took them to the old burying ground—highly recommended as a treat—where Casimir the Great was supposed to be buried, but wasn't; to the stone residence of the Synod of the Orthodox Church (here a bribe of a hundred *zlotys*); to a Roman ruin with late-sixteenth-century and seventeenth-century additions. Tony and Archie held film rolls and measured distances, and Asta worked her camera, studied light meters, exposed a roll of film. She was humorless, dedicated, absorbed as she worked.

At the house of one of the first members of a historic *Sejm*—parliament—she photographed marble columns and said, "My fingers are getting numb. I don't feel anything above the knees."

The driver said, "*Pani*, you are frozen."

Archie, sniffing miserably in the cold, hinted to Tony that they'd better find a saloon and some native raisin vodka, but Asta insisted she had one more roll to go. Tony was getting acclimated to the bitter Polish winter, but he could see his two companions were close to the freezing point.

"Better call it a day, Asta, or you'll ice up so solid you'll break in half when we carry you in, like St. Indeghilda."

"One more, Pedlock, just one more."

"One ear looks stiff already. Feel anything?" Tony asked touching her face.

"No. Say, should I?"

"Archie, take her away from here. There's a department store on Sobieski Street, the driver says he knows where. Buy her some long woolen underwear, baggy drawers, and warm her ear back to life."

"I don't like baggy drawers," said Asta, shivering, her hands trembling. "Where are you going?"

"To the People's Artists offices. See you at the hotel."

"Do we get drunk again tonight?" Asta asked. "I don't much care for it. I mean, every night."

"Force yourself," said Tony, pushing her into the car.

When they had gone off, Tony watched two men who had been in the doorway of a pork butcher shop inspecting ghastly sides of pink pigs. One stayed where he was, the other ran off toward a small Opel and was soon moving in the direction the hired car had taken.

Tony grinned. He hoped the Security Police had a one-way mirror into the dressing room when Asta tried on the baggy drawers. It would be a pleasant sight, he decided, and the thought kept him warm till he reached the People's Artists building. He didn't go in. He waited till the man following him was again in sight, then went down the badly cleaned street a block to the Security Police building. The building didn't look dangerous or depressing. Of pink brick, it had a marble frame around the doorway, as in a Gogol short story. It had once been some merchant's palace.

Tony went inside. A man wearing a military jacket without any insignia asked him to wait. He sat sown on the old-fashioned bench of golden oak. Formidable-looking men in fur caps, with black-holstered pistols slung over their greatcoats, came and went, but they seemed more like football players than police. A stocky girl with black bangs across her forehead came out and motioned Tony to follow her along a hall hung, oddly enough, with Japanese prints—courtesans, kabuki actors, geishas, scenes from wars fought by two-sword samurai in crablike armor. Captain Kura's office was a former hothouse built behind the merchant's palace. Snow covered the glass ceiling of half the room, and the glass side walls had been whitewashed. It was very warm—tropical-hot. Captain Kura in pajamas, his red hair uncombed, was reclining on a sagging sofa. His naked feet looked very clean, almost parboiled like the pork in the shop windows.

"I'm sorry to greet you like this, Pedlock. Had a late night of it. *Meshuggener* room, this is, isn't it? But the warmest in the place. Former owner, papal knight as a matter of fact, grew bananas, pineapple here, Care for a banana?"

Tony looked at a dying plant in a pot with a dozen green, finger-sized fruit. "Not just now, Captain Kura."

"Oh, the trouble we've had with Washington over you! The United Nations even." The captain sat up, looking thin and boyish in his pajamas. He gulped at a cold glass of tea. "People worry over you. So you're free."

Tony sat down on a low stool. "I'm getting into something I don't want to get into. You say you could toss me into a prison for good if I don't help you. Maybe so."

"Why maybe?"

"Jailing me—that wouldn't help you with your gold and currency smuggling."

Captain Kura said, "You see my socks anyplace?"

Tony handed the captain a pair of heavy red socks. "You put me and my friends in prison, but you solve nothing. Let me find the child and go home."

Kura walked in his stockinged feet to a small desk and sat down and rumpled his red hair. A large painting hung over the desk, a lapidation of Mary Magdalene. "You want advice from somebody who likes you? Don't trust Gillman. We get him and the priests. We know about the Hebrew ritual relics."

"What are my chances of getting Leah out of the country?"

"My God, or whoever is up there, you are stubborn." Captain Kura went to a little round mirror hanging on the wall, rubbed his face and began to lather it thickly from a cup of creamy soap warming on a radiator. He rubbed the lather briskly into his chops and smiled at Tony in the mirror.

"It's as you think. Leah Ellenbogan goes with you only if you help us, not those people."

"I see."

"So rest here. I will be back soon. We will work it out."

Tony was left staring at the green finger-sized bananas. Man, he decided, needed new values of communication if he was to accept all of the last half of the twentieth century. Huh. Tony the boy philosopher.

There was a fine radio in the wall over the shaving mirror. It had international short-wave bands, special police bands, and some Tony couldn't figure out. He wondered if he could tune in some of the short-wave broadcasts from America. He was feeling edgy; the unreality of his situation had taken over again. He began to fiddle with the short-wave indicators, got a snatch of gourd music from Brazil, then a hissing voice that announced itself as Tokyo X42. *Yaren no kamone ni shiodoki kikeba . . ."*

He felt cut off from the United States, from all the American Pedlocks, in the predicament of a dreamer trying to run and finding, no matter how quickly his legs moved, that he was not making any forward progress. Sweating in the hothouse atmosphere, he turned the selector wildly. There was a sudden blast of rock 'n' roll music—Rock Father—Roll Mother. Beyond it on the dial came a voice, American with the crisp edge of New York to it: . . . "of it all. Sudden death figures prominently in grand opera. The methods employed to dispatch the characters are varied. This year's opera season is definitely a stabbing year. There is very little gunfire. Mario Cavaradossi, the ill-fated artist in *Tosca*, falls before a firing squad. Manrico in *Il Trovatore* is burned at the stake, and Rodrigo in *Don Carlos* is shot by order of King—"

He turned it off.

The stocky girl came in, scowled at Tony and said, "*Przepraszam!* Warmonger."

When she went out, Tony tuned in a local station. A professorial voice in German was droning on in a deeply involved presentation of some philosophical concept. From it, Tony, as he sat waiting, made out only that the entire cosmos is dead matter—only protoplasmic cells contain life and consciousness. He felt like shouting, "Thanks a lot." He turned off the radio and just sat, staring at the little green bananas. There are times like this, he thought, when life starts coming through the rind. His early morning queasiness, like that of a pregnant bride, was back. (I should write my father a long letter and my grandmother a letter—and Jacob, who got me into all this, I'd like to mail him a curse.)

The hothouse heat, the tiredness that overcame Tony caused him to doze off. He came awake, sputtering, to find the stocky girl with the bangs shaking him, and behind her two very large men in gray coats showing the now overdramatic holsters. It was at that moment that Tony knew the full searing bite of fear, the awakening of an almost gibbering fear that comes to a man with the shock of recognition that he is involved in something which his reason cannot fully comprehend and in which he can only appear as a damn fool.

"*Bardzo mi przyjemnie*," mocked the stocky girl. "Come."

"Where?" Tony could not move from his chair. Fear is of many kinds, he thought. I have been too casual with this thing, and now it is on me like the panic of dying on a frozen slope with a broken leg; the fear of being crushed and torn in terrible ways when the brakes on a car give out on an icy mountain road; fear of a madman who is sure you have stolen his skiing medals and insists you have followed him around the world to do him harm in a public exhibition . . .

This one was the worst fear that had yet enmeshed him —a cold, ink-black pool of despair. Tony knew the thin hairline between courage and abject fear can be as simple as the turning of a key in an iron lock; fear could take over even from a light slap in the face, the rattling of papers from an official folder among which one recognized an early photo image of oneself—certain letters and newspaper clippings. (Lord, does the Store exist? Will I ever shop its sleek counters again?)

Painfully he forced himself to get up. The stocky girl, her face shiny, expressionless, motioned him to stand between the large men, who were so tall and wide they made Tony feel like a schoolboy being taken to the headmaster's office to be given the ritual tonguelashing for some infringement of school rules. They knew Marcel would never come down to the school to protest or protect.

As they left Captain Kura's warm nest, they turned to the right and came to stairs of hard brown stone, steps that screwed downward into the earth counterclockwise. (The reason for this, he had once read, was so that invading swordsmen in the old days would have to fight left-handed.) At the bottom of the stairs Tony was assailed by the smell of wet rat dung, decaying stone, sewer seepage. Bluish light bulbs hung from the barrel-vault ceiling. Before entering a doorway flaking off yellow paint, the two men went over Tony's body with their hands, searching for concealed weapons. They knew their job; they hunted the bands that held up his socks, handled him between his legs where a crotch gun is sometimes hidden in James Bond stories. They tapped his armpits, even went through his hair with thick stiff fingers. How could a Jewish boy get in such a situation?

The stocky girl said to Tony, "*Prosze*," and pointed for him to precede her as the door was opened. The little room was full of the sweaty smell of soiled shirts, cigarette smoke, unwashed clothes. Three men in a kind of triangle sat facing a fourth man, all seated on chairs. The three were leaning forward; the fourth seemed cornered and smaller. Tony half expected a spotlight on the man in the center, the way it is in old gangster movies on TV when a suspect is grilled. Here only two bluish light bulbs hung from the ceiling, and the scene could have been in a shabby bus station when the prep-school team goes to play baseball with its rival school.

Tony saw that the prisoner was the little fox-faced man whom he had followed from the hotel suite. He was more than a little battered; his upper lip was cut and puffy, and through his half-open mouth a gap, raw and purple, showed he had lost two teeth on the left side recently. He was holding a soiled handkerchief to his bleeding nose, and his head and eyes were lowered. Tony noticed the prisoner did not shake or shiver or show any reaction to his plight. Pain flashed in Tony's own head. Could Washington, the United Nations, Judith reach this cellar?

Captain Kura, one of the men facing the captive, turned as Tony pushed closer. "Ah, identifying witness. A chair for Comrade Pedlock."

Tony felt the hard edge of a chair hit the back of his knees and he sat down in a hurry. The two other men, their faces in deep shadow, did not bother to give Tony more than a glance. They had solid square heads that seemed roughly hewn from wood. The fox-faced man looked up and stared poker-faced at Tony.

The young woman in the military-cut blouse was seated in the corner. She was wearing black slacks, and Tony saw she was running a tape-recording machine. In stories she would be ravishing; she was merely plump and frowzy.

"You recognize this man?" Captain Kura said, in German, to the prisoner, pointing at Tony.

"Yes," said the prisoner, sniffing and pressing his dreadful handkerchief to his nose. His voice was low, steady, almost polite. Tony's head ached.

"From where do you know him? Speak up!"

"*Przepraszam*— excuse me. I broke into his hotel suite."

"To contact the smuggler, Gillman?"

"No. He followed me to the monastery school. That was our only meeting. I was *not* hired by the American Pedlocks to arrange anything."

One of the hard-faced men turned to Tony. "*Prosze*, is that correct?"

"Yes. I'm just here to get a relative's child."

"Have you anything to add?"

Tony rubbed his forehead. He was getting a fearful migraine, losing part of his vision. Under great stress this migraine could be very painful and set off crazy patterns across his optic nerves.

"This man took me inside the monastery school when I accused him of ransacking the suite. He took me to an old man who, I presume, ran the monastery. We talked about—"

Captain Kura said crisply, "We haven't asked you, *panie, what* you talked about. This is the man, you are sure, the one you followed?"

"Yes."

The prisoner looked up. "Could I have a drink of water?"

One of the men handed him a small, very small glass of murky-looking water. The prisoner sniffed it and swallowed it quickly.

Captain Kura laughed. "A knowing fish. It's all right. It's not drugged. Cigarette? Now, if you weren't hired by American Pedlocks, who are you and Gillman working for?"

The prisoner nodded, accepted the cigarette, again sniffed it and held it in an unhurt corner of his mouth while one of the men clicked a brass lighter to set it on fire. The prisoner inhaled twice, sighed and looked up; his image blurred in Tony's vision.

"Ask me what you want. You don't have to use police pressure."

The captain said, "*Papisha*—who has suggested torture? The People's Police feel a guilty conscience will clear itself, given time." He looked to see if the tape recorder was getting all this banal nonsense down, officially.

"Getting my teeth kicked out," said the prisoner, looking directly at Tony, "that was an accident?"

"Very much so," said the captain. "Begin by giving us name, background, country of origin."

"My name is Isadore Kubellik. A stateless national. Born thirty-eight years ago in Kaunas, Lithuania. Father was the chief Hasidic rabbi of the Baltic states." Tony's eyes went wide. "Germans murdered him at Buchenwald when it was run by the man who is now chief justice of a high court in West Germany. My father was eighty-six years old at the time, *olva scholom*. I escaped from Lithuania, got on a boat for Palestine. British put us behind barbed wire in a concentration camp in Crete. Sent back against my will to Zhitomir in Soviet Territory. Spent six years growing up in a work camp at Yansk on the Lena delta in Siberia. Became an expert mechanic of lumbering machinery. This what you want to hear?"

"Go on."

"Escaped later from a *kolkhoz*, farm, and after knocking about here and there went to France where I repaired water pumps."

"You met a Father Wallin?"

"Yes. Father Wallin." The prisoner looked up boldly, but had not raised his voice.

"For how long have you known Father Wallin?"

"Seven years."

"Did you know Father Wallin in Hungary when he lived in the Ferencvaros section of Budapest?"

"No. Never met him in Hungary."

"Do you deny you were in Hungary five years ago? Attended the Pazmany University, joined the Hasidic groups of Rabbi Zandor Beckwitz?"

"I don't deny."

"Good. A phone call to AVO, the Hungarian secret police, says you were questioned at their offices at 60 Stalin Street, for trying to carry a million *forints* black-market money across the border into Austria."

"True, but that's only nine thousand dollars in American money."

"What was the money for?"

"Father Wallin. To get Jewish children held in monasteries to Israel. Didn't meet him. Was imprisoned."

"Where were you to meet him?"

"Heiligekreutzen Monastery in Austria. Near the old Esterhazy estate. Church claimed Jewish children were Catholics now. A lie."

"Who collected the rest of the money? The American Ped-locks?"

"Don't know. I was picked up at the Hotzwald Kammgarnfabrik —a textile factory in Pest."

Questions, names, names, answers. *And the charities of the Ped-locks involved.* Judith and Nathan were both active in recovering Jewish children kept hidden in monasteries; a hell of a time for it to come out. He was losing all detail in the center of his vision, and when he closed his eyes, strange darting images appeared like tele-vision test patterns. He wondered if he dared ask for aspirin.

The prisoner, Isadore, seemed at ease, foxy face relaxed, wounded mouth firm with the cigarette smoldering over the bruised lip.

One of the men asked, "What kind of rabbi was your father?"

"A leader of the Hasidic sect, a student of the cabala. Wrote some well-known commentaries on the works of Maimonides and Jehuda Halevi."

Captain Kura snapped his fingers. "Did he know a Jacob Ellen-bogan?"

"Never heard of him."

"Katzenellenbogan?"

"No." Tony thought, Is he lying?

Captain Kura frowned. "Was the Hungarian project his?"

"Whose?"

"Have you ever met this Ellenbogan before coming to Cracow? On the Vistula when it was frozen ten years ago? In the Warsaw prison on Nalevki Square eight years ago? At the Bristol Hotel two summers ago?"

"Never."

Tony looked up in amazed wonder at the questions. Jacob!

"You an agent for any country, large or small, Isadore?"

The prisoner lifted his arms and hands in a sign of indifference. He dropped the cigarette butt on the floor and stepped on it. "I have said no. You have means, sure, of making me say I am an enemy agent. I am not an agent of any country, large or small. I smuggle—nonpolitical. But if you use your usual methods on me I will confess to anything you want. Another drink of water? A large drink?"

He was handed a small glass of water. Captain Kura turned to Tony. "You look ill, Comrade Pedlock. What do you think?"

"I have a dreadful migraine headache. They come over me sometimes."

"Too bad. We get you headache pills." He addressed the stocky girl. "Vera, get our friend headache pills, a car to take him to his hotel."

"I'm sure my family is not involved," said Tony.

"You help us. We help you." The captain took Tony's arm and walked him to the door. "Frankly, we have an important fish here, thanks to you. He's a liar, of course. He's in contact with Father Wallin, we're sure. And here in Cracow. A few days sitting thirsty will press vital information out of him. Smuggling is political to us. And you—my advice is to rent a car, you and your girl. Go visit winter countryside. Take skis. Enjoy, enjoy."

"You'll excuse me, Captain, I can hardly see."

"We want to watch if Gillman leaves Cracow when you and the girl do. Is an order. Vera, take the comrade's arm."

As the door closed behind Tony and the girl, the last image he caught in that inner room with a corner of his sick vision was the face of the prisoner, mute, expressionless, yet giving off a despair so great that it seemed to be almost an indifference to life. One of the men was taking off his coat. (Was Jacob involved in this dreadful moment?)

Vera said, "Questioning will continue all night."

When he got to the street, Tony was surprised to discover that twilight had fallen, the snow was crystal blue with deep indigo shadows, and the cold was so biting that his teeth chattered and his vision grew worse. ("*You and your girl. . . . Is an order.*")

At his hotel room he lay down, a damp towel over eyes and forehead) the pills the girl had given him and his prone still position helped drive away the migraine. He lay on the bed, feeling just the edge of the ache. When he heard movement in the living room, he sat up, put aside the towel and brushed back his hair with his fingers. He saw it was Asta in the living room, bending over a map spread out on the table.

She looked up. "Rumors you were under arrest."

"No, no. They asked me to identify a hotel prowler. Where's Archie?"

"Gone. Bags too. Now listen. The Lupescu Ice Show and Circus has been touring in Poland all the time we've been here. It *never* went to Rumania."

"You mean they've been lying to me?"

"That's right," said Asta, smiling. "Traced it through some buyers here, furs, furniture, to the towns of Bielsk and Makow. *And* Leah is with the show." Asta pointed to a section of the map near the Czech border. "I figure you and I can go down there, present our legal papers and get her."

"The police want Archie. It's serious."

Asta shivered and took Tony's hand. "No skin off our ass, Pedlock. But something's very wrong. Maybe they don't want us to leave."

"They said they don't object to us hiring a car and playing tourists."

"Good-o. What a crazy trip Pedlock & Sons sent me on."

"I'll make it up to you."

"Don't try. You look shaky."

The image of Isadore filled Tony's mind: that sad, broken, little fox face in the cellar of the Security Police. He saw himself and Archie and Aster in that cellar, begging for a drink of water, wiping their own bruised faces. The idea of Asta's body, so white, being hurt seemed dreadful. Now? To Bielsk or not to Bielsk. How to decide?

Tony went down to hire a car for the trip, wondering at the same time how to avoid hiring a police spy. After looking over the three drivers that were recommended by the hotel clerk as being able to produce cars that could be driven over winter roads, he decided on an evil-looking fellow with a two weeks' growth of beard, red-rimmed eyes, two fingers stained yellow with nicotine. Anyone this disreputable-looking, Tony felt, no doubt was a spy. Hitchcock would have hired him on sight. It was one way of keeping in touch with Captain Kura.

The hotel clerk said Stephan, the driver, had a good Russian-built car, and he handed Tony a letter. Tony looked first at the stamps: It was from the right country. It was an airmail letter from his father. He shoved it into a pocket to read later. He was excited over the idea of taking a trip with Asta.

CHAPTER 20

◦§ "Pardon, *panie*." The driver, in a filthy sheepskin coat, cap in hand, smiled down at Tony. His English was fair, so he was beyond a doubt a police spy. "I need a couple hundred *zlotys* to buy petrol for the trip."

"Tell me, will you turn your earnings over to your wife as called for by the new law?"

"*Panie*, she just open mouth and tell me about new law I knock teeth out, that is if she had teeth."

Tony grinned and gave the driver the money. The driver rubbed his unshaved chin and said for them to bundle up good, it was "very cold on road." Once in the car, Asta seemed too numb with cold to talk.

They passed larch and birch in frozen attitudes, leafless on the great snow plain. The roads had been scraped or packed down, and the chains on the hired car—a Russian-built Pobeda—rattled and sang their metallic song as they moved past huddled snowbound farms, a solitary twisting column of wood smoke turning with the rotation of the earth or torn to bits by a scattering wind. Often there were cattle standing under a shelter, a bundled-up peasant moving toward a barn. Now and again they passed some huge lorry, but otherwise there was little traffic in the great cold. Asta said, "My God, so much snow!"

Their wet-nosed, unshaven driver, the agent of Captain Kura, drove badly but with style. For Tony all that mattered was Asta beside him in the back of the car, both of them under a huge dusty bearskin rug, very close together for warmth. Because of the bulky sweaters and jackets they had on under the big bearskin they could not get close enough to exchange any comforting body warmth.

"Pedlock, it's cold."

"Call me Tony."

"I'll try."

They experimented by interlocking legs, hugging, putting their cheeks together, and finally either the weather relented or they began to warm each other. Soon they were very cozy, and Asta was making little sucking sounds of pleasure. Tony didn't know if it was relief from the cold or a personal ache at their closeness, but he knew why he felt so good. He was raunchy. Slowly their warming process turned to a kind of parody love-making, a nuzzling intimacy, nearly satisfying but hampered by their cocoons of clothing— hunting intimacy in each other's pockets, aware of the protection and defense in layers of clothing, buttons and zippers. In the end, frustrated, they just dozed in each other's arms as the clanging car chains set up a kind of repeated chant that made them drowsy.

They stopped for dinner at a low-lying inn, half cement blocks, half logs, on the edge of a gloomy Polish forest of wind-tormented oaks. The driver said they would have to spend the night. He had to repair the chains and hunt up petrol in this end of the world.

Asta said, "I bet there are wolves in the forest."

The driver went off. Tony was sure it was to find a private phone at the gas station and report to Captain Kura. He didn't give a damn; he was fed up with all the games and dangers. Let Archie Gillman risk his skin, let the whole Security Police drop through a hole cut in the ice over the next river.

Inside the smoky inn Asta sighed, stretched, unzipped and unbuttoned down to her leapard-skin jacket and basic ski pants. She said she wanted to wash up before dinner. Tony sat in the raftered dining room of the inn before a fire of great logs, sipping a steaming glass of *krupnikof* punch. Black hams hung overhead and dried herbs stirred in the rising heat.

It was all coming into focus for Tony: This game of chase and hunt was not his game. He would find Leah Ellenbogan and get out of Poland. He would wonder about Asta. The thought of Asta made him wriggle in masculine comfort. Whatever the future held, the next few days would, could, or *might* be very wonderful.

Asta came down from above. She had changed to blue slacks, a knotted yellow scarf and a velvet jacket with big brass buttons. "They bring up the hot water to you from the kitchen, in pots, for the bath. And the john in the hall is heated by a flue from the fireplace."

"We're lucky," said Tony, getting up. He motioned to the plump man who stuck his head out of the kitchen. "*Day yeshck*— serve the food." (The guidebook did help.)

They ate on a heavy black wooden table, first *borszcz*—a thick vegetable soup. Then a big clay pot of *bigos*—hunter's stew in which one could recognize rabbit and wild boar and little birds (better not to think of them). All with a pale-green wine, and finally a carp in raisin sauce.

Asta ate as if she would not see food again for some time, and Tony asked the waiter for brandy. Asta's face reflected a rosy glow from the fireplace. She smiled at Tony and took his hand.

"Pedlock, don't try and get me looped. You'll be out on your face long before I feel a thing."

"I don't want to get you looped, honey. Just understanding and kind." He kissed her hand.

"It would be so unjust to Jules in Paris, don't you think?" The tears came into her eyes.

Tony said no, it would not be unjust. After all, they worked, the three of them, in some way for Pedlock & Sons, didn't they?

"Yes, that's a link between us. You know what the name Pedlock & Sons means in European buying offices."

"I don't give a damn, Asta."

"Power, money, good jobs, security."

They had a few more drinks. Time passed. It grew cozier because outside it was so savage and cold.

Tony could hear the wind like demented creatures roaring around the walls of the inn, hear the stamping of heavy boots on the back staircase. He felt overheated and was aware he was standing in a low-ceilinged room with a wide feather bed and a dresser of raw lumber, a fogged distorting mirror nailed over it, a smell of goose grease, bedding insect powder, unpainted wood full of rosin.

Asta was unknotting her scarf and looking at him with her Mona Lisa smile. "You're in my room. Is that fair?"

"How'd I get here?"

BOOK VI / 215

"We were drinking that plum brandy downstairs, Pedlock. You tried to get me drunk."

Tony sat down suddenly on the bed and nodded. "Yes, I did."

"It's no good."

"I can't help it, Asta. I'm a man, a healthy man, and you're so—well, you know, in the Village they'd say well stacked. . . . I'm sorry I can't say what I really want to say, so maudlin drunk. Wait till my head clears up."

He stood up and went to Asta and put his arms around her. "You see how it is with me?"

"You're making a problem for me." She didn't move, just stood still, all of her relaxed, not tense—those big black eyes under the hood of dark hair. He buried his face in her hair, smelling of cigarette smoke and auto fumes, but deeper, deeper, the essential odor that was Asta—woman, armpits, sweat, body powder—and that aroused him afresh. Brandy or no brandy. Muffled by his posture, his voice said, "It's so good to be here, snug, all that kooky crap with the police and my crazy mission out of sight."

"You're not helping me, Pedlock."

"In what way?"

"My personal problems. We can't be en rapport."

"Oh." He lifted his head and kissed her cheek, her neck, and when she turned, he bit her lightly on the chin and laughed as if it were a child's game of some irresistible simplicity.

"You can't, Asta, be thinking of Jules if you're thinking of me."

"Very true." She was on the verge of tears, and he understood, suddenly, that even for a woman who had had two husbands and lived like a man of the world, there could be agony and pain in love, the sorrow and depression of parting from someone held very dear.

"It's a fine thing you're doing, Asta—giving Jules up. You know these French Catholic family units."

"I didn't know anything could be such misery."

"I'll take your jacket off. It's getting warm."

"That's the brandy."

She had only a slip on under the jacket, and he fumbled at the slacks, but the zipper defied him. He shucked his own jacket. The flue from the kitchen kept the room neatly warm; they mutually discarded more of their clothes, bit by bit. Woman, he decided, is the universe made conscious.

He kissed her then on the mouth, and kissed her hard and brutally. He was very much aroused and frankly in love. *Yes*, in love; that rare state his friends mocked as square. Neither of them had stirred from in front of the dresser. He removed the slip from her shoulders. His head was clearing. Now it was his body that was drunk with some new white incandescence. It had never been like this with the chicks in his Village pad.

There was a hard knocking on the door, mood-shattering.

"*Panie, panie!*"

"*Kto tam*—who's there?"

"Me, *panie*." It was the voice of the driver.

Tony shouted in English, "What the devil do *you* want?"

"I need some *zlotys* to pay for the petrol. The swine here don't give credit."

Tony in his underwear released a glassy-eyed Asta, hunted up his ski pants from the rough wooden floor, found his wallet and took out some bills. He went stiff-legged to the door, opened it three inches and shoved out the bills.

"Here. Go away."

"*Panie*, we'll be ready at nine tomorrow morning to start off. Good—" The rest of the message was an obscene congratulation on premarital intercourse.

Tony slammed and locked the door and turned back to Asta. She was in the bed, deep under a vast feather comfort. She said in her sleepy dopey voice, "Good night, Pedlock. Go to your own room."

"Oh, hell!"

He picked up his outer garments from the floor, and, feeling the full-length fool in his underwear and socks, he started for the connecting door to the next room. At the door he turned.

"Can't we take up where we just left off, honey?"

"Be understanding. Be kind to me."

"I want to be. Very much."

"Good night. Oh, these feather beds are so-o soft." She appeared to fall asleep at once.

He went with taut suppression into the next room, sat down gingerly on the bed, kicked his clothes away from him. It wasn't fair. He looked around, thinking of the direct attack, a frontal assault military style—Gettysburg, Waterloo. Deep down he was a romantic, wanting to be wanted.

To punish himself he thought of the scent of her: wonderful, dainty sweat and honey. Her skin, the soft yielding parts of her body and those places where it didn't yield to the touch but was finely muscled. He rubbed his lips, still tasting of her mouth. He saw again the slacks sliding, slipping down, coming to rest, to dangle around her feet like some sultan's captured beauty held in silver leg chains (an Ingres painting in his father's galleries). The slim strong white (so white) legs, hairless as an egg. He moaned as he remembered the feel of those magnificent breasts. He was a fumbling idiot—let's face it, he told himself. Most of all he suffered because he was so alone with such images, and because he was human and he could have been so happy with another human being in an old and ardent connection. Passion, he knew, had been traded for a comic situation. This was the basic stuff of fast-moving bad plays. He wondered if he could sleep in his state of mind, body and nerve ends. That wind was growing in fury, roaring among the trees of the nearby wood. A knob rattled in the lock of the connecting door. The door opened.

Asta stood there in her finger-length sleeping robe. She said, "I'm frightened of the noise, Tony. Bring your pillow with you." (She had called him Tony!)

She turned, a ballet of exposed rounded rump, and went back to her room. Tony, with nerveless fingers—in avid expectancy and despair—picked up a pillow from the bed. There was an ethic about this. Should he go now, having been once rejected? Should he go because now she wanted him to, or was she a tease? Should he give in after being told to go? What should a man do on the periphery of the unknown?

Tony laughed. Why the hell was he thinking about ethics and codes and manners at a time like this? This was no ski meet for points. He beat the pillow into a new shape with hard blows, pulled off his socks, underwear, and stood looking down at the bed with a new smile. He went to the low door and passed through just as some wind-loosened bricks fell down the chimney and the shutters banged against the walls.

She was on her side and he gripped her and turned her on her back and she said: "Just be kind."

"If you want kindness," he said, and he began to bite at her mouth. She was strong and was as driven as he was, he felt, for she began to push her tongue between his teeth, and he grasped her as he had never grasped a woman before, with a firm direct hold, one arm—the left—around her torso, the other holding her head under his, her breasts alive and bobbing, mashing themselves against his naked chest. He was for the first time not ashamed of his condition, his erectness, raw-red and firm. (As he had been ashamed with his few other women, with the Chicago girl, the first obscene feeling of her leg, the shy shame of going above her stocking tops and touching beyond the garter belt—Everest at last!—the struggle on the dusty couch with a self-proclaimed tribal virgin in his Village pad, at last to reach the jewel she held so sacred, the long late hour he had spent, panting and struggling just to remove her panties, her girdle, slip, skirt, blouse, tit harness, and the final victory, so discouraging and wet with tears—the wails of Cossack pogrom and rape, and her speech of the sacrifice of the family maidenhead that had been made to him *without* marriage and no more than a vague promise.)

"What are you thinking of?" asked Asta, pleasure sweat on her upper lip.

"Of you, Asta." And now he was, no shame as before, no guilt, no feeling of violating Israel, the laws of Moses, the moral foundation of the Old Testament. Just two young lovers, a marvelous body and his own body and the two of them engaged in byplay, close wet contact in certain ways; now he did to her, now she did to him, not feeling that he was a degenerate, doomed, perverted, depraved. No, no! Now he was on her, he holding out her arms spread-eagled, their hands clasped together. They were merged, at least at the most obvious pressure parts, and the main splendid deed was in progress and it *was* beautiful. It was breath-taking; never before, in the few hurried, dark, fumbled encounters, had it been for Tony the true act of man and woman done well, the grace of it muscled with such pleasure of nerve ends, groan and gasp. The final explosion shook them.

"Was I kind?"

"Just comfort me. Don't pull out."

He grasped her nakedness, felt her react, respond, shout, "*Oh!*"

Later, much later, when the atmosphere of the room no longer throbbed, she flexed the body held in his arms and she said savage, amorous sweet things with earnest directness. There was a diffused white light in the room, reflected up from the snow, and the bed seemed to float rather than rest on the floor. Their bodies, under the feather comforter, were like old friends gossiping with little gestures.

"The wind has stopped," Asta said, her mouth on his ear.

"I didn't notice."

She laughed deep down in her throat. "Neither did I."

"It's a white world."

"You mustn't think, sweetie, this is just a light caprice with me. You have such broad shoulders from skiing?"

They compared anatomies, settled deeper into the drug of the feather bed. Asta sighed. "A cigarette would taste *so* good."

"I don't want to leave you, honey."

"There are some in my bag, there near the bed."

The cigarettes were Turkish and strong. They lay side by side, shoulders, hips, knees, toes just touching as they smoked, eyes on the rain-stained ceiling, greedy to get the tobacco smoke into their lungs.

Asta addressed the ceiling. "Always I've been a schnook, a fool about this. I mean I never played it right. I shared, but nobody really ever gave me a proper shake."

"That's over now." He kissed her shoulder, executing with his fingers a quick sketch (say by Rodin working in clay) on her torso. "Believe me."

"What a way for it to happen, Ped– Tony. Crazy place, crazy trip."

Tony was carried away by love, by the feeling in his relaxed limbs. He wanted to confess something, anything. "You don't know the half of it. Archie, he's some kind of a smuggler."

Asta laughed and choked and coughed. He had to sit her up and pound her with pleasure on the long shapely back. "Oh, Tony, you are crazy."

"He's really here to smuggle out some Talmudic relics and gold and currency."

"You're serious? You sound serious."

"You bet your sweet toes I am. That's why if we find Leah, we'll scoot across the border and leave Archie Gillman to stew in his own schemes."

Asta laughed and buried her face on his shoulder. "Oh, my poor Tony, don't you see, Archie has been reading paperback thrillers, pulling your leg."

"The Security Police don't think so. They questioned me about him back in Cracow."

Asta shivered and handed him her cigarette. "Hold me tight. I hate police. All Europeans do."

He mashed out their tobacco in a clam shell left as an ash tray by the bed and took her in his arms. She said softly, quickly: "For generations my people, like you Jews, have been running. From Turks, Greeks, Russians, Germans, Marxists, Fascists. And here we are *again*. Our driver, is he a police spy?"

"No, no," said Tony weakly. He had been wrong to talk to her of this—to tell her any of this crazy story. But get a man in bed with a woman and he'll forget to put a sock in his mouth. Tony calmed her after a while with carresses, and that roused something else in them. Just before dawn they made love again in the wide feather bed. Then, sated, they slept with the contented and innocent smiles of wise children after erotic games.

The driver, coming to wake them up, knocked. He gave up after a while and went down to find breakfast, swearing at the habits of the people he drove—should he report *all* this in detail to Captain Kura next time he phoned in?

They left the inn at eleven.

In Bielsk they stayed at a clean little place called Lieber Freundhof, run by an exiled German who projected *Gemütlichkeit* and snarled at the servants with the manners of a *Gruppenführer*.

"*Ach, ya,*" he said to Tony in a coarse German. They stood in the lobby while Asta was testing the genuine, very hot bathtub upstairs. "Jean Lupescu, the circus man? I know him. Never trust him, but who trusts a Rumanian? *Nein?* Not that I believe in any of our *alt* German nonsense of inferior races, but once a Rumanian *always* a low dog."

"You know his show and circus?"

"Do I know it! Does Heinz Pufendorf (at your service) know it? The troupe still owe for two weeks of meals. I'll tell you the difference, Herr Kall, between a Rumanian and a Hungarian. They will both sell you their mother, but the Rumanian will deliver. *Ja.*"

"Where is the show now playing?"

"In Makow, I hear. Held there for the rest of the week."

"I have business with Lupescu. Is my car driver around?"

"In the kitchen. These Polish *bauern*—you can't trust them in any room where there are rugs on the floor. They spit. *Himmel!*"

Tony went to find Stephan, who didn't object to driving to Makow just so long as the road was fairly clear. "The car chains are wearing out. Maybe I get some in village."

Tony gave him some bills to go hunt for chains. The bundle of traveler's checks Pedlock & Sons of Rome had sent along was getting pretty thin.

CHAPTER 21

◄§ As he waited for Asta to finish bathing and for the car-chain problem to be solved, Tony remembered the airmail letter from his father. How far away it looked, as from another planet, this letter on good paper in an envelope of fine bond. The crest of his father's art galleries, with a thick gold imprint in one corner. Tony began to read his father's careful up-and-down writing:

DEAR TONY:

Your cable that you were healthy and free again sent us all into a pleasant mood, from your grandmother down to the smallest Lazar-Wolf child. The family has been aroused as they haven't been for a long time, as reformed as a solid unit of infantry. The Polish Embassy in Washington explained it all as one of "those mistakes," and we accept that. The suffocating presence of some sinister dread is gone. Thank God, as Jacob said.

Somehow I seem to see Judith's new husband as a kind of irritant that is causing family disorder among us, and then again I feel I'm just too sensitive about the atmosphere in which our family exists and moves. But he *did* get you involved in this crazy adventure to find his daughter, and Judith has become obsessed with a feeling that she has been destined to erect some kind of a monument in Israel to Jacob's special and daffy view of the godhead. It has caused much friction among us, and Judith and the lawyers, for she holds the control of more stocks and shares in Pedlock enterprises than all of us put together—in the Store and the Bank. I'm sure it will come out all right, but I keep thinking of the instigator of it all—Jacob, spry, artful, charming, his wispy beard waggling, his eyes bright as jet buttons, always alert, saying wise ironic things at times and at other times blanketed in some Hasidic or cabalist mumbo jumbo I can't penetrate. At first, believe me, I nearly thought he was a *dybbyk*, one of those spirits that enter a human body, or so the legend was, and work their evil from within some innocent frame. I still wonder at times if he isn't a demon. But that's nonsense, of course, in bright daylight. He's just a wiry little Jew who feels we're all lost because we don't follow the Union of Orthodox Jewish Congregations, and he proves Reform and Conservative sects aren't Jews at all. ("There is a goal, but no way.") He's witty on the subject when he's had a few brandies too many and your grandmother is patting his arm and encouraging him. ("To lose one's faith in one's youth, Marcel, and spend one's life looking for it—isn t that all art is?")

As you can guess, there's all this, and your Uncle Tom getting a divorce and his daughter Nancy insisting she be ritually converted to full Orthodox Judaism if she decides to marry Dick Lawrence (it's off and on). He used to be Dick Lazarus. Frankly, I think Nancy, who doesn't understand us, is in for a surprise. Dick is resigning from the Jews, as I see it, and wants anything but a believing Jewish wife. It's all very much a Chinese puzzle, isn't it? Or rather a Pedlock one. We have a way in the family of pushing passion to eccentricity.

The lawyers and Uncle Tom are working out the settlement Mabel is to get. The Bank will put up the cash, but only on the condition, of course, that Judith comes into the agreement and signs some papers at the same time to keep her holdings from being buried in some project out of the country. It's a very clever lawyer set-up, I suppose—Tom and Judith, a double package of our family problems. Old Addison figured it out. He's a Dionysian rogue playing at being bland. So we'll have peace again. Old Nathan is planning to absorb the Ganzler Fairs chain, Tom will marry his so pregnant redhead, Nancy will have Dick, and Jacob will have his daughter. And you, Tony? What will you have? It's all like a Dickens novel, isn't it? The way, too perfectly, it works out. I suppose I see it so because my insomnia is on me and I exist in bed, writing to you like this; for life is *never* like a novel at all. You can't skip the unpleasant parts, or the dull sections, or gloss over the deep dark secret things that revolt each of us at times within himself. And nothing comes out neatly at all in life—there are always raw edges, joints that don't dovetail. As Jacob quoted somebody at dinner the other night: "There is no irony like God's irony."

As you see, I'm obsessed with him. He's beginning to frighten me; see how I keep coming back to him, even in this letter to you? I was thinking of something just now (it's two-thirty in the morning): He makes me feel like a line in the Eddas: "The magic spring was guarded by a giant in a deep mountain cave, and when asked if one might drink of the spring, he said: 'Yes. The price is your right eye.'" Jacob has that effect on me. He knows the fearful price of *everything*, and seems to hint he can get it for you. I suppose that is what makes him supernatural to me. Perhaps he is Mesheach, the one who comes for the dead. Alone, here at night in this big bed, my bones aching, it could be he has come for me. I'm old, Tony, even in the middle of my fifties. I've aged quickly. I sense the damned unpredictable failure of body and mind may not be too long delayed. I have developed a heightened sensitivity to mortality. I think, frankly, that is why I have made such an effort of late to become very close to you. It's not the nonsense of having a Kaddish son to mourn for me. It's that before I never seemed to feel like being a father. I lacked the sly facility to make you like me when you were a child. My life has been ludicrous incongruity, temperament, sterility, gestures, I now see. What is art but childish marking on walls, little games of critics and fecund, overheated creators of scratches and lumps. None knowing too much. And as for life, I haven't lived it. I can't even say with that Frenchman: "Our servants do it for us."

As for women: almost nothing. I can be frank with you, Tony. I have never had much sexual drive, and what there was I detoured into reading and collecting of objects, canvases, gadgets. Fame—Milton calls it "That last infirmity of noble mind." (So many lines by other people in my mind—I am a cultural dustbin.)

When you get back, Tony, we must take a long trip, expensive, foolish. I want to show you what I have cherished all my life, the places, cities, walls, wines, chefs: things neither poignant nor perceptive. And you must teach me to live the way you do, under the sky; let me peer into your world, the Village, the hip places, the way to tear off restraint, catch the outrageous irrelevancy of which your generation is aware, that life never pays back what it costs. (Just took two sleeping pills.)

I seem to be the only one aware of what your grandmother's new husband is infecting us with: doubt, a perception of our ostentation, our pride in ourselves, our desire for the display, which is still after so many generations *parvenu*. (We hold ourselves, as is written, above rubies.)

I think Nathan feels something is wrong, but he is outside us in a way, a half brother, and Uncle Tom is merely sensual—perhaps it's enough to be a virile animal. He's always trying to cauterize his conscience with a new girl, yet all his life he hasn't been able to stabilize his relations with women. No, it's not envy on my part. (The pills are working.) If my desires don't pump hard enough at the idea of four legs in a bed, well, perhaps I've been spared the agony that a love object can inflict on one, so much deeper pain than a stranger.

You must be smiling, thinking, What's the old bastard mewling about? Isn't there a slogan in your set: If you don't like it, don't knock it? I know so little of your emotional life, except for that Chicago girl who seemed to work out so badly for you. Now that you're free of any attachment it would be a good time for me to show you something of a world of surface delights that had failed me, but can at times be a pleasant journey. From nowhere to nowhere, the scenery is fine. Write me in great detail of how things truly are with you.

Your father,
MARCEL

Tony folded the letter with its faint redolence of shaving soap. Poor old bastard. How I loved him as a kid, and still do. And he didn't give a shit about me. Shoved me into a rabid Presbyterian prep school and then to a faroff college, gave me money, sent me a lousy Lautrec etching or Picasso drawing every birthday, asked me was I "having fun."

He imagined Asta naked and put away the letter. We could get married in Rome and ski for a month in the Tyrol. Well, better get the car. He went upstairs and Asta seemed pleased when he said they'd get Leah at once and leave Poland. She brushed off his kiss casually and told him to mind he didn't drop her dressing case and its mirror.

"Maybe, Asta, we can get Leah and have the driver take us across the border at once."

"That would be mission accomplished."

"I can't believe it's this easy. We're in luck."

"Suppose, *mon cher*, Leah doesn't want to go with you? Suppose they won't let her go?"

"We've the law on our side. Legal papers."

Asta showed him half an inch of pink tongue. She looked ready and fit, even if her eyes were a bit ringed from love-making. "The law? Who will you call to help us, the Security Police?"

"Don't be a killjoy, Asta. And wear a warm coat."

"Stop talking like a goddamn husband. I have my new long underwear, *boychick*."

"Who taught you that word?"

"It's around the Rome buying office."

The roads were in bad shape. The car bucked and skidded. Twice the driver wanted to give it up and Tony had to tip him to get him to go on. Makow was a big town; there was some kind of power station there and an industry. Tony couldn't guess what kind, but it left a lot of the outskirts shabby, the streets unpaved and the jerry-built houses crooked on their shaky foundations.

Asta pointed to a high fence where posters gleamed under a skin of frost. The driver translated. " 'The People's Artists present Lupescu's International Ice Show and Winter Circus.' "

Asta said, "Do you see any dates?"

"No, but Leah's name is still featured."

Tony tapped on the driver's shoulder, and the man sniffed through his cherry-red nose. "Sputnik Hall, driver."

"Khrushchev Hall, once," said the driver.

"No, the poster says Sputnik Hall."

"Oh. They must have changed name since last time."

The hall was an impressive place, built sometime in the last century, Tony guessed, as a smaller version of the Paris Opéra, but with additions of its own. It was not in good repair under its green copper roof, but somehow its style inspired one to think it would sink into a fine ruin, like an old beauty, a woman aging and wrinkling, but still retaining some of her fine bone structure. Tony and Asta got out of the smoking auto and went up an alley along the soiled brown path worn in packed snow. The stage door was easy to open, and a bell rang somewhere as Asta followed Tony into the dark interior backstage. There was the bark and smell of seals and their attendant herring, an odor of grease paint, unwashed costumes, old steamer trunks. A half circle of ice surface had replaced the stage, and an old man was fumbling under a work light with some leaking amonia pipes.

He looked up, pulled on his mustache and spoke. The driver said, "No visitors, he say, backstage. This ice-making machine blow up at any minute."

Tony extended a bill and the old man blew air through his tobacco-stained mustache and hid the money quickly.

The driver said, "He say, 'How can I serve the Herr Graf?' "

"We'd like to see His Excellency Lupescu."

"Second door to the right. Watch your head on those sandbags."

They avoided the hanging tie ropes and bags and went past a cage of three seals hooting in a tin bath of dirty water, past four miserable and obscenely sniffling poodles dyed yellow and pink. A very wide young man in darned yellow tights was sewing gold braid on a red jacket. At the proper door Tony looked at Asta, shrugged his shoulders and knocked.

A voice said something in Polish. Tony opened the door.

The room was filled with steampipes, racks of costumes gay but soiled with grease and wear, all repeated by reflection in the cracked mirrors on the wall. At a small table sat three persons at lunch with checkered napkins tied around their necks, a man and two women. The man was portly, smooth even in his flannel undershirt with his braces up. He had oily black hair, a round face with deep-gray eyes. He was chewing on a knuckle of salami. One of the women was mature and busty, her red hair worn piled on top of her head. She wore a Japanese robe and was sipping coffee that smelled of chicory. The girl, Tony knew at once, was Leah Ellenbogan. She was bigger and thinner than he had expected, flat-chested, her hair blond, nearly silver-colored, and she was wearing a blue sweater over a ballet skirt and ivory-colored washed tights. She stopped spooning up her soup as Tony and Asta came over to the table.

Tony said, "Anyone speak English?"

Still chewing, the man said with a Bronx accent, "Jean Lupescu at your service. But say, this is no time to call on me and my little family."

"Wipe your mouth, Jake," said the woman, taking a swallow of coffee.

The man took up a corner of the tablecloth and followed orders. "So?"

"I'm Tony Pedlock. I wonder if I could talk to you privately, Lupescu."

Asta said to Leah, "Cute as a Degas drawing."

The coffee drinker asked in a British clipped tone, "What is this bozo, the tax collector?"

Asta said, "We've come to take the girl to New York."

"New Yok," shouted the man. "The Hippodrome, Roxy's!"

"They've all been pulled down," Tony said.

"Masha darling," said the man, kissing the coffee drinker. "New Yok. Ah, meet my stars. Mash (The Cat) Nanson. We are to marry soon. And Leah, like our own daughter. No? Yes? Speak up."

Leah flushed and put up her pert face. "I want a Hollywood hairdo if we go to America." She looked spoiled and pampered, Tony thought—a little bitch.

Tony began again. "If we could talk . . . just for a moment—"

Masha (The Cat) Nanson said, "What you have to say we can all bloody well hear. Jean and I are going to get married as he says.

In New York you Americans like things moral and respectable. Very—"

"New Yok," said Lupescu, closing his eyes.

Tony took out some papers from an inner pocket of his overcoat. "I have here Polish legal papers issued to Jacob Ellenbogan for him to take his daughter, Leah, out of Poland, and a letter appointing me his representative."

"The hell you have," said Masha. "He wants our star, the blinking sod, that's all. Just like *that*—" she snapped her fingers—"you take her away?"

Like a bird observing, Leah looked around her from face to face. "That Jacob, that's my papa, isn't it?"

"That's the arse-faced bastard," said Masha, rising, showing her soiled silk underwear as the kabuki robe opened. "He walked out on your mother in London, off to chase some Yid pipe dream— God forgive us all, and he never sent us a shilling to support you. He didn't give a good goddam until Jean and me we made a star out of you. The world stinks, mister."

Jean Lupescu was using the tablecloth to wipe his face again. "Justice is not dead. You can't break our hearts, Mr. Pedlock. This is the people's state. The old capitalistic horsecrap don't work here." He burped garlic and put his arms around Leah, who grinned at all the excitement. "Who trained Lily, brought her art out? Got her silver skates? Who sat up nights with her cough, her scarlet fever?"

"I bloody well did," said Masha, examining the papers and wiping coffee stains off them. "Now stow your gab, Jean. Save your voice. We do a show tonight. Legal is legal. We'll call our lawyer chap in Warsaw and get legal too. Leah, ducks, go out and practice your figure eights. They're weak."

"They are not! You can't do them better, so there."

Tony didn't like Leah's tone of voice at all. She lacked her father's charm—but the daughter of a *dybbuk*, what could you expect?

Masha said simply, "You're not too big to get a slap in the head, my little lady."

"It's about me," said Leah, sitting down, arms folded. "I'm entitled to hear. The new Poland is here for us youth. We're the future."

Jean swore softly in Rumanian, smiling all the time, and looked at Masha for orders.

"Yes, we'll get our own lawyer. People's justice is all we ask against American imperialism. This isn't Cuba, you know."

Asta said, "You may not like the justice when you get it." She turned to Masha, "Look, doll, we can work this out."

Jean shrugged, "You have money? American dollars?"

Asta smiled. "Within reason. Win or lose, in the end Leah has a father she belongs to."

Tony said, "He's old."

"Good," said Masha. "And a hundred other bones to break yet, I hope. He's a spook, that's what he is."

"Don't talk that way about my daddo," said Leah.

Masha lifted her hand toward Leah, who quickly moved away.

"We are just poor proletarians," said Lupescu.

There was a tap on the door and the stagehand stuck his head in with some bad news. "Herr Lupescu, *kaputt, alles kaputt.*"

Lupescu picked up an end of salami and threw it at the old man. "Can't you see we're talking business?"

CHAPTER 22

❧ It hadn't been all that Tony had expected. It was imbecility and singular greed. Driving back to their hotel, Asta turned to Tony. "You're not going to pay Lupescu two thousand dollars for Leah's contract? If there is a contract."

"I may have to. I'll cable my grandmother."

"That Lupescu leaks greed like a roast goose drips fat. And Masha, what an *outrée* Cockney bag."

Tony felt the car buck a snowbank and go on, with a banging of chains against the mudguards. "What do you think of Leah?"

"Very spoiled. If she travels with us, I'm sure I'll give her a few slaps. I dislike precocious puberty."

Tony took Asta's hand in his. Even through their gloves he felt a current between them. "What will happen to us?"

"Us?" Asta reared back in the seat as if to get a better look at him. "Damn it, what's wrong with us now?"

"Nothing. Just want to keep it that way." He tried to nuzzle her covered neck and shoulders.

She laughed. He'd never heard her laugh so loudly and strongly. "You're happy, Asta?"

She turned a serious face to him, the big black Mediterranean eyes, the too white face, the blue-black hair—all again as he had first seen her. "Let's not kick any talk of happiness around, Tony. You know what my first husband's definition of happiness was? A limited amount of contentment. He smoked opium."

"That's certainly limited."

"You get a limited contentment and you've made it."

"Doesn't seem enough."

"I always say, take everything as it comes. Either duck or grab. Darling, I think our driver is crazy."

They had skidded to a teeth-jolting stop in front of the German hotel. Tony told the driver he might want him later. Inside the hotel lobby they shed their outer layers of clothing. The hotel owner, Herr Pufendorf, joined them in a drink—"*Ist das nicht ein schönes Kümmel?*"

Asta said she was going to take a very hot bath and get warm again. Tony wrote out a cable to Pedlock House, Norton-on-Hudson, and Herr Pufendorf said he'd have it sent right off—if the post office of the People's State was open. Tony decided he'd have another kümmel and then take the bottle up to Asta's room. The German came back and said, of course, the whole bottle, and what *Mumpitz* about paying for it, but if Herr Pedlock wanted it on the bill, of course.

"I tell you, Herr Pedlock, we don't get the proper visitors here any more. Now you, I'd say, have some sort of personal mission. Don't tell me. *Eins, zwei, drei,* the police have me in a cellar asking me what you said."

"I have no mission—I mean any political one."

"Ach, of course not. But if you need anything, ask me." He winked and looked into his kümmel glass. "I know all the smugglers who cross and recross the border. If you want a crossing in a hurry, just slip me the wink. *Ja?*"

"I have all my arrangements made. I mean for traveling."

"It's easy to slide across the border. Ach, a man like you, you could ski. Now if you're smuggling ikons, I can have them sealed waterproof. If it's black-market money, I can get you a better rate of exchange than the Greeks. Any merchandise can be handled."

Tony laughed. "You have me all wrong, Herr Pufendorf. I don't have to be smuggled across a border. I don't carry any of what you call merchandise."

The German winked and put a fat finger to the side of his potato nose. "*Ja,* I should have known. It's women, *nein?* The one upstairs, that is sample of the merchandise for say South America? Pedlock & Sons, a famous firm."

Tony picked up the bottle. "What did you do during the war?"

"*Schweinerei.* A salesman for Krupp. I sold gas furnaces to the concentration camps for them; quality goods is Krupp. Handled hot Picassos, a ton of coal here and there. I was a *Dummkopf.* The really big stuff got away from me. And now this Robert Kennedy, he has given all seized Nazi assets back to the old firms. I missed out."

An elderly woman's voice sounded from the kitchen in rasping country Polish. Herr Pufendorf excused himself. "My damn wife. *Ich komme schon, Liebchen.*"

Tony went up the stairs, knocked on Asta's door and entered. It was really only half a room. A thin plywood wall had divided a bigger room. Tony had the other half. There was no door between the divided parts, just an opening and a dusty rose-colored curtain on a rod.

Asta was in long woolen winter underwear. "I'm glad you brought something to drink. What is it?"

"Kümmel."

Tony got out of his jacket and sat on the bed, drinking. He kissed Asta's cheek. She shook her head. "Tony, don't make too much of all this—what has happened between us. We got a bit emotional, that's all."

"You love me, don't you?"

"There's more to life than love."

"Marry me." It seemed a loose, foolish statement, but he was feeling loose and foolish.

"There are a few problems, Tony. But it can be worked out." She patted his hand. "Wouldn't that bug out the eyes of the Rome office? *Mrs.* Pedlock. Where would we live, *if* . . ."

"Asta, you ever been in the American desert? In the Southwest below Palm Springs? We're building a big store there. It's still, however, the way it was. I know a knoll on a mesa under a mountain ridge. We'll build us a house there. Fieldstone with a good tile roof. We'll keep horses. The view a hundred miles in any direction, any way you look. You never saw such colors, such sunsets."

She leaned against him, sipped her kümmel and sighed. "Don't tempt me. At heart I'm a slob, *boychick,* for romantic talk."

"This isn't just talk." He ardently unbuttoned the top three buttons of her woolen longies.

"Tony, grow up. Peace, intimacies, companionship—that's romantic crap, just talk in this rotten world. Survival is all. Jules used to say—he reads Sartre and Camus—'We betray each other and ourselves.' Jules was always moody with me, and after a while he'd want to kill himself." Asta began to weep.

"Why bring Jules in?"

She scowled and dried her eyes. "Moods, I think, were Jules' kicks, that's all. He knew he couldn't kill himself. The Church was against suicide, and he was pious, but he'd see how close he could come. Good Lord, sweetie, not in the afternoon!"

"Close your eyes."

She whispered, "What will we do at night?"

They made love in leisurely detail and with great contentment. Later she said in a low voice with a kind of desolate awe, speaking into his shoulder, against which her lips were pressed, "Tell me again all about the desert, the mesa, the house, the horses. Tell me all the time. I need all that dream talk. You're such a sweet fool, Tony. It's a good thing I'm loyal to the Rome office. What if some scheming bitch had found you?"

There was a small Telefunken radio on in the room. It was playing a version of "Tea for Two" from East Germany, very schmaltzy and sweet. Then there was Victor Herbert, and they lay and listened, half asleep, half hearing as the cold day outside darkened. The radio news came on, the usual details of plane crashes, storm warnings, snide diplomatic items. A girl in Dresden had started a plan to bring Lennie Bernstein and his Dixieland jazz band to Poland. The winter rye and clover crops were doing well. There had been an explosion in a government building in West Berlin, a faulty furnace valve, or a Red plot. A new European snowstorm was due.

Tony got up and turned off the radio. "I suddenly have a feeling, Asta, those Rumanians are going to bilk us. I have a feeling they're smuggling Leah out of town."

"What can you do?"

"I've got about six hundred dollars in traveler's checks. I'm going over to the hall right now and make a down payment on what we promised them."

"If they see and taste real money, Tony, maybe they'll say yes."

"I'll take them and Leah out to dinner. You want to join us?"

"No, no. It's getting too cold out there. And I have to wash my hair. You climbed all over it, cowboy."

"You must take me seriously, Asta."

"I'm trying, darling."

Tony went through the curtained opening into his room and dressed. He wondered if the German, Herr Pufendorf, like the car driver, was a spy for the police. He went to the window and opened the latch. There was a balcony beyond it and steps going to a kind of yard leading to a side street. He decided he'd walk to the Lupescus. This would be a good way to get back to his room later, without the German or the driver knowing just when he got back. Tony left the window latch undone.

Asta, in her room, pouring water from a basin, called out, "Tony, don't let those Rumanians sell you the circus at dinner."

"Bring you back some cakes and tarts. Most likely come in late." Tony went to her and rubbed his cheek against hers, and he felt a fool to go out into the cold on an errand he didn't give a damn about when he could be warm and in bed with the woman he loved. His big problem, as he saw it, was how to get water up to that mesa house in the desert, the one he was going to build. There was enough green around, he remembered, to suggest some hidden spring. Would Asta fit in with the Pedlocks? Well, honest doubt is the greatest faith.

Asta turned the radio back on to the East German station: "Many American youngsters who complain of weakness, headache and dizziness are suffering the effect of glue sniffing, a physician who has made a study of the problem declares. Seldom, says Dr. Ignacy Sokoli, chief physician of the People's Health Section . . ."

After Tony left, Asta tuned in a radio station playing Chopin.

Tony's plans for taking the Lupescu ménage out to dinner had to be changed. There was, Tony found, great activity at Sputnik Hall. A muzzled live bear stood backstage, on roller skates, scratching himself with dusty vigor. Half a dozen naked-legged girls, blue with cold, some with runny noses, huddled around an electric grill. Jean Lupescu, in ring master's outfit, was raging at the old stage hand. He threw his arms around Tony—"Comrade American!"— and was ready to kiss and hug him in true Rumanian style. But dinner, he said, was impossible. "Just now not to be thought of."

"Why?"

"Ah. We never eat before a show. And the damn People's Artists, those stinking comrades, make us give two shows a night. But later we three, we celebrate—*mamabeja* and *drob de miel* at a real Rumanian place."

Tony explained he'd like to show his good faith by handing over the six hundred dollars in traveler's checks.

Lupescu said, "No, *no!*" and pocketed them with a bow. Tony said that Pedlock & Sons, Rome, would sent the rest of the promised money. "And I'd like to see the show."

Lupescu bowed again and cracked his whip as he stood up on the splintered wooden floor backstage on ice skates. "Yes, yes, you go back and bring your young lady. You *must* see the *second* show. Our best one. Then you can buy us all a big dinner. Masha, Masha!"

Masha and Leah came out of a dressing room, both in blue tights, wearing little cat masks over their eyes. Leah was not yet fully developed, being thin and long-legged, but was very pretty. Masha was a bit over-curved, over-bosomed, but a magnificently built woman.

Lupescu said to Masha, "Pan Pedlock and his lady will honor us from a box at our second show. Two passes for them, please."

Leah grinned and did a little toe dance on her ice skates on the wooden floor. "America!"

Masha handed over two bits of paper taken from an old wall desk, after adding some wild marking in purple ink. "Here you are, Pedlock. For you, jolly well free, but there is a bloody people's tax of a hundred *zlotys*—each."

"Later, collect later," said Lupescu, as stage lights went on. "Damn it, who chained that bear up so close to the curtain? He's going to scratch the ass off those girls. Masha, the seals stink. Why isn't the water ever changed? You see, Comrade Pedlock, everything on *my* shoulders—they forget I'm an *artiste*."

Masha made an abscene comment.

"See you all later," said Tony. "Leah, I sent a cable to your father."

Masha said, "Be on time. Our second show is at nine o'clock."

The customers could be heard out front, talking, rustling their programs and coughing, aided by the seals backstage.

Leah hugged Tony and hung on his arm. Even on skates she had a few inches to grow. "You think my daddo will be glad to see me?" She was flirting with Tony, blinking her eyes. Her body was crowding against him too closely, too intimately.

"Oh yes. Jacob has missed you."

"Is he very rich now? Like they say, a Rothschild?"

"He doesn't care for money."

"He'll buy me the American clothes then?"

"Don't worry. You'll go to school there. You'll be just like other young girls, have a fine normal life."

"Give up being part of the theater? Must I?"

"Yes. Don't you want to?"

Leah pouted, scowled, gave a weak smile. "Maybe I'll stay here with Jean and Masha. They're fun when they're not scratching their eyes out or getting drunk."

"They are being well paid."

Leah put a hand on her hip. She looked unreal in her costume—not at all a child. "I suppose after all the old bastard is my father."

Tony felt a concupiscence in Leah, of an unhealthy sort. Maybe Marcel was right. If so, this was the child of a *dybbuk*.

Tony said he'd be back with Asta in time for the last show. He went out, just escaping the chained bear's swipe at his head with a huge paw. A light snow was falling again—people were standing in a stringy line—and he wished he were far away from the nasty child, only with Asta at his side, skiing down a good packed slope with the surface just right and at the bottom a warm room with a fireplace, and a good meal at a table set for two, and a few drinks, a very big soft bed, and, being young, sweet and dedicated pleasures. The last, at least, was available back at the German's hotel.

Walking back to the Lieber Freundhof Tony felt the snow falling harder. It had the soft thickness of wood, but no warmth. The hotel was almost hidden by the snow, which merged with its dun-colored wall. Tony looked through at the well-lit lobby; the double glass doors showed Herr Pufendorf trying to light the short stub of a cigar, talking earnestly with the driver of their hired car. Tony decided to go up the back way to his room, the way he had prepared for himself, just in case these two were actually reporting his actions to the police. Perhaps he'd catch Asta still soaking in the big tin bathtub.

It felt good to be crunching in the deep snow in the alley behind the hotel, protected from the wind, the cold less sharp than it had been. A steep wooden staircase led up to the little roof by the balcony of his room. The steps hadn't been cleaned, but the snow was not too built up. On the balcony, Tony stopped to look around

him. Everything was muffled and silent and gleaming crystal-white.
He touched the unlatched window and it gave inward. He stepped
softly into the room and smiled as he thought of the woman just
beyond the plywood wall, the dusty curtain.

Images of sensual detail, a need for warmth and companionship
filled him. The radio in her room was tuned to some gypsy music,
so low that he was suddenly aware of voices, the creak of an occupied bed. He stood very still in surprise, his mouth slightly open,
not daring to move his heavy shoes on the worn rag rug.

". . . of you getting here." (Asta's voice, sultry, warm, slow.)

"Almost never got here at all." (Archie Gillman! No!)

"Been so damn dull here. Without you, sweetie." (!)

A kind of amorous stirring sound came to Tony's ears; more *ping
twang* of bedsprings. Voices intimate, so low he couldn't hear.
Asta's little coughing laughs when passion overcame her. (Oh
God!) Followed by Archie's goatlike hoot.

"Archie, *mon cher*."

"It's been too goddam long between *trenning*." (Vulgar.)

"God, yes." (Eager.)

Strong breathing, amorous inhaling. The catch and sob of slob-
bering kisses. Tony stood there, hands at his sides, forgetting to
take off his gloves or open his fur coat collar. Aware of sweat pouring down the sides of his torso under his shirt, of the strong dry
heat of the room. Of the tortured breathing next door. The sound
of the bed in three-quarter time, the expelling of air from wet lips.
A mounting series of coarse personal sounds, basic animal pleasures
not meant for a third set of ears. The steady jingling—a duet of
two sets of limbs and purposes. A long sigh like an expiring whistle.
Silence . . . Tony wiped his face with the back of a glove. He
stood in darkness, a faint light outlining the dusty curtain to the
next room.

"Cigarette?" (Asta.)

"Where the hell are they?" (Archie.)

Tony could not move. Nothing could have moved him just then.
He was petrified, turned to stone. Only stone flesh would not hurt,
ache so, feel that the end of the world had just been acted out on
a Polish bed on grimy gray sheets, in a second-rate hotel room
smelling of Asta's sweat and Schiaparelli perfume.

"Sweetie, matches." (A sense of farawayness in the voice, but a
hope of recovery.)

"Lazy bitch." (Archie coughed, then the sound of kisses as if in reward for something well done.)

"How long do we stay here?" (Asta's voice, gaining volume.)

"Till I hear for sure they'll deliver."

"In *this* snowstorm?"

"That's something we didn't figure on. We better get dressed before the jerk gets back."

"Gone out to dinner with the Lupescus. God, Pedlock is such a square."

"Don't know what Captain Kura has told him. We're lucky to have a *putz* like him with us."

"A deadly bore, Archie. I've had a time keeping him entertained. He's horny as hell."

Tony stiffened and clicked his teeth together; it didn't seem to help the pain.

"I bet." (A sound like the delivery of a strong but playful slap on someone's rump.)

"Suppose you were trailed here?"

"No, no."

"What about our driver? He'll turn us in."

"He takes money. Don't get up yet, you *nafka*."

Tony covered his ears and began to pant, quietly, silently, the way a dog will after a heartbreaking run after game that has confused him. Then he let his hands fall.

"Archie, did he ever talk to you about his goddam mesa and sitting around looking at the desert sunset?"

"Huh? We need him. The Pedlock name is magic."

(Intimate scuffling noises of renewed copulation.)

Tony turned, opened the window and stepped out on the balcony. Asta must have contacted Archie in Munich, told him that she'd been assigned to Tony by the Rome office. Old lovers, of course. He felt confused, betrayed, very much in pain, a kind of dry pain with no visible wounds. They had planned from the start to use him. . . .

He went down to the alley and out to the side street and just stood there. Suddenly he ran—ran off in a kind of Indian lope, ran into the snow—remembering a fragment of Philosophy II at Princeton: "Men have ideals, women have only illusions." Nietzsche. He was shaken by spasms of pain, frustration, betrayal, and Asta's mocking voice—"His goddam mesa."

CHAPTER 23

❧ In his flight Tony Pedlock froze to death, and in time was buried. He knew just how it began; he had decided to freeze to death. Somehow, in his heated mind, full of the humiliating tragedy of his betrayal and shame in love—tragedy? no, vulgar comedy —he had decided to sit down and freeze solid so that in the spring they would dig him out of some snowdrift, hard and dead as firewood. Two things could have defeated his spur-of-the-moment despair. Or was it crushed vanity? The snowfall had raised the temperature and he had not frozen as quickly as he had expected. He was also a healthy, warmly dressed young man. Something in him had fought for a long time for survival. (He had not unbuttoned and helped nature.) But he died and fully experienced his death.

He knew he was dead because he could sense only a void of blackness—and space is death, a modern artist had said—a relaxed tingling in his limbs. That could only mean that peace had been granted him. Would he lie in the Pedlock plot or be buried here? The feeling of the grace of the grave when he was buried was very comforting. The dead in other graves around him were chatting away. He would introduce himself later. Just now, he wanted to enjoy the comfort of being a corpse and the awareness of being . . . being *what?* An unmoving body, conscious and at rest, with a desire to laugh one note short of a scream.

It was hard to believe he had been in love with that bitch, Asta. Or, frankly, that he'd been hurt enough to destroy himself. Tony chuckled; the spiritual bookkeeping and recording even on the

239

other side of life was as faulty as on earth; technically he knew he should be listed as a suicide by the family. And, had he answered his father's letter? No. Just technically a suicide, of course. He hadn't meant to freeze fully to death—not really; deep down there had been a spark that spoke for survival and struggle to keep the blood pumping; the facetious clichés in mind—"Men have died and worms have eaten them, but not for love."

The people in nearby graves were chatting away. Polish. Hearty and insensitive to a man getting accustomed to his new grave. Here at last was the complacency of the noncombatant. A calm place, the grave, even for a long rest. The grave was much lied about, Tony thought. He didn't feel anything himself yet. But most likely the dead went through a period of adjustment, toughening up—like a course in a new gym.

There was the sound of a coffin lid opening and shutting, the thud of heavy overshoes moving on newly packed graves. Tony opened his eyes and stared at Captain Kura, bending over him. He was wearing a grat black fur hat, his face unshaven.

"Ah, the dead awake," the captain said in English.

"You have no right to walk on my grave," Tony began, then saw he was lying on the earth floor of a low-ceilinged hut built of rough timbers, stretched out by a glowing little wood-burning stove.

"If my men had not been watching hotel, you'd have got off and frozen out there. Were drunk, maybe?"

Tony sat up and someone handed him a bowl of hot *borszcz* soup and a big spoon. He fed slowly, not minding that the soup was very hot. There were six men in the hut. He saw automatic pistols, shotguns, Bren guns and a portable short-wave radio with a yellow-haired boy wearing earphones bent over it.

Captain Kura squatted down as Tony handed over the empty soup bowl. "I didn't think I could eat anything." He smiled at the captain.

"You've got a tip of ear frozen, a couple fingers. This to happen on my weekend off. My wife very angry with me."

Tony felt his ear. "Yes."

"Now. You seen Archie Gillman?"

Tony didn't want to answer that directly on the nose. He hadn't actually seen him, just heard him. "He was up in—in Miss Chauessian's hotel room last I knew."

"Still is."

Tony stood up and ached. The ear really hurt. He rubbed it.

"Don't rub hard. Keep letting warm blood in."

Tony looked around at the men. They were smoking, adjusting their weapons. He accepted a small glass of vodka and a plate of raw, fat herring filets. Between the drink and the salt fish, he realized he wanted to live, eat, and get out of Poland, out of his grave, to become a Pedlock like Nathan or Judith.

"I'd like to pick up Leah Ellenbogan and leave the country."

"I promise you, you will. We are waiting to arrest your friends when the stuff is delivered to them."

"How do I fit into their scheme?"

"They may have planned to leave you behind, *if* you lucky."

"What do you mean *lucky*?"

Captain Kura cocked a hand like a pistol to his head and pulled an imaginary trigger. "As my young son says playing cowboy, 'Biff-biff, dead is dead.' No, *yingle*?"

"Miss Chauessian wouldn't—I don't think—"

"Why? Because you made love with her? Don't be an American *yold*—who hasn't?"

The boy at the short-wave set was busy talking into a hand mike. The stove hissed. No one seemed to pay much attention to Tony, back now with his personal agony. A map was examined at a pine table under an oil lamp. He felt his ear and fingers ache, felt the bottom of his world was long since fallen away. He couldn't get over Asta's betrayal. It was, of course, very simple. He had been bemused, made stupid by passion, had accepted love (or whatever it was that had driven him) without any mature thought. He looked up. Captain Kura began to button his heavy fur-lined coat.

"We going to surround hotel now. Bring more Security Police." He turned to the radioman.

"I'd rather stay out of it," Tony said.

"Yes—you stay in car. Come."

There were four heavy dark-gray army cars in the snow outside the hut. It appeared to be a deserted farmhouse. The captain motioned Tony into the second car and bundled heavy sheepskin rugs around him. They started off into the silver-blue night. Lights were dimmed. The snow was drifted about them, but it had stopped falling. A grill on the floor of the car gave off a dry warmth that was comfortable.

"It was clever in this sense," said the captain. "Gillman and

Chauessian, deeply involved in smuggling, had perfect pigeon in you, as they say in America. A decent person, a real honest reason to come into Poland. To find lost daughter. Even legal papers. And their jobs—Pedlock & Sons, Rome office, buyer—he a journalist. With you as front they make contact with black market here. We arrest key man, thanks to you."

"Don't forget that," said Tony. "Don't ever forget it, Captain Kura."

"A gold star on your record, but Gillman never lose sight of you."

"The driver of the car I hired is working with them?"

"Yes. Stephan work both sides. What matter?"

The cars were moving in single file along a narrow trail, all lights out as they approached the hotel. Captain Kura saw to it that the cars were parked out of sight. The radioman had his portable set working and was issuing whispered orders that he read from a sheet of paper Captain Kura had handed him.

Tony looked over the desolate village. The night was milky white with deep-blue shadows; all the sharp edges had merged into soft forms. Only thick-snow-covered houses on all sides had a pattern of their own, and the naked tree limbs were etched a sooty black.

He fell asleep. He missed the death of Archie Gillman, who tried to escape over the roofs. He was stiff in all his bones the next morning. He had finished the night sleeping in a chair in the hotel lobby.

Life seemed one big anticlimax as he came to Sputnik Hall in the bright of noon. Last night seemed untrue. The images of the events no longer were real. It must all have come from some tightly plotted dream, experienced comfortably in a warm doze. He blew his nose and knew he had a devil of a cold from the night's doings. His nose, throat and ears were all inflamed. He coughed, pulled his overcoat collar tighter around his neck as he went down the alley to the stage door of the ice show. Of course last night was just a kind of nightmare. He had missed the violence. He shook his head. The bullet-mutilated body of Archie Gillman had certainly been real enough, and gory, and also Asta in her fingertip-length bed jacket howling in the snow outside like a wolf bitch in a steel trap, screaming: "Pedlock! Pedlock, do something!" Tony coughed and felt every tissue in his body inflamed and sore. He hadn't wanted to do anything, and couldn't have.

Backstage, the seals still smelled, but the great brown bear slept, curled up in a ball exposing only a wet black nose from a pile of mangy fur full of sawdust.

It was Jean Lupescu who wept as Leah buttoned the collar of her new gray karakul coat. It was Jean Lupescu who held out Tony's travelers checks and shouted, "Take it all back; I can't let Leah go! It's like asking me to eat my own heart in sour cream."

Leah whirled around for Tony's benefit. She looked gay and childishly excited in the daylight—why had he thought her evil? "It's all new, Tony. Am I fit to travel with?"

Masha, in a pink feathered robe, was laying out a gypsy fortune hand at the table, cigarette in a long paper tube dangling from her teeth. "You ungrateful brat. Ought to clip you one on the lug. Get out of my sight."

Lupescu wiped his eyes. "Ah, who knows, who cares what happens to us true *artistes*. Tear us apart. Sell us like Uncle Tom."

"Get the money, you mangy sod," said Masha, placing a red ten of hearts on a queen of spades. "*Get* the money."

The dressing-room door opened and Captain Kura came in, closely shaved, refreshed by four hours of sleep. He was wearing a smartly cut overcoat and a gray fur cap. His boots were polished.

"Come, Pan Pedlock, the Warsaw-Berlin express will stop for you two only ten minutes."

Masha said, "The money we were promised, *Papisha*."

Captain Kura grinned, looking again the redheaded Jewish farm boy. "What *chutzpah*. Artists don't need money. Besides, I've good news. Your show has been graced by interexchange of People's Artists groups for Siberia tour at last."

Masha threw down the ace of spades and spit on it. "A black year on all *artistes*, all audiences, all police captains, and *all* Rumanians." Lupescu looked hurt. Masha kicked his shin and he howled.

Leah tried to kiss her aunt, and Masha suddenly burst into tears, pulled the child to her, and kissed her on the cheek. "Ah, Leah, stay young a long time, ducks. Live, live, and stay away from pimps from Bucharest."

Lupescu made a sad face and waved his hands about. Tony blew his nose. Captain Kura looked at his wrist watch. He put his arm around Tony's shoulder and led him out to the stage entrance.

"Mr. Pedlock. Notice I return you to your own side of world with Mr. There is a Mercedes-Benz car out front. You find a prisoner in front seat in handcuffs. You might want to say goodbye to prisoner." He looked at his watch again. "You have four and half minutes. What *rebbe* said, 'Better to walk behind a lion than behind a woman'?"

Tony didn't answer. He frowned, beat one foot against the stage door, then stepped through it without looking back. The big blue car was in front of the theater, and the driver, out of the car, was joking with the ticket girl at the nearby theater entrance. Tony felt a slow degeneration of all his faculties.

He went to the car and opened the door on the side of the steering wheel. Asta looked up. She was very pale, terror-sticken, her eyes darkly ringed. She was wearing no hat and was bundled up in her heavy brown coat. She smelled of fear and personal odors. There was a slight quiver of her bruised lips as Tony slid in behind the wheel. He saw she too had a cold—her perfect nose was red. She tried to hide her handcuffed wrists, and he saw that a steel chain led from them to the steering column and a padlock there completed the captivity. He felt like a mourner at his own burial— no, that was last night.

She sniffed. "I'm happy, Pedlock, you weren't really hurt."

"Stupid of you to get into this, Asta."

She shrugged her shoulders in despair, too weak, it seemed, to regroup her emotions. She looked at him, moving her head closer. She kissed him directly on the mouth. He wanted to put his arms around her, but he didn't. He just kissed back and then moved his head away.

She moaned. "You love me, Pedlock. Help me now."

"Nothing I can do."

"Swear to them I had nothing to do with any of this."

"But you did. As a buyer for Pedlock & Sons you had a side racket—and a pal, a lover."

"Lover? Only you and me are here now. He's dead. We matter."

"Archie was your lover. I'm just a square—a horny square with a goddam mesa."

"Oh! Christ, you *heard* that? That bastard Archie, I hated him.

He blackmailed me into bed—said he'd expose me, get me fired."
She made an oval of wretched fear of her mouth. She sniffed and
nodded. "He's dead. Terrible way to die. All death is terrible. Does
that matter? You still love me, Pedlock, I know."

"Always love you, Asta."

"Save me."

"I can't save you."

"They'll shoot me."

"Shoot you, or lock you up for a long time."

"It will haunt you—me in a dirty stone prison cell for years and
years. I'll grow old and wrinkled and dirty. Pedlock, you can't let
that happen to living flesh you held in your arms. Think of all
those lovely nights, all those fine times."

"Goodbye, Asta."

"È troppo! Captain Kura will listen to you. He expects you to
plead for me. After all, I work for the Rome office of Pedlock &
Sons."

"It would be only a gesture. No help."

"I'm asking, lover, for my life."

She glanced about her, at the driver still talking to the box-office
girl, and at the other car in the stage alley, the one that would take
Leah and Tony to the station. She whispered to Tony in a graphic
drama of moving head and limbs. "The car key is in the lock. Start
the motor, drive like mad down the street, turn to the right. At the
border there's an underground smugglers' garage where we can
hide. Save me."

"Asta, no more melodrama."

"Damn you, I can't drive these fancy manual shifts, but move
over, I'll try it myself. Give me a chance for all I gave you."

Tony didn't move. "Tell me, Asta, how did Archie die?"

"How? Like we all die. He stopped breathing. Pedlock!" She
rolled her head, her eyes seemed larger, wilder.

Tony watched the driver approaching the car. He kissed her
cheek. "In my heart there will be a corner just for you. Not that it
matters."

"Pedlock!" Asta's eyes were full of terror as the driver stood at
the car door.

Tony could not speak. He got out of the Mercedes. Leah and
Captain Kura were coming out of the stage door. The driver had
slipped into the seat behind the steering wheel. Asta stared at

Tony, her lips drawn and then, her face a tight despairing mask. She choked up some sounds, animal sounds so like . . . He turned away to face Leah Ellenbogan. The car started off and he never saw Asta again. Much later, after he was married, he heard she was serving fifteen years in Lvov prison. He felt their love had been little more than a battle between technicians.

BOOK VII

SONG OF SONGS

CHAPTER 24

◆§ Dov A. Ganzler was considered a rather dull man—with transitory phases of bad manners—who had a great cunning in business matters. In fact, he had racked up two billion dollars in assets, controlled an empire called Ganzler Family Limited, a Delaware corporation. He lived in Santa Barbara among a vast art collection of very safe, overpriced paintings: rare Impressionists and Postimpressionists. Marcel Pedlock, who had helped form the collection, knew better than to suggest to Dov Ganzler any painting or bit of sculpture that wasn't as accepted an investment as U.S. Steel, A.T. & T., or Ganzler Fairs Department Stores. He was also chairman of the board of Coastal Tidbits, which canned fish, mixed paints and poured cement, and controlled the melon crop of the Fresno Valley. He held the presidency of Wonder Waters, which bottled no-cal soft drinks and imported scotch. The Ganzler holdings in secondary newspapers and popular magazines were impressive.

Dov Ganzler wasn't. A sad-eyed, puffy little man with a wife and eight children. Marcel Pedlock said of him: "No vices, not even a hope of any, a dull, self-made man who has the gift of turning everything into money. He is uneducated and, like most self-raised men, he has a respectful opinion of all culture, art, philosophy that he doesn't understand, and a hatred for the menace of organized labor and big government. He has no taste, no religion, but as a successful agnostic has raised his children in the Reformed Judaism of the coast—heavy on folk dancing and lectures on Samuel Beckett."

Tom Pedlock and Dick Lawrence, of Lazar-Wolf and Pedlock Brothers, waited for Dov at noon in the Mink Farm Club, where Ganzler enjoyed the sight of half-naked waitresses, with breasts falling from their scanty costumes, their little real-mink tails dragging, waiting for any customer to grab and yank. Dov Ganzler, a faithful, unardent husband, never yanked. He just liked to hold these little meetings for business—just as if he were only a *small* millionaire.

Dov followed the hostess, three paces behind, watching her tail wag. He greeted Tom, whom he knew, and shook Dick's hand.

"Ever see such a crazy place? Gotta come here every time I get to town. So, what's drinking?"

Tom held his Beefeater's gibson; Dick, his blond scotch on the rocks. "Auld Scratch brand, Mr. Ganzler. Your own."

"I only import it, I don't drink it. Miss, buttermilk for me, a plate of large prunes, real large ones?"

"Yo' not drinking nuthin', sir?"

"Buttermilk."

Dov looked up at the mink, her printed name pinned under a bobbing breast: Bobbie-Sue.

"Buttermilk, Boobie. You fellas ordered?"

"The cutlet," said Tom.

"The same," Dick said. Dick clicked the ice cubes in his glass. "Had a good trip, Mr. Ganzler, from the coast?"

"Always have a good trip. I don't keep a couple *nudniks* on the payroll to fly my jet to have a rotten trip. Tom, you look pooped. Got *vobb*—wife trouble, I hear?"

Tom smiled at the crass way Ganzler put it. "It's being settled."

"Knock wood." Dov Ganzler did. "Married thirty-one years. I don't chase no chickens. Thank you, Boobie. It's churned?"

"It's buttermilk, sir. All we have of it."

"Got a good stomach, wanna keep it that way. *Nu, tocus offen tish.* Somebody talk."

Dick Lawrence took a pull on his glass. Only the vein beating in his temple gave him away to Tom. Dick looked at Ganzler, trying the old trick of staring at a man *just* between his eyes, on *one* fixed spot. Ganzler didn't seem to mind as he poured buttermilk over his prunes and began to spoon them up.

"Mr. Ganzler, here's what's come up, and I'm handling it for Tom here and for Mrs. Judith Pedlock Ellenbogan."

"You're not representing Lazar-Wolf, eh?"

"No. As a matter of fact I'm leaving the Bank at the end of the month. Now, with an option on Tom's holdings and Mrs. Ellenbogan's, or part of them, you can control Pedlock & Sons Department Stores."

"This I didn't have to go to no Hebrew teacher to know. All right, Tom plays with me, but that old lady, she's got the strength of bulls. No offense, Tom."

"Yes, she's a strong-willed person," said Tom, pushing aside his cutlet and hunting his pipe.

"Now with Tom's stock *and*—" Dick leaned forward, casual, comradely to the great businessman—"with an option on Mrs. E.'s shares, you could bring on a proxy fight and seat yourself on the Pedlock & Sons board, control it."

"Chairman of the board, maybe," said Dov, spitting out a prune pit on the floor.

"That's up to you after you get the options."

"I don't want just Tom's bit—no offense—unless I get the option on the old girl's. That's clear, all understood?"

Dick nodded. "She wants two million within sixty days for a six-month option to buy."

"Ha, my grandmother wanted nuts so she could be my grandfather. Give her a million in sixty days, say for a year's option to buy at the going market price. I don't *hondle*—that's for Arab rug peddlers."

Dick looked at Tom, who remained expressionless, blowing air through his pipestem. Dick said cheerfully as he rubbed his chin, "Option to buy at a price halfway between the market low and high if it goes below today's price. What could be fairer, Mr. Ganzler?"

"A lot, young fella." He reamed his hairy left ear with a finger. "A hull lot. Oh Boobie, you got spongecake?"

"Sir, we have boysenberry pie, banana-cream, mocha and choc-fudge."

"Go look, dolly, maybe they got an old piece spongecake in the kitchen. You want anything, Tommy, Dickie? It's my lunch."

They both said no.

"Place like this with all the mink quiff running around and all the business they do and you can't get a piece spongecake. My mother—rest her soul, her *yur* is next month—she could make spongecake. From bones she'd make a feast, for soup a little greens, a marrow bone, a few matzo balls, a whole *pesach*. We were real poor people."

Tom carefully filled his pipe from a pouch of oiled silk.

"I gather, Dov, you agree to our plans?"

"Poor? My father was nothing. A *narr*—a fool, sickly. It was my mother carried us, six of us, to make something of ourselves. . . . Look, when I see the legal option papers, we got a thing going. I'm plain as rain, and I don't need lawyers. Oh, I got them, but a thing is a thing done with me when I personally handle it. So show me the option papers, I'll have the nine hundred thousand—all right, a million—for the old lady in sixty days."

Dick said, "Of course, Mr. Ganzler, this has to be kept very secret. A leak and who knows what can happen?"

"Look, family fights I don't like it. Trouble I don't make unless people they ask for it. The Pedlocks are salt of the earth. All right, so they did me a dirty thing in that store in St. Louie, blocked *my* store's view. That's business. We eat each other, eh, and God eats us. Boobie, you call *this* spongecake?"

"It's all we have sir. Kin I get yo' somethin' else, sir?"

"No. Here's five dollars, get yourself something to keep from getting a cold. . . . Such a nice young thing, eh, Dick? My daughter, Miriam, is just about her age. How can people send a girl out to do this with all these degenerates looking at her? You'll pardon me, Tom, Lawrence. I gotta go. We're introducing a new scotch, pale pale Highland Lass, and if I told you what some Madison Avenue publicity *momser* is charging to do it all wrong, you'd say Dov Ganzler he's throwing his money around. So I gotta go and shout a little. I always shout, even if I'm wrong. They all jump. And things get better right away. . . . Please, Tom, please. Young fella, you ever need a job, knock on my door. I gotta a lot of blond *shabbos goyim* from Yale, Stanford. For what? *Tzum vishen dem tocus mit*." He was gone after shaking his head at the mink.

Dick wiped his face fully, carefully with a handkerchief.

Tom was puffing his pipe slowly. "He's a monster, isn't he?"

"No, I rather admire him, Tom. The window dressing of a genuine slob works. As he said, he just shouts and screams and everybody trembles. And why? Because he's a clever slob. You don't pile up a two-billion-dollar fortune, perhaps more, by just worrying over spongecake. Bobbie, the check."

"All taken care of, sir. The cute lil' old man, he never like his frens to be handed no bill when he comes in. Yo' all want mo' coffee?" They both shook their heads.

Tom said, "I'm jumpy. When the Bank tried to palm me off with only half of what I wanted, you came up with this. But you're sure Judith is willing?"

"Tom, believe me, you don't know how rock-hard and stubborn she is. She's got this bug to build this school in Israel for her husband and his friends. And if it means doing it this way, she said all right she'll do it. It isn't as if she's taking a loss—my God, you know what Ganzler will pay for all this?"

"It's not like Judith, and that worries me. The Store, the Bank—she always held them above everything."

"When you're old, I hear, all that matters is leaving something you feel will remind people of yourself. How do you think colleges get all those fancy donations from the big thieves?"

"You're really leaving Lazar-Wolf?"

"Yes. When Nancy and I get married, frankly, I want to be with a different kind of house."

"A Christian firm?" asked Tom softly. He despised his future son-in-law, yet he knew Dick was a comer, one of those who would do big, worthless things. As for sex outside the house, Nancy wouldn't have to worry on that account. He wanted position, not . . .

Dick leaned back on an elbow. "Hotchkiss and Westover, most likely. They've made me an offer—but don't let it slip out."

"A very good established house. Aren't they rather anti-Semitic?"

"They want to broaden their base. For bringing in a share of Dov Ganzler and a bit of your mother's holdings they'd give me the key to the uncircumcised washroom. They have become very tolerant."

"You promised Nancy you wouldn't operate on your nose."

"They want me, hook and all."

Tom watched the hostess, Mother Mink, waggle past. What

magnificent divided buttocks. She seated a party and turned. Tom gave her the expected eye. She gave him the answer. He was rarely wrong in reading a glance as a signal, an interest. But Rita's clothes were in his town flat. He looked at Dick. No, one didn't borrow a future son-in-law's place for something like this. Mother Mink walked slowly past—on tiptoes, in her high-heeled shoes. . . .

It was Founder's Day at Pedlock & Sons on Fifth Avenue. The annual event rocked the fashionable city street. It had been heralded for a week on radio and television, sent out in a fifty-page flier to half a million addresses. *Der Tag*, Nathan Pedlock called it in his memos to heads of departments. For a month the Store had been putting the screws on buying offices, jobbers, manufacturers, importers for special deals. Ships had unloaded bales, boxes, goods from strange ports. All-night store crews had worked in the deep subcellars and in the Pedlock warehouses in Queens, in Hoboken, up in Connecticut, unloading, stripping, unpacking, ticketing, numbering and stacking. The Store was like a city preparing for siege. Fatigue and terror existed.

An extra task force of two hundred salespeople was on the ready. There was a first-aid station on each floor, and Brinks had sent extra private police. Pictures of known shoplifters and sex degenerates who mingled in crowds were handed to every section manager. Lists of counterfeit bills, numbers and defects were also issued.

Tony Pedlock—as Tony Peters—reported to work at the Store at eight o'clock. It was his second month with Pedlock & Sons. His father had been amazed that Tony, on his return with the girl, Leah, from Poland, had asked to be put to work in the family business.

"Good Lord, Tony, it's the last thing I expected of you. You seemed predisposed to sports."

"Oh, it seems best, Dad, to get into the family work."

"You wouldn't want to be here in the galleries?"

"Art doesn't mean anything to me. Oh, Dad, I know all the big names. And it's fine on a wall, I suppose. But no, to me it's like playing with dolls. I want to be one of the Sons in the firm's name. Art is *too* fashionable these days."

"Did something happen in Poland?"

"It was dull, really."

"All right. I'll call Nathan. You don't have to start as a sweeper or packer, you know. But you do have to eat in the employees' cafeteria. Clean but tasteless food."

So here he was, Tony Peters, one of Mr. Mingler's crisp, neat young men in the stockroom of the shoe department. Mr. Mingler was a middle-aged man with mint breath, broken feet, a fresh flower in his lapel. Pacing up and down on Founder's Day as if commanding his old raiding party in World War II. "It's the big one of the year, Founder's Day, 1853. We want to go big this year in *shoes*. Twenty-four thousand, seven hundred and sixty-five dollars last year. We'll do better, much better. Groton, comb your hair. Hill, remember don't let them put the shoes back in the boxes, *you* do it. Palmer, always their left foot to try the shoes on. You all know the code sizes, so no matter what they ask for in sizes, just smile and fit the nearest you have. Everything is a bargain today. Oh, you, Peters, it's vital that at the packing counter every slip must check. So you be there." (He "knows," Tony thought.) "Well, in twelve minutes, war—ha, ha, the tribes break out of the reservation."

Nathan had been at the Store since just before dawn. The Negro and Latin crews were just finishing cleaning. The work lights were on. Special brass grills covered the lower half of the street windows. Several elderly women and a man with a whiskey bottle in a brown paper bag were already at the main entrances. Nathan spent the next two hours trotting up and down the stairs, inspecting shipping, phoning to warehouses. He saw to the rolls of paper and bags for packing, the serial numbers on the salespeople's order slips (so no ringer could fake charges or items; Exchanges and Complaints was closed on Founder's Day). He sniffed the coffee perking in the lower-floor cafeteria and had two big cups himself. He ran up to the roof garden to see if the stage lights were in order for the fashion show called for at noon with an unemployed but once famous TV comic as M.C.

At nine, the sales help was in place, comfortable shoes on. The Store's trucks could be heard underground in the deep garages under part of the building, bringing up reserve stocks. At nine-ten, the telephone line to the main offices failed, but there was an extra switch-in plug for just such an emergency.

Tom Pedlock came in through a freight elevator at nine-twenty-

two. He stood in the balcony of the book department (JOIN THE
PEDLOCK READERS' CLUB—ALL BEST SELLERS 40% OFF ON OUR DIVI-
DEND PLAN). "Bennett Cerf can go jump in the Plaza fountain,"
Nathan had said.

Tom, in the shadow of a fake columned portico, looked down on
the waiting counters, the salespeople, the special police. He could
hear the outside sounds of some of their men trying to control the
crowds, the tapping on the closed and locked doors on all three
sides. At nine-twenty-nine the public-address system rang out with
the first bars of some music—Mozart. (Tom, his churning stomach
at rest with a cup of coffee and two bourbons, had almost expected
"O Captain, My Captain.") Mabel had tried to kill him that
morning. He had spent the night at home in Scarsdale, having to
get some papers from the library safe, and Mabel had come into his
room at three in the morning with her father's West Point sword
(Major Carter Ormsbee, 1882-1934). It had been quite a session,
wrestling it from her, her stinking of brandy and not making much
sense. He had sat on her while the butler phoned Dr. Tebbel to
come and give her a shot in the arm. He hadn't been able to reach
Nancy. She had left school and gone to live in the Village.

The doors of the Store were open, and the mob came in from
three sides as if following Dante, he thought, to hell: east, north,
south. They were a strange array of people direct from the Bronx,
Brooklyn, the Jersey cities. Mostly middle-aged females, some
younger. All threw themselves at the counters, Tom thought, as
if on lovers, swarmed like bees or army ants up steps, moving stair-
ways, bunched before elevators like lynch mobs. Dust rose, the
smell of excited humanity. Tony Peters, busy in shoes, thought it
was the odor of women's urine.

Nathan was in the furniture department, where he had discovered a whole series of Swedish Moderns incorrectly priced; the con-
sumer would have overpaid by three dollars on each item. "All that
should happen," he told the department head, "is Gimbels should
hear of that."

Like strong-hocked mares, the women pushed forward. By noon
things were in turmoil. Two show windows had been smashed on
Fifth, brass grills or not. Six shoplifters had been caught, and one
had pulled a knife and wounded a Negro guard. Screaming women
in the menopause, wearing Birch Society buttons, had tried to dis-

tribute hate literature. Anti-Semitic booklets were found in the third-floor ladies room. Nathan said, "Is it worth it? The *tummel?*" He had some soup at noon.

Tom ate a sandwich as he stood behind a tower of Irving Wallace and Irving Stone in the book department, drinking a double martini that Rita Burton brought to him in a paper cup. She was feeling morning sickness and showed a bit in front—but not so you would notice it if you weren't looking. "I've got this damn TV crew up in the Gift Shop and then they go to the Fashion Show. It's bedlam up there. The models are afraid to undress. How are we running? Two furlongs under the mile?"

"Christ, Rita. Let's leave at four."

"You can, boss man. But the Store stays open till nine today. And we all go down with the sales slips."

She looked at Tom with love, hatred, admiration, scorn, lust, distaste. Maybe it was the strong gin, Tom thought. He gave her a quick pat and decided to be loyal, loving, honest, true-blue. He'd tear up the phone number of the hostess at the Mink Farm. He'd find Nancy and make her go back to college.

Tony Peters was a bit dizzy after bolting a Founder's Chicken Pot Pie Special, two slices of pie and a paper carton of vile coffee. The shoe department smelled of stale feet, bad breath, foot powder, processed leather. A little Irish woman was standing in front of Tony in her stockings, holding up a pair of new tennis shoes.

"Two left feet, two left feet the devil sold me, I'm tellin' you."

"I know, I know. We'll give you a certificate. No exchanges today."

"Shove yer certificate up yer arse, you young hellion. I've lost me own shoes in the crowd. I can't walk to Queens, now kin I, in two left shoes, kin I now?"

"It's a store rule on Founder's Day—*no* exchanges."

"You kin shove that founder, too, up the spout. Where's yer effin' slogan now? 'The Customer Always Comes First'? Or is that just a hur-house motto?"

Tony loved her; he handed her a pair of brown shoes. "Here, I'll pay for these myself."

"What trick is this now? I'm signin' nothin'."

"No signing." One had to bend a few irrevocable rules from time to time.

The counters were a mess. Crews were trying to bring order to torn frocks, mismated pairs, beltless dresses. Unstrung cultured pearls crunched underfoot like snails in a garden. A fire was discovered in the fifth-floor Religious Objects section, but a thoughtful floorwalker had it stamped out in a moment under the calm eyes of Mary and St. Francis. That section was called the *shlock* floor, for it contained departments that were failures or in the process of being reorganized, so it was not as packed as the rest of the store. No panic resulted, but Nathan could scarcely catch his breath at the close call.

The M.C. who was to do the roof-garden show had been smoking pot all morning. The fashion show was a great success, but a Paris original by Orloni was stolen—someone had put it on and left a soiled pair of red Capri pants and a loose yellow sweater in exchange.

The mob seemed to thaw into purely sensory enjoyment.

The afternoon did not calm down, and there was soon an ugly roar on the ground floor when an Italian woman was called a nigger by a woman tugging at the other end of a girdle they both claimed in the Chic Spot. It passed. A society woman from Rye was arrested with a bagful of lace stockings, a carton of Tampons and a pair of marble bookends. She insisted she had bought them at Lord and Taylor and that her husband was a friend of Nelson Rockefeller and that she would sue Pedlock & Sons for one million dollars. Her husband was found at the Princeton Club and went bail.

Tom deserted his post at four-thirty and crossed to the Whalers' Bar on Madison Avenue. Nathan couldn't eat any dinner. He left the tray of tepid food on his desk and swallowed two pills and drank half a glass of soda water. He was having difficulty breathing. The plumbing had failed on two floors. Tony Peters just sank into empty boxes in the stockroom and took a nap. Mr. Minton, aware of Tony's absence, felt, What if he had, he was one of the Pedlocks making it the easy way. Floor clerk to vice-president in six easy months. (Boy, if I only had him in my old army outfit for two weeks. *Zowie!*)

In Sports, a salesman, a former member of the Bavarian Alpenkorps, wearing an Alpine hat, had a nervous breakdown.

At six-thirty, the store doors closed for an hour. The customers were encouraged to leave. Most did, but several diehards hid in the rest rooms or refused to leave the lunchrooms. Observing the bundle-carrying customers, Nathan remembered Jacob saying: "We all wear Gogol's overcoat."

A crew moved in to sweep up, replace counter goods, bring order to stock and racks, refresh the shelves, issue new sales books. The accounting department was rushing figures to Nathan like runners in a battle. They were $83,000 behind last year's Founder's Day figures until an error was found in an IBM machine ("So they're not human after all!") and it was only $5,098 behind last year. Nathan asked for a recount and began to feel his pulse. It seemed very fast and he was aware of every breath he took. The tendons of his ankles felt overtight and very painful.

The Store reopened at seven-thirty-six, six minutes late, and again it was thronged. The regular help was trying to keep up, smile, but the extra help was goofing off, not giving a damn about it. Time and a half or no time and a half, thirty off cost or no thirty off cost on what they bought for themselves. They had had it. Their feet dragged, their tongues were coated, their sales writing grew stranger. They made errors in adding, and checking their slips took a long time. Customers, no longer gay, snarled for service.

Publicity had announced for a week special door prizes (West Indies cruises, piano lessons for life, five-hundred-piece china family sets), and Rita Burton was lying on her office couch with a damp towel on her head. She had fainted suddenly, and her assistant had to attend to the drawing of the numbers for prizes; there was a suspicion the special sales tabs that were to contain the winning numbers were being counterfeited in the shipping department by some Store traitors. Rita tossed off the towel and phoned Tom's department, then his post, his office. She got through to him at last at the Whalers' Bar. He told her to come on over and forget the store. She decided she had better—pregnant, dizzy, unmarried, her dad due for a visit from St. Louis in a week, and Tom in a mean mood these days; she'd better try to hold on, hold on tight. She couldn't get into the packed elevators and made it at last in a freight car, wedged in between sweating packers trying to hold broken, rejected and torn items from smothering them all.

Rita got to the bar and sat in a booth decorated with fishnets and plastic coral—with Tom, drinking and holding hands. She was a stupid dame to get fouled up like this with a married man. He'd better get his difficulties settled before her dad got to town or she'd take a bottle of sleeping pills and *that* would certainly make a cute publicity mess for the Store. Tom said love was a hard thing to figure out, but there they were owning each other enough to make threats. He looked at his Swiss wrist watch that rang the quarter hour and donged the hour and said, "In twenty minutes Founder's Day will be over."

Tony was back from the stockroom, and a very fine-looking girl, with dark hair and black cotton stockings, was there by the lizard slippers. He knew her. Of course! Nancy with dyed hair. Cousin Nancy.

She was looking at her fingertips. "This is Weirdsville. I just came to buy a bargain. But they're all gone."

"Hello, Nancy."

"Tony, don't tell me you're working *here?*"

"Yes—sh-sh, it's a secret who I am."

"This will teach me never to come above Sheridan Square. And when I think of the subway back, oh my aching back! Dad cut off my allowance when I quit college."

"It's been a tough day all around. I live in the Village too. Come in my taxi, Nancy."

"I don't get it. Why this work? Shoes?"

"I'm doing a survey, Nancy, really, for the firm."

"Really?"

"How's Dick?"

Nancy wrinkled her nose. "Who cares?"

There was a hissing sound over the public-address system, then an Orwellian doomsday voice: "Pedlock & Sons thanks you for making its Founder's Day Famous Sale a bigger success than ever." There was a Bronx cheer in the glasswear department. "We have gone way over last year's total, and the savings to the public is . . ."

Tony Peters took the dark-haired girl's arm. "Come on, let's go."

In the big office with the old furniture from the old Store only a dim light was on. The intercom box glowed. A voice came from it. "Hello? Yes, Mr. Pedlock? Mr. Pedlock! Are you there? The latest figures, not final by any means, show we have gone over last year's figures by thirteen thousand, five hundred dollars and eighty cents. Mr. Pedlock? Is anything the matter, Mr. Pedlock?"

Nathan Pedlock lay on the floor, on the rich thick carpeting, where he had fallen out of his chair. His face was scarlet, his lips blue. He was breathing with a roaring, gasping sound. The girl from his outer office knocked, then came in and looked down in horror.

The store doctor, a young intern from Columbia Medical in the main-floor first-aid section, knew what do to. He gave Nathan a big jolt of Adrenalin and asked who the old man's regular doctor was. No one knew. Tom Pedlock couldn't be located. The doctor, taking no responsibility, sent for a city ambulance and felt the irregular pulse. He told everybody to get the hell out. He wasn't going to get caught with the death of this big shot on his hands if he could help it. He phoned Nathan's apartment, got some stuttering Swede to blurt a doctor's name: Bernard Zimmerman. The doctor's answering service was snotty. However, the name Pedlock helped, and service said they'd locate him.

Tom and Rita lay in the big bed in Tom's apartment, in each other's arms, feeling nothing, boozed, but having each other. Tony and Nancy were in a Village joint, the Tender Womby, listening to modern folk singers ("Rock Mother, Roll Father"), and Nancy was telling about the way-out novel she was planning to write— "Oh, way, beyond Salinger. He dates so."

Nathan lay on a white bed, and a strange doctor and his own Dr. Zimmerman looked down at him, and a great burning belt of pain ran across his chest, and they had a tube in his nose, and they were dripping something without mercy into his veins through another tube. He heard Dr. Zimmerman say, "So . . . from . . . you . . . under . . . yes, yes . . ." And the world whirled away and Nathan wondered if this was the end, the everything now here, all of it. . . .

From Marcel Pedlock's journal:

Jacob has been talking of his youth when he went from Poland to Russia as a student. ("Now at this time, while I struggled with my own problem, Russia was groaning and big with trouble.") Strikes were appearing in the factories of the big cities. Men spoke of new forms of government. Some few of the Czar's officials were blown into fragments by amateur students of chemicals; the trains to Siberia carried more passengers; literature thrived in the turmoil. ("All was not well with the Little Father of all the Russias, or the Russians. They had Jews to burn, as the saying was.")

A simple remedy that had always worked in the Slavic past to give the people a chance to blow off steam was unleashed. Orders were issued, the Czar nodded and agreed—a new series of pogroms against the Jews: street riots, village murders, the moving in of Cossack regiments, the encouragement of the ultra Pan-Russian groups like the Black Hundred. It was neat, simple, and always an exciting circus. ("Except, naturally, for us Jews. Still, 'God must have chosen them for something,' said the grand dukes, and to be the safety valve of the Holy Russian Empire was no small honor.")

The evil rumors began to reach to the village near Kiev where Jacob and his friends lived. Earnest young Jews came from St. Petersburg and Moscow with suitcases full of pistols and bombs to help organize a defense corps. If there were to be slaughter and pogroms in the village, the young Jews with their suitcases wanted the Jews of the village to fight back. They had many villages to visit, many defense corps to set up. So they turned over the suitcases to Jacob and left him to organize the Jews of his village against the pogrom. Bribes to officials in Moscow had revealed that the village was to be the site of a bloody pogrom, and very soon.

Jacob went to his Socialist friends; they were young and loud and active. But they looked at him and shook their heads. "This is no way to bring the Socialist message home to the Russian workers. We are their brothers, even to the Cossacks; we can't fight against them. We have plans for a great republic of all Russians, workers and peasants. Tolstoy's saints."

"You mean you'll not fight the Cossacks—the Black Hundred— when they come with a pogrom?"

"Don't talk nonsense, Jakov. We don't fight our fellow Russian people."

So Jacob went to see the "South Africans," those who were planning a republic of Jews in the Dark Continent.

"Leave us alone, Jakov," they said, "with your talk of Russian troops and killings. We are leaving here in a year or so. We don't care what goes on in Russia. We shall found a Jewish homeland in a new place. This is no longer our problem."

"But suppose they kill you first?"

"There is always talk of pogroms here. We have been lucky so far."

"Only so far."

Jacob went to the inn where the anarchists hung out. But they laughed at him. "What do we care about a few Cossacks to kill? We're planning a big thing. A big bombing of an important man close to the Czar. All the world shall hear of us. This is a blow they will never forget."

"But you're Jews. What about what happens in this village?"

"You're no intellectual. You're kosher calf meat."

They threw Jacob out into the mud outside their clubroom.

He went at last to the rabbis, who sat drinking tea with lumps of sugar between their teeth, and they listened to him. The holy *rebbe* ben-Russel stood up and pulled on his beard and took snuff from a battered silver case. He filled both nostrils and sneezed.

"We Jews are not fighters. We are students and scholars. They that live by the sword shall perish by the sword. We love our Czar. We are his children, even if he is hard on us."

Jacob shouted, "You fools! You will die like dogs. And *why* aren't Jews fighters? They always were! I throw in your teeth Bar Kokba in the mountain gorges slaughtering the Romans! Maccabeus the Hammer fighting on the plains of Eretz Yisroel, Gideon's war trumpets shattering the nights! We are a great people of warriors who have stopped fighting!"

Reb ben-Russel sucked tea from his tall glass over the lump of sugar held in his teeth. "You are no longer one of us Jews. You are a police spy working, I'm sure, against us, and waiting to turn us in. We say nothing against our beloved Czar. We don't fight."

So Jacob went down to the river and sat a long time watching the water carrier fill his barrels. He went home and buried the bag of pistols and bombs in the cellar of his house, and it was then he began to read seriously about the Hasidim. ("I met my first demons, I talked to spirits, I crossed borders few men had seen; otherwise I was *aleyn*—alone.")

He prayed and prepared himself for the judging ordeal of Czar and Cossack. Who shall die and who shall not? Who shall be poorer or richer? Nothing could change now. Sobbing and tired at the end of the penitential days, the population of the village all went down the muddy streets to the river, and there they prayed under the gray sky that their sins might be cast into the waters . . . and that they would be swept away to the sea. ("This ceremony I *never* forgot—a now timid Jeremiah.")

The awful sense of doom sat on them, hung like black wings around them all. Jacob forgot the happy holidays. Now everything was sacred and awful. In the house where he lived a white candle burned all night. The woman there waved a live, shrill fowl over her head and said a prayer that in atonement for their iniquities all the evil would leave them and go into the living fowl. Services began at dawn. The old men appeared in their grave clothes; they beat their breasts and confessed and swayed. No one ate. The big fast was on them. The *schul* filled with the odor of the people lamenting and praying, their breath fouled by hunger. They sank down and mourned their past. They smelled strong scents to keep from passing out. At dusk they went home, tired, weak, cleaned of sin. What could be done?

They ate the last of the white *chollah* and the cold fish on the table. They prayed once more and ate. Doom had been averted for another day. ("We lived each other's death and died each other's lives.")

And as Jacob read, alone, of the Hasidic lore, probed the cabala, the sacred numbers, the pogroms began to be heard from. The news of slaughter crept down from Moscow and up from the Polish border. The Jews of the villages gathered in their *schuls* and lamented and groaned, and collected enough money to buy in Kiev a great silver clock with golden hands. They put this clock in a red velvet bag. Reb ben-Russel and the wisest and longest beards of the village (Jacob refused to join in) went to see the governor of the district and gave him the clock, and when he asked for ten thousand rubles more, they sold their horses and their silverwear and their teapots and mortgaged their future to a moneylender, a one-eyed Greek. ("And there was no pogrom in the village because of the clock with the golden hands.")

There was slaughter ten miles away in a village on the canal. They murdered a few children at the grain farms along the river. The Cossacks raped the pregnant women of the hamlet where they wove woolen cloth. They cut open the women's bellies, and then the old men were forced to dig their own graves and were cut apart by sabers. But the village of Jacob was spared.

The pogroms failed in their major purpose: Russia was moving toward the great unrests and revolts, and even a war with the Japanese could not turn the Russian peasants from their troubles. It is interesting to record that in 1938 I saw the silver clock with the golden hands in a Bond Street art gallery in London, where it was misleadingly listed as: "Presented to the Czar by the grateful Jews of the village of Lemkapoff on his visit in 1914 to inspect the damage done by a windstorm."

("So, go, believe in history, Marcel; all we knew was that we did our dying as we went along—we knew you can't start a lawsuit against life. . . .")

CHAPTER 25

꒰ Leah Ellenbogan was happy—a little too happy, a bit too gay.
She had all the new clothes she wanted. She was permitted to go
ice skating at a fashionable uptown rink. She said she was seventeen, not fifteen, when anyone asked her to have a drink or go for a
ride. She didn't take to discipline or to Judith, and her father
would shake his head, stroke his little beard, and point a finger at
her and speak a fast Polish Yiddish. "Grateful no, polite no. Is this
the way you repay *Shana* for giving you a home? Is this the way a
father is thanked for bringing you out of misery and into a future?"

"I *shank* you such a future. *There* I was a star, got applause, took
bows. Here I'm a schoolgirl."

"What's wrong with being a schoolgirl? In my youth girls had no
schooling, in my youth—"

"These *shtunks*—they don't understand an *artiste.*" Leah was inspecting a pair of leotards and chuka boots.

"You need a *potch* to rock your teeth."

"Look, *tattala*—little father—don't begin again about the hard
Russian winter, the pogroms, the scholars in the lousy *schuls*. It
gives me a pain in the *tocus*. You're not that pious, that honest—I
know you Hasidic loafers."

Her father made the gesture of offering her a blow, changed his
mind, and went quickly out of the pink bedroom Leah occupied at
Pedlock House. He went down the stairs past armor (from what
crusade?), family portraits. He glared at Judith's first husband, ignored her grandfather, and set himself down in the library, the

resonance of his anger still strong. Hardly a Hebrew book in sight, he noticed, among the two thousand red- and green-bound books, mostly in sets. He spun an old globe of the world. (Watch the world spin; so we all spin while we come to the truth with which at the end of our lives we hang ourselves.) Did he have to bring the girl here? Did she have to be a shrew, a witch, like her mother? Jacob sighed. To be even a bad father is a task. He had seen Dachau, Belsen, and nearly been sent to Buchenwald, but there, in his catatonic state of acceptance of all things, the blows never penetrated too far. Yet an ungrateful child (sharper than a serpent's tooth) could ruffle the philosophical calm with which he tried to live most of his life.

Judith came in, sailing like a full-rigged ship, dressed for the mild spring weather, pulling on gray gloves. She seemed bigger than ever. "You're ready, Jacob?"

"For what?"

"We're going to visit Nathan. I told you."

"Ah, Nathan. Yes, poor man on his mattress grave."

"It's not that bad. He's making a fine recovery. It's the first day he can have visitors. It's been a bad few weeks."

"He's the best of your sons."

"He isn't my son, only a stepson. You keep forgetting. But I agree. He has something mine lack. I think frankly, Jacob, I dominated the early years of mine too much. What's good for the character of a woman is bad if a man gets too much of it. Our genetic pool of inherited characteristics is all mixed up, going *way* back."

"Don't mumble me any science, *Shana*. If there's one thing worse than Dostoyevsky's nonstinking monk, it's the way modern Jews take the jargon of science like the pure word of God."

"*Mal à propos?* Explain it to me in the car. Your snip of a daughter behaving herself?"

"Leah is Leah."

"I've had to give her a few solid backhanded slaps this morning. She called Nora a—never mind. Where do they learn such things these days?"

"She learned in the ice circus to hear these things, to take blows. I'm thinking maybe I should send her back. She's a *chiya*—a wild animal, not a child."

"Nonsense. I'll tame her, educate her, marry her off. What do you think of my grandson Tony for her, eh? He has a gregarious pliancy."

"He doesn't like her. Didn't like her, he told me, from the first moment he saw her in Poland."

"So they don't like each other," laughed Judith. "With that one agreement between them a marriage has a chance."

"Spoken like a *rebbizen*—a female rabbi. So let's go see Nathan." He rebrushed his beard, flecked invisible crumbs from his jacket, and followed Judith down the hall. (*Moisha Rabainow*—acres of woman and *all* his.)

Spring on West End Avenue meant a little more light, a little more dust, a heavier thud of traffic, the glimpse of a loose-hung sky between two stumps of apartment houses, the sound of street jackhammers, the bang of riveters downtown expanding the city upward.

The sick man lay in his apartment on the rented hospital bed pushed to the window of the high-ceilinged room, a room of heavy, massive furniture of no special period, out of style by nearly thirty years. The nurse would be back soon to commit some indifferent indecency on him. But now, with the drugs working, the poached egg and toast digesting without heartburn, he could rest, wait. There was a story by Tolstoy he had read in his youth—about an Ivan Something-or-other, a man who has been important to himself and his society. He suddenly sickens and then slips with horror into dying, aware that all his material graces, honors, struggles were foolish and nonsense. And so, calmly, cut off, he dies.

Tolstoy was a fool, Nathan thought; a man does what he thinks is right, does the foolish little duties that make a world, a people, a family. If it's all nothing, then an aware nothing is what we are here for. And with this warm nothing a man spits in the eye of the universe. Notice me or not, destroy me, but I *know* I am here now; the universe knows of nothing.

So what is wrong in material things? If one knows they are hollow, mere décor, and one has a duty to them, no more *just* a duty . . . He moved a bit and felt his heart flutter. The mind is the real world—we only move in this one. Ha, the heart again. It is only poor plumbing. The true heightened sensitivities come to a man from the harmonious conceptions of memory—like now, when only the present is inadequate. Like an item at the Store, battered, broken, beaten down; it must be put on the bargain counter marked "as is." As is. An idiot could make a whole philosophy of life of it.

He grunted, wet his lips, swallowed, turned and sucked up some foul-tasting liquid through a glass straw. White sales, spring bargain week, garden month, basement price picnic—not his worry now.

He was aware of the abyss of nothingness he faced, but he had been duty's child all his life; the one who did what had to be done. He was not as bright as his father, nor cunning as his grandfather, nor a bold pioneer like his great-grandfather, the founder. He was just Nathan *here*, Nathan *there*. That said it all. The perfectability of man had escaped him. All his life had been for this end, to become, and die, the fullness of being the Store. He had not wanted much of women, gambling, trips around the world, art, or the insides of books. He had followed a path where nothing began and nothing would end. The Store would go on. He had never had the call young men have to set the world free, only to save it money and give it service.

But then, as Jacob Ellenbogan had once said, "As the years go, the risks cost less." The crowded years contract to thin images of no present value.

The nurse stuck her chinless birdhead in the doorway. He said, "Go away. I don't need the glass duck."

"We have company. The Ellenbogans are here to see us."

"What are you waiting for, Miss Fogel? Let them in."

Judith carried two bottles of wine, Jacob a basket of hothouse grapes not too well cleaned of their sawdust packing.

Judith kissed his cheek. "*Nu*, Nathan, you escaped chicken soup, the Jewish penicillin. It always has the taste of burned feathers to me. The wine will do more good. Sandeman Three Star and some Dom Perignon." She bent over the bed and kissed him again. "Get well."

Nathan tried to avoid the kiss smelling of sweet fennel and said softly, "No no, please, not again. I'm not a child."

"You look a bit thinner," said Jacob. "But better, much better. A woman in confinement couldn't have it better. Warm, clean, washed, combed."

Nathan gave a small laugh. He had been warned not to laugh

too hard. "I'd rather be up, but Dr. Zimmerman says not for another four weeks. Judith, something worries me."

"That's bad; no worries when on your back. Anyone will tell you that."

"Besides," said Jacob, nibbling on a grape, "what's a little heart strain? Today is like a bad cold. They could bring a *golem* to life with their tubes and pills. What they've learned of medicine since King David collected foreskins from the Philistines!"

"Judith, what worries me is something is going on and no one will tell me."

"What could be wrong but this happening to you? Don't try to participate by vicarious bystanding. You rest."

"The newspaper I read has stock-market pages missing. Something is happening to the Store, to the Bank. It's worse, Judith, not knowing."

Jacob took up a bunch of grapes, ate, spit pits.

Judith sat poker-faced, arms folded. "Your imagination. They don't want you to play the stock market, that's all. The Store was there before you, and the Bank, too. You have *mal du pays*."

"It will be there," added Jacob, "when you're . . . when we're all gone. The Psalm read, 'Because I was flesh, and a breath passeth away, and cometh not again.' "

"Thank you, Jacob. How's your daughter, Leah?"

Judith said, "A child. Headstrong, but nearly housebroken. You should hear her talk French, Hungarian. Jacob, don't eat grapes. It gives you wind."

Jacob wiped his fingers on the fruit basket, looked around the bedroom. "When I was in the last German concentration camp—no details, please—at the worst of it I began to keep myself sane by using a magic cabala formula for raising up a spirit, the undead, the unhuman of Prince Reubeni of Khaibir."

Nathan laughed again, softly, and sucked on his glass straw. "On West End Avenue a spirit wouldn't dare present himself. He'd never get past the Irish doorman."

"No, no. Don't laugh. The Germans were beating us to death with clubs. It was three days before the Americans broke into the camp. We hadn't eaten for a week. We were in dark underground cellars, little air, faint light. I drew a circle of water—the cellar leaked—on the floor, a circle of water six feet across, and I recited the words in the text of Baal-Shem-Tov in his extension of the

work Sefer Yetzira. He quotes Simeon ben-Halafta on spirit raising. You recite *Shekhina! shekhina! shekhina!* three times." Jacob
stood up and waved his arms. "Then I calculated *gematriot,* a
theory of cabalistic numbers. The year of my birth, the day of my
arrest, the Hebrew month of Shebat—tears and lamentations, the
number of my major sins." Jacob stood beside the bed swaying from
side to side, fingers out as if sowing something on the rug. "I drew
the mystic signs of God's ten emanations, the *Sefirot.* Then I did it
all over again and again. For two days, every half hour, while outside the Germans hung the last rabbis on piano wire. Two days."

"And?" asked Nathan.

"Really," said Judith.

"On the third day a spirit came to me. No, it wasn't hunger, fear,
darkness. No hallucination. As I said, a last *shekhina* and there was
a blast of light—"

A faroff rumble came through the partly opened windows. Nathan smiled. "They're blasting for the new under-the-river tunnel."

Jacob sat down and wiped his face. "I'll send you my text, and
when you're alone here, Nathan, in the night, you can test yourself.
But take it seriously. You may be one of the chosen. I have tried
since; I am now impure in some way—but you, perhaps."

"That's all he needs," said Judith. "A bed partner who's a spirit.
We'll go now, Nathan. Not too much excitement the first day.
When you get up I hope you're not going back to the Store right
away. Take a year, a year, even for a mature man like you, it's
sweeter, shorter than a youth's year."

Jacob said, "You can tell a spirit—the whites of the eyes are red;
it casts no shadow or mirror image—but the ears, *watch* the point
of the ear."

"What would you suggest I do," asked Nathan. "Go traveling
with Jacob's spirit as a companion?"

"Jacob is only entertaining you."

Judith hunched forward and placed a gloved hand on the shoulder of the prone man. "Believe me, Nathan, you haven't been permitted to breathe. Always for the family you're in the Store, for the
family doing the work no one else would do. Now play the game
inside out. Let them run things. Give your other side a birth.
That's what Jacob really means. A spirit, that's your other self.
Gamble at Monte, dance a bit, sit on hotel terraces, look at ruins,
enjoy sinful thoughts when the young girls pass on those fine long

legs—*mains froides, coeur chaud.* Pray in old *schuls* in far places.
Do something against your nature. Raise up Jacob's spirit—watch
the points of the ear."

"With my heart plumbing how far would I get?"

Judith kissed Nathan's cheek.

Jacob said, "How far do any of us get? Place one foot before the
other, repeat it, and after a while it's a journey."

"You're kind, Judith. You, too, Jacob."

Jacob smiled. "And you can visit us in Israel."

"Israel?"

Judith rubbed her gloved fingers together. "We're planning to
go by summer. Be well."

Judith took Jacob's arm and steered him from the room over
mixed goodbyes. Nathan lay very still. Ruins, girls' legs, wines,
gold coins, Monte Carlo? It must be fine to enjoy such easy-to-get
things. Or Israel. The trip, the two of them. Ah, the talk of a
school of Hasidic learning. That was what they were keeping from
him. Judith's holdings, the fights with the lawyers over legal papers
against taking her assets out of the country. He reached for the
buzzer. The nurse came in, led a full three inches, or so it seemed,
by her nose. "Miss Fogel, the glass duck, my pills. I have to get well
ahead of plans."

"We are more cheerful today, aren't we?"

"I didn't notice."

She pulled back the sheet and brought up the indecent glass
form. "We're going to have white chicken meat tonight and we're
going to sleep all night—and without a pill, aren't we?"

He wasn't listening. He made a calculation of probabilities. In
two weeks they'd let him ride a wheel chair. Another week on a
cane. Meanwhile he'd get some of his spies in from the Store. Yes,
he'd take a journey back into the life he had always led; *that* was
his girl legs, his wines, his red or black at Monte Carlo, his win or
lose. As for ruins, he chuckled, wasn't he a pretty fancy ruin—one
of Dr. Zimmerman's prize packages?

Miss Fogel smoothed the sheets. "We are now going to try and
take our teeny nap before dinner, aren't we?"

"Tell Dr. Zimmerman I changed my mind. I'd like to have a TV
set."

"No, he thinks that's too strong for us just yet. But maybe we
can have a radio."

"All right, a radio. And order the wheel chair."

Miss Fogel was carrying away the glass duck under a linen napkin. "We *are* feeling better."

Nathan closed his eyes. He saw Jacob in his German horror cellar. We are all prisoners, no matter where—at Buchenwald or on West End Avenue. We are *all* waiting to be taken out to be clubbed to death. And no one knows from which direction the clubbing will come. We can imagine we can raise up spirits. He felt, rather than heard, the boom of blasting and men digging under the river.

"*We* will have a teeny nap before dinner and eat *our* white breast of chicken like a good boy, shan't we?"

The Store, like a great zoo animal, lived on, not caring who fed it, combed it, cleaned it, saw to its needs.

Tony was promoted to display work, assisting in the dressing of the Fifth Avenue windows at the Store. At lunchtime he waited at the 59th Street entrance to the park, where spring was far enough advanced to send the green buds on the trees into leafing. The few remaining horse-and-carriage men with their battered top hats, red noses and stable smell were still where he remembered them from childhood. In those days, once a month, Dad would take him for a ride around the park, pat his lap, pull the robe over his knees as if he were protecting an investment in some lost fertility. He'd ask him was he "a good boy," and not wait for an answer, give him a dollar or a half-pound bar of chocolate—"Share it with your little friends"—and be free of him for a month. When he was older, he'd come in from prep school, Lawrenceville—"A grand school, isn't it?"—every other month and get a good lunch, a musical-comedy show, visit some museum, get new clothes, a fifty-dollar bill and a taxi to Penn Station. "Good seeing you, lad." How the hell did the old man think he could make up for it now? Anyway, Tony had other things on his mind besides a father who had suddenly discovered the loneliness of the aging process. Don't sit on *my* shoulders, old man.

Nancy Pedlock was just getting off an uptown bus. He waved and she waved back to him. When they met, face to face, they smiled at each other and held hands. She was letting her hair grow back to its blondness, had given up the black cotton Village stockings, and on slim, sheer, high-heeled nylon legs, she had less of the hip, beat, jet conformity.

Her first remark, she knew, was so banal.

"How come, Tony, you can get off?"

"I have to go to some studio to order some Japanese screens. Besides, I know all the big shots at the Store. Like your father."

"Tony, let's be serious. These meetings are awful."

"I know," he said, "I know. How about lunch? I don't have to be back."

"God yes, it's been slim rations since I left home. This family thing—what makes it so important?"

"Well, they just put a bronze plaque on the house where I was born. It reads, 'Con Edison.'"

She looked at him earnestly. All she said was, "I'm really hungry."

"Doesn't Dick feed you?"

They were crossing the street arm in arm, and Nancy frowned. Both had been avoiding Dick's name till today. "It's like this, he's very busy these days, and . . ."

"And what, Nance?"

She gave a jumpy laugh—half a sob. "He's kind of cut up about you—me seeing you."

"He knows we're first cousins." He kissed the back of her neck. "All in the family. Oh God, Nance, we're lousy to each other. Let's relax."

"I told Dick they're trying to work up some kind of romance between you and that Leah bitch."

"That! A firm no there. Come on, tell me, you really can't go for Dick, can you?"

"You make us sound like a lousy soap opera."

They both laughed and the tension began to ease. In the shadow of the Plaza, he put his arms around her, in front of everybody passing, and said, "For the first time I feel real, meeting you. So we're first cousins. That doesn't mean our kids will have three tails. That's tired-out folk legend. Besides, Jacob says he can cast spells."

"Tony, I've got the shakes. Look how I'm trembling."

"I'll shoot my week's salary on stuff Judith talks about. *Bisque de homard, crêpes beau meunier.*"

He took her arm, for the first time really as an owner, and they went to a splendid place for lunch.

Only the fact that he gave the Pedlock name got them into the Colony. They began with a solid Beefeater's gibson, and Tony was very earnest over whatever it was they ate; he never did remember. He felt in an expansive confessional mood.

"What I've been trying to do is deceitful, Nance—wean you away from Dick Lawrence. He's bright, much brighter than I am. He'll go places. But he'll break a wife's heart. His ego is unadulterated what's-in-it-for-me."

She said slowly, looking down at the table, "I fell out of love with Dick weeks ago. For me he's not fish, fowl or Jew. He wants to be an abstraction."

"Good Lord—is he that unsure of himself?"

"White Anglo-Saxon Protestant. It's so safe—and so false."

"He'll make it, too."

"How about some tacky fancy dessert? You know, lots of whipped cream. *Coupe à marrons?* You like fat women in bed?"

"Honey." He took her hand. "Don't build me up. I haven't been to bed with a lot of women. I'm pretty much a man with only a little experience. Don't expect an experienced stud."

"You're not a virgin. Christ, I wouldn't much care for that touch of character, Tony."

"No, I'm not." He felt himself growing red. "You're embarrassing me."

"Just one thing. I was had by my high-school music teacher. V*ery* unsatisfactory. And there's a summer thing. Under canvas up in the Berkshires; marvelous smelly fishing guide. It was all physical and a girl discovering herself. But it was not love. I had a bit of love for Dick, never beyond kissing. But the real, how do you say it, the whole *magila*, it's for you. Why Tony! I think you're shocked!"

"No, no, I'm not really shocked. Just, well, do we have to talk here?"

"Look, buster, I didn't say my name was Morningstar."

He laughed. "Our big problem is the family. This first-cousin thing is traditional or ritual or whatever the hell they call it."

"Tony, sweet, you're still shocked by my girlish experimenting. I don't want you to think I'm like my father. Tom has a kind of disease of the libido. He has to prove himself with everything available. Not me. With you I'll take, teeth gritted, the ranch-style shack in Westchester, the station wagon, a French poodle, four kids, members of the temple, pure P-TA, League of Women Voters. Give me a try."

"I better ask for a raise at the Store." The waiter refilled their coffee cups, and he felt a choking sensation and for a moment had a vision of a dark world, of a white face in a Polish prison.

CHAPTER 26

◆§ Judith had taken command. She had moved Nathan, his wheel chair, Miss Fogel, and medical bottles and pills to Pedlock House. She had given him the yellow bedroom in the river-facing tower, had installed a railway lift that ran along the main staircase so he could ride up or down at his ease. She had built ramps to the garden, the river path. The cook was ordered to bone up on invalid cooking and salt-free dishes. The cook, proclaiming degradation, protested. "*Yoi istenem*, Mrs. Pedlock, what good is food with no taste? What brings out taste? Salt, garlic, paprika. *Nem yoh, nem yoh.*"

Judith in her rose dressing gown trimmed with feathers just stood unblinking in front of the Hungarian cook, whose bulk almost matched hers. "Do as I say, Marta. And none of your damn inconsistency!"

"I do, I do. Willie, *teh bulund!* Where are my plucked chickens?"

Judith nodded, pleased at her grip on necessities. She went back to the hall, riffled through the mail and left it without much interest. Her friends were all long since dead. Their children and grandchildren were going to the devil in their own way in this jet age. The begging letters went to the Bank for answering. She didn't need sales catalogues. There wasn't anything she wanted, nor could keep for long. She doubted if she wanted to live past ninety-five. All right, ninety-six, ninety-eight; she wouldn't disagree with God if he slipped in an extra year or so, like a baker giving an extra bun. Time is a force operating on one in spite of oneself.

Leah was in the sunroom in flimsy blue pajamas, barefoot, painting her toenails a fire-engine red. "This red, Tanta Judith, *is* red."

"Don't do those things here, Leah. You have a room. Ladies don't scratch themselves in public, or make up. You have an extraordinary capacity for doing the wrong thing."

"I'm not a lady. I'm an ice-skating star."

"You are my stepdaughter."

Leah painted a big toe, staring as if into great interspatial depths. "You're much too old to have a daughter like me, Tanta Judith."

"You're not too old to get a good slap across the face. I'm adopting you. You're to call me Mama."

Leah carefully closed the little bottle of red liquid and waved her toes in the air to dry the polish. "I'm not going to. I have a real mama."

"She's dead. You're too full of guile. Now go get dressed. You're getting too old to run around in flimsy pajamas like that."

"Who sees? Willie? Ha, he's sleeping with the cook."

"Leah, watch your tongue."

Leah was gone, swishing up the stairs. Her slim girlishness had a kind of perverted impishness about it. It was piquant, reminiscent of other times. Lord, Lord, thought Judith, at my age to have a little bitch like that on my hands. And it hasn't made Jacob happy having the snip here, not at all. No matter how wise the man, a woman or a shadow of a girl can make a simpleton of him. Reason seems logically inaccessible between the sexes at times.

The sound of an electric motor came from the top of the stairs, and Nathan, in a bathrobe, seated in the elevator chair, descended like an actor playing a god in a Greek play. Miss Fogel, in her crisp nurse's white, paced him. She carried a folded blanket, a popular novel, a rubber pillow.

"Good morning, Mrs. Ellenbogan."

"Good morning, Miss Fogel. Morning, Nathan. You're looking healthy enough to chop wood."

"Our *first* day," said Miss Fogel, "out of our wheel chair."

"Morning, Judith." Nathan felt not at all happy, but the sun lamp and the garden sessions had given his hide a bit of glow. The forced feeding of seasonless pap had filled him out a bit. "Lazar-Wolf sent me a box of fine cigars. Doesn't he know I can't smoke?"

"He's got his mind on other things. Miss Fogel, go for a walk. Take my arm, Nathan."

"I'll manage, I'll manage."

They walked out to a side porch where the sun felt good on their faces. There was a light, Roquefoot-green spring sky, the usual chatter of lawn birds. The tea-colored river purred by, and Nathan sensed the undulation of all breathing things. They sat with the sun just to one side so it didn't shine directly into their eyes. Judith lit one of her little black cigars. "You don't mind me smoking, Nathan?"

"I don't mind. It's good and pungent after that sawdust breakfast."

"We have to keep you with us, Nathan, a long time. It's frightening when you get older and everybody familiar drops away. It's not just old friends. People you didn't like, even they are precious. If you can't work up a good spot of hate for somebody, life, it's like your food, without salt."

Nathan watched a tugboat push three barges filled with old brick and rubble upstream. Without taking his eyes off it he said, "Judith, I know what's going on."

"*How* could you?" She carefully shook off ash into her cupped palm. "I've been wasting my self-denial and penitence on you."

"I have my ways. There's the radio, stock reports, and let's just say I have ways. The back pages of the *Times* carry the story of the proxy fight over the Store with Dov Ganzler."

Judith flicked ashes into the air. "You can't find an ash tray around here even with six in help. Nathan, one thing I learned, never admit a mistake. But I had no idea Dov Ganzler was trying to take over Pedlock & Sons. I thought a little investment in us would be healthy."

"Dov would sell you his mother and deliver. He stands a good chance of taking over the Store, depleting our stock issues. This Dick Lazarus or Lawrence, he undermined us from inside the Bank. Got all our files and secrets from there. I tell you relatives are the worst things to have in a firm. Lazar-Wolf's own nephew doing this. Arranging a betrayal. Jacob is right. All earthly beauty is corrupt because of the abjuration of the devil."

"I felt, Nathan, what's wrong. The boy, he's engaged to my own son's daughter. And if you don't trust anyone, how can you get things done."

"You gave Ganzler the option to buy all your Store stock?"

"No, only forty thousand shares. Something didn't seem right, some dimension seemed wrong. I told Dick I'd think over optioning the rest."

Nathan sat fingering the blanket placed on his knees. "You're going ahead with this thing in Israel?"

"It's not a thing, it's a Hasidic school we plan, the best in the world. The only one of its scope for the teachings of Reb Israel Baal-Shem-Tov."

"Judith, you're a pagan, always were. You have as much use for the *schul,* the Gemara, the Midrash as a wooden post."

"So I'm a pagan. But I feel something, Nathan, something I didn't have before—the vanity of palpable society. Is the world made for pleasure, for doing what one wants if it hurts no one? Or do we owe someone something? Is there a mystery we can't ever understand? Do we have to balance the good with the bad, the things regretted with the things done without selfishness?"

"You don't believe a word of it."

"As we grow older, Nathan, we do grow full of cant. We begin to think: I've had my fun, I've done my deeds, now let me ask for a little grace, forgiveness. If there is something beyond this life, I've hedged my bets, if there isn't anything out there but hydrogen, what have I lost?"

"You're still a heathen. *You* wondering what is sin? No?"

Judith sat silently, threw the stub of her cigar into the still-bare rose garden. "You've found me out, you *momser.* The sense of sin, eh? Nathan, what would you know of it?"

"One observes others' pleasures."

"Pleasure, I always used to feel, is natural and should be like something beautiful one loves: a dress, a tree, a child, *pardon,* a man. But it addicts one to more pleasure, and the sense of sin—believe me—makes it more interesting. A feeling at the height that some stern punishment is waiting gives it a bit of bang. No wonder the English go in for whippings and get to need them, demand them. But this talk isn't for you. Neither are the stores now, believe me."

"Judith, I've got to get back to Pedlock & Sons. Lazar-Wolf can't fight this alone."

"Out of the question. Dr. Zimmerman says it would be suicide for you to go back to work. And my doctor agrees."

Nathan smiled. "Zimmerman's a better doctor than I gave him credit for. But he's too pontifical. He has to support two Rolls-Royces with Jewish patients. It's nervewracking."

Lazar-Wolf's house in Great Neck was a big colonial barn of fieldstone and ripsawed timbers placed under oak trees with the sound simpering below it, triangular sails skimming the slate-blue waters. It had been build in the twenties by a popular novelist who, as Saul told it, went first to Hollywood, then to drink and the dogs, and last to Forest Lawn. It was a monster of a house, half Mount Vernon and half Rhine River beer-baron castle. Lazar-Wolf had added red bricks, white columns. Green ivy beards climbed toward chimneys. He added a circle of bluestone drive and a lawn falling gently to the sound. Lazar-Wolf had modernized it year by year, put in oil heat and air conditioning, rewired it, cleaned the six fireplaces, moved in dubious antiques, modern reproductions of Americana, a model of his navy PT command, *and* his family's feather beds and brass candlesticks. He also placed the sacred little signs of a Jew's house, *mezuzahs*, little metal cases containing a scrap of parchment and a prayer, on the doorways.

Saul sat heavy with a cold in what was called his library. It was a pine-paneled room that contained a huge color television set, a stock board, shelves of bound *Wall Street Journals*, Dun and Brad-street reports, outdated *Who's Whos*, the model of his PT boat, his campaign ribbons and medals and Gertrude's collection of Tang Chinese figures. He himself had fallen in love with a series of ceramic Tang camels bearing on their backs red-bearded, hook-nosed riders: Chinese records of the first Jewish peddlers to push into the vast mysterious land of Cathay before Marco Polo. Saul Lazar-Wolf's family insisted that early Lazar-Wolfs had been among the red-bearded Jews who opened trade routes to China, dealt in amber, silk, paper, spices, erotically carved ivories.

Lazar-Wolf sat moody and low in his contour chair, blowing his nose, smoking a cigar that had lost its savor. Dusk was falling like pollen over the sound. The damned birds were bickering in the oaks as they ruffled feathers and prepared to kip down for the night. From elsewhere in the house came sounds of animation: Dinner being prepared in the kitchen by the help.

Gertrude was upstairs on her reclining board, her head lower than her feet, thinking blank thoughts. She was attending a new series of lectures on general semantics at the New School, and the blank mind, ass higher than nose, was a recommended combination for non-Aristotelian grace.

Mendes, her eldest, was away at M.I.T., dreaming of the moon. These days, who knows, he might get there. . . . Sharon, in her high-school cheerleader's sweater was necking with the young Mexican gardener in the potting shed and wondering if she should ask him to please remove his hands from her budding breasts. He looked so like Lennie Bernstein that she didn't, just sighed and shivered and felt her nipples respond. As the Sunday-school lesson said, "Value yourself above rubies." Nahum was in his room making a model of the clipper ship *Flying Cloud* (Boston to Canton and back, seventy-two days). Dave and Sheila were reading *Mars Monster Comics* in the closet under the stairs, which was their secret, private kingdom. They called it Kondoma. It smelled of old rubbers, raincoats and a dead mouse. They were nibbling on forbidden chocolate creams that undermined their gold-bound braces. Joanne was watching the cook's tiny Japanese television set in the pantry. The two shared an admiration for the deeds and wit of Yogi Bear.

The mood was broken by the ringing of the front doorbell, which, as the salesman had promised, donged out a bar of Debussy.

Ursula Canack, the surly, sour-faced German maid, put her head into the library door. "Herr Doktor Shindell."

"Send him in, send him in."

Dr. Shindell, in too youthful Ivy League tailoring, was thin, balding, middle-aged, with wet blue eyes, limp white handshake, slightly sour breath and the large nose of a man who suffered from allergies. Lazar-Wolf shook the white hand, pointed to a deep comfortable chair, closed the double doors, offered a cigar and sat down facing the doctor, peering into the bland unexpressive face.

"I've a cold, but I felt it's nothing to delay our meeting. You understand, Doctor, this is a visit I don't want to talk about. When Dr. Newberger said he thought highly of you—"

"Look, Mr. Lazar-Wolf, beyond my professional duties I don't pry. You are, I gather, seeking psychotherapy, the full three-year analysis perhaps?"

"Doctor, you let me talk."

"Overvocal reflexes. Perhaps a trauma set up by something that bops you? Say carried over from what we'll discover. You are, I'd guess, the anal type. But of course you'll have to come in for testing and then, *then* we'll go into a correlation of symptoms and syndromes. How long do your colds last?"

"Dr. Shindell, me personally I agree with Sam Goldwyn: Anybody who would go to you people for help should have his head examined."

"I don't understand, Mr. Lazar-Wolf. You phoned and said this was very very vital."

"Have a cigar, a brandy? All right. Here's what I want to talk about."

"You mind if I make notes? The consequence of error at this stage, it could bollix the whole *smeer*."

"I mind. It's about my mother-in-law. She's very old—well over eighty, we think. She's done strange things of late. We don't want to be crude about it, understand? Try the cigar, real Havana. My mother-in-law. It comes out that the family is really alarmed."

"You want to get her to a laughing farm? You see I like a patient who levels."

"Doctor, you don't sound like a real head shrinker to me. What kind of jazz talk is this? I'm frankly disappointed in you."

"Ha, you expected the little Vienna beard? The horse-*drek* about Freud, Adler, Jung? The Gestalt gimmick? Not Lennie Dory Shendell. If you came to me, you must have had high recommendation."

"Dr. Newberger had me read about your testifying in the Montross murder case."

"Yes, yes. A Dostoyevskian apocalypse, wasn't it?"

"The judge was impressed by your knowledge of legal medicine, states of what-was-it?"

"The temporal side of the unconscious; the secret, exquisite guilts of the id; the euphoric malevolences; the perverse demons that lurk in all us jigging cats."

Lazar-Wolf, wary, nodded, put out his cigar, blew his nose. He took some nose drops and gagged. He was baffled. A frustration, talking to this kook head shrinker. "Look, Doctor, it's not like an uncle of mine hiring an arsonist to set fire to his shop. I want the best man. If I didn't know Dr. Newberger so well . . . I don't know, frankly, about you."

"Say what you have to say, Mr. Lazar-Wolf, don't fight your doubt. It's a normal aspect of life."

"What are the chances of getting my mother-in-law certified as mentally incapable of handling her own affairs? Because, say, you find a real senile condition?"

"Crudely put, but I catch the melody. More than a question of mere idiosyncrasy. She controls the loot, is that it?"

"Please. You worry me. Still, the Montross case . . . She's the major stockholder in Pedlock & Sons and has a good bit of Lazar-Wolf and Pedlock Brothers too."

"Over eighty?"

"Just married, a man years younger than her. Talks of moving her assets out of the country, has been giving options of some of her holdings to a rival chain of department stores. Don't think it's just the money or the Store or the Bank. She may really need help."

"How does the rest of the family feel about this loss of center of gravity?"

"My wife, her daughter, I can handle. The other daughter and husband, they're out of the country, going around the world. The sons will go along. There's a stepson. He's our problem."

"Common desire to replace his father in his stepmother's bed. Normal. Hell, any high-school chick knows that set-up. I'll handle him."

"He's laid up with a coronary. The family law firm is with us."

"Us. That means you really want me to tee off?"

"I don't know. . . . What a heel this makes me appear."

Dr. Shindell patted Lazar-Wolf's knee. "Not at all. I see you have a war record. Led a free life, courted death. Very interesting. Now you think of yourself as a heel. Just delayed feedback from the war. Most men in my field would call that a guilt fixation, a fear syndrome resulting from overburdened family feeling. But I suspect alienation and isolation caused by your navy years. Tell me, in your dreams, any intimations of some strange desires?"

"I didn't ask for myself."

"What is a recurring dream you have? Just as an example. Level with me."

"Hmm. I sleep like a brick wall. But sometimes there is a dream.

I'm in a place, strange to me, but still familiar. I mean I know it, I don't know how I know it. I could draw a map of it."

"Good. Just relate it as you remember it."

"First let me take some more nose drops. . . ."

Upstairs on the pink bathroom floor, Gertrude had succeeded in making her mind a perfect blank. She snored slightly on the reclining board. In the potting shed the young Mexican gardener had failed to get into Sharon's pants. She had simply hit him over the head with a clay pot and giggled with tension and worried she had hurt him and so let Chico kiss her but kept her lips tight together. Nahum was setting the foremast and the mizzentop into his model of the clipper *Flying Cloud,* his tongue between his teeth with effort and his best jacket stained by the plastic glue used in model building. Sheila and Dave in the closet under the stairs were near the end of their *Mars Monster Comics* and were stabbing each other in the ribs with imaginary ray guns, both feeling a little sick from the chocolates. They would eat hardly any dinner. Joanne had left off looking at Yogi Bear on the cook's TV set and had wandered into the dining room, where the German maid, Ursula, was setting the table with a banging of silverware and tossing of napkins into place. Grumbling inside that she was working for these foul Jews when her own brother had been an S.S. commander. Her brother, now a judge in the Bonn government, had written her that the old spirit wasn't dead, the days of the long knives would come again.

" . . . So in the dream I'm trying to get home, get back here. Sometimes it's by train, sometimes it's by subway or old-style elevated, sometimes I thumb rides. I tell you, it's an obsessive thing."

"Time present or past?"

"I don't know. Everything is pretty vague. The odd thing is, nobody I meet will tell me where I am, men or women, or where the train or bus is going. I try to head in the right direction. But I'm never sure I'm on the right train, or headed for home. I always wake up before I know if I ever do get home."

"Let's outline the symbols you remember. A dream can only be explained by another dream, I say. The trains, the people who refuse to give you information. By the way, can you call all the articles of a woman's lingerie by their proper names?"

There was the bong of a Japanese gong struck by Ursula with an angry arm. "Dcotor, we've gotten off the tracks. So if I dream, I dream. You'll stay for dinner?"

"Can't. I'm lecturing tonight. 'Homosexual Images and Motivations in Modern Jewish-American Writers.' Don't worry about your mother-in-law. I've methods for these things. She'll be made happy and meet new faces. We'll have lunch and you can give me details."

He's crazier than his patients, Saul thought. "Take some cigars. You can't get them any more."

This is the third time he's offered me a phallic shape, the psychiatrist noted. "Thank you. We'll be in touch. Oh, if you'll write down your dream when you wake. Just a few notes for a countdown. The singularity of our being, believe me, is a gasser. Sorry I can't stay. Smells damn *geshmak*."

The Lazar-Wolfs began to gather for dinner: cream of leek soup, a white fish stewed in prunes and ginger, a good chuck roast with buckwheat groats, swimming in fat, sliced onions, a baked-potato pudding three inches thick with a very hard brown crust.

"Don't breathe over the children with your cold," said Gertrude.

CHAPTER 27

From Marcel Pedlock's journal:

I have not been able to sleep very well for some time, but of late it seems I lie awake all night repeating a haunting little phrase of a violin, and doing this writing, trying to relate observations to experience to keep me company. There is an incipient danger in night broodings. I have become addicted to this journal, for my days are no longer real to me, just a collection of symbols, the tasks of a spectator, faces that melt away. To begin with, my son, Tony, wants to marry Tom's daughter, Nancy. It appears a splendid idea, but the ritual of racial, tribal mumbo jumbo seems against it. It's not really forbidden, just hardened custom. They will marry anyway, I'm sure, but the talk of breeding three-legged children and idiots goes on. Tony is a petulant fellow; he'll do what he wants. I am courting him shamelessly.

The symbol of the stock market is replacing what was once something so solid in our lives—the Store, the Bank. Tom has gone over to the Ganzler interests; Lazar-Wolf has been betrayed by his nephew, Dickie, who has changed his name from what it was to what appeared to Dickie would help move him to what he would like to be, a fake *goy*. How the proxy fight over the Store will come out I don't know.

And Judith, too, has engendered special symbols—some ritual nonsense from a ghetto past of wild dancing rabbis in a Polish tale, of shouting fanatics who in Hasidic frenzy think they have founded a mystic new approach to the godhead. For this she, too, is ready, it would appear, to wreck the symbols that are the Store, the Bank, the Family (all capital letters).

Is it a temporary aberration of Judith's brought on by Jacob Ellenbogan, the *dybbuk*, the false messiah, or death himself, the Meseeach, the very breath of death? Or the Devil? I begin to think so more and more. Jacob is molecular, not human, and he is eternal; some punish-

286

ment sent to punish or destroy us, the Family. A flight of formless shadows, an indeterminate force.

I have been going with him into strange parts of the city, for he has begun to organize his *schuls*, his Hasidic followers in their colonies in Brooklyn, where in ear curls, beards, black alpaca coats they live like layers of pious survivors among dangerous Negro neighbors. I remember my first visit to a decaying synagogue in the Bensonhurst section. I stood by Jacob's side in prayer shawl, an unwilling actor, racial memory in my entrails.

"Oh Lord our God, forgive us for the sins we have committed . . ."

The eve of the Day of Atonement. The yellow candles burned with red centers, hunting for oxygen in the humanity-packed *schul*. I stood among men and boys in their white socks, bent, draped in their fringed shawls, shouting out prayer, punctuating their sins one by one in shrill calls as they enumerated them with a closed fist beating hard against their breast bones till I thought they would fall stunned to the broken wooden floor.

From behind the calico curtain that hid women came an echoing lamentation even more shrill; women did not sit with the men, Jacob said, as "in the pork-eating temples of the shaved Jews on Fifth Avenue or out on Long Island among the Volkswagens."

Jacob, sweat running down his beard, beat his chest; moored by stocking feet to the old board floor he leaned forward, then backward, as he joined in the prayer, swaying to the words, glancing at me to see my reactions.

"We have trespassed, we have been faithless, we have robbed . . ."

Under prayer shawl, under alpaca jacket, the people about me were sweaty in atonement. The air was strong with gasping breath from coated tongues and rasping throats, digesting spiced garlic-scented foods that proceded the fast. The candles wavered and seemed to expire like little dancing yellow spirits in front of my eyes.

"We have spoken basely, we have committed iniquity, we have wrought unrighteousness . . ."

The lean old man at my elbow lifted his head to the velvet-draped ark, and there came from his lungs and throat a great cry, deep-toned and agonized and out of an unrelated past.

"We have been presumptuous, we have done violence, we have forged lies, we have counseled evil, we have spoken falsely, we have scoffed, we have revolted, we have blasphemed . . ."

A man struck himself a blow fit to knock out a light-heavyweight. With each blow he seemed to break away some crust of the past, open a little more the passage to atonement, payment for a miracle, for what else? I didn't know.

"We have been rebellious, we have acted perversely, we have transgressed, we have persecuted, we have been stubborn, we have done wickedly . . ."

A young man with fluttering lips, a rash of beard, repeated, "Wickedly!" and fell, folding up, fell to the wooden boards, his limbs twitching, a spasm disfiguring his features, his skinny legs kicking out. Two black-bearded men picked up the fallen angel or sinner. I lost contact; was it Brooklyn beyond the dirty windows and the tattered drapes, a world of traffic and normal guile? Others fell, were lifted by the armpits and dragged away; the rest went on with the prayer as the stricken sinners were removed.

Jacob cried out in a voice from a mountaintop, "We have corrupted ourselves, we have committed abominations, we have gone astray and we have led astray . . ."

But the Pedlocks were not there to repent.

The droning prayer, rising, echoed as the hoarse voices overflowed the dark-brown *schul,* hunted escape among the ancient rafters. A cloud of snuff-colored dust, dislodged from the once solid rafters by the concussion of prayer, floated down on us. I felt abased, not exalted, not a miscrable sinner, yet I felt redeemable, so redeemable, as Jacob took up the call:

"O Lord our God, forgive us for the sin we have committed," he shouted, "in our hardening of the heart!"

I looked about for escape, for the heat was unbearable, the candle-wicks sputtered and stank like cheap frying oil. I ran from the place to the ritual refrain of *"Dayenu! Dayenu!"*

But I could not escape; I went again and again to the place with Jacob Ellenbogan as my sponsor.

"I am not a ritual Jew," I said.

"*Fahrblunged*—lost," said Jacob, grinning, pulling his little Satan's beard. "But a true *nashuma*—a soul. Come, come."

The synagogue where the *chalutzim* danced the Hora—given to the Ashkenazic ritual—was not a fashionable *schul.* It was housed in a decaying lopsided little building on the fringe of the Negro section of Bensonhurst, a middle-class slum. Jacob told me the synagogue had been founded in the late nineteenth century by a Hasidic sect, Russian, Polish, Austrian refugees fleeing death, starvation, rape, torture, pogroms; fleeing nobles hunting them down like foxes; escaping recruiting sergeants of the Czar or Emperor, foul tax collectors, the anti-Semitic bishops and cardinals, talk of Jewish ritual murders of Christian children for blood needed to make matzos. Such a *goyische* Europe, the Jews said, a black plague on it. The *schul* had not prospered, but had not closed either. The men remained tailors, sweepers, sweet-potato hot-corn peddlers, cobblers, some *schnorrers*—all students of Talmud and torahs, the Shomronim growing old and more outlandish.

"In the present century of progress, tolerance, Marcel, there have been more refugees. These later exiles disliked the Negro-Jewish ghetto, the semi-slum synagogue. When the German Jews arrived with their precise pride, high-assed snobbery, the last refugees had come. The men shaved clean as a *maydela*—little girl—and with a nose for manners, hope, a new world. Some were *idyutts*, not lovable, but Jews of sorts. They soon moved into the better parts of town, West End, Riverside Drive, Park, appointing their own rabbis imported from Berlin for the holiday of Tisha Ba-Ab in their new Temple; they did not care for the word 'synagogue.' The whole *magila*: a basketball court, swimming pool, modern-art *tzatzkes*—gimmicks. The deserters of this *schul* soon merged into middle-class American life; some grew rich, important, intermarried with the *goyim* families, worshiped material things—Yankees.

"Yet it was to this old *schul* I came, carrying a *yurzeit* glass to light in memory of my father. Judith's temple, modern as a supermarket or a jet plane, had not ever impressed me as having any religious significance. It remained a status symbol where the Pedlocks and their friends came not for a Kaddish—the prayer for the dead—but to be seen, Marcel, in furs and jewels for a Bar Mitzvah, Channukah, Yom Kippur, Rosh Hashana. Reb Simon-bar-Yohai would have called it *trief*."

I could not escape Jacob Ellenbogan.

The *yurzeit* glass with its wax and wick (gift-wrapped by Pedlock & Sons High Holiday section) was under my arm. The old warped *schul* doors of a blistered brown were open; the interior was dark and throbbing; fluttering orange-cored candles burned before the open ark, which held the two torahs in their gold-red covers. The old men and boys paid no heed to me as I slipped in. A bearded figure on the platform was reading from the Midrash, the exegetical literature, with a quavering singsong, strong and fervent. Jacob unfolded our prayer shawls, adjusted my black silk cap. I felt I was a debased minor Faust in the grip of this bright-eyed little Mephistopheles.

"To show you all the arts which I possess I'll give what no mortal yet has seen . . ."

I stood among the radical followers of the Hasidic cult of Rabbi Israel Baal-Shem-Tov of the Ukraine. A man gestured, shook his fist, raised his voice, and in the end spit in disgust and walked away, twirling his prayer shawl over his shoulder. "You see, Marcel, any fool can talk, but to think, that's something they avoid. The true cabala is hidden here, Marcel, not in your temples. The *misnagdim*, they think only of modern décor."

It was comforting in the drone of the sacred reading, the shuffle of old slippered feet. I relaxed, head bent, muttered, in the midst of a smell of dry rot, moldy drapes, faded reds, the glint of copper and the silver of the branched candlestick, fat with drippings. Jacob, now on the platform, was reading from the scroll; he stopped from time to time to take snuff up his nostrils from a pinch on the back of his hand, and voices whispered, "*Eretz Yisroel*."

As a man came in he touched on the doorway the little tin *mezuzah*, the narrow metal object nailed up on a slant. It contained, Jacob had said, a scrap of parchment with twenty-two lines of text, a talisman against evil. The newcomer eyed me as if I were out of place.

Voices were calling the third benediction, Kedushshah—holiness of the name—and the whole congregation was giving the responses. Jacob joined in, getting, as he told me later, just the right wailing note, that proper falsetto resonance into his voice. He was swaying back and forth, lowering his head at each forward sway, repeating and calling out clearly. He was part of this drama, this place, the joy of these poor, hard-working mystics. He beat his heart with a closed fist (as called for) and shouted out: "*Shema!*" in the confession of the faith. "Hear, O Israel. The Lord our God is One!" ("The decisive moment is always ahead, still to be endured.")

Suddenly I realized the old men and the young boys were all looking at me. An old man with protruding eyes said in a soft Yiddish so like my old governess long ago, "Why did you come here?"

"It's my father's *yurzeit,* Mordechai Pedlock. I have a lamp."

One of the little boys with long ritual curls growing alongside his ears came near me. I was beardless, yet fully adult.

"Will you do it for me?" I asked.

The old man smiled. "You light it. For this you don't have to be a *rebbe.* You do it."

Jacob led me to the place before the ark where the two torahs rested. Other memorial lamps were burning there. I lit my glass lamp from a candle in a brass holder and set it in place. I could hear them muttering the prayer for the dead behind me. I wanted to say something—just what? The men and boys were back at their reciting, swaying in prayer. I went toward the open doors and put down some bills among the tattered prayerbooks.

I remembered how Jacob had explained to me the wonders of the cabala—the received. "They got God by renouncing the world's snares, the mere traps of the senses. We, too, must, like them, substitute intuition for reason, spirit for flesh. The hidden for the visible, the unknown for the known. Only so, only so, Marcel, can we make a bridge between this place of tears and God. You believe it can happen to you?"

"I don't know."

Back in the 57th Street galleries, among well-dressed, fine-smelling people buying nonsense painted on canvas, little games of lines drawn on paper (how right for the Old Testament to deny the use of images), I felt better, more myself, less drugged. What had the *other* Mephistopheles said: "Gray, my friend, are all theories. And green the golden tree of life."

I have had dinner with Tony and Nancy, and when they left I did not cheer up. I have been living on Benzadrine and sleeping pills too long. I have been writing this in bed, and at this late hour, as Nancy would say, am bugged for sleep, confused by barbiturates. I know Jacob Ellenbogan is an unliving spirit who has come to destroy the Pedlocks. Can one with bell, book and candle remove a *dybbuk?* Will a bullet kill him? Does it have to be a silver bullet? I am frightened of the fearful little man, his dancing movements, his bright burning eyes. I shall dream of him. But will I proceed? A silver bullet and a crying out of *Dayenu, Dayenu?*

Tony and Nancy were not eating dinner. They were at his place in bed together, making wedding plans. It had shocked Tony the way it had come about. Nancy had appeared at the door of his pad with a brown paper bag of food and bottles. She stood there smiling, legs far apart.

"Post time. I've got bourbon, gin, corned beef. We're getting a bit looped, then I'm going to see if I like being married to you, the *whole* works."

"Listen—"

"Listen my foot. Who shot me when I was a child? Who put a trauma on me with a twenty-two Remington. How can I be cured except by being taken to bed, undressed, made love to in leisurely detail by my lover, by the man standing with his open mouth there who is going to be my husband?"

He saw she was not as calm or as flip as she was trying to appear, and his heart went out to her (or was that too poetic a picture?). They had two big martinis, badly mixed, but tasty anyway, and she stood against him, head on his chest, saying nothing. Slowly, all thumbs, he unbuttoned her dress, unzipped something when she pushed a flank against him. She said softly: "The most wonderful thing should be unbuttoning the shirt of the man you love." And she did. He knelt and put his arms around her hips and slipped off and pulled off the rest of her clothing.

She said: "I have a desire for children." She stood naked, looking like a painting to him. Her body was so fine and young, the breasts not too large, the watermelon-pink nipples aroused.

"Be gentle with me, Tony. I'll see you become what you can become. Oh Tony, you need someone to make you to do what you can do. You're so honest and so simple sometimes."

He was all over her, like a starfish opening an oyster. She was kissing his mouth, eyes, nose, throat, biting at his sterile breast buttons, running her hand down beyond his flat hard stomach, encouraging him with a sweet sound.

When she could breathe easy again she said, "Now you've shot me again."

BOOK VIII

SUSANNA AND
THE ELDERS

CHAPTER 28

⚜ Every weekday morning Nathan Pedlock, attended by Miss Fogel, came down from Norton-on-Hudson in a shiny black Lincoln. Judith had offered to take her old Hispano-Suiza off the blocks in the old coach house and have Willie put it in working order, but Nathan had refused. He would arrive at ten-thirty every morning, go to his office, work till twelve-thirty. He would have a dismal, tasteless, saltless lunch, lie down for an hour, Miss Fogel taking his pulse, temperature (by mouth), and telling him, "We're not taking it as easy as Dr. Zimmerman would like. We're *not* going to shout this afternoon at anyone, are we?"

"Who ever shouts? *Me!*"

He usually got rid of her by giving her discount shopping rights to some bargain in the Store, or sending her out on an invented errand. At three-thirty Miss Fogel would announce crisply into the intercom on Nathan's desk that no more calls were to come in. "Mr. Pedlock is leaving for the day. He is *not* to be called at Pedlock House."

Nathan submitted, for he knew a bad report would cause Dr. Zimmerman to insist on a sanitarium, and there was so much to do. Not just the final Spring White Sales and Easter Closeouts, the coming Vacation Specials, the Summer Picnic Sports Shows, the long planning for the Fall Fashions Festival, the College Shops expansion, the Thanksgiving Parade. And the *big* one, Christmas, when the entire inventory, showcase space, selling areas, publicity and windows had to be rebuilt from the subbasements up. Famous was the annual Joy of the Season Concert, and Circus Day in the parks, a Pedlock special that outranked the Macy's parades. Then, also, came the Big Three Scholarships for worthy boys and girls, awards from the Pedlock Foundation. Headaches would be the dealings for new union contracts with the teamsters', window dressers', tailors' and garment workers' locals, electrical and maintenance unions, the threat of a strike by the mailing and shipping departments. An increase in graft was expected by the fire, police, health, structure-inspection and zoning boys, who came up from downtown and said, "The Pedlocks were always white Jews, and the boys around City Hall have to have a little more this year—everything." Said Manosha Rooney, the Tammany bagman, to Nathan, "Ke-rist, it's going sky-high. The boodle now has to be split so many ways, Mr. Pedlock, The departments are going dishonest —playing footsie with numbers rackets, dope, hookers, syndicate boys, bookies. The clean stuff, honest boodle, doesn't suffice no more, know what I mean? Thank you, Mr. Pedlock. You need anything, just yell for ol' Manosha Rooney."

The big-city graft no longer annoyed Nathan. The greed of the political fat cats or the various public licensing and inspection services—no store, hotel, restaurant, loft or business could exist without laying it out, and there was always the greedy union shop steward or organizer who did not mind if his kid got a Pedlock piano, or the family suddenly had a new color television set. The excuse was: "It's human nature."

But these were normal problems for the Store, traditional almost, when it came to doing business or living in New York City. The biggest cloud, the major conflict over Nathan's head was the coming battle with Ganzler Fairs Department Stores. Nathan and Lazar-Wolf had mounted a counterattack, were fomenting trouble inside Ganzler's own empire of paper, steel, soft drinks, food processing. They were buying stocks, alerting that little group of troublemakers among stockholders who were the bloodhounds at all meetings of corporations and holding companies, questioning Dov Ganzler's overdone expense accounts, unethical bonuses, his sons-in-law in fat lazy jobs, certain preferred stocks held by the family, the Ganzler Crafts and Artists Foundation that wasn't really a foundation, just a hidden hive of untaxed assets. How it would all end, Nathan didn't know. When he left the Store at three-thirty-five, he had pains in his chest, a bit of high-powered pill dissolving under his tongue, a drugged night ahead. He thought, Tomorrow and tomorrow and tomorrow, what *then?*

As his car left the underground garage he saw Tony coming along, carrying a flat package. He tapped on the car window glass and had Willie stop the car, despite Miss Fogel's frown.

"Tony."

"Uncle Nat. How are you?"

"How is an old Jew? Surviving. How's Marcel?"

"Dad hasn't been sleeping well. I think this proxy fight has him worried."

"It should. Worrying isn't enough."

"Now, Mr. P., we mustn't talk business after hours, must we?"

"Oh shut up, Miss Fogel. Look, Tony, tell your father to call me. Things are coming to a head. You have a sales slip for that package?"

Tony grinned. "Yes, Uncle Nat. Just some stereo recordings I bought at my regular store employees' discount. Want to see the slip?"

"No, no. So when's the wedding?"

"When I get my two weeks off. We're going hiking down in the Blue Ridge country, the Great Smokies, with packs and camp gear."

"Gypsies, eh? Well, with *mazel.* What would you like for a wedding present?"

There was a honking of auto horns behind them, blaring up the traffic tunnel leading underground.

"We talked too much today, Mr. P. I shall call doctor and report you shouted at us."

Nathan winked at Tony and waved to Willie to drive on.

Tony watched the car move off, blue exhaust mixing with the various fumes of the polluted city street. He had a new Coltrane arrangement under his arm, also some pioneer Bird sides. Nancy was down at the pad cooking dinner. He'd run some old skiing film on the eight-millimeter projector and they'd finish the bottle of Beefeater's and . . . Poor Uncle Nat—old, sick, worried-looking. Tony hoped he'd never get like that, old, sick and worried-looking.

Sin, Judith dreamed, is not a condition, but a personal act, consciously transgressing God's law. But did sin exist? Or God?

There were times now when Judith felt her years, but there were other moments when God did exist—when she became ignited by the visions of what she would do for Jacob, what could be done with a Hasidic school in Israel. Nora let her sleep later than usual. She brought the tray of black coffee, the rye toast, the two coddled eggs up late. She ran the bath but not as hot as herself used to like it. Herself was slowing up, or burning herself out with the family matters. It was hard to tell. Herself had lived life and enjoyed it more, and had no sense of harm in the process. Nora laid out the morning robe, long, form-fitting, with a bit of train, and compared its shape in her mind with the browning pictures in the big velvet-covered album downstairs among the Biedermeier and Louis Seize: pictures of a younger, thinner herself with bright dark eyes and the grace of hips and the breasts on her that were an open invitation to a man. Nora crossed herself piously. In Catholic countries a wife was a closed package—nonexchangeable, you might say—but the Jews, now, were beyond the grip of the Holy Trinity. Herself could outstare any hairy Hebrew god who dared question her for her past. "Oh, macushla, it's better than the bland sincerity, *that* Protestant sin."

"Nora, Nora! Irish!"

"Coming, coming, I've only two hands and heads."

"No head at all. Has Mr. Ellenbogan gone out?"

"Oh, early, and Miss Leah now—bad cess to her, she sassed me—she's gone to the ice-skating palace. Mr. Nathan has gone to the Store, and a bit shaky in the pins, I put it."

"You're better than a newspaper, Nora. I'll just rest a bit more and perhaps have lunch in my sitting room. Some Malossol caviar on crackers."

"Dr. Newberger, he says a plain soup and toast and a dish of stewed fruits."

"If he says that, let *him* eat it. Put on the record."

Nora knew what record, which one. She put it on the player and left. The rasping faroff voice of Richard Tauber struggled through the worn grooves of the recording, singing *"Dein ist mein ganzem Herz."* Judith closed her eyes. More and more she was drifting between reality and fantasy, and it frightened her how she would often, if aroused, suddenly have difficulty in separating the two. The music brought on memories of Madame Sacher's Viennese bentwood chairs, the scent of Dimitrinos cigarettes, the lobbies of Shepherd's, the Meurice, Claridge's, candlelight Mozart, a man undressing, some royal events in Paris with the wedding march from *Lohengrin*.

She slept, or was in a trance, as Nora often feared, mouth open, breathing strongly, powerful heart pounding, strong lungs inhaling. Only the mind was puzzled why things went so quickly—the years when she knew Colette, the writer, and fought her father for the right to live as she wanted. "All women feel guilty, my Judith," Colette had said to her, "for not being born sons." And everything was past, past, past, nonobjective and reticent to the point of evasiveness.

"Madam, the doctor is here."

Medallion of goose pâté . . . *soufflé de grenade à l'orientale* . . . Judith opened her eyes, angry, confused, *very* hungry, to find Nora and Dr. Newberger looking down at her, the new doctor behind them, eyes like the cats in the Goya painting.

"Ah, Mrs. Ellenbogan, taking forty winks? Good."

"What, Doctor? You dare come into a lady's sitting room!" She smiled, he was so handsome a young devil. "I'm fine today, none of your damn monkey tricks."

"Of course not. Oh, I was on my way to the hospital in Dr. Shindell's car and he wanted to see you again. Dr. Shindell, Mrs. Ellenbogan."

"Yes, yes, I remember—you think I've lost my memory?" Judith looked up at Dr. Shindell. A loose, casual view of women, she decided, a beady eye, a sensual mouth, a turf of beard, Freudian or beatnik. "Vienna, ha?"

"That's true. Also Rome, London. The whole *magila*."

"A Freudian? Touched by Jung?"

"You're so on the nose, Mrs. Ellenbogan."

"I can smell the lint off your couches. Psychoanalysis is still only a lousy theory, isn't it?"

Dr. Shindell admitted it was with a smile, a gesture of spreading his hands apart, palms up. "You've read Mr. Big well."

"My only reading these days is Escoffier's *Guide Culinaire*. I have fantasies. I smell food I ate two, three generations ago."

Dr. Shindell seemed pleased. He pulled up a Louis Seize chair. "Ah, madame, give it to me, all about it, in detail. We must share some dishes in common."

"A tureen of sorrel soup, the best sole with creamed lobster sauce. *J'ai un grand appétit.*"

"You actually can smell all this? You're putting me on."

"Of course I smell it. A soufflé Armagnac. *Merveilleux*. With a Bollinger '04, *extra* dry."

"Mind if I make a note of the year? I keep a few bottles, for laughs. . . . "

Dr. Newberger bit his lower lip with his upper teeth and said he'd leave them to talk of food. He'd go down and look at the pictures in the ballroom. Nora put a hassock under herself's feet and went to warn the cook that the usual prescribed lunch would not be acceptable—"Not when she's talking soufflés."

"Some silent people," said Judith, "converse through their organs. A lot we possess is so precious and incommunicable."

The doctor agreed and made a few more notes.

"Would you mind turning on the gramophone, Dr. Shindell? They call it a record player these days. I miss the big buttercup horn of the old Victrolas. Did I tell you I knew the Kaufmans, who gave fine dinners? Sari was always trying to impress me with her love for a tenor in the Viennese operetta. One day she said to me, 'Judith, I must confess to someone. I'm having an affair.' And I said, 'Are you, dear? Who's the caterer?' She started that rumor that I had a very racy, vulgar streak."

"Wasn't that a strange answer to make, Mrs. Ellenbogan? You knew she meant something else."

"It served her right."

"You confused the logic of her remark."

"Doctor, you lack a sense of humor. Perhaps you should have stayed in Europe. Like plants, some men suffer in having their roots disturbed by transplanting."

"I never thought of it just like that. Do you have many ideas like this?"

The disc spun and a ghost sang. *"Dein ist mein ganzem Herz."*

Leah Ellenbogan skated expertly across the wide glassy rink of the Uptown Swiss Ice Palace in her short skirt and professional skates, wearing a little yellow cap with Chinese letters, black tights, a cashmere sweater. She was a graceful sight as she spun into a figure eight, then twisted and, gaining power, did the backward glide, one leg up, a pose which she had used to end her act in Poland. There was scattered applause and she almost made the professional bow, kissing her fingertips and tossing them out toward the audience. She stopped herself just in time. Why waste it on these cement heads?

She skated to the edge of the rink, where booths were set up, and stopped before two seated skaters, a man and girl drinking hot chocolate.

Leah said, "You were sent to spy on me, weren't you?"

"Oh, nonsense," said Tony. "This is my cousin, Nancy. Nancy, this is Leah Ellenbogan."

"Hi, Leah."

"You've been following me. I know. Just because you brought me out of Poland doesn't mean you own me—or your old *yenta* of a grandmother."

Nancy laughed. "So this, Tony, is what you dragged out from behind the Iron Curtain?"

"And don't think there aren't times I don't regret it." Tony made a spanking gesture at the back of Leah's short skating skirt. "Nobody is following you. I just wanted to introduce Nancy to winter sports, that's all. Go get lost."

Leah made a pouting mouth. "You can tell Judith and Jacob I'm not meeting any men here. *Not* that I couldn't." She made a forward, backward, difficult step, stuck out her tongue and skated off.

Nancy watched her go. "She's got a big crush on you, Tony."

"Don't be silly. She's only a kid. Fifteen, sixteen. I'd rather be loved by a cobra."

"That's the age, fifteen, sixteen; I had a crush on some idiot who picked his blackheads and collected matchbooks."

"I once wrote a letter to Shirley Temple."

She took his hand. "It's going to be fine being married to you—"

"Thank you."

"You're so square."

Tony didn't appear annoyed. "Well, I realized that when I came back with the brat from Poland. I'm a Pedlock, I said. The true breeding tells, as in dogs, horses. Dull, devoted to Pedlock enterprises, trustworthy mostly, no fireworks."

"My dad isn't like that."

"Perhaps not Uncle Tom. But I'm a true throwback, like Uncle Nat. I tried to escape into skiing, international games, the pad in the Village, *and* in Poland . . . well . . . It's not for me. I want to be married, have kids, help run the Store, pass on something solid that isn't *avant-garde* art, or a wild sex life, boozing, snobbery. It sure sounds dull. But that's me."

Nancy leaned over and kissed his nose. "You're a stern, serious young man, Tony, and I love you. That's important. So you're not a swinging cat. But you know what you are?"

"Dull, I said it."

"You're comfort, shelter, honesty. You're safe. You're all I never had in the fancy poolhall in Scarsdale. I'll be the wild one. I'll swing from cloud nine. I'll drive you nuts, but I'll give you an exciting life in exchange."

"In exchange for what?"

"For honest love, for wanting me always, not a whim, a quickie, a fast shack-up. Christ, you don't know with what terror I've looked at life around me and felt: Where are the old corny virtues, where are the rinkydink traditions people once had?"

"You're a little mad," said Tony, grinning. "You've got what Grandma has: a thumb at your nose. The old gal has had quite a life, so I hear. But we both lack something she and her times had. She had a floor under her feet. It's no longer there for us."

"Oh dear."

"I'll bat you right in the ear if you look bored. Just listen. We're all living on jello, the entire world. Only Jacob Ellenbogan seems fully aware of it. So if we can give each other a little courage, a little comfort . . . Oh, nuts, I'll teach you to ski this fall. You've got the legs and behind for stretch pants."

"Now hold me up and show me why I should go out on the nasty ice with you."

Arm in arm they rose and looked into the mass of skaters, some good, some bad, a few expert. Nancy started off, gingerly, holding Tony firmly to her.

In the powder room of the ice palace, Leah Ellenbogan sat watching a solidly built girl bat her false eyelashes into a mirror as she lit a cigarette. She had a long torso and slim legs with overdeveloped calves. "Imagine you knowing the Fondue skating act! In Rumania now, you say? Well, Maurice Fondue was grand, a fascinating hunk of man. He was getting on, and he couldn't get billing in England no more."

"You know, Wanda, soon as I saw you skate today, I said that's a real pro."

"Thank you, ducks. You're not so bad yourself. Thought you'd tear somethin' doin' that split, know what I mean?"

"You will put a word in for me with the Wonderland Ice Tour? I've been skating in shows since I was eight."

"How old are ya' now? No malarky—how old?"

"Nineteen. Honest. I work in the line, I do a specialty clown act as a cat. I have a solo to Chopin music."

"We use Rodgers and Hammerstein mostly. Very sweet, schmaltzy. And you've got no parents or nothing?"

"Just distant relatives, and they're tossing me out. I have to get into the Wonderland Ice Show. Wanda, I'll make it up to you. I'm smart. I get by."

"It means touring in the tank towns of Canada, ducks, and then overseas to Japan, Australia, Hong Kong, all them gooks and Ay-rabs. Bunking with six other girls, no laundry, starchy food. And pinchers—a black-and-blue arse."

"Anything to get back on skates and into the show world."

The long-torsoed girl inspected the back of her head in the three-way mirror. "Eager little thing, aren't you?"

CHAPTER 29

◆§ The sky was colored like Neapolitan glazing—a set of china he owned. We do our dying as we move along, thought Nathan. He picked up and read the report in the New York *Times* as Willie drove the Lincoln downtown in the smoky morning traffic toward Wall Street. Nathan liked the report. That ought to show Pedlock & Sons was working at being Pedlock & Sons, and at being in a better position in the coming proxy battle with Dov Ganzler, the *pupik*-picking *momser*.

PEDLOCK & SONS STORES TENDERS
OFFER ON PREFERRED

Pedlock & Sons Department Stores will offer to repurchase all of its outstanding 3.75% and 3.40% preferred stock, Nathan Pedlock, president, said Monday. The firm will offer $91.50 for the 3.75% series and $83 for the 3.40% series. There are 298,240 preferred shares outstanding. The bid prices this month were $87 for the $3.75 series (1955); $76 for the $3.40 series (1958).

Pedlock & Sons Department Stores has arranged for the private placement of a long-term note to provide the necessary funds, Pedlock said. The company believes the offer price will provide sufficient premium over current market prices to encourage substantial interest. Any accrued dividends would be added to the price.

The law offices of Addison, Foote and Kalish, with their modern glass, wall décor of collages of rags and copper strips, Swedish furniture and framed Daumier prints of shark-headed judges, did not impress Nathan. He preferred his own lawyer's dusty, paneled, Charles Dickens offices. To Nathan, lawyers were men in whose hands reason was oxidized away.

As senior partner, Peter Addison had the corner suite, below which the ships, the sea tramps and cruise liners, skidded past the Battery and headed for the Narrows, the Kill Van Kull, the breasting Atlantic surge. Nathan felt seasick, an asphyxiation, just thinking of it. He sat down, and Peter Addison pulled at his canary-yellow waistcoat with its chain bearing his Phi Beta Kappa key, Harvard ceramic piggie, family seal—"a gorged fish hawk," Marcel had reported, "on a field of jade-green spinach and the line *Fide, sed cui vide*, Trust but take care whom."

"Well, Nat, dear man, I'm pleased you're about again. Not over-doing it, I hope?"

"I'm doing it, Peter. Somebody has to."

There was a tap on the fumed golden-oak door. Lazar-Wolf came in, followed by Don Kalish carrying several brown cardboard folders under an arm. Don was wearing tweeds, smoking a long tan pipe. A bald, miserable-looking Jew he seems, Nathan thought, and yet he remains in this nest of fancy robber *goyim*, who are tax and estate specialists and do a brisk business in upper-income marital infidelity.

Lazar-Wolf shook Nathan's hand. "With *mazel*, you're up and about and in Wall Street. No, no thanks. I'm over a bad cold in the chest. We'll lunch at the Bank?"

"I don't know. How long will all *this* take?"

Addison leaned back in his chair behind the cleared glass-topped desk. "Let's get to it, then. We've put Hendler and Otis, the proxy poll-taking people, to work on the Ganzler thing, and their report shows . . . " He slid black-rimmed half glasses over his New England nose and opened a brown folder. "Hmm, yes. In a proxy stock fight, Pedlock & Sons should get twenty-four percent of the proxy votes turned in, Ganzler twenty-two, the rest undeclared and or undecided. With a top-notch hard-sell organization to work we can snap up five percent more proxies perhaps. Ganzler is spending a hundred and fifty thousand dollars in a proxy-winning campaign. We would recommend that Pedlock & Sons do the same."

Nathan poured himself a glass of water from the silver urn on the desk. "You recommend, Peter. Who pays? The Stores, or we Pedlocks?"

"I'll have Mr. Munster, our expert, go into it and see how you'll benefit most, tax-wise."

Don Kalish nodded. "Munster, Uncle Nat, he's the only man in town who can keep the Washington tax people from taking nearly everything. Works sixteen hours a day with a full staff. I'd advise, Uncle Nat, no matter under what conditions, Pedlock & Sons go after the extra proxy votes. You'll need them."

Lazar-Wolf sucked on a hollow tooth. He got up and went to the bank of windows and looked down at the shipping on the lead-colored tide. He thought of his first sight of America, of coming in on the reeking, rusting ship, the scribble of shoreline, the heave and toss of the Greek tramp ship, the smell of bile, vomit and worse. He remembered his first sight of that copper lady with the torch, and the way he felt. He did not turn around as he spoke. "Nat, there's one more way to bar this thing. Just hear me out— don't judge, just listen. A way to declare Judith's stock option to Ganzler void and prevent her optioning the other half of her holdings with him."

"If there is a way, Saul, I haven't thought of it." Subtle nuances he didn't expect from Lazar-Wolf.

Lazar-Wolf turned and came over and put his hands on Nathan's shoulder. "We shouldn't even bother you with details."

"Never leave out the details, I find, or you're holding the *pish-teppel* for some stranger. So?"

Addison looked away. Suddenly his fingernails needed attention.

"Judith is very old," Lazar-Wolf said. "And she's failing, Oh, not physically—*Gott sei dank*. But her memory, her ideas about *things*."

Nathan said nothing, he just sipped the tepid water. Let the bastard sweat, he thought. He's got the Bank—how do I know he doesn't want to swallow the Store?

Addison, his nails getting a passing mark, fingered his chain of status symbols. His voice was ironic, amused, precise. "Had an old aunt up in Boston, on Dorchester on the Charles. Lived to be a hundred and one—no, two. Bright as a new penny up to the very end. Yes. Shoveled her own walk in a snowstorm. Had the impression, however, she was Priscilla and the Negro furnace man was John Alden. Yes, fearful scandal. She left the darkie half her estate, Mary Baker Eddy the rest. Took years to break the will."

Nathan looked at Don Kalish, who looked away and chewed a

bit of skin off his right thumb with his irregular yellow teeth.

They *all* know—it's a show for my benefit, Nathan decided.

Lazar-Wolf pressed his fingers deeper into Nathan's shoulder. "The truth is it's for her own good. We must prevent her from doing what she's doing: harming the Store, the Bank, the Family."

Nathan closed his eyes, counted slowly to five, put two pills into his glass of water, watched them hiss and dissolve, then swallowed the mixture. "Stop *shtupping* around, Saul. What's going on?"

"We're preparing a medical report by prominent doctors recommending Judith Ellenbogan be declared incompetent to handle her own affairs. Don't look at me like that, Nat. It will not harm her. She'll remain what she is, honorary head of the family. Only we'll handle her affairs for her."

Look at them: a wolf, a fox, a pig. Nathan spoke a Yiddish word: *Rachmunes. Rachmunes.*"

"Uncle Nat, it's for—"

"Haven't you any feeling? No heart? You want to kill her with your dirty legal cruelties?"

"Nonsense," said Peter Addison. "Judith, knock wood, is solid as an oak tree. Bury us all. *Pereunt et imputantur.* Nathan, this is sort of a backfield play to be used only if we can't pass or cross the line, as it were, in four downs. Don't intend to use it if we don't have to."

The sonofabitch dog-molesting football player. Nathan pressed his breastbone with a blunt thumb. God should strike me dead— God forbid—right here before I'd let these bastards go ahead. "Doesn't this scheme have to have full family consent?"

Saul Lazar-Wolf waved in the direction of heaven or the thirty-fourth floor overhead. "Details, details, Nat. Gertrude and Naomi love their mother. Who doesn't love a mother? Tom too. Yet they've agreed *something* must be done."

"And Marcel?"

"He hasn't said no, hasn't said yes. Marcel he hasn't been well. Insomnia. And seeing Jacob Ellenbogan."

Nathan nodded. "*Fahrblunged*—lost, lost." He looked up and smiled. "But you don't need my signature. She's not my mother, my relative. I'm only a stepson, remember? I'm a markcd-down item, slightly cracked—what the French call *un sale youpin.* Yes, I used to go to Paris on buying trips."

"Nat, old boy, as a lawyer and friend, I know—if there's anyone closer to her than you, I don't know. Blood ties even aren't as strong."

"Uncle Nat, without you, why, the Store wouldn't be the same."

"Yes, the Store; glass and steel and modern shithouses and bargains on every floor, fashions nearly new before they're designed. Forty, fifty stores, I don't remember all. And every Pedlock & Sons full of things from a spool of green thread to a Picasso, eh? The Store. I'm sick of the Store, I'm sick of all of you. I'm, I'm . . . " *Don't die here at their feet. Walk away.*

"Nat, don't, your health."

"I'm sick of your big words, of lawyers, doctors, consultings. What kind of kockamaymee medical report are you preparing?"

"Now, Nat." Lazar-Wolf worried at Nathan's color. "Dr. Shindell, Dr. Newberger, they're big men in their field. They hold respect."

Nathan stood up and eyed each of them in turn. Addison smiled, amused at these Jews—so damn emotional. No New England starch in them. "Nat, old man, don't think we intend to use this. Last resort, as I said. Why not just rub it out of your mind? If we do proceed—most unlikely—you'll be told. Can I have a sherry poured for you?"

"An old lady's drink. Sherry. But not Judith's. She's, she's Judith." Nathan started for the door. "She's not my mother, mother-in-law, aunt. Cut her up, divide her among you. And please ring the parking lot for my car."

Nathan went out, slowly shaking off Don Kalish's hand. The door closed behind him. Lazar-Wolf's stomach gave a great rumble. Don Kalish polished his pipe bowl alongside his large thin nose. Peter Addison picked up a small gold-plated ruler, then threw it down on his desk. He showed his well-fitted dentures from between a surgeon's slit of ironic mouth.

"Gentlemen, we didn't do so well. Not even a field goal."

Lazar-Wolf hunted his cigar case. He remembered Dr. Shindell had told him to cut down—"It's only a desire to return to infancy, sucking the maternal tit." He closed and put away the leather case. "What *now?*"

Addison rocked back and forth in his desk chair. "You think he'll inform Judith of what's going on? I sense more than an attitude of querulous hostility."

"No," said Lazar-Wolf, "he'll just sit back and wait for us to tell her or inform her. What way is it done, Don?"

"She's served a paper to appear for a hearing. It can be done neatly, privately. Judge's chambers—all that."

"Uncle Nat will tell her to be on her guard."

"He's such a sick man—and this added to everything else. Peter, I'm worried."

Addison pressed a lever on the intercom. "Miss Munday, I'll be through here in time for that lunch with Jenkins Pomrey. Yes, Princeton Club. . . . Oh, Saul, this isn't a hint. Not near noon yet; time to mull on this. How shall we proceed?"

Saul knew it was the brush, the cold sonofacodfish. The true Pedlocks he treats with respect, but me, Saul Lazar-Wolf, I'm just out of the ghettos, still a sheeny to him. "We proceed on both fronts. Proxies and this other thing, if we have to. Did you hear Nat say the word *rachmunes?* That's Jew talk, Pete, means *pity*. My grandmother said it to Kolchak's Cossacks before they po-gromed her entire family—raped and murdered her six daughters. Well, a good lunch, Pete. Bye, Don . . . remember the word for pity—it's *rachmunes*."

From Marcel Pedlock's journal:

I'm slipping into a trance, like a rabbit under the eye of a cobra, incapable of any action. Jacob has me hypnotized. I am conscious of returning to a different world. Have I or have I not been through a traumatic religious experience? I have not, or have I eaten as if of Leviathan in the halls of heaven? In the shabby little synagogue there I am different, and when Jacob's eye is on me I am—I am lost.

The practical art dealer during working hours fights off the mood. God had shown no sign, sent no demon to tempt or destroy me. After talking of Degas, Pollock, Pop art, in my father's library, I read, in translation by Moses Mendelssohn, the Pentateuch. I also found there volumes on the cabala, Maimonides' *Guide to the Perplexed* and Jehuda Halevi's text of Khuzari. My father had once given us Hebrew lessons with an old *malamud*. I knew the Hebrew letters, I read the old texts again, and they meant nothing to me. Then one morning, like Dr. J. awaking as Mr. Hyde, I awoke to find a prayer shawl, the unused phylacteries for morning prayer. It was a shaky experience, me winding the black straps around my arm, putting the little black square of sa-cred rite on the forehead.

Did I dream or did I really recite the texts, bowing and swaying? I am either mad or have made a startling discovery: When Jacob made the magic circle it was a *dybbuk* that entered him—the real Jacob no longer exists, only the *dybbuk* in his form. Help me if I am sane. Aid me if I'm mad.

Fridays I go with Jacob to the old *schul* to make up the *minyan*—the quorum for services. Once I even read from the platform a commentary on Ecclesiastes. Jacob discussed the Gemara, the old men offered snuff from their snuff boxes. I was, to my horror, to them one of themselves.

Jacob, is he really Ahasuerus, the Wandering Jew, come back as the spirit?

Jacob bought me a clock, Hebrew characters on the dial. I sat on a Sabbath eve in a poor cold-water flat while a wife blessed the candles in their brass candlesticks. Jacob ran his finger through his little beard and broke the *chollah*—the egg-varnished white braided Sabbath bread—into proper chunks. Would all this pass and would I change back to my former self if I destroyed this *dybbuk*? Was I already possessed by him? *Is it too late?*

Preparing Judith for bed, Tom Pedlock had once said, was like the ceremonies for the burial of an Egyptian queen. At ten, Nora turned off the large, outmoded television set in Judith's bedroom, standing in front of the screen like an unresolved irritation, facing her mistress.

"Now herself knows the doctors want her in bed asleep before midnight."

"You think the damn nonsense on the telly interests me? All that innocuous trash—it's just I don't want to lie down."

"A bath now would make you sleep better."

"I'm sleeping sound enough. Any of the old bath salts left?"

"The new ones are just as good."

"Everything is just as good when you're old. But nothing smells right, tastes right—you can't pin the past down like butterflies. Just as good, just as good. Ha!"

"Come along."

In the veined black-and-gold marble tub Judith floated like a great sea creature, her vast bulk at ease in the green-tinted water pool old Tobias had built to his own measurements. Only a side bracket on the wall in the shape of a sea satyr was lit. Judith remembered the wonderful body, the magnificent figure she had once been, and didn't care to overlight the bloated remains.

Bathing in pungent salts, bath oil, Italian castile soap, she felt marinated like a herring. She was pulled from the tub by Nora, toweled, sprayed, powdered, helped into the flimsy nightgown of another period, then seated before the mirrors. Nora, comb in

hand, was a hundred-stroke maid. The tired, dyed, stringy hair got
its one hundred pulls, Judith howling, "Damn you, Irish! Trying to
pull my damn head off! *Il faut souffrir pour être belle!*"

"Herself still has hair on her head. Mrs. Norton Weinberg,
Mrs. Plotkin Bright, *they* wear wigs."

"They never had hair, even when young. Nora, dear, when I die
you're to have the gold-and-ivory toilet set Baron Franscani sent us
from Rome."

"Herself mustn't talk that way. It was Giorgio Chiabrera sent it.
The baron only sent us his bills."

"I've made a new will. The set for you is in there. And ten thousand a year for you. Stop sniveling, you stupid girl. One must be
ready to accept defeat in the end—rules of the game."

Nora sniffed and made two braids of Judith's hair under her
skilled fingers. "It's not something I like to think of, passing on."

"Dying, *not* passing on. Look, even kings and popes die and
stink like the rest of us. What will you do? Become a nun?"

"No, my thoughts aren't that pure. There's a little pub on
O'Connor Street in Dublin, an old uncle has it now. He's getting
feeble on his feet. The O'Casey House. I'll be pulling up ale and
stout there, and help send two nephews through the priesthood
and a niece into the Sisters of the Sacred Heart of the order of St.
Nestora of Blessed Memory. It's little enough I can do to salve my
sinful soul."

"You're a fool, Nora. You'd be better off to go to the Riviera
and get yourself a small hotel and maybe some strong French handyman and have a little fun. You were always a girl for a bit of slap
and tickle."

Judith settled in bed and looked about her. The two pillows under
her were laid just right. The plug was in the electric blanket in case
she got cold during the night. The tray with the glass of warm
milk, which she began to sip as she examined the chicken sandwiches under glass (on rye bread, crust left on as she liked it), the
thermos of fruit juice, the ash tray and a box of her little black
cigars in case she couldn't sleep and woke up for a smoke and to
empty her bladder. The volume of poems by Alfred de Musset
were at her elbow. So were *La Prisonnière* and *Albertine disparue*
and *The Jews of Cochin* by David Mandelbaum.

"This milk tastes rotten."

"It's skimmed milk. Dr. Newberger ordered it."

"Ha!" Judith opened a drawer in the night table and took out a bottle of brandy and added a good jolt of it to the milk.

"I need it. The nights are full of terror. Poor Marcel, he too has bad dreams. Lower the lights. Turn the radio on low."

"It's clocked to go off in half an hour. It's set on the all-night classical music station."

"Good night, Nora dear."

"Good night, sleep well. God protect you with His grace."

Nora leaned over and kissed Judith's cheek and Judith kissed the maid's and pressed her arm. They understood each other as friends, as women, both aging. They glanced at each other, expressionless, aware they were old, aware they were lonely women full of secrets, knowing it had all happened too quickly, too quickly, this wearisome mortality. The radio purred through some Debussy, the small bulb burned in a little lamp with a crazy shade. There was a sense of exquisite response, almost too poignant to face.

Nora went out into the hall and crossed to Jacob's room and knocked softly. "Herself is ready to go to sleep, sir."

There was a mumbling throat-clearing sound and Jacob came to the door of his room. Silver-rimmed glasses on his nose, a book in hand, finger keeping his place, his bathrobe open, exposing his old-fashioned European underwear, pipestem legs ending in too large red slippers. He looked tiny, ludicrous, grotesque.

"*Nu vu den*, Irish."

Nora, who could gabble a Celtic-flavored Yiddish, sniffed and went away to her own room down the hall, connected with a buzzer to herself's bedside.

Jacob scratched his remaining disordered hair, put down the book and knocked on Judith's door. He liked the funky, perfumy smell of the place, the low light, the sight of the woman in the bed. She had lit her last little black cigar of the day. Smoke, like a temple offering, rose in lazy ribbons from her nostrils. He approached the bed and bent down to kiss her chin. She pressed his hand.

"*Sluff gezunt*—sleep in health, *Shana*."

"*Sluff gezunt*, Jacob. You have a good day?"

"A fine day." He sat down on a little chair by her bedside, not letting go her hand. "And your day?"

"*Götterdämmerung* it wasn't. The banal leading the banal."

"I've had a marvelous idea. You know every year we Hasidic followers perform the ceremony of tashlik."

"With the cocktail lemon and the palm leaf?"

"No, no, that's *another* holiday. This is when we go to a stream and empty our pockets of everything into running water. Empty out our sins, our doubts, fears."

"Where will you find a stream in Brooklyn, Jacob? *Il s'en faut de beaucoup.*"

He patted her mottled, still firm and steady hand. "You'll see. I want you to come and join in."

"Of course, Jacob. That will please you?"

She put out her little cigar in the silver ash tray. They exchanged face kisses again; it had become part of their good-night ritual. He waited till she put her head down to the pillows, wriggled her body, sighed from a suffocating pressure, turned to beat the pillows into submission with a heavy fist, sighed again and muttered something too low to catch. Jacob put out the single light in the room. A faint sliver of a glow remained from the inch of bathroom door left agape. Judith tried out a small snore. She was not yet asleep, but these little sounds helped, as she said, to cork off.

CHAPTER 30

⟨⟨ Dov Ganzler, a bundle of coarse, strong tensions, tissues and fluids, was a man who liked to do things for himself. When he had a big project "on the fire," as he would say to his vice-presidents, sons-in-law, company lawyers—those schmucks—he liked to "finalize" it himself. His Bentley pulled up before the building of Lazar-Wolf and Pedlock Brothers, the car radio playing a muted version of Mahler's Second Symphony, the Resurrection. He had no feeling for good music. He usually hummed the "Anniversary Song" from the movie *The Jolson Story* when happy, but he liked to have "high-class" sound in the car when he was alone. The chauffeur opened the car door for him and Dov Ganzler told him to use the bank's parking lot. A stranger would mistake his expression for one of imponderable sternness.

Dov Ganzler didn't care for the old-fashioned look of the bank's interior, but it had quality and tradition, and he was trying to get some of that himself now, curb his own lack of restraint. The board room, the one called the Golden Oak, on the fourth floor, was where Lazar-Wolf had suggested the meeting. Well, he liked to swallow organizations, not build from the ground up.

Ganzler didn't think much of the room: no size, none of the modern-art crap that made a man feel he was buying the present, that gave the place, well, a feeling you could afford to piss away your money. Just crumby paintings of old Elijah, old Tobias, old Mordechai. As a *glitz*—low Jew on the Cultural totem pole—there was something baneful for him in once German Jews.

Lazar-Wolf, a Polack, a *litvak*, one of the lesser breeds, was looking very dapper in a well-cut suit, an almost naval jacket. Peter Addison was in dark serge with his French honors, a thin sliver of red, in place on his lapel. Dov Ganzler's own lawyer, Sam Krinzmodel, was also there.

"Right on time, Mr. Ganzler," Krinzmodel said, as everyone shook hands with a superficial, Hemingwayesque he-male pressure.

"Where's Nathan?"

Lazar-Wolf motioned to the big leather chairs. "Can't get away, but Peter is representing the stores. After all, Dov, this is just an off-the-cuff meeting. No elaborate etiquette."

"Sure, sure. Addison is a white *goy*." He laughed. "You don't mind, Mr. Lawyer."

"*Touché*, Mr. Ganzler."

Lazar-Wolf laid out his gold pencil, a leather pocket case of cigars. "So, can't this be better than public lamenting?"

"Now, Mr. Ganzler," said Addison, touching one side of his chin, "both the Pedlock Store and the Bank feel that a costly proxy fight would be foolish, from both sides."

"Don't worry about me. Cost is a soft mattress to me."

Krinzmodel said softly, "Mr. Ganzler, what Mr. Addison is trying to say is that we can't get anywheres here today, unless we—"

"Krinzmodel, I know what Addison is saying. But what he's saying isn't the point of this meeting. Keep your eyes open, Krinzmodel, and your mouth closed. *So?*"

"So," said Lazar-Wolf, "if that's the attitude, Dov, we might just as well shake hands and forget this meeting. How's your girl, Bernice?"

"Fine. And your son Mendes? M.I.T? A good school; no *hucmas* wins there."

"Gentlemen, gentlemen, a public fight would be of the utmost indelicacy, and a rather unfair incident to the communities of Jews across this nation. If I sound corny, forgive me. How else express it?"

Dov Ganzler sat back and looked over the paintings on the wall. "You should have the paintings cleaned and revarnished, Saul. Otherwise the steam heat, the air conditioning, will crack them and ruin the colors."

"Van Gogh they're not, Dov."

Peter Addison didn't show he was upset. He was, of course.

Marcel had once said: "Addison has admiration and contempt for the Jews he serves. To him we have a strange tribal culture with its own habits and methods that he's never bothered fully to dislike, and our greed for life he envies." Addison rattled his watch chain; he was wearing his snuff-colored waistcoat.

"Mr. Ganzler, you base your desire to control Pedlock & Sons on an option you hold on some portions of the holdings of Judith Ellenbogan, with the hope of getting the rest of her holdings under another option."

"You add good, Mr. Addison."

"We have asked for this meeting as the family has begun legal and medical proceedings to have Mrs. Ellenbogan—because of her advanced age and certain pressure from exploiting interests in her own family, and *other* considerations—declared senile, incompetent to handle her affairs, retroactive to the time of her marriage, to before she signed any options with your interests."

Dov Ganzler smiled, tapped his hand on the table, whistled shrilly, reamed his right ear with a finger. "You see, Krinzmodel, what a good gentile lawyer can say with words." He turned to Addison. "He's my son-in-law, but needs a good couple years with a Christian firm."

"Mr. Ganzler," said Krinzmodel, ignoring the last remark, "we can take it to the highest court. Our first option is legally sound. We can demand the second option be put in force, and of course tie all this up in the courts for years."

"Please, Krinzmodel, you think they'd have me come here just to break the news of what they plan? No. Go on, Mr. Addison. Like the fella says on stage, I'm all ears."

"A team of well-known doctors, specialists, have agreed to certify her as being unaware of the reality of events around her, and we have started proceedings for all her contracts, holdings and assets to be frozen. They'll be held until a family group is court-appointed to handle her affairs fully. Now we have asked you here— really, Mr. Lazar-Wolf insisted we sit down with you; you're both on the board of Brandeis, the U.J.A. My own advice was not to inform you of anything we planned, but to have the deed—if I may call it that—fully accomplished. But Mr. Lazar-Wolf—" Addison shrugged politely and put the tips of his fingers together— "he has high regard for you, Mr. Ganzler, and your sense of fairness when, as he put it, the cards are down and it's eyeball to eyeball."

"Thank you, Saul; once a *landzman* always a *landzman*, eh? So just what do you want from me?"

"We'll buy your holdings, Dov, in Pedlock & Sons stock at the market price *plus* ten percent. End the whole thing to avoid something that isn't good, let's face it, for the Jews."

"And take over the Ellenbogan options?"

"Naturally," said Addison.

Dov Ganzler stood up, knocked on the table before him. "You think you're playing with little *boychicks*? Go ahead, lock up the fine old lady. Point to her, say in the streets, she's a *meshuggener*. A fine respect you have for her. For your own family. Elijah, Tobias, Mordechai, must be spinning in their graves. *Olva scholom.*"

Lazar-Wolf said, "Dov, we don't want a public thing of this. Some place along the line we should be able to work out *something.*"

Krinzmodel opened his mouth. Ganzler placed a finger on the fat lips of his son-in-law. "You'll say the wrong thing, I'm sure. A lawyer thinks from lawbooks and the fee. Saul, let me mull on it. I see your position. The full pound flesh I don't want. Still, I have you by—never mind. So I'll mull it. We'll be in touch. No hard feeling, Mr. Addison, I mean my crack about lawyers. Couldn't live without you these days between taxes, and Washington favors, eh?"

Addison laughed as he shook hands. "You're damn right you couldn't, none of you could. Anytime you'd care to lunch—the University Club—give me a call."

Lazar-Wolf walked Dov Ganzler and Krinzmodel to the elevators. Addison gave his image on the tabletop a corner of a smile and excused himself. Saul decided to have his after-lunch cigar before lunch, cursed his nephew, Dick Lazarus Lawrence, and felt sour toward his dear sister, Rifka, for bringing such a monster into the world. He sat smoking his cigar, looking at the reports of Dr. Shindell and Dr. Newberger. He flipped the pages, picking out a line here and there.

"We detect, at times, in her recounting of her meals decades ago in famous eating places around the world, a lessening of perception between reality and fancy, and a humbling of her ego by such statements as 'One is just a drop of human consciousness, even if St. Paul held women are of their nature without souls.'

"Gregarious and rhetorical at times, at others she is withdrawn, opaque to reality and events around her. . . . It is the studied opinion of both doctors that her fetish for a proper funeral plaque, the care of the gravesite, is more than just an old person's desire for proper burial; it is a senile frenzy of apprehension. . . . She is under the influence of her husband, a much younger man (beyond a clinical definition as yet). A report is attached (section B-3) on the curious stealth with which he has invaded her mind and sanity. The subject, not known for her religious beliefs, has become like a hypnotized creature full of metaphysical speculations. (Quotes from tape recordings are in B-4, which have no meaning in the normal sense of things.)

"There are long periods when the subject appears to be transported back to an earlier life. At such times the past and present merge for her and it is difficult for her to state the actual day, month, or year (tests in C-2: direct quotes). . . . A baneful influence is also projected over her mind and actions by her maid, Nora O'Donoghue O'Hara, who bullies her mistress, forces her to bathe and carry on the common decencies, and is the true dictator of the household. Miss O'Hara should be removed from the subject, whom she often cows into full hysterical submission, so that the subject releases herself in oaths and strong language. . . ."

And a lot of fancy words and strange languages that sounded obscene by their sound: ". . . the first signs of mental regression."

Everything all cocksyturvy, Saul thought. Nora dominating Judith; *that* would be the day! And as for Jacob, he never demanded anything, everything had to be forced on him. Lazar-Wolf sighed and coughed on his cigar smoke. So what is right, what is wrong? Does one save a family, the stores, admit one's own bit of greed? Or does one protect a fine old lady? There was a bitter taste in his mouth, and he didn't know if it was the lawyers, the doctors, the mean times ahead, his own consciousness, or the damn cigar. The age of the good cigar was over, like many other things. He had a moment of morbid self-absorption, then called Addison's office instructing him *not to file the proceedings against Judith Ellenbogan until they heard once more from Dov Ganzler.* If God wanted to, he could intervene in his own mysterious fashion; if not, not.

"Tony Peters," who had, his Store report noted, no outward eccentricities, had been promoted to the testing laboratories of Pedlock & Sons. The lab did little beyond claiming Testrue products, Pedlock's own, were better than brand-name items. It was a custom when a young Pedlock came into the firm for him to take a name like Peters, or Preston, or Patterson, and while the secret of his identity soon spread, it did serve as a kind of coy system of make-believe that the youth was quickly working his way through storerooms, window dressing, testing labs, buying offices, shipping, advertising, merchandising and price comparing on his own merits.

There had been few Pedlocks in the last generation to introduce into the firm. In the past, Tobias, Mordechai, Nathan, Tom had all come through the step-by-step education and shown their merit. Marcel had never attempted it. Samuel, son of Elijah, had found Wall Street more interesting; he finally founded the Bank there. Once there was a nephew of Nathan's wife, but he, a stupid egotist, went on to Hollywood, after a disaster in a shoe sale, and he became head of a studio. There were at the moment no younger Pedlocks, except Tony, available. Lazar-Wolf would provide some apprentices in time, it was hoped. Mendes would go from M.I.T., if science didn't hold him, to the Walton School of Business and into Pedlock & Sons. It was hoped Nahum and David would become the young blood of Pedlock & Sons' future, but they were not Pedlocks except through their mother. They were Lazar-Wolfs, and they would, Nathan used to think during dark moments, take over the Store as their father had already taken over the Bank. They had that tangible drive of all latecomers with strong appetites.

It would be up to Tony and Nancy some day to provide the young and earnest Pedlocks who would continue the line of management: that intangible heightened perception and pride in shopkeeping.

Tony liked best after a day's work to stand on the first balcony as the Store emptied. He loved to watch the counters being covered, the lights dimmed. He would inhale the great smell, an odor of dust and packings and the breath of all those who had been there all day, added to the subtle perfumes used in air conditioning and restrooms to sweeten people *en masse*. The cleaning crews had not yet come; the watchmen were not yet checking their posts. It was like the night before Genesis ended, he felt, and he was there—perhaps because his adventure with a woman in Poland had frightened him back to Pedlock normality, perhaps because . . .

Department heads below and above were checking their last sales figures. The Store police and plainclothesmen were locking exits and checking bundle passes. The shrill night crews of the limp-wristed who dressed the windows were coming in, the trucks leaving soon for express offices. Piers and post offices were still silent under the basement floors.

Tony liked to lean on the bronze balcony railing and feel the mood and the strength of the atmosphere: the place. A crazy crazy thing to do, he'd think. What the hell am I, some kind of mystic nut? But I can't help it. My father, grandfather, great-grandfather all made something of the name Pedlock. It's a kind of special sales item, a bargain at times, a little better, a little cheaper, a snip more fashionable. Something with more guarantees, returnable, exchangeable, services better than any other store in the world. At least *we* like to think so.

Pedlock & Sons is an infection and I've got it. My father used to say he never had the disease called Pedlockitis, but Uncle Nat did, and he's right. He has it and I've got it now. A capacity for middle-class visualization. I suppose because I'm like Uncle Nat—too serious, a too cloying sense of loyalty, a way-out idea it all matters *who* sells and *what* sells and *how* it's sold. Tradition is a force operating on a man in spite of himself. No wonder Nancy says I'm square. So what the hell, I'm a square and I'm going to stay here and be the Store and, if I make it, run the Store. There isn't anyone else. Whatever I may lack in brains and other qualities, I do have purpose and a sense of dedication.

He looked at his watch. He was to meet Nancy at the Roma di Notte, and he was late. He hurried to the side-street exit, was politely saluted—a subservience touched with guile—by the first watchman on duty. As he left he had a sense of a gigantic tired animal at his back—the Store, snapping its teeth at his rump for attention, like a friendly but demanding dog.

CHAPTER 31

꿏 The day dawned gray. The sun did not come out. Winds beat themselves to nothing on tattered flags at the remains of the Brooklyn Navy Yard. The police on duty at Brooklyn Bridge Plaza wore raincoats, and at eight in the morning the rain came down slowly, fruit-green in color. By noon it was falling with the persistence of an all-day rain. There was a slight grayish vapor when people passed out breath in the chilled air, their heads held deep in their coat collars. The sky gave off a metallic, feeble thunder.

At one o'clock the rain suddenly broke off and the host of cars on the Brooklyn Bridge splashed through the puddles mixed with black moss: ancient dirt that collects on bridges no matter how often they are swept and painted. The traffic police beat gloved hands in superficial, jocular boredom.

It was the day Jacob had picked for the ceremony of tashlik, the tossing of the old year's lint and sins into moving water. He had been up early to go to the old *schul* in Brooklyn. Marcel and Judith would meet him at the bridge at two-thirty. Meanwhile there were to be services in the *schul*, and the members, old men, young men, children, the wives, sweethearts, were all to join in the event. It was to be an amazing drama, for Jacob had decided they would all march to the center of the Brooklyn Bridge and perform the ceremony *there*. He had asserted that the East River was running water —a bit soiled, but certainly an impressive body of polluted water. What was better to carry off the sins of his followers?

321

"We are a becoming, as well as a being."

Two battered buses waited outside the *schul* to carry the congregation to the bridge, but first there were the special services. Jacob was impressive in his black alpaca jacket with the flaring tails. Instead of the ritual little silk cap, he wore a hat trimmed with a red fox skin which he had bought from the widow of an old Polish rabbi. Jacob's little beard was in disorder, his eyes sparking embers. He could hardly control his gestures as he saw to the children and went to check on the two buses for the sacred journey. They would keep warm with the contents of the two dozen bottles of Pilsporter Goldtropfchen, a crate of gin, slivowitz and Noilly Prat Judith had donated. Some of the pious from other poor *schuls* were joining them.

The Brooklyn Hasidic court of Jacob Meshulam Berish Katzenellenbogan, also known as Ari Hakodesh, the Holy Lion, once of Poland, Russia, Galicia, England, numbered more than a hundred in students and attendants this day. The Hasidim arrived by bus, by train from New Jersey, the Catskills, hungry, wrinkled, dry in the mouth, their beards and black alpaca coats damp with rain.

Jacob welcomed them, offering brandy from a brown bottle. They all sang Hasidic chants. The Jersey rabbi broke into a whirling Hasidic caper, kicking his torn shoes in the dust, spinning his ragtail coat into bat wings. His unkempt black beard was waggling, his uncut hair falling into his eyes. His face was white and lean from fasting and never going out in the sun. He snapped his fingers at Jacob:

> "*Hava nagila v'nism'cha,*
> *Have N'ranna v'nismcha!*"

"Yankel," said Jacob, donning a moire caftan, "not so fast."

"*Tottala*, in the text, Lamed-vov, it says that when a man doesn't dance, he walks sideways toward God."

"True," said Jacob, "true."

The Hasidim laughed and snapped their fingers and chanted. Jacob ordered another bus. The rain had let up—a proper miracle.

On the platform of the Ark of the Law, scrolls unrolled. Jacob recited of the Unutterable Name of God. Followers, armored against turmoil, material temptations of fleshly lusts, bent and kissed the fringe of the curtain that hung before the ark. The candles on the Menorah stand were thick with old wax drippings and smelled like a sinner's breath.

Jacob prayed for the pilgrims from Jersey and the Catskills, for the faithful, for all those in Israel, and for those Jews still "scattered over the face of the earth among the unbelievers, the counters of coins, the uncircumcised, the godless scientists, the bigots, adulterers, the lighters of pogroms, the pork eaters, the violators of maidenheads, the Dr. Kellers, Goldwassers, Beverly Hills rabbis."

They danced and chanted. Dust rose from the floor and the last candle sputtered out with a black sooty plume.

The procession for tashlik formed after black tea and unbuttered hard bread. The Hasidim were joined by the women with their children. They began to fill the old buses, singing loudly.

Later there was no sense of reality to the day. Few who were there remembered any feeling of pain, only a great sense of being.

Judith had gotten the Hispano-Suiza off the blocks. It had been oiled, serviced, newly tired. Willie drove to the bridge, proud to be behind the wheel of one of those now legendary cars. People stopped to admire the wonderful car, its great coiled silver pipes outside the slightly moth-eaten leopard-skin upholstery.

Judith sat with her son Marcel, whom they had picked up at the art gallery. Marcel wondered what wild dream he was dreaming, how he was cauterizing his conscience. He must have fallen asleep while working on his journal, and soon he'd wake up and *not* be riding in this fantastic car.

Judith patted his hand. "The truth is, Marcel, I forgot the damn auto was upholstered in animal skin. But it runs fine, doesn't it?"

"It's a well-made car. But so bizarre. I could have taken my own car."

"No, I want to ride in this one. The handles are solid silver. Chico Hernandez Marmol had a silver Virgin Mary put into the glove compartment when he built it to tour Spain. You didn't know Chico? He was from the Mexican Embassy in Madrid. I bought the car from him."

"No, Mama, I didn't know Chico. Where is Jacob performing this ceremony?"

Judith laughed. "At the Brooklyn Bridge. Don't stare. It's not mad. Jacob wants to dramatize the failure of our American Jews to perform their ritual duties proudly."

Marcel felt a band across his chest, an invisible tennis ball stuck in his throat. "But on the Brooklyn Bridge?"

Judith pressed a button and a cabinet in front of them opened, showing a collection of dusty bottles. "Must be something to drink here. I'm coming down with some kind of virus, Dr. Newberger said. Alcohol helps keep it under control, I say." She found some silver cups, blew dust from them and inspected some four inches of brown liquid in a brandy bottle. "You'll join me, Marcel?"

"Not just now."

The buses were unloading on the Brooklyn side of the bridge. Traffic Officer Barney Swartz, in his heavy raincape, came over and politely touched his cap. "Pardon me, *rebbe*, what's the *smeer* here?"

Jacob said, "Chappie, you look like a good Jewish boy."

"I try, *rebbe*, I try."

"It's the ritual of tashlik over moving water."

"And this mob is with you, *rebbe*?"

"Come join it. We're walking over the bridge."

"All of you?"

"It's a law against it? Jews can't walk like the *goyim* on a bridge?"

"Who says so! You got the same rights as any good citizen." He blew his whistle as a Hispano-Suiza came off the bridge too fast and in the wrong lane.

Jacob pointed to the car. "*Mein vaub.*"

"Your wife? In that fancy crate? *Rebbe*, you got class."

Judith descended, followed by Marcel. She was wearing a brown wool dress and over it a light sheared-seal coat. On her hair, magnificently rinsed red by Nora for the event, was a small tobacco-colored hat with a nose-length veil.

Jacob beckoned on his followers with his furled umbrella, motioned to Judith, to Marcel and to the policeman. They formed a double line and went onto the footwalk of the bridge. Traffic began to pile up, and Officer Swartz, commenting, "My father, mother, shoulda lived to see this" moved them on their way, whistling shrilly. The skies frowned, turned darker. Raindrops began to fall. The procession began to chant: "*Have N'ranna v'nismcha!*"

In the middle of the bridge, Jacob stopped the procession, umbrella handle high. Marcel shivered and thought, Why don't I wake up from this dream? It began to rain, a cold pelting drizzle. Judith stared out over the river waters at the little tugs below, at the falling rain. She felt holy, redeemed, recovered. The haunting sense of irremediable loss was gone. She had a bottle of rum, found in the car bar, under her large coat cuffs. She coughed and took a big swig. It was impressive: the rain slanting down, the crowd of Hasidim with no addiction to remorse, the Jews in black coats, the children, the women with shawls over their heads—all dancing and shouting. Jacob prayed. All the rabbis, as his guests, prayed. Judith felt chills and then hot flashes, which she fought with rum. Here was a community of interest, a mutual plea to the godhead. It was glorious and Jacob was *so happy*.

The people lined the rails of the bridge and Jacob recited from the Prophet Micah:

"And thou will cast all their sins . . ."

They all answered, "And thou will cast all our sins . . ."

"Into the depths . . ."

"Into the depths . . ."

"Of the sea."

"Of the sea."

Judith's voice was louder than most. Marcel looked around in the lashing rain.

They all began to empty the contents of their pockets into the East River. Nutshells, newspapers, laundry tickets, bits of tinfoil, old letters, clippings from magazines, soiled handkerchiefs, a few loose kernels of corn, a rusty key, a few copper pennies. Marcel turned out his pockets and began, with trembling fingers, to shake from them the lint, stray crumbs of good tobacco, pellets of gray paper, tiny fragments of red wood from a pencil. Judith threw over a compact, a cigarette lighter, keys, unanswered letters.

Jacob cast cleansing herbs into the East River and recited, "May the water wash from us greed, misfortune, hate and envy for the coming year."

The Catskill rabbi dug deeply into a twisted pocket of his coat. He brought out a silver dollar and, shouting and sobbing, he cast it into the stream. "So cast we out all our sins into the depths of the waters . . ."

Jacob frowned. He suspected showmanship.

The Catskill rabbi fell heavily upon the bridge, rolled back his eyes in his head. His arms and legs twitched. The Hasidim stood around him with respect, with envy, with awe. Jacob seized the moment, his arms raised high: "Let us sing, V'*taheyr Leebeynu.*" They shivered and sang as the sound of a police siren rose over the tops of a traffic jam on the bridge. Marcel sneezed. Judith was in ecstasy.

BOOK IX

Serve ye Jehovah with gladness:

Before his presence come with mirth.

CHAPTER 32

⋅§ Marcel had once said of Dov Ganzler: "There is a streak of kindness and a desire to be liked in the man that he has worked hard to fight down. Dov Ganzler is a new kind of American Jew, risen not from ghetto or sweatshop, pool room or Seventh Avenue cloaks and suits. There are no dynasties of cut velvets and trimmings behind him. Dov is one of those who worked his way up with some education, and with his cunning, brightness, aches and pains had gone into fields none of his kind had tried before. He made his fortune in Western industry, savings and loan companies, canning, woodpulp, newspapers, distilleries. Soon his tiger's paws were bared in sudden stock raids, in the destruction of old firms to make better ones. Dov feeds an inner emptiness with mergers."

Dov Ganzler lived with a pained expression that may have meant ulcers, heartburn or constipation. He had piled up two billion dollars in assets by the simple rule of attack, always attack. "Buy enough shares, *boychick*, to ask for control, then seize it. Expand in all directions. Never show mercy to your assistants. Overpay them, sure, overbonus them with *gleckloch*, bells, but always put the spur to the seat of their two-hundred-dollar suits. Always step on the toes of their hundred-dollar alligator shoes. Make 'em rich but make 'em earn it."

Close up, to some, the harassed face of Dov Ganzler, the lonely isolated eyes, showed a frightened man who wondered in his dreams if his stocks were printed on snowflakes.

The Ganzler Foundation was his hope of salvation—a tax-avoiding scheme which afforded him the power to give away bronze statues, schools, scholarships, whole museums of industry and science, at no personal cost—sometimes for a fat gain in terms of his tax structure. There were also his family trust funds. A million here, a few million there, to his daughters', a bit invested for the grandchildren, present or still in genetic pools.

"But," Marcel said, "for all that, Dov is just a frightened Jewboy who wants to be feared, and is ashamed of wanting to be loved. Given to take-home philosophy and the use of words he has no knowledge of. He's impregnated by concepts fed him by a team of left-wing intellectuals who brown-nose and fawn on him, and tell him he's a thinker, a modern Medici. Dov, so alert to the sound of money, able to hear the dropping of a stock option clear across the nation, lets his two Trotskyite monks inflate him during long weekends at his Santa Barbara museum and ranch house, a place complete with electric barbecue pit and Roman bathtubs cut from solid marble blocks. He isn't a man any more. He's a distorted mirror image."

Dov Ganzler got out of his special Mercedes-Benz in front of the Waldorf. Ahead of him were the two lawyers carrying briefcases and a male secretary carrying a dispatch box that held a small tape recorder. They stopped, then followed him into the lobby of the hotel. He had a large suite, always open, in the tower, held in the name of one of his foundations, but it didn't seem to be the proper place to finalize the Pedlock deal. *Finalize*, a splendid word, like *know-how, brain-storming, consumer-wise, survey-tested,* and a few others with which he managed to carry on ordinary conversation with his staff. Those fine words plus a few oaths and obscenities.

The first lawyer in the retinue opened the golden-oak door to the suite. The press called it the Arab Chief Suite. "Too large for the new African nations, too small for a Russian trade and cultural exchange mission."

The living room of the suite was furnished in a neat gold-and-rosewood Regency, with a false fireplace. No long conference table, no glass tops on anything, no rows of ash trays; there was no hint that business was conducted in the room.

Nathan and Saul were standing at the windows looking down on

Park Avenue. They also were accompanied by two young lawyers. Both sides had tacitly agreed not to bring their main guns to this action. Dov had called it "a friendly meeting of scouts—so?"

Dov threw off a topcoat, not looking to see who would catch it behind his back.

"This isn't bad. Nobody is smoking, good."

"I am," said Saul Lazar-Wolf. "But later. So, Dov, you think here we can come to an understanding?"

"Why not—and before the proxies are counted at the big open public meeting."

Nathan shrugged. "I'm for letting the lawyers handle it. But Saul said, 'Listen, Dov Ganzler is not the devil. After all, we're all aware of the image of the American Jew.' So I'm here."

"Image? Lawyers? Let's face things as friends," Dov said earnestly. "Forever we're not going to live. What's material grandeur? It's a polish; just a wax job a man puts on his nakedness." One of Dov's Trotskyite monks had recently talked to Dov about Martin Buber and a popularization of the Jesuit Chardin. "So sit down. I'll sit down. Everybody sit down. Comfortable?"

Saul sat down in a red silk chair. "*Tocus oif dem tish*, Dov, ass on the table."

Dov waved off two briefcases offered him. "This meeting is a mission of mercy, you could say. But it's more. It's a peace offer. I can't swallow Pedlock & Sons, scales and bones and tail, like a herring. Surprised? Well, this is the moment of truth, as that schmuck Hemingway said. But you Pedlocks, you're a target to make the mouth water—overextended buying up stock, taxes due, new stores. And the proxies can give *me* four new members on the board. I can chicken-grease three more members—this way, that way—and demand chairman of the board. Oh, oh, don't wave fingers. I know maybe you can still beat me down. But it means a dirty fight, a Ganzler special—no new shopping centers, and think of the court costs, years of lawyers eating *our* bones and marrow."

Nathan was very calm. He had set himself to accept what had to be. "Judith Pedlock's options are not firm in your hands. They may not hold up in the courts."

"Better than four acres, believe me. But I'm not here to put your heads into the meat grinder. I'm giving way, *half*way."

One of his lawyers made a neighing sound like a pleased horse.

Saul took out a cigar and examined it. "Push us so far, Dov, and an inch more and I'm going to do something to stop you that the family will hate me for."

Dov's eyes gleamed, opened wide, his mouth just hinting at a smile. "You'd hold a sanity hearing? Have her declared senile? You'd void my options that way?"

"You're goddam right. Nathan, *not* a word from you."

Nathan nodded. "Saul, I'll be no part of it. But you have the Bank and the Store to think of. We had a hard time keeping Judith in bed—she wanted to be here."

"A *litvak* stand-off," said Dov smiling. He was happy. He was pleased at his tolerance, his understanding, his willingness to go only halfway. After all, these were the Pedlocks. "Here's what I offer you, and you'll take it. Sense you have, and you don't want to put the old lady into the hands of the nutcrackers and head shrinkers. Agreed?"

Nathan made a gesture that could have meant anything. There was a quick hand knocking on the suite doors, a banging as if they were being struck with a blunt instrument. Nathan thought, No! It couldn't be! Not her! Yet . . .

Judith Pedlock Ellenbogen stormed into the room, cane in hand, her nose red from a cold, her face puffy with fever. The rain on the bridge had done her no good, but where else would she be? Here, of course!

When she spoke her voice was hoarse, a croaking from conjested lungs and an ugly sore throat. She swung her gold-headed cane in the direction of Dov Ganzler as if aiming a rifle at his heart.

"You are frankly a no-good sonofabitch. *Du bist am Ende was du bist!* May your liver be full of worms, and every worm carry poison!"

Dov merely pulled out a chair for her. "My dear Mrs. Ellenbogan, I didn't want to bother you with these details, but *nu,* if you came to sit in—"

"*In!* I'd rather sit with rattlesnakes, even Germans, Jesuits, than sit with you! I just came to say you tricked me. No, I wasn't senile. I wasn't soft in the head, you *mauvais drôle!* I just had this idea that Jacob's dream of a great Hasidic center in Israel was more important than *anything* about the stores. But to this I didn't think it—would come—" She gasped. "I can't breathe so well this . . ." She coughed, swung her cane, sweeping water glasses, a vase off a table. "And you, you know—what I think you are? What my first husband called a kike. Always slipping in a little deal here, taking a pinch there, eh? Slicing off the tasty belly part of other people's lox for your own greasy mouth."

Dov smiled. "To me, being called a kike, it's a call to go on to show them. I came here only offering peace terms, with no scandal, no swallowing up of the great line of stores. And for *this* I get called—never mind. Only look, I'm *not* angry. No."

Judith stood there, staring at Dov, breathing through her mouth, flushed, no sense in her stare. She said softly, "You may start the music in the ballroom. Only please no Strauss waltzes—Ravel, yes, yes. . . . There will be fifty sitting down for dinner. Have you seen to the wine? *En grande tenue!*" She went around slowly in a circle. "I can't breathe. Open the French windows. At this time of year Rome is so dreadful, isn't it? The swamps full of malaria . . ." She suddenly sat down, head sunk on her chest.

Nathan went to her and took her hand. "You've got a fever. I'll take you home. Here is nothing for you to do."

"*Es ist . . . rein aus mit . . . uns?*"

Saul picked up the phone and waved back the lawyers, who were coming closer to the stricken woman. "Hello! Get me the house doctor. Get *anybody*, damn it! Get a doctor up to the Golden Suite. And an oxygen supply if you have it. Don't ask goddam questions. Do it!"

Judith lifted her head with great effort. "No panic . . . I'm not dying, not yet." She pivoted her head slowly to face a blanched Dov Ganzler, who was feeling his ulcers begin to bite at his stomach linings. She said softly, thickly, hardly heard by the rest: "You're . . . what I said. I know you are, Ganzler, nothing else. Crawl back to your money, your holding companies. . . . Pull them around you, they can't . . . keep you warm. You're a dead man already. I know the signs. . . . Ah, there is no irony like God's irony, Jacob says. . . . God lets horrors like you talk big, talk fancy . . . pile up *what?* Junk . . . then one morning—*faire bonne mine*—with a flick of a finger that you use to brush away a fly . . . He'll kill you, Ganzler."

Nathan patted her hand. "Judith, no more. Nothing matters but you."

A woman in a nurse's uniform came in. "Dr. Sales will be here in a moment." She opened Judith's coat collar, as Judith struggled to breathe. The nurse took her wrist and Judith pulled it away.

"No, no . . . just some air. What are they playing in there? I said no Strauss."

Saul was on the phone again. "I want an ambulance right away. No waiting for the city crate! The best private service. Pedlock, that's who for! Mrs. Pedlock, now Mrs. Ellenbogen. Judith Pedlock . . . Yes."

The nurse shook down a sliver of glass she took from a pocket and pushed it into a corner of Judith's unresisting mouth.

Judith cocked her head, her flushed swollen face to one side, and smiled at Dov standing facing her. She spoke from one side of her mouth in a whisper. "No two trees . . . sound alike . . . in a strong wind."

The nurse and Saul caught her as she pitched forward like a great stone falling from a height.

Later Judith refused to let the ambulance take her to a hospital. Not for just a bad cold in the head, she said. To keep her from protesting so loudly they took her home to Norton-on-Hudson, where they put her to bed and sent for her doctors. Nora did her hair while they waited. It wouldn't do for herself to be seen with such a mess of mixed-up curls.

GANZLER MERGER VOTE BY PEDLOCK & SONS PREFERRED SET

Holders of Pedlock & Sons Series A and B Preferred Stock will vote on the firm's proposed merger with Ganzler Industries, Inc., at a special meeting in New York, Dov Ganzler announced Tuesday.

The merger agreement is subject to approval by holders of two-thirds of the 147,897 shares of the stock eligible to vote. The Pedlock & Sons board approved the merger agreement at a Tuesday meeting, according to Chairman Nathan Pedlock.

The plan provides that Pedlock & Sons holders will receive one share of Ganzler Series A $3 cumulative convertible preferred stock for each Pedlock & Sons preferred share. Common shareholders would receive an amount of preferred equal to $17.25 per share of Pedlock common stock. The Ganzler preferred has full voting rights.

So *this* was the price of peace. He felt pain enter the scapula, penetrate, lodge in the thoracic cavity. Nathan Pedlock knew the news item by heart. He threw the paper down on the floor of the sunroom at Pedlock House and he looked out at the whirling weather. Another year, another season of life for him, another banal appraisal of banal philosophy. What for? Sitting and watching time crowd him, waiting for the final blow, *Gottanu*, in the back of the head. The abysmal incompetence of death was shocking; try and run a store that way—sheer waste. He hadn't done anything to resist this final settlement between Lazar-Wolf, representing the family, and Dov Ganzler's interests. They had prevented a great proxy battle. It had stopped having to have Judith— still in bed upstairs—declared too senile and incompetent to handle her own holdings. It had—but why think of that, of anything. . . . He had broken free of an overwhelming obsession. Pedlock & Sons and Ganzler's holdings merged would become nothing like the original units, but a combination, a vast collection of impersonal, clean, well-lit, characterless shopping runways: everything tricky, tasteless, overpriced, oversold, made to wear out quickly with too many high-cost parts to replace. There would be a conformity of styles and patterns from Vista Mesa to the Bronx, from Utah to Key West. The Pedlock touch would be gone, the personal tone lost. Computers, the whores of IBM, would take over everything. Cellophane and plastic would wrap all things tighter. The package would be all, and the product nothing, *nothing*. Dov Ganzler was a garbage shredder, and it all *kocked* out pure gold.

Miss Fogel came into the room and set down a glass of milky mixture. She watched him while he swallowed it. She was aware now, he knew, that it was a battle to the death between the two of them. He would defy her more and more, press her, harry her till she left. Even if she didn't, he would live the rest of his life his own way. Nathan's eyes gleamed. He smiled as she left, carrying tray and empty glass. It was a game. It was a project near at hand. He had something left in life, in his oddly ticking body and all the empty days and months ahead (who could dare to think in years?). War with Miss Fogel to decide whether he'd live like a blind puppy wrapped in cotton wool, or if he'd live what remained to him of his life the way he wanted to do. And evil take the heartbeat, the blood pressure, the clogging waxy veins leading to the brain, the sugar content of his urine, the white blood count. A cholera morbus take them all! It was all nonsense, this pampering of human plumbing. Man had so many years counted off, as Jacob said, and it was best not to know the final addition. He reached into the padding under the seat of the club chair—he had rolled the wheel chair into the river the week before—and took out a hidden cigar. Nathan lit the cigar carefully, rolling it round and round, drawing in the pungent smoke. Miss Fogel would be away twenty-eight minutes—he had computed the average timespan of her absences—doing her bathroom duties, taking a shower, soaping that horrible, sluglike body.

Jacob Ellenbogan came into the sunroom in scuffed red slippers, bathrobe belt carelessly tied, pliant, yet bristly as a small hairy dog.

"How's Judith, Jacob?"

"The cold in the head still bothers her. Now it's in the chest. If I had goose grease I'd make her rub it into her skin."

"That trip to the bridge in the rain, then to the Waldorf, it was insane at her age."

"No, no." The little man sat down on a bench and rubbed his knuckles together. "It was fine for us—the papers took pictures on the bridge. It showed that some Jews still act like Jews. Can you think of a ceremony like that being real in your gay, insubstantial Fifth Avenue or Los Angeles temples?"

"No, I guess not. We wouldn't let in those wild bearded followers of yours. What's new with Leah?"

"She was in Toronto. By now, ha, she must be flying to Tokyo with that ice show. I had hoped for spontaneous affection—father, daughter—but she's cursed with my own restless destiny."

"You want me to talk to the State Department people they should get Leah back here?"

Jacob cocked his head to one side, closed his eyes and made a grimace. "Ah the truth is, Nathan, as a father I'm a *schlemiehl,* even a *schlimazel,* a luckless idiot. Why should I think she'd love me? Why should I think she'd be lovable, respectful? Why?"

"Because why—because parents always hope so."

"Leah was a devil, is a devil. I knew it the moment we were together again, I had picked up a red-hot coal. No, it's better she goes her own way. I'm not the proper father. She's not the proper daughter. There's something in both of us that doesn't follow patterns other people set up. We're incurably inaccessible to normal life. I feel at times the cry of the cabala: *Ato bra golem hachomer v'tizim torfe Yisroel!*"

Nora came in with a vase of loose yellow roses. "Better if herself didn't see these, she'd be thinking people were sending them as if she was a corpse."

"Is she resting?" asked Jacob.

"The cough bothers her deep down. But I'll get a coddled egg and some rusks in milk into her."

"Has Dr. Newberger been?" Nathan asked.

"Doesn't want to see him. Says he's done things behind her back that she'd shoot him for if she was a man."

Jacob rolled his eyes at Nathan. "Not me. Not from me she heard. I didn't say a word about the report on her, what they were up to. *Shana* didn't hear it from me that they called her senile, a *hock in kop*."

Nora dried her damp hands by waving them in the air. "It's that sod Willie. He's always been a regular third eye for herself. They gossip at times like two Dublin biddies."

Nathan said firmly, "Call Dr. Zimmerman. Nora, I want him to see her today."

"She's not likely to trust another doctor ever again."

"Give me the phone. I'll call him."

Jacob stood up and fingered his little beard. "I'll go sit with her. A Jewish house and not a drop of medical goose grease. A scandal."

Nora rubbed her forehead, and when Jacob was gone, she looked Nathan directly in the eye. She wanted to say something, but changed her mind and went out.

Nathan dialed the phone number slowly. His memory wasn't what it was—even for simple numbers. He looked up at the ceiling. Judith's room was just overhead.

Tom Pedlock came out on the deck of the *Queen*, the forms of the palpable sea world still edged in mist, shipboard dimensions and echoes still strange to him. He was wearing a little cap with a buckle in back, left over from his sports-car days, and a camel-pile, snuff-colored topcoat. The faroff sea horizon, a crayonlike blue, shifted. The line of chairs on the scrubbed deck was empty on this cold and chilly day. A steward came by with a can, looking for ash trays to empty. A very slim girl with marvelous legs passed, walking firmly with solid heel tops. Twice around the deck one way, twice around the deck the other way. Tom thought with his *cojones*, as the Spanish say, as she passed, heels hard on oak deck. He'd meet

her at the big heavy glass doors as she came to the end of her walk
and he'd invite her down to the Pickwick Bar for a morning coffee,
gin or brandy. Rita hadn't been on deck since the boat had sailed.
Mrs. Thomas Pedlock was heavily pregnant, seasick, cursing the
day she decided not to fly to Europe on this delayed honeymoon.
The best of life's moments, Tom mused, are the impermanent
ones. He was earnest and nervous. It had been a hell of a year: a
divorce, his daughter defying him with that Dickie, then Tony, the
damn stores merged with Ganzler's. At least he had made a lot of
money. The new issues of stocks would make him rich enough
never to have to work anywhere again. With Rita. Rita the rest of
his natural life. Yes, he swore it, this had to last. He was getting too
old to try marriage again with someone else. This one, he promised
himself as he moved to the glass doors, would take, would stay,
would be permanent.

"We seem to be the only bold ones today." He held a door
open.

"You har muss kind." Her accent was thick, strange, exotic.

"Not at all. Bit nippy, isn't it?"

"Mack my nuss red."

"Not at all. Pretty nose. Besides, a good hot coffee will do you
a world of good. May I offer you one as a fellow walker?"

"Vhy net?"

The small deck messenger, an underbred Cockney dwarf in brass
buttons, monkey hat, saluted Tom. "Message for you, sir. Radiogram. New York."

"Ah, nipper, so it is." He gave him half a dollar and took the
flimsy envelope.

"Message, always she mins trouble."

"Of course not. Business. Miss—?"

"Sharkasiak. Toovanda Sharkasiak."

"Pedlock. Tom Pedlock."

He held open the bar door for her, noticing her fine hips,
haunch, calf, ankle. They walked arm-in-arm into the atmosphere
of saddle wax, oak paneling, salt peanuts and spilled ale. He put
the radiogram safely away in his coat pocket. Except for *this*, he
thought, we only grasp understanding of an experience in contemplation long afterward.

In her cabin Rita was vomiting up oatmeal.

The Cumberlands were cold and blue. Buchanan County, wise to winter, was beginning to gather its woodpiles for the coming cold. The town, more a village than a town, was called Java. Tony and Nancy, in heavy walking gear, knapsacks on their backs, found only one hotel, the Original Indian Penny House, and were pleased to find that there was hot water for Mr. and Mrs. Anthony Pedlock, N.Y.C., on only half an hour's notice.

"Well, Mrs. P." Tony rubbed a three-day beard. "It's too cold to go on walking."

"Been a marvelous three weeks. I learned to scale fish, open a can of anchovies with a sharp rock, and find out my husband talks in his sleep."

She lay prone on the rickety brass bed, ski-panted legs apart, hair in a tangle, hands bruised, nails chipped, skin chapped. She felt essentially passive, pleased, compliant, hungry, and wanted to be made love to again.

Tony slipped off the top sweater he wore over two others. "An Irish whiskey would go good. But here they don't even drink whiskey. They make moon. Corn dynamite."

"I'll bathe. It's a marvelous tub. All tin, on lion's legs of brass. And the john is three marble steps up and has a six-foot chain to pull. Lee is still defending Richmond, according to the plumbing."

There was a tap on the door and a fat girl came in with a red tin Coca-Cola tray on which were two steaming bowls of rice and okra soup. "Yo' bath watter be right hot in fifteen minutes. Yo' Mistah Tony Pedlick?" she asked.

"Close enough."

"Message left yere last night yo' was to call some number we got wrote downstairs."

Nancy sat up. "It must be Dad. Something has happened to him and Rita."

"Nonsense. I'll go down and put through the call. You take a bath."

Marcel was sitting in his private office in the galleries, not listening to one of his salesmen, Bertie Ironspinner, explain that someone wanted sixteen Grandma Moses. "But they all have to be snow scenes."

Marcel was trembling. He held a gold pencil in his fingers to try and control his shaking. "Bert, go see what is holding up that phone call I placed last night." He tore off some markings on a desk pad. "This one."

"The Moses matter?" asked Bertie.

"Moses was in the cellar when the lights went out. Or so my mother used to tell me when I was a boy."

Bertie lifted one narrow eyebrow and went out, walking with a slight quiver. "Really! Talking of Mother. Og!"

The phone made a polite low-keyed *ting*.

"Java, West Virginia, calling Mr. Marcel Pedlock."

"Speaking. Put it through."

He waited, hearing the dull roar in his ear like his seashell with the letters "Atlantic City 1914" when he and Papa and Mama rode in the boardwalk chair and the green pickle on the pier was called fifty-seven.

"Hello, Dad? Tony."

"Hello, Tony. I've been trying to locate you for two days."

"Sorry. Got rained in a few times. Anything the matter, Dad?"

"It's Judith. She's down with a serious virus pneumonia."

"Very bad? Dad, they've got all those miracle drugs these days. Besides, she's a fine tough old peacock."

"Those drugs don't help with this kind of virus. Tony, she's in an oxygen tent. Dr. Zimmerman says it can go either way. She got soaked in a rainstorm and she'll die. *Die*."

"Good Lord. No, not Grandma. She's so eternal."

"You and Nancy better fly back. Nathan thinks we should all be here."

"Uncle Tom?"

"His boat docks today in Southhampton. Naomi is already here. Gertrude is under sedation for her blood pressure."

"We'll get to an airfield somehow."

"Yes. How's Nancy?"

"Marvelous. This will hit her hard. She's so proud of Grandma. Look, Dad, people have made amazing recoveries from these things as long as their vital organs are all right. I better go now and find a way of flying out of this place. Bye, Father."

"Goodbye, Son."

Marcel hung up and stared at his desk top. Ever since Jacob came things had been happening, happening. Happening.

. . . Comes the time out of mind . . . out of sleep out of
being, when this is the dream and the dream is the brevity of
poignancy . . . here now waking the mist departing a hole in time
a woman me the bed the faces the forced air strong too strong the
plastic tent over all . . . now I am me here breathing is hard . . .
is this the way the thing that comes the business of dying *Yigdal
Eloheem chai v'yishta* bury me in the black chantilly lace over the
bright-blue silk chalk my cheek like nectarines but you only you
Irish wash and handle me let no one else touch the secret corners
of me . . . going going down in the white soft sleep with blank
walls all wonder, sun, joy, piquant details lost lost . . . dancing
così così when . . . the truth yes . . . the whole truth never
. . . again a clear lens the faces over the bed beyond the plastic
tent feeling Judith Judith in her bed Judith fed bred set the eyes
sad the mouths hurt with fear the smell of strong medicines tanked
air washing alcohol old raddled flesh destined for extinction . . .
on going away by boat train and yacht the sound of the music of
Jacques Offenbach I am *enceinte* with my first-born belly-proud
with Marcel and the family came to see him with hothouse fruit
and say he is beautiful and the talk runs around the teacups "It is
significant Einstein was immediately preceded by the Russian Ballet." . . . The B'nai Brith sent a ring of stale roses when Gittel was
born she will die as she was born crying . . . the prick of pain is
near the heart the chest very full of hurt the ingoing outgoing the
little deaths in hired beds, Tom used to come running to me on
baby legs and say, "kiss my hurt," and me dressing in a lake of mirrors going out to a ball citron-green Paris gown wearing the Pedlock diamonds . . . and the studio of that artist *l'art des noirs* all
those sensual Congo carvings me in his arms bells ringing from the
Church of St. Thomas . . . Doucet the couturier made the gown
he tore in his greed need seed to get at me skin to skin . . . now
why are *they* so sad? It was in another country and besides the
wench is dead . . . sticking that tube into my face the needles
into my arm the drip drip from the bottle high in the ceiling dark
dark the smell of frangipani and Mordechai in a 1910 top hat
laughing alive alive eating an *omelette au rhum* under an oriel window and World War One was just hinted that afternoon in the
Hotel Drouon where I bought the Degas drawing *merde* I said
coyly . . . it's beautiful and all the men laughed *that crazy American beauty* and the tall one who looked like Prince Myshkin, Dos-

toyevsky's Idiot said I was the sin he wanted to commit . . . *C'est une vraie aubaine* . . . I asked with happiness? He said happiness is the absence of unhappiness . . . Jacob Jacob look at him Talmudic Second Empire beard in disorder tears in his wise eye corners pernickety perverse *Shana Shana* faintly I am generations infinitely removed from all of you now . . . in me some *schoirah*—merchandise they're losing *Zuloscho hagolil* . . . *Mah lee umee lee?* Who am I . . . what am I . . . it's getting stone-gray cold the wind comes out of Zion I'm driving the children home from the picnic with the fat farting pony the basketwork chaise a storm coming over the Hudson will we reach the house before we are all killed in the summer lightning Tom laughs Marcel weeps Naomi wets her drawers and Gittel holds the puppy to her fat stomach . . . on the steps solid the provider Mordechai waits for us laughing smoking a good Belinda cigar gold watch chains proudly Pedlock gold gleaming on the round merchant stomach . . . oh I feel a pain a smother that leads to a need to know . . . is life *I* and love *we* . . . ?

CHAPTER 33

◄§ The family was gathered at Pedlock House, Norton-on-Hudson—those of its members that had responded to the phone calls, cables, those who had by modern miracles of motor cars, fast trains, jet planes been able to reach all that remained. The large high-ceilinged rooms were stuffed with several generations of memories, furniture and pictures. Nora sat in odd corners, handled holy medals, scapulars, rosaries to benefit Judith's soul or recovery—whichever it was to be.

Tony and Nancy were in the library before a tray of coffee cups for which, as yet, there was no coffee urn. Nathan paced the hallway and Lazar-Wolf took his arm and led him into the big sunroom. Tom was missing. He had cabled, "Rita too ill after rough crossing to leave her now." It was just as well, Lazar-Wolf muttered: "The *momser* and his women, his worshiping of the female pudendum. He was the one who brought on most of our problems with his selling out to Dov Ganzler in the first place."

Gertrude clung to her husband's side. She was in a too tight dark-brown dress salvaged from a hamper, it being not too gay or stylish for visiting at such a time. Judith, if she rallied, would not notice lapses and gaucheries.

"Saul, Saul, don't blame anyone for anything, not now."

"Just how serious is it? Mendes, stop biting your nails."

They had brought the older children: Mendes summoned from school, Sharon, Nahum, Dave. Joanne, they had decided, was too young to understand. It was their birthright to be there at such a time, if a final mortality was at work on the family monument.

Naomi and Mark Penrose, marvelously tanned, came into the library.

With a slack hopeless gesture of fear Naomi was fingering the slim strand of pearls on her black silk gown. "Oh. Sorry busting in. Tony, Nancy. How nice. I mean not nice—sad. We haven't sent you a wedding present yet." The women kissed. The men shook hands, eyes down, in that respectful silence reserved for solemn events like wars, bankruptcies or the suicides of friends.

Tony's clothes felt too tight. "Uncle Mark, did you have a hard trip?" It sounded, as he asked, like a stupid question in his ears.

"Flew in a rotten little two-engine job out of Trinadad—rather, St. Elmo's Island, near Trinadad. Drunken pilot, I'm sure. But of course—" Mark Penrose made a gesture. "How sick is she? It can't be true."

"Very sick," said Nancy, sniffing back tears as Willie came by with two pots of coffee and trays of small currant cakes. "Poor Grandma, she looked so solid and permanent."

They could hear Gertrude crying in the hallway, and Naomi, dropping a bursting tear, went to comfort her sister. Mark Penrose pressed his trembling lips together and Tony almost smiled. Uncle Mark hated what he called "hysterical Jewish blubbering."

Mark Penrose retained a good Anglo-Saxon grip on himself and stood in his gray London suit, coffee cup in hand, emotions firmly under control. "She's so full of years," he said. "Absolutely unique. Full of years. I feel I should put on a prayer shawl."

Tony found the coffee too hot. "Who's to say so, so full of years? The insurance statistics? She should go on to be a hundred. She's so alive and alert when everybody else in the family is so dreary and respectable. Some people never live, they only exist, but Grandma, it's unfair. . . . I'm sorry for what I just said about the family."

Nancy captured his free hand. "Darling, you're making a speech."

Donald Kalish passed the library door with averted eyes. Mark Penrose sighed. "The legal sharks are gathering. I suppose the will is in order. Unless, of course," he leaned over, "they've gone ahead with the reports of the medical head shrinkers and—" He tapped his own brow. "Well, her condition can change, you know. She'll live."

"No," said Tony, "we don't know."

Buffet tables in the sunroom held tea, coffee and small brown-bread sandwiches of cream cheese and chopped nuts. The cook had an idea that these were the proper Hebrew pre-funeral meats. Ger-trude hiccupped, wiped her red eyes and clung to her sister. Naomi rubbed her sister's broad neck and back and arms. She, too, was weeping. She had expected to be calm, collected, properly sad, but not this emotional flood of sound and feelings.

"Gertie, Gertie, don't cry."

"I neglected her. I avoided Mama when she was angry. She could say such cruel things. But we'll be *lost* without her. There was something so precious and incommunicable between us and her."

"She loved us, Gertie, loved us for all our faults. And we loved her—for all hers, even if hers were full of character. *Outré.*"

"Oh, Naomi, don't get intellectual now."

They clung together and the voices of Mendes and Sharon were heard from the hall debating about the identity of a portrait that hung there:

"That's so Grandpa too."

"Don't be a drip. That's Uncle Samuel. Granduncle Samuel from the Bank."

"No, he had a square beard. This one's pointed."

"Oh, have it your way. But this lovely thing, who's that?"

"Grandma, of course. When she was very young. Who's it by? Rembrandt?"

"Oh no—Rembrandt! It's by John Singer Sargent. Signed right there. He charged plenty, too."

"How beautiful she was. We don't seem to have inherited any-thing from her. Even if they say I look like her; I mean, you know, we lack poise, that kind of thing."

"You really think she looked like that? Society painters they al-ways made the subject sorta grander than actual."

"Not in Grandma's case. You can still see all that's in the pic-ture, only older, wrinkled, know what I mean, Mendes?"

In the sunroom, Lazar-Wolf, Nathan Pedlock and Donald Ka-lish sat drinking small brandies in square diamond-cut crystal cups. Lazar-Wolf tapped Kalish on the knee. "She leaves the major por-tion of her estate to Ellenbogan?"

"I don't know, Saul. Mr. Addison has the will in his private safe. He's in charge of the major estates in the office. I'd imagine it's something like that. Oh, it's going to be something." He smiled as if awed by the prospect of the idea. "Going to be a hell of a tax problem. But we're ready for it. I guess we—the firm—have probated more important wills than any law firm on the street. Yes."

"You think there will be complications? We've got to think of the family." Saul put down his glass.

"Oh, the state and Washington will give us a hard time. They're always ready to make ridiculous demands so you'll settle. But our tax department section at A.F. and K. is A-1. As Mr. Addison says when he's setting up a trust, 'We don't give Washington a red cent more than they can press out of us,' and he points to the stealing by the big oil men who run Washington."

"I don't mean that," said Lazar-Wolf. He picked up his glass carefully, still with an inch of brandy left in it. "She was in an acceptable legal condition when she made it? Forget the *chazzereye* you and the doctors cooked up."

Nathan said, "That nasty business of the head doctors comes out and I'll rally the family, Saul, to such a damn fight you'll regret it till the day you die if you use *that* on the will."

"*Yoisheer*, Nat, *yoisheer*. Can't a man ask a simple question? It never entered my head to question anything I haven't seen. It's just I've got the Bank on my mind, the merger with Ganzler. If an estate is involved for a couple of years . . . I'm sure, Nat, you see our problems." He placed his hand on his heart. "I'm made of flesh and blood. You think I came out of the navy untouched? Who loved her like she was—like my own mother?"

Nathan said softly, "You don't have to use the past tense."

"Nat, we're not pleasant to each other. Let's not bicker."

"Where's Jacob been all morning?"

"He hasn't come downstairs."

"Where's Marcel?" asked Donald Kalish. As a lawyer he didn't want to be witness to a disagreement between relatives.

"He'll be here. Phoned he overslept. Those damn sleeping pills," said Lazar-Wolf. "I'd outlaw them. A warm bath, a glass of hot milk, I sleep like the Czar, as my father—in peace in his grave— used to say."

Nathan looked out over the river. "The Czar, he sleeps like anybody else who has just died. You don't hear even him being permitted complaints."

The Angel of Death—so he did exist—intricate molecules becoming organic—there he stood by her bedside. Judith smiled. He was a splendid thing, a proper male, with the torso and arms of one who wore with ease huge gold and red wings, wings that came high over his golden head and tapered down behind him to his naked feet. A kind of black cloak was around him, and there was the smell of spices and temple lamp oil and eternity. Mesheach, the Angel of Death, held out his arms. Judith swayed, her head off the pillow like a sick child. She wet her lips. She coughed up difficulties from her throat and lungs, wanting to word something bothering her.

"You don't understand. I want to go. But I can't go because they still need, need me. Don't shake your noodle at me, mister, and insist. You see they are a swineless lot. I've held them together as a family. I've kissed their little wounds. I've . . . I've patted their heads, wiped their behinds. I've said go, go, *kinder*, face life, do your little tasks. Without me, believe me, there is a dismal insufficiency—they'll be nothing, wasting their portion of the family holdings, going their crazy ways to despair, to ruin. I don't ask mercy, I don't beg for myself . . . you're such a handsome angel, Mesheach, an exhilarating phenomenon, and I'm soooo old . . . but wait . . . just a little longer . . . there are a few things still to be done."

The Angel of Death smiled at her. He bent over the bed and pushed aside the plastic walls that separated her from the present, from the living. And she, in metaphysical speculation, was now, for the first time, afraid. He smelled of rotting graves, old moldering bones, black coffin moss. He smelled of the billions upon billions of dead he had come for since the days of Genesis. But she would not show her fear—she had never shown fear, and if the angel would not listen to sense, no wonder the universe was such a disaster, life such a mess. . . . The world was sick of being sick; for they ran things badly in the universe. . . .

The Angel of Death did not come closer. He waited, like a mountain range, she thought, that had come out of the sea to dry itself.

Everything in front of Judith's eyes focused into drapes flapping and strong voices singing: "*Yigdal Eloheem chai v'yishtabach mimtso eyes el m'tsseuso!*" She was back to her beginning; the cry of Godhead in her ears.

The living God we praise, exalt, adore!
He was, He is, He will be evermore!

Echod v'eyn yocheed k'yichudo

No unity like Him can be . . . can be . . . can be . . .

The Angel of Death again offered his arms. The drapes were parting. A red-glow came through from behind them. There was a blinding yellow light. Beyond it, Judith saw the massed *tzaddikim*, the holy rabbis, the wonder-workers: Moses, Abraham, Rebecca, Esther, Ruth in the alien corn. She must enter eternity now. In a flutter of drapery and a great beating of wings there was the Angel of Death with a flaming sword barring Judith's path.

"Are you ready now?"

"Not ready. Just resigned . . ."

"Be then with the *sephiroth*—with love, compassion, intellect."

The Angel of Death swung his flaming sword at her. His cape fell away and she saw that it was Jacob, a young, black-bearded Jacob.

"*Shana, Shana* . . . my heart . . ."

She sighed, and thought, thought of *what*, of *why*, of nothing . . . was no more but a memory to those still on their feet. . . . She went quickly, for she had on special occasions very good manners. Her last flicker of consciousness was an awareness that it was no longer her scene. . . .

From Marcel Pedlock's journal:

I have just returned from the burial, not at all a fearfully vulgar ceremony for all the dreadfully crowded place where the Jews seem to huddle each other in death as they did in life, raising up pompous monuments over themselves. Overhead a plane was writing something in the distance: "Shop Xmas early"—it would have amused Mama. There was a diaphanous gauze sky and that plane. I have had to take two tranquilizers on doctor's orders, but they seem only to have made me feel a spinning dizziness. Perhaps writing now will calm me enough so that when I take the Seconals I'll sleep till morning. I'm very tired. Also I think a little mad, but controlled madness like an ephemeral dream I only half believe in.

The grave has been given a beauty treatment, the earth, fresh-dug, hidden under false evergreen grass; the cold day, Venetian blue and gold, called for banners flapping. The tent erected over all stirring over our heads. We standing in the bitter blue cold, no flowers on the huge pine casket that Judith had insisted on as being ritually orthodox; no blooms, no rare wood or silver handles. Everything, for all its sleek ease, that Horwitz and Gringold Parlors could do only making it worse. Their kosher Uriah Heep sad-eyed whispers, the black gloves, the proper padded folding chairs for the weak or old, all a sophism to make one's image of life and death lack any reference to space and time. A sort of Broadway theater party.

Jacob, a strange creature in red-foxed rabbi's hat, his own rabbi of the old *schul* there as a standby, bearded to the eyes and ears with a black Assyrian growth. Several of the followers—the Hasidic brotherhood—in their thin long coats and wide hats. Naomi had insisted on the Beverly Hills Reform rabbi, Nathan's brother, fat, clean-shaved as a castrated harem guard, trained by the late unlamented Wise. A copious extravagant personality, known to television and interfaith orgies for his rolling *R*s, his ability to drink martinis over our justified grievances.

Tom at last, flown in by jet at the last minute, looking rather exalted between tears. I thought, some new woman, and I brushed aside the stray thought as I looked at Tom in his black flyfront Burberry, bowler hat; it's not his fault, he is what he is—he's Mama's son; she, too, had the wild strain, but she had quality and grace.

Nancy and Tony helped me not break down at the grave. How I love them. I want to share their warmth, their marriage; they don't need me, I feel it. Gertrude with a bad cold, her children bored, frightened in turn, then pinching each other. Nathan, scarfed, overcoated; he had insisted against doctor's orders he had to be there. He is the best of us. Behind him a landscape, perfectly Euclidian I thought. I couldn't keep my mind on the death of Judith, her burial, unless I related it to some era of art; it was too much to expect of me. I'd sink into impenetrable darkness if I had to face the true ugly facts of death.

The Beverly Hills rabbi, Cousin Charlie, has done his routine, has clasped together square hands that look parboiled, rolled his last greasy *R*, looked about as if wondering where the cameramen were. The Brooklyn Hasidim have begun their chant, and Nora O'Hara lets out one keening sound for Christ and his saints to protect herself, and falls to the turf to be pulled to one side by the cook, Marta, and Willie, who push a leatherbound flask—once Mordechai's—into her gaping mouth. She is shaking and her limbs twitch as in the act of physical love—it's all I can think of suddenly, and I'm ashamed.

"*Yisgadal V'yiskadash shmay raboh!* Hallowed and magnified be the name of God!"

The casket-dropping machine began to sink the pine box below eye level. Mama! Her cold remains descend slowly; lost! Lost! We stand overcoated, cold, sad, Lazar-Wolf looking about as if to see who has come, counting the house. Addison, Kalish, other members of the firm. In ranks behind them important families, Jews, gentiles; here a Strauss, there a Lehman, there a Warburg, there even a Guggenheim, a Rockefeller grandson, an upstate judge. A few editors of Yiddish papers and magazines that the Pedlock Foundation helps, the splendid *schnorrers* from Brandeis (Who can spare us a gym? A lab? A collection of Daumier prints?), U.J.A., the sisterhoods, the dark, brooding Irgun fighter called Avrom with the maimed hand wrapped in black cloth (she had helped arm them). All knew her, all came to express a gesture. Stray words: *here; gone; sorry; sad.* Old pensioned store buyers, Yeshiva loafers from Friday nights. Chaim and Hersh from the Home for the Hebrew Elderly (*"Sh'ma Yisroel adonoy*—why is a rabbi at a grave like a goose with its head in a bowl of *kasha?"*).

To the left a group in slight discomfort, the gentiles of her *other* world. A thin rank of thinning generations. Edwardians, Jamesians (Henry), Fitzgeraldians (F. Scott). The man from the French embassy, dying himself, growing a cane from his navel to lean on, the sharp Gallic head, the cheekbones thrusting through the flesh; the manager of that hotel who was a busboy at the Ritz when Judith first tipped him; a New England novelist rattling his dentures (was she the Sari of his now forgotten novel, *Soufflé à l'orange?*); a disciple of Gertrude Stein's in men's shoes. The rest I don't know. They all seem out of place, just as her life, her other world with them was never real to us.

The smooth leader of the burial detail, functional Mr. Horwitz, the funeral director himself (I suspect him of blossoming piles), makes signals . . . Jacob takes up a wild cry: *"Shema Yisroel adonoy!"* He tosses it down after her and looks away. *"Eloheynu a donoy echod!"*

We pass by the pit, family first. I don't look down. I shuffle my too thin shoes on the false grass, lumpy over the red raw earth. Two men in rough gray coats wait—off stage—behind a tombstone next door, their red unshaved faces distorted by wads of tobacco stuffed in one cheek. I see long-handled shovels and turn away. (The only true grave scene is in *Hamlet.*) Gertrude has begun to wail and cry out, "Mama, Mama!" Her children surround her and cry too. Lazar-Wolf's eyes are streaming and red (a good man for all his greed). Tom is deadly pale and he hurries to a waiting taxi, to some bar, to some waiting bed, a woman. He once confessed to me that tension is best released in violent fornication—that this is what kept him sane, poor Tom. Poor all of us. We are alone now.

Naomi and Mark followed by the chauffeur with the black sealskin car robe have gone. Nathan and his capon rabbi brother Charles have gone, the bearded one and his Hasidic followers and Jacob are drinking from a flask of slivowitz near the gates. Tony has gone to get the car and I stand by Nancy's side. (Tom has given her only a hasty kiss and a "See you soon, kids," and she seems hurt.) I hold her gloved hand and she smiles and presses my fingers. The tall wall is marked by the obscene chalk words of children, suggesting it is the barrier to the underworld.

I must sleep; my pains are now anesthetized but will return stronger.

All the half dream was of Byzantine faces from Ravenna in a lilac afterglow and Judith's face was always turned away. I have slept some; I fell asleep writing, the sleeve of my robe stained with ink. I use an old Georgian silver inkstand (Geo. Rex II) that once belonged to Samuel Johnson, but no feather. I have my father's old Waterman fountain pen; its sac no longer works but the broad nib is perfect. . . . I have come around to the truth, to a point of no return. I am going to murder a spirit, a *dybbuk*, a supernatural being or an evil ghoul. Perhaps I'm insane, as I feel at times. But I don't think so. My pulse is a bit fast, normal for me. My temperature (oral) is nearly ninety-nine, but the dizziness is gone. I'm no anchorite piddling with visions and temptation. I have the gun—a pistol, really—we keep downstairs in the packing department. A Smith & Wesson .45 with six chambers, six bullets (none of silver). Jacob I am sure is a *dybbuk*, an evil spirit that entered him during his concentration-camp era—by invitation—sent or created in some way to destroy the Pedlocks, to hunt us out and do evil. He killed Judith in the rain on a bridge, he seduced Tom to betray the Store, he injured Nathan's heart, he failed with Tony only because Leah, the female *dybbuk*, tasted the pleasures of lewd life and ran off. He brought forth Dov Ganzler. (How did Ganzler have the sense not to appear at the graveside? His telegram was at least silent even if the prose was banal cant.) And me? *What has Jacob reserved for me?* Me he has driven mad, has seduced with ancient rites, ancient incantations from the cabala, the Hasidic lore. Those Brooklyn Jews are demons sent to tempt us. It is the Sabbatian heresy I am sure. They are able, they tell me, to find *shekhina*, God's radiance. The Messiah will not come till they call him. I must destroy Jacob. (I am insane, I think— and don't really mind.)

I am insane? Or is it just that the truth is too much for me? I live with a sense of apathetic dread. I will dress, will take the pistol, will go to the *schul* in Brooklyn. Jacob is there, the demon, the *dybbuk*, the Hasidic spirit that has ruined the Pedlocks. Oh, for the moment we are still rich, but the Store is in other hands, Lazar-Wolf has the Bank firmer in his grip. We have nothing but the future, a future I am tired of already. I must say my paranoid glow is exciting. What I once thought of as a temporary aberration, Jacob among us, in my idiot's self-complacency, is now *what?*

BOOK X

Make ye a joy'- ful sound-ing noise

Un - to Je - ho - vah, all the earth:

CHAPTER 34

◄§ From the last will and testament of Judith Pedlock Ellenbogan:

. . . and being clear in mind and purpose and feeling that the years are piling up on me—with no great belief in nirvana and samsara, or any questioning of the eternal and the temporal—I do declare this my last will and testament: the last words I shall leave as a text on this earth. So without any introspective comments on the problems of material possessions I do hereby dispose of them.

I want to begin with some personal gifts, not to be thought of as mementos. To my dear and long-time companion and friend, Nora O'Hara, who upheld my spirits and saw to my flesh as much as anyone of my girth would permit, and for all those years and places we shared —all our irrelevant actualities—I leave her through my personal trust with Lazar-Wolf and Pedlock Brothers a sum of ten thousand dollars a year to be paid her till her death. Also my diamond earrings called the White Drops, made for me by Lalique of Paris in 1900; my silver-mink coat and any of my album photographs she wants copies of. The only advice I can add is for her to stay clear of nunneries, elderly retired military men and fortunetellers, all those who try to mitigate the shock of human society. The only pure thing is the eating of fruit. . . .

To Marta Nemenyi, who is more than my cook, and if judging by my size less than a friend, I leave the outright sum of fifteen thousand dollars, the blue evening gown by Worth she has so often admired, and the small photograph of myself with Lady Elsie Mendl and the chef Monsieur Alexandre Dumaine. . . .

To Wilhelm (Willie) Izekman, a true rogue, for his serenity without smugness, his virtuoso unrespectability and because his driving once saved my life on the Bavarian Road to Regensburg on the Danube, I leave the sum of fifteen thousand dollars and the ruby-and-garnet sporting pins known as the Fox Hunting Set. . . .

Five thousand dollars to the following people whose last-known addresses are listed with my lawyers: Gregor Narrak, Athens, Greece; Everard von Hebra, Venice, Italy; Aulkeen Dowd, Brown's Hotel, London, England; Major and Mrs. Jared Rutledge, Fenn Manse, Kent, England; Alexandre Taunton at the Au Bon Coin, Orléans, France.

To Mark Dorsey Jones of St. James's Park, London, the sum of twenty thousand dollars with the understanding that this does not acknowledge his mother, Molly Chatham, now dead, as the child of my late husband, Mordechai, the matter having been settled in 1917, in the legal papers on file in Somerset House, London. This is in no way to be taken as a criticism of my husband, who had little time for the anonymity of modern love or the enigma of our physical actions.

Now, as to my own family. We have been told too often all is vanity —but to enjoy vain things is a pleasant weakness. Life should be— Bergson told me once—the putting of the infinite with the finite. I regret leaving the world, but I also regret leaving all of you, for I feel you still lack the placid simplicity, the firmness to exist without me. If this is ego on my part it is balanced by all I have had to do for you, the steps I have had to teach you, the wounds, invisible and visible, I have bound up. When you read this, loss, bereavement, parting and agony will come over some on you. I have never explained myself, blamed myself too much, or given way, as some of you have, to a stark masochism. Life and the universe, I have always suspected were made by a drunken conjurer, and my dear Jacob and his texts have only strengthened that impression. But the Creator is not a fumbler. All my life he has been taking wonderful rabbits out of fine hats for me. I have tried to avoid spleen, hatreds, those sour wines of old age. Nature itself has no significance, no sadness, no triumphant goal.

You will bury me simply. I want to lie between my two husbands. I am a Jewess and have remained one, but I do not follow rules set up by mere men who accept mythomaniacal texts. All the rituals of any faith, sacraments, rites and gestures I see as fine little games we play when we are too old to sleep with a light in our room. My family is related to Spinoza, and with him I agree: man is God, God is man. So protect me when I am no more from any erroneous notion that I was deeply pious. I sat at Trimalchio's banquet rather than near Abraham's bosom. I did follow Jacob's words eagerly, but only with the hope of finding some small clues to the never-to-be-solved mysteries of the universe. I am against extremes in anything: Theology or science picking at cosmic nits. Society, from being in my time a fine surface civilization, has become a psychological puzzle, a regulated barbaric despair on one side, all cant and banality on the other, and everything seems made of plastic. It is in this world you and your children must live. Try for the infinite diversities of living; but remember the mind does not really act, it conditions action, some of it shameful, some of it doomed to frustration. In the end you will find when you are old that everything is a limitation, a compromise. So pamper your sensibilities. I can't remember who once said: Man would be better if his gods were happier.

To my son Nathan Pedlock—the word "stepson" is an absurdity. He has devoted a lifetime to our selfish comfort, interests and undeserved care. Of material things he needs nothing. In my home, Pedlock House at Norton-on-Hudson, so full of the history of the family, I leave him any objects he desires for himself; paintings, furniture, family papers, anything else. And if he should desire to live there the rest of life, he is to have that right. I leave to him, to destroy, certain personal journals and letters marked A, B and C in my private bedroom safe. He is to destroy these unopened and unread. Dear friend, I could not destroy them myself. They were another part of me created at the same time as my Pedlock life. It would be an abject humiliation to my ghost and to certain families if they ever were exposed to other eyes.

To my son Marcel, any paintings, objects of art from Pedlock House he wishes. I am sorry, Marcel, you never found life to be as it can be: a sweet sedation, an addiction to wonder, pleasure, feeling, even a proud duty. Art is nothing but décor, a nonsense of fallacies. No fully mature person should waste a full life in it. It is only for leisured moments and status seekers.

To Marcel's son, Anthony (Tony) Pedlock, I leave two hundred thousand dollars with the wish that he leave the Store and go abroad with his wife to see if he can't find something that really excites him, and her. I also leave him my Biedermeier and Louis Seize furniture, and to Nancy my long double string of pearls now in the Tiffany vaults.

To my son Thomas Pedlock, I leave a regret he thinks he has taken certain traits from me and debased them into a strange sensuality. I don't blame him. What we become is between our nerve ends and our dreams. I don't pay much attention to the trash of psychoanalysts, that false new Jewish religion. To whatever wife Tom has at present, I give my gold bracelet made by Wolfer of Brussels.

To my daughter Naomi (Fuderbloom) Penrose, I leave the Viennese bentwood furniture of the sunroom, my Art Nouveau Galle diamond armband, my square diamond ring, my emerald pin, my ruby sunburst made, I think, by Guimard. To her husband, Mark (Moses), I give all the tins of Malossal caviar in the ice vault and the lapis-lazuli watch seal of Tobias Pedlock. You are an anachronism, Mark, so I add Mordechai's long razors, seven in a rosewood box, one for each day of the week. An uncle cut his throat with Friday. Fashionable people now seem as impersonal as eunuchs. You both cultivate the vice of gentility, a belief in your own infallibility. But I know you have doubts. Cultivate those.

To my daughter Gittel (Gertrude) Lazar-Wolf, I leave the sable coat, the chinchilla, the Serrurier-Bovy furniture on the second floor of Pedlock House, the John Singer Sargent painting of myself, and my diamond necklace called the Royal Collar, now in the Tiffany vaults. Also the short triple-strand pearl necklace, the narrow emerald bracelet, and the diamond-ruby pin designed by Ranson of London, now in my bedroom safe.

To my son-in-law Saul Lazar-Wolf, I leave the books in Hebrew in the library at Pedlock House, the collection of ancient torah covers in the glass cases, and the old business ledgers and private papers dating from 1853 connected with the Store and the Bank. You have a humane suppleness, Saul. You restrain your desire to acquire all our assets. You have made Gittel a good husband, and your children, once they escape the usual smothering Jewish family life, will do well. You both forget life is the total of what you have to pay for it. The American Jew, like yourself, is trapped, Jacob tells me, between the poles of aspiration and realization. "It's all Dead Sea fruit. Rosy on the outside, dead dust inside."

To my grandchildren, Mendes, Sharon, Nahum, David, Sheila and Joanne Lazar-Wolf, I leave trust funds of twenty thousand dollars each, to be paid them on the day they become twenty-one, *or* the day they marry. It is not enough to ruin them—a lump sum of no great amount to begin their lives as they please, without pressures of family or tradition or need forcing them into grooves they do not want to fill. Each of them is to pick some bit of jewelry for himself or herself in the small case marked *D* now in the Tiffany vaults. The only advice I give them is not to take any advice from anyone—even myself. In an incoherent universe they will learn to read their own omens.

All the rest I have and own, except for the items noted above, all my stocks, holdings, jewels, and other assets, I leave to my husband, Jacob, for him to dispose of as he sees fit. He has shown that reality is only that which is outside ourselves—the smallest part of being. Perhaps he is right in saying God will find each of us, even behind a thousand walls. *Sholom aleichem.*

This part of my last will and testament is not intended to be any rite of purification for myself, nor a rationalization of an irrational but, in the main, a well-filled life. It has all been a dim hovering of dreams in my last days. Life, I have found, is remorseless but not disappointing. There have been times in my life when some have said they would die for me. *However, that is one task we must each do for ourselves.* When you have set me down for the last time, come back to the house on the river and Willie will bring up from the cellar the last bottles of Laffite-Rothschild of that special year. Let my family sit around and drink a toast as they remember Goethe's line: *Die Natur weiss allein was sie will. . . .*

From Marcel Pedlock's journal:

Am I too sick to know I'm sick? In my mind a fixation has become a reality. In writing of the supernatural we are only writing from our point of view, and the vast majority do not any more believe in *dybbuks*, spirits that capture or inhabit human form, slip into human frames. I cannot share what I have discovered with anyone else. . . . After the will had been read and we all turned to see how Jacob Ellenbogan took his millions, he merely rose from his chair in the library at Pedlock House, made a small clawing gesture in the air in front of him, looked at my son Tony and said: "I've got to think something out." Then he went upstairs.

I had the pistol in my topcoat pocket in the hall. I went to get it, and was waylaid by Don Kalish, who wanted me to sign some papers to get the jewels out of the vaults. By the time I went up to Jacob's room he was gone. The maid said he had called a taxi and gone out the back way. I knew where he was going. To his nest of mystics, that *schul* in Brooklyn where with his followers, the seers of the cabala, the latter-day Hasidim, all looking as if painted in soot by Chagall and steeped in Martin Buber's texts, he would be sitting under the tattered ark, drinking glasses of tea, sucking it up through lumps of sugar held in the teeth. Waiting for the *minyan*, the quorum needed for public worship, while the sun sank over the dreariness that is that dismal borough.

I got into my car. In the cold air I was sweating and I did not dare take my pulse. I knew it was racing. There was this middle-age strain on the heart after fifty that ran in the family (that and a bit of sugar in the urine). If I was to drop dead, I wanted to kill my *dybbuk*, my *golem*, my demon first. There were still Pedlocks left he could harm if he wanted to complete his work in the destruction of a family. How I wished I could have told Nathan or Tom or Lazar-Wolf. But they would have turned me over to their head shrinkers, the society doctors Shindell and Newberger and Zimmerman, talented charlatans. The East River was frozen lead, tiny ships far below the bridge were skating. At least Leah, the female demon, was gone. Ships skating slowly under thin funereal plumes of smoke that the wind tore to bits. People walked bent over, noses red, necks turtled into collars. I drove and drove, remembering little. The street of the *schul* was littered with broken glass, torn cardboard—either because of city neglect or because there had been another riot between the Negroes and the Hasidic families. It is safer than attacking the Anglo-Saxon Protestants. And what was one more pogrom to people who had been big-leagued in pogroms?

The *schul* was open. The front doors do not fit well any more and at night a chain is looped through the rusty iron handles of the portals and padlocked. Now it was open. I went into the dun interior. Several candles made golden holes of feeble light, the red velvet curtains of the ark were half in shadow. Two old men, bearded, *yamikas* on the backs of their heads, were sipping slivowitz from cleaned-out *yurzeit* glasses. "Eh, eh, *who*? Oh, *him*. Yes, yes."

They told me Reb Ellenbogan was in the storeroom out back, and would I stay for prayers—for the *minyan*. I went through a door once painted blue and down a hall (roller skates, a battered samovar, rotting mops) and to a pine door chalked with the Hebrew letters that spelled out the Yiddish phrase *Vuszhe vilsstu*—what do you want.

I pushed open the door with a shoulder and went in. On a long wire a naked electric light bulb hung from the dusty ceiling, and on nails driven into the plank walls hung prayer shawls, raveled tablecloths, discarded curtains. Piled along the baseboard were worn-out prayerbooks, a teakettle with a battered snout, several pairs of moldy over-shoes, a broom, a spray can of insect repellent. The room smelled of a sick cat, candle wax, old paper.

Jacob was packing a straw-covered suitcase with the contents of a wooden locker. A blue sweater, some shirts, a suit of his long European underwear, cramming on top several heavy volumes with calfskin bind-ings. I felt under no pathological stress—I just had difficulty breathing or talking.

Jacob looked at me, his little beard like the devil's horn in the harsh light; eyeball centers black as ebony, highlights blazing in them. I wanted to shout a prayer of protection (*"Ribono schelolum"*), but I just stood there, hand in coat pocket, fingers on the pistol butt (a Jewish Gary Cooper).

He said simply, "I never grieve, but I don't forget. You look tired, Marcel. Sit down." He pointed to an empty grapefruit crate (Florida Delights—Pink Centers). I remained standing.

"There's something I want to say to you, want to bring out in the open." *High Noon* in Brooklyn.

"Don't look so solemn, as if you're about to kill a man, or start another pogrom." He placed the pair of worn slippers into the suitcase. "Something ended today—something began."

"What are you packing?"

He turned around to face me, sat down on a backless kitchen chair, extracted from a pocket a cigarette with a long cardboard tip, lit it with a wooden match. After puffing it alive he held it in the European man-ner, between thumb and forefinger. "I'm packing to leave, chappie. You're all kind, but I have no reason to stay. She's gone."

"You can't get the money that quickly. It will take some time to probate her will. Oh, it's legal. Mama was very bright and her lawyers are excellent."

"What's the matter, Marcel? You look strange. As if you'd seen the false Messiah. *Shana* felt you would miss her the most."

Perhaps I had seen the Messiah. I put a finger on the trigger. I'd fire through the pocket—I didn't have the strength to remove the weapon from the coat—aim and nakedly fire. I felt petulant, no longer erratic.

Jacob studied me closely and smiled, the eyes remaining dark pools of power with a glancing scrutiny. I felt sweat on my brow but didn't touch it. Whatever powers he had, I didn't dare take my eyes off him.

"Marcel, Marcel, you don't know Jacob. I'm always the stranger. You think I'm going to run with the Pedlock cash? Burden myself with all that nonsense of stocks, bonds, holding companies, and legal *drek?*"

"Aren't you—"

"My *yold*. I'm not legally entitled to it, that's why not, to begin with. I saw to that when *Shana*, rest her soul, made the will."

"What the hell are you talking about?"

"Chappie, you are upset. I didn't know money meant so much to you. You, a sensitive fellow, an art lover who knew art is—what? Only man added to nature. I expected better of you."

"It doesn't mean a damn thing, the money. But you . . ." I'd count five and fire, right at the gray sweater he wore under his unbuttoned vest under his open jacket. I noticed it was the sweater he'd come from England with.

"In the will it says, a dark truth—as Saffed the cabala master, Chayyim Vital, puts it, with the black breath of the devil—that *Shana* leaves *everything to her husband*. You notice it doesn't say to one Jacob Ellenbogan or Katzenellenbogan. Ha?"

"What's this mumbo jumbo?"

"I don't think you're in a condition to hear me. Marcel?"

"You're going away. Why?"

"Don't get me wrong. I'm going away because I want to be among Jews I feel comfort with. Here you're all a fine people. But all Jews here, you're no longer Jews, you're Americans. A fine people, too. I've seen you and the shaved Reformed and Conservative creatures you call rabbis, social directors, project planners, the pool tables and the lessons for folk dancing. Very American. But Yiddish, no. Hebrew, no. Services not in the mother tongue. So I'm lonely. I want the smell of Jews, the look of Jews. They stink, they look gray—life is as God said, a trial."

"You're going to Israel?"

"No, no—you didn't hear me. There it's just a fine healthy zoo for people who need help. They're strong, they're happy. They have plans for cities, for material things. In two, three generations they'll be Israelis, like you're Americans. But not Jews either."

"You're the devil. I don't want to hear your—your cunning lies."

Jacob smiled. Eyes crinkling up, beard bobbing, cheeks wrinkling, face wearing a big Chinese smile. "You don't understand, Marcel. I have to be—it's my destiny—where there is dirt, poverty, where Jews are being ground down, picked apart. Where they gather in their rotting little *schuls* with bruises and shake and pray to God direct. Wherever Jews of this kind are left I want to be a part of them. That is our purpose, to suffer for the whole world. Judaism is passing away. Sad, sad but true. Yet here, there, will be a group of us who'll hold onto it, make out magic circles, dance the Hasidic dance while the barbarians drop atoms—we being a little of the sense of Nathande-Zizitha the Exilarch, as told in the Ma'aseh Nissim of Tunis. You all have traded Moses for Dr. Teller—I spit—Abraham for Freud, David for Marx, Job's boils for Einstein's haircut—"

"You're a *dybbuk*. You want to return us to the ghettos."

"To our duty."

"*Dybbuk!*"

"Ah, there is hope for you, Marcel. You believe in *bubba meinsahs* —granny tales. But to get to mundane things. I was explaining the will. *Shana's* will says her husband is to inherit, *not* Jacob Ellenbogan. Jews should not get fat, rich, accepted. The God who made us put us here to serve and ache."

He gave a witch's cackle. (I counted, *one*.)

"Ask your son Tony why I insisted on that wording."

"What's he got to do with it?" (*Two.*)

"What's he got to do with it? When he went to Poland for Leah—may God strike that land down and its anti-Semites—the police showed him my dossier. He told me."

(*Three.*)

"And in it your son saw something he kept back from you all. He didn't want to (*Four*) hurt his grandmother. You see I still have a wife, Surah Honnah, living in Bialystok (*Five*), and so I'm not *Shana's* husband—legally, as they say."

I had started forward, mouth open at his news, and my finger, remembering an earlier message, pressed the trigger. The pistol went off, twice, in the little room, but in moving (and I had never fired a weapon before) I hadn't aimed well. The slugs went into the wall over Jacob's head. Plaster fell; the sound of firing had been harsh but not *too* loud.

Jacob stood puzzled, almost grotesquely lackadaisical, his head to one side, cigarette burning short in his stubby fingers with nails like seashells.

"Marcel, what's the harm in it? It made her happy, didn't it? I am entitled to nothing, I'm not her legal husband. Don't you think you're acting the *narr*, the fool? For this you shoot a person, could do him harm?"

I turned, smelling smoke, burning cloth. The door opened and two bearded faces appeared in its frame.

"*Rebbe, rebbe, vos ist doss?*"

I pushed past them, beating my hand on my smoldering pocket. I ran through the *schul* and into the street. Behind me the beginning of the evening prayers, the outcry of someone calling for the police. In the car, me trying to get at the pistol, it fired twice through the floor.

CHAPTER 35

ᴖᴥᵹ At the very moment that Marcel Pedlock, who had been writing all night and part of the morning, put away his journal, put down his pen, and took the two sleeping pills, Tom Pedlock was at New York's International Airport waiting to board the transatlantic jet. He was standing in one of a bank of phone booths talking to his wife in London.

"I'm waiting for the call to board, Rita. Damn it, yes, of course I missed you. . . . No, I didn't expect more in the will. I have enough with my exchange of stocks with Ganzler's company. . . . How do I feel? What kind of question is that? I feel pretty lousy, that's how I feel. How else can I feel . . . No, it's not because I'm coming back to you. I want to come back to you. . . . Of course I want us to have a great life. . . . Sure, sure. I know. I know all about that; I've had a child, have a child. I know how messy it is. . . . Okay, have it your way, I'm only the goddam stud. . . . Yes, I love you. . . . Look, I have to hang up, old girl. They're announcing my flight is ready . . . Yes, dear, soon. Me too."

Tom hung up, stood in the booth wiping his brow, feeling numb and lonely. Poor Rita. He could understand her worries, her discomfort, and being alone in London. He looked up at the soiled, interminable expanse of sky he had to cross.

He went down the passage toward his plane, resolved that the loss of his mother, the end of Pedlock & Sons as an independent company must, should, would, change his life. He felt depleted, consumed, listless. The three bourbons in the airport bar hadn't done anything but make the world appear a deeper insolvency. With Judith gone, the Store gone in some fancy-sounding merger, there was really only Rita. Somehow the old yen was dormant in him, and for a moment he had that clutching fear of all males in their fifties: Was this the real impotence setting in—the failure to function to the full of one's potential? He walked behind two South American chicks—South American by their coffee color, their swift slurring Spanish, high-heeled, high rumped, swaying. Oh God. Could it really be he wasn't randy any more? No. Must be just the shock of Mama's death, the mess of the will, loss, loss. Nothing is permanent. There are inevitable cruel changes brought by time. *Les grands nerveux*—sensitive beings, an actress had once said to him in Paris. So it's Rita, Rita, wine and roses all the way. . . .

"*Dispénseme usted, lo siento. Thees de jet to London, señor?*"

"Oh, yes."

Nice set of eyes, one of those half-breed Indian shapes and no girdle.

"*Muchas gracias. Me gusta.* My seester and I first time crossing ocean to Urope. She no speek English."

"*Hace buen tiempo.*"

Well, that was better. He could still get a charge out of a beautiful dish. But nothing else. No. He'd get back to Rita and they'd take a villa someplace below Nice. Near a good French doctor—if they exist—a good doctor. He'd, well, he'd find something to do. Maybe just sail, swim, fish the first year. When the kid was old enough to be left with a good solid French nurse, they'd well, they'd find something to do: see Japan, ski, collect coins. Hardly mattered once you gave up tomcatting.

In the interior of the plane the two South American sisters were across the way, a seat ahead.

"*Un pedazo?*"

A brown hand with rings and a ruby bracelet held on open box of rich-looking, sick-making chocolates toward him.

"No."

The jet's pods were being turned on. Tom Pedlock sank back in his seat on his spine, closed his eyes. He felt relaxed, hungry. Not yet as sad as he would be later, and later.

Naomi and Mark Penrose were in their adjoining bathrooms, he in the shower and she in the rose-marble tub. Steam, bath oils, scented soap filled the air like a temple incense. Through the open door between, they talked as Mark shut off his shower and began to towel himself with a brisk vigor, swaying like a figure in a prayer shawl. But for the slight paunch, Florida-tanned, he was pleased with himself. He was deep in Gestalt psychology and it kept weight down.

"What happens now?"

"What, dear? I've got water in my ears."

"I mean to Mama's estate?"

"Oh. Seems simple."

"How?"

"He isn't her husband. Wasn't, that is."

"I'm happy she never knew. So?"

"Have you any extra dental floss?"

"Top drawer, right-hand side. You've got a pot, Mark."

"Little handball at the club will attend to that. Addison assured Lazar-Wolf your mother's estate goes to her children. Share and share alike."

"Hand me the towel."

"You're a skinny bitch."

"What do want, a fat *yenta?*"

"What's a *yenta?*"

"Ha. Don't go *goy* on me. Where were you raised, in a nunnery?"

He slapped her on the slim tight buttocks, making a pleasant sound. She smiled over her shoulder and hoped he wouldn't upset her hairdo by going into rut. She couldn't get an appointment with John-Thomas for a new one before three days.

Nathan Pedlock stood in the dark interior of his clothes closet puffing on a thick cigar with great relish. The old air vent to the roof of Pedlock House would carry off the smoke. He kept the closet locked, as a rule, telling Miss Fogel it contained private papers. He smoked slowly, with relish, against doctor's order. Judith had been so right. He had denied himself the full sensual life, the wider wilder shores of living. He'd go out tonight "for evening services at the White Plains Temple," but instead dine at Grosbeck Inn. A bottle of Anheuser moselle, Veal *saumone*, a balloon of Fundador with another cigar. If the heart couldn't enjoy living, that was it's problem, not his. He wouldn't live out whatever was left as an idiot child wrapped in cotton wool. So what was life? A geometry of chromosones, an animated carcass, unless you made it more.

He was down to the last two inches of cigar, a genuine hard-to-get H. Uppman. Yes, we hoard symbols, as Jacob said once, that shield the truer parts of ourselves from consciousness. Nathan hadn't been able to escape yet from the loss of Judith. The circular movement of memory still spun. He felt like one of the doomed cities beyond Genesis when he thought of his loss. He himself should have married again, begun another generation. But he had devoted himself to the Store.

What a mockery that was. He was on the board of Ganzler-Pedlock Department Stores. But it meant nothing. Printed paper, a chair reserved for his ass a few times a year. He tried to think of women he had once desired, but failed to do more than merely produce dim shadows. Each apparition of a woman in our lives, he thought, is a hope that does not become fully real. My fault, a kind of indifference in translating a vision, or version, of something into reciprocated love. Not that he had really cared for this business of two people eating noses, or four legs in a bed. We all drown, each within his own depth. But a man had a duty to that ludicrous gesturing, and in time, in time it could become a florid delight—man's flesh caught unaware and exposed. The cigar was tasting sour.

He took a last hasty puff. Judith in her wilder moments—God forbid he should criticize her now she wasn't here to speak her part—never felt any guilt. But he himself always had sensed there must be purgatory, because there never can be full atonement for one's actions.

He opened the closet door a crack, looked around sniffing the air. He locked the door behind him. Going to his bathroom, he flushed the cigar butt down the toilet and stood there panting a bit, looking at himself in the half-length mirror. He was thinning out on the saltless baby pap they fed him. There was too much flush in his cheeks. Well, no form or force of permanence exists, as Jacob once put it. All living, in time, becomes shopworn, ready for the bargain counter. Do we grasp understanding of an experience only in contemplation long after the events? Well, at least that would give him something to do.

Miss Fogel rattled the doorknob of the bathroom.

"Are *we* all right in there?"

"Are *you* all right out there, Miss Fogel?"

Gertrude Lazar-Wolf was lying prone on her reclining board, having good empty thoughts as her general-semantics class advocated for complete nonverbal relaxing. Mama was gone, the Store merged with cheap Jews. "The map is not the territory," she said softly, to change her thoughts. If only not to be harassed by an incapacity to fulfill. What's six charming children and two miscarriages, and a secret abortion? That's no incapacity, that's capacity in spades.

Gertrude found to her amazement that she was weeping silently on her reclining board. At the loss of her mother, at the fact that they had not been close, that they had not understood each other, that she, too, was getting old and aware we are not impenetrable and hollow in our secret self.

Saul came into her room, pulling down his yellow waistcoat. He stepped over her, bulging in the crotch, preparing to be driven to the Bank.

"This vest? What do you think?"

"It's nice, Saul."

"You think it's maybe too colorful, so soon? Just a navy blue, brass buttons."

"You feel bad, don't you?"

He bent down. It wasn't easy. His girth was greater than it had once been. "Of course I miss her. The kind of life I came from you think I'd not know something like Judith is special? With her I felt solid. Everything else is often unreal emotions. You know, like the habits of a dream."

" 'Gertrude,' she'd say to me—"

" 'Gittel.' "

"She'd say to me, 'Gittel, you lack adventure, you'll never play a tamborine.' She knew I only practiced the piano for two years."

"Gert, I think I caught Sharon kissing that *shkutz* gardener."

"Did you or didn't you?"

"It's your duty to talk to her."

"No, a father is for these things. Besides, she's still a child. What's sixteen? Their illusions have no disillusions yet."

"When a girl has breasts she's no longer a child. You talk to her. That's *all* we need, her making out with some spic."

"Tush, you imagine things. I'll talk to her."

Gertrude's thoughts wandered again. Why am I so lonely as if I had a twin that died at birth?

The Store was filled to overflowing. It was the morning rush for the Pre-Holiday Sale in china, house furnishings, linens and imported crystal. The Fifth Avenue windows were featuring Holidays of America's Past. There were mannequins dressed as colonial folk, whiskered and beribboned, Forty-niners, sedate Civil War home scenes, the gaudy nineties of the best carriage trade, the splendor and grace of life before the Great War of 1914, the jazz and speakeasy décor of the twenties, flappers, comic gangster types.

Tony and Nancy, walking down from the park, looked at the packed sidewalks, peered inside at the Store. The few men in the crowd seemed, to Tony, like survivors of some Indian raid.

With a hand on her shoulder, he stopped Nancy's forward movement toward a store window. "It doesn't look much different does it?"

"Why should it?"

He pointed to where a crew on thin steel-rod scaffolds were raising a new metal sign, overshiny with chrome, into place above the main entrance.

"There's a big change."

"Mr. Ganzler didn't waste any time."

The surface of the metal plaque caught the sunlight:

THE FIFTH AVENUE FAIR

A Ganzler-Pedlock Store

"Oh, Tony, they put Pedlock last."

"It's usual: from A toward Z."

"I'm glad we're going abroad."

Tony pulled her to one side to avoid a crush of customers getting off a bus and charging toward the Store entrances.

"We're not going abroad. I'm going to report for work tomorrow. Here, at the Fair."

"You're putting me on. Come on, it's a rib."

"It's true, honey. I've been made assistant advertising director, now that the former Miss Burton, your stepmother, has gone to live abroad. The whole department is being reorganized. You know what I'm going to do?"

"Not any more, mister, I don't."

Tony's face broke into a grin and he put his head to one side as he looked at the Store's upper floors. "I'm going to bore from within. I'm going to stay. I'm going to promote, politic, shove, show them I can run things, get things done."

"But whatever for?"

Tony rubbed his chin with the back of a forefinger and shuffled his feet like a perplexed loose-jointed hero in a cowboy film. "I guess I've got what Uncle Nat calls the *cholleriya*, the infection. I'm going to run the whole damn thing someday. Make it again what it was. A pure Pedlock project. *Our* Store."

"When did this come to you?"

"Just now as we were walking along here. Let's face it, Nancy, your husband is a born square. The perfect hero of soap opera. I'm not unusual, or brilliant or different, except that I can ski pretty well, and that goes with your hairline, your breath and your twenties. What else have I got but you? Hell, honey, you ought to see it, you're a Pedlock."

"You're not just square," said Nancy laughing. "You're a goddamn cube. Let's go in and see your new office. And I need some nylons. Might as well use our discount as store employees."

Tony was not aware that he had discovered that one moment of time when the direction of everything changes. It was Nancy, as they pushed their way to the main entrance of The Fair, who sensed more than he did the idea that the past dies yet is continuous. The best bony parts survive. Only the soft stuff of the piling up of generation upon generation withers away. . . . Our advance is a zigzag, but we grow, like the Great Barrier Reef.

Placed against the window, to the right of the main entrance, was the old sign that had just been removed from over the door. The four great screwholes in it were green with patina, the sign itself dented and scratched:

PEDLOCK & SONS

EST. 1853

As they entered the Store Nancy wanted to touch the bronze surface for luck, but one must hold back something when bargaining with the gods. Inside the Store there was a mooing sound like a cow in parturition. Silhouettes—half wraiths, half shoppers—filled the lower floor. The counters and protruding balconies were buzzing. Tony had the feeling he was looking back in time, at the founding storekeepers as though through reversed binoculars. The banks of elevators, the heavily loaded escalators were pumping humanity upward like bees rising in a hive. There were more people in the store, he thought, than had seen the Red Sea crossing.

He gripped Nancy's arm as she bore him toward sheer nylons. The remark Jacob Ellenbogan had made to Uncle Nat just before the will had been read came back to Tony:

"Each inside has an outside—streets, cities, fields, the whirling by of time, marked out by night, by day—all of it in the wrinkled corner of one little universe. The meek shall inherit the earth and be too weak to refuse it."

Cheerfulness and light filled the Store. Outside the weather remained briskly cold. There was the hint of real snow for the holidays.

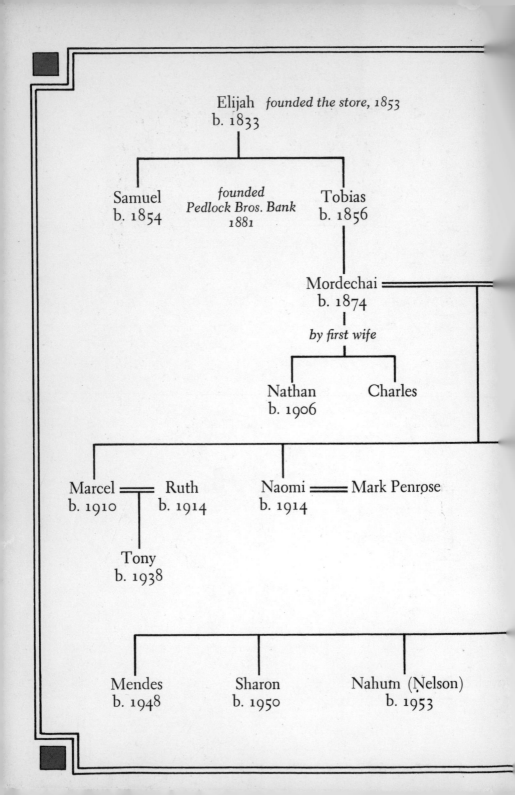